BROKEN COWBOY

THE MONTANA MEN SERIES BOOK 1

JAMIE SCHULZ

OTHER BOOKS BY JAMIE SCHULZ

BROKEN COWBOY

COPYRIGHT

Broken Cowboy
Copyright © 2021 by Jamie Schulz

ISBN: 978-1-7362226-1-4

For information contact: www.thejamieschulz.com

Book Cover design by Les/Germancreative & Jamie Schulz

For my Mr. Wonderful!
Thanks for everything, sweetie!
I love you!

CHAPTER 1

Addison Malory let out an angry shout as she kicked the front tire of her old Ford pickup with the rounded tip of her cowboy boot. It hurt more than anything else, but she couldn't have stopped herself from kicking something. She groaned at the painful throb that shot through her toes and into her foot. Resting her forehead against the chipped green paint, she took a deep breath and tried to calm the anger and frustration building up inside her.

How was she going to do her regular job and take care of the farm all by herself?

Anger flared again.

"Damn you, Ted Ballinger!" she shouted as she kicked the tire again, though less intensely. Slapping the green fender with her palms and letting out another frustrated, wordless growl, she pushed away from the truck, yanked open the driver's door, and crawled inside. She pounded her fists against the steering wheel, then wrapped her fingers tightly around it and took a deep breath.

You're acting like a child, Addie, she told herself sternly, then took another deep, steadying breath and released it slowly.

"I can do this," she said into the empty cab of her old truck. "I'll go down to Tri-Cities to find help, take out an ad, or do it all myself if I have to. I may lose half the crop, but I won't let them win."

She pulled the key from the pocket of her blue jeans and shoved it into the ignition. One turn and the old Ford's engine roared to life. She threw it into gear and headed toward her long driveway.

A cloud of dust kicked up as her truck rolled over her dirt-pack dooryard, her mind returning to her troublesome ex-employees. She doubted Ted or his two buddies were around to bother her or her property, but she kept an eye out anyway as the events from an hour ago played through her mind.

Ted's unwanted attentions had started small, a look, a hand on her shoulder, a word that said he knew better. All of it had simultaneously made her want to cringe and dig out her high-heeled boots for the extra height. Today was an all-new practice in frustration for her when Ted had presumed to crowd into her space and kiss her! When she'd pushed him away, he'd only grinned and stared at her ample chest.

"Come on, honey," he'd said, dropping all pretense of professionalism, "you know you want it."

"No, Mr. Ballinger," she'd replied tartly as revulsion churned in her stomach, "I don't want *anything* from you."

He'd tried to coerce her by wrapping an arm around her waist and dragging her toward him. She'd used the momentum to drive her knee into his crotch and then, as he doubled over, she slammed her elbow into his jaw, dropping him to the ground.

Thank you, self-defense classes!

Glaring at her from the barn's hay-littered floor, Ted had gritted his teeth as he crawled to his feet.

"You're fired, Mr. Ballinger," she'd said in a cold voice. "Get off my property, or I'll call the authorities and have you removed."

That made him chuckle, and she clenched her jaw. She and the sheriff's department—well, one member of it anyway—were not on good terms, but she hoped they would, at least, do their job.

Ted cupped his groin as he glowered at her, clearly attempting to use his few extra inches of height to intimidate her. "You don't want to do anything you're going to regret."

Fury bubbled to the surface—and a little fear, too—but Addie stood her ground. "Get out."

"Sure, whatever. You're a pity-fuck, anyway," he said, and she blinked. "A fat girl should take what she can get." He laughed at her soft gasp. "You sure as hell won't do better than me."

She'd frowned and hardened her expression. "Go. Now."

Surprisingly, he left, chuckling to himself the whole time just to irritate her—though not before his last comments reinforced one of her biggest, and most secret, insecurities.

Nearly every man she'd ever met commented on her self-assurance and 'pretty face,' but she saw the truth in their eyes. They liked her, even admired her to one degree or another, but most of them never saw her as beautiful. She had smarts and a ton of confidence, but her weight—and how men often perceived her—had been a life-long struggle.

Addie knew she might be a little on the heavy side, with a lot of generous curves, but she wasn't unattractive, and she wasn't stupid, either. No matter how much she needed Ted and his friends' physical strength for the farm, enough was enough. It had actually been a relief to kick him off her property.

The bad part was that his two coworkers went with him.

"We're a package deal," Ted had said, grinning at her as the three of them climbed into his truck outside the barn.

The youngest of the three, Jorje, hadn't seemed to want to leave. His soft brown eyes had looked apologetic when the others grabbed his arms and hauled him into the truck. She wouldn't have minded Jorje staying. He seemed different from the other two, but maybe that was just her wishful thinking.

"We'll be back for our pay," Ted said as he started his truck.

"You just got paid yesterday," she replied and then waved a hand at the barn, "and it doesn't look like you did anything that I asked you to do today. So, don't plan to get paid for not working."

He'd glowered at her and spun his tires in the dirt, throwing debris into the air as he sped out of her yard and down the long drive.

The whole incident could have been much worse, but it still left her with more work than she could successfully handle on her own and, among a myriad of other things, a leaky barn in need of repair.

Reaching the end of her mile-long dirt driveway, Addie took a moment to breathe and calm herself. She stared out her windshield at the wide expanse of pastoral land that had been fenced-in long ago by one of her neighbors. The low rolling hills in varying shades from light brown to dark green went on for miles until they culminated in the higher ridge known as the Manastash, which wandered westward and arched around to the northeast and into the Cascade Mountains. Together they formed a horseshoe-shape that encompassed their little valley of farms and ranches, and the growing college town where she was now headed.

Feeling more relaxed by the peaceful scene outside her windows, Addie sighed and turned her truck onto the dust-covered road to town. She didn't mind the drive; it was beautiful, and this time of year, there were all kinds of crops and things to see along the way. Mostly tall stalks of corn and huge, swaying fields of dark green Timothy hay grew on either side of the road beyond the fences and irrigation ditches that hugged the roadside. Green, leafy shrubs or trees grew in patches here and there and she passed a few other farm buildings along the way.

Even though she'd grown up in the suburbs of Seattle, she'd always had a country-girl's heart. Her plan to move over the mountains and find a way to make both of her dreams work—farming and writing—had never been far from her mind. This year, with a little coaxing from a friend in town, she'd finally done just that.

She'd become a freelance writer after college, working on some ghost writing and even managed a few books of her own. She now wrote for an assortment of magazines and online sites all over the world, as well as putting out another novel tow or three times a year. All of it allowed her the freedom to work from anywhere. She'd done well enough to scrape together the funds to buy her rundown farm with a little left over. It had been a good deal and in a great location; she just hadn't realized how unfriendly most of the town's folk would be toward an outsider.

She wiped the perspiration from her forehead with the back of her hand, making another mental note to get the truck's air conditioning fixed. It was hot and dusty, but with the windows rolled down, the loose tendrils of her hair furled in the wind, slapping and sticking to her neck and face. Too late again, she wished she'd thought to bring a hat for this trip. *Maybe I should just start leaving one in the truck.*

She turned right at the next lonely intersection and had just shifted into third gear when she saw another truck parked on the side of the road ahead. The truck was about ten years older than hers—which at times seemed older than dirt—and had its fair share of dents and scraps in its blue exterior. The hood was up and huge, white clouds of steam billowed out from the engine.

She slowed down to see if they needed some assistance, but the driver's seat was empty and no one was in sight. She hadn't seen anyone on her way here, which meant the driver must be hoofing it back to town.

"They've got a long walk," she muttered. The highway entrance was about a mile back the way she'd come, and the center of town, where the stores and service stations were located, was another several miles the other way.

Shifting gears and speeding up, Addie went back to her thoughts and was surprised by the first thing that popped into her head.

If Jared had listened, I wouldn't be in this mess...

She shook her head. Where had that stupid thought come from? Even if he had been an adrenaline-junkie, it's not as if Jared wanted to die. They'd met during her final year of college, snowboarding on the slopes of Stevens Pass, and that look she'd come to expect from men never entered his eyes. He'd been handsome, funny, reckless, and a little wild, and she'd been instantly smitten. His death two years later had left Addie's heart in pieces, but she'd picked them up, locked them away, and gone on with her life.

She used to think she missed Jared because she had loved him so much, but lately, she'd begun to wonder.

Though capable of taking care of herself, she missed the feeling of a man's hard body beside her at night, of having someone to lean on, a partner.

She pressed her lips together as she stared out the truck's dirty windshield.

Right now, I'd settle for a decent man's hard, warm body to keep me company tonight, she thought wryly, then tilted her head. *Okay, maybe that's a little*

5

much. It's not as if she'd ever had men knocking down her door—attention from men like Ted Ballinger excluded. She wasn't as fit as some women and she'd never be a swimsuit model, but she did okay when she put forth the effort. But that was the problem… *She* always had to make the effort, and she hadn't felt up to that effort for some time. Men never chased after her like all the romantic stories on TV or in books. She was just the girl-next-door who usually ended up being a friend rather than a lover. It was depressing.

Her shoulders drooped. She was tired of being alone. Tired of dealing with the never-ending problems that began when she'd refused the advances of her closest neighbor Mark Harden. He'd seemed like a nice, solid guy, but…

She sighed. Right now, she was just plain tired.

She shook her head to clear it of her difficulties with Mark and sat a little taller. She had more important things to think about than Mark Harden. Such as how to find workers for the farm. She barely knew anyone here, having just moved in about three months ago, but she did have one good friend. Veta, her best friend from college, had settled here and opened a café with her sister only a few blocks from the school they'd both attended. Veta had started Sisters Coffee Café right after graduation. Her sister, Lana, was in her second year at the same college and had always treated Addie like a sister, or a long-lost aunt.

Addie only got to see them maybe once a week, and she wasn't about to take advantage of their generosity by asking them for help with her farm. Veta would offer to ask her husband to aid Addie's troubles, but he had his own work to do and the sisters had their own business to worry about, too.

Few laborers existed around town who didn't already have a job that kept them plenty busy. And she wasn't about to take Mark Harden's offer of assistance, either. *He'd be worse than Ted, and how would I get rid of him after the harvest?* She sighed; he wouldn't leave her alone, even if she demanded it. She'd already tried, and so far, he'd kept his distance since their last…disagreement.

Brushing a loose strand of her blonde hair from her face, Addie focused on the long stretch of pavement in front of her. The last thing she needed was to have a problem on the road. That's when she noticed a man strolling along the rock- and dust-covered verge in front of her. Tall and lean, he wore cowboy boots and Wranglers that fit just right. The wind plastered his blue western shirt against the hard planes of his back, outlining every shifting muscle. He had that cowboy walk—loose and sinuous, but all powerful grace—that she'd always loved. That was one of the reasons she loved country-life. She smiled as a little tingle of attraction warmed her insides.

He didn't look familiar, but considering her short residency here, that didn't mean all that much.

Maybe he's with the rodeo, she thought. The town was full of tourists and cowboys from all over, and had been for the last few days.

Her eyes drifted over his body, impressed with what she saw as her truck rolled up to him and continued right on by. She glanced in the rearview mirror and noted that his front looked almost as good as his back, though she couldn't see his face due to the tilt of his head and the wide-brimmed straw hat he wore.

Hmm... Without realizing it, her foot had slowly backed off the accelerator. *I wonder if he's single...?*

"Whoa!" Her head snapped to the front and she straightened up in the seat, adjusting her steering so she didn't run off the road.

A deep breath steadied her nerves.

"Where the *hell* had that come from?" she muttered to herself. Yes, she was lonely, but she wasn't really interested in one-night stands, either. At least, she didn't think she was. She'd never had one, never even thought about it...not until now, apparently. *Down, girl.*

The truck slowed and then lurched, the engine trying to die, and she jammed her feet on the brake and clutch pedals. The truck came to a sudden, idling halt, and she looked back over her shoulder.

Maybe he could use a job. That would solve some of her problems, but he was a stranger. She couldn't trust him. Could she?

The cowboy had glanced up briefly, but then dropped his eyes and continued ambling along as if her truck hadn't almost stalled out only a few yards away.

"Oh, what the hell." She shifted into reverse. "He can't be worse than

Ted or Mark." She'd find out what he was doing here, and if he had any experience or references she could check, she'd offer him the job. With his rundown boot heels and lack of transportation, it looked like he could use a little help.

Maybe he could solve my loneliness problem as well?

She froze in her seat.

Wow! Am I that desperate?

"Let's just start with a ride," she told her inner harlot.

Ignoring all the voices in her head telling her that this was not a good idea, she backed up the truck and skidded to a quick stop, kicking up dust as she did. The man halted, turning away from her and waving at the debris that clouded the air around him.

"Sorry about that," she shouted out the open passenger window.

The man coughed and when he looked up, her heart fluttered and flipped stupidly. He was handsome—more than handsome, with a rugged appeal she couldn't ignore. Her mouth went dry when she met his bright blue eyes. He frowned at her, looking both alarmed and confused.

She smiled, hoping to alleviate his concern. Opening her mouth to speak, she prayed she didn't sound as nervous as she felt. "Need a ride, cowboy?"

CHAPTER 2

Caden Brody dropped the rag he'd been using to troubleshoot his truck's steaming engine, mumbling a string of curses at his own clumsiness. Rounding the truck, he yanked open his passenger-side door and fished a bottle of water out of the cooler sitting on the truck's bluish-gray bench seat.

"Ah," he moaned once he'd uncapped the bottle and poured the cold liquid over the burn on his hand. *God, that feels good.* Though, not burning himself would've been better. He'd been careless as he checked wires and hoses surrounding the engine, his thoughts so preoccupied with all his other problems that he hadn't been paying attention to what he was doing under the hood. The back of his hand contacting the sizzling heat of the manifold focused his wandering mind instantly on the present.

"Serves you right," he told himself as he examined the back of his hand. The burn wasn't too bad, but it still hurt like hell. He poured the rest of the cool water over it, tossed the empty bottle on the passenger-side floorboard, and then grabbed his leather riding gloves. Something he should have done sooner.

As he pulled the gloves on, movement on the ground caught his eye and he looked down. A trail of greenish liquid slowly rolled past the dusty toes of his worn-down boots.

Another curse escaped him and he shook his head. "That's just great."

He'd known the truck had a cooling problem, but all he could do was watch the temp, keep a store of water on hand, and refill the radiator whenever necessary. It made travel tedious but kept him on the road.

After filling the gas tank that morning, he'd scarcely had enough cash to refill his thermos at the coffee shop in town. If he'd had the money for the parts and the tools to repair this issue, he could've done it himself right there on the side of the road—though the county probably wouldn't have liked that. But thanks to circumstances beyond his control, he had no way to fix it, and in its current state, no way to move the truck, either. He didn't have much of anything—no house, no garage, and few friends. Fewer still, if he counted those he could actually trust and rely on. And no family. Not anymore.

A pang of regret struck him, the weight in his chest tugging him further into misery, but then a wave of anger replaced it. No, no family. His mom had died when he was in college, and his father a few years ago. His brother... Well, his brother may as well be dead for all Cade cared. At least, that's what he kept telling himself.

Cade pushed those thoughts to the darkest part of his mind before they could drag him any lower, and then went to the front of the truck. Dropping to his knees, he crawled under the big four-wheel-drive to assess the damage.

Not only had one of the radiator hoses he'd already patched with duct tape sprung another leak, but the water pump had blown for good, too. Hot water gurgled out of the seams to enlarge the puddle already muddying the ground below.

"Damn," he muttered, rolling out from under the truck and getting to his feet. Wiping the sweat from his brow and dusting himself off, he glanced up and down the road. No cars in sight and no houses nearby. If he still had phone service, maybe he could call someone, but he'd had it turned off months ago. *And you've got no money. Let's not forget that. Besides, who would I call?*

His chin dropped to his chest and he sighed. "When am I going to catch a break?"

You could call home… Go home again, a soft voice muttered inside his head. No, that he would not do, not ever again.

Shaking his head, he started walking back to town. He had an idea where to find the auto parts store and knew he had a long walk to get there. What else was he going to do? He had no funds, not even a credit card, and, aside from some of the cowboys at the fairgrounds, he didn't know anyone in this smallish college town. All he had was himself.

Maybe he could convince someone at the auto store or a mechanic's shop to let him work off the cost of the parts and beg for the use of their tools.

"Or maybe one of the ranches around here could use an experienced cow hand?" He chuckled to himself. Not too likely from what he'd seen. Those few men who appeared to be available also seemed to be less than desirable. Probably unreliable as hell, too. Not that many places looked in need of extra help right now. He'd be lucky to find a dishwashing or serving job at a restaurant or bar in town. It was a college town after all, and the bars—even in late August—were busy.

Maybe some hot college girl will drive by and give me a ride. He chuckled to himself. *Maybe she'll have a rich daddy and fall in love with me, too,* he thought with a smile, but then it slipped away. *Sure. Stop dreaming, boy. When have you ever been that lucky? Besides, what girl would be interested in a rundown loser like me?*

Shaking his head yet again, he quickened his pace. He was better off without that little fantasy coming true anyway. He didn't want to get involved. One wild night and a goodbye kiss before breakfast, that he could do. But getting to know her? Exchanging numbers? No way. He'd had enough of women. The last one had ripped his heart out, stomped all over it, and tore his world apart. He wasn't in any hurry to risk that again.

The burn on his hand throbbed. Stopping to yank off his gloves, he tucked them into his back pocket—wishing he'd thought to leave them in the truck—and examined his wound. Luckily, the burn didn't appear to be blistering, but he could use some more cold water. Yet another thing he'd forgotten.

He glanced behind him and was surprised at how far he'd come. His truck was a tiny dot in the distance, but he still had a long way to go.

He started walking again.

A few cars had passed him already, but no one stopped. Most of them looked like families on their way back over the mountains to Seattle after enjoying the rodeo and fair, or maybe on their way in. As shabby as he looked, he would've been surprised if any of them had stopped.

Aside from those who worked in town, the locals appeared to have made themselves scarce once the rodeo started. That he understood. A bunch of strangers invading their little town during the four days of the rodeo, mucking up traffic, doing who knows what, getting into trouble and fights. He didn't blame the locals for staying home. It just would be nice to get a break for once.

Another truck rolled by, but Cade didn't lift his thumb or bother to look up. It wouldn't do any good, anyway.

A moment later, he heard the engine almost stall and he paused to glance up. The driver must have jammed the pedals down, because the truck began idling normally again. Strangely, it had stopped in the middle of the road. Hope lit inside him, but he snuffed it out. In a minute, they'd put the truck in gear and continue on their way. He dropped his head and started walking again and, just as he'd predicted, the driver shifted, the gears caught, and the truck began to move. Only backward instead of forward.

It came to a stop beside him, and he turned away from the sudden dust storm the skidding tires kicked up.

A light, feminine voice shouted an apology from inside and his stomach gave a little flutter at the sound. He looked in through the passenger window at a cute blonde about his age, with a huge smile and generous curves. The peach-colored tank top she wore did little to hide that fact, but he refused to ogle the display. Still, his throat went dry when he met her twinkling brown eyes, and her brilliant smile was addictive.

"Need a ride, cowboy?" she asked in that melodious voice that made every nerve in his body tingle with awareness.

"If you're headed into town, I sure could use a ride to the auto parts store."

She hitched a thumb over her shoulder. "Was that your truck back there on the side of the road?"

He nodded. "Yeah, it finally gave out on me."

"Well, I'm headed into town. Hop in."

He pointed to her truck's bed. "You want me to climb in back?"

She frowned. "Why would I want that?"

He shrugged, heat crawling up his neck that had nothing to do with the hot August sun.

She chuckled. "Nah, just hop in the cab. It's not a long drive."

Pulling off his cowboy hat, he climbed inside and set it on the seat between them. He ran his fingers through his sweat-dampened dark hair a couple of times before he settled into the seat and rested his arm on the open window.

The woman held out her hand to him. "I'm Addie Malory."

He glanced at her hand then into her eyes. She was still smiling and the way the sunlight struck her face gave her eyes an amber glow.

He swallowed hard, wiped his palms on his jeans, and took her hand. "Cade Brody," he replied and she shook his hand once before releasing it.

Her hand had been so soft and warm, with just a hint of calluses. Disappointment twitched in his chest when she let go. It had been a long time since he'd touched a woman. That had to be the reason he was feeling so damn aware of this one—even if she was cute.

"Nice to meet you, Cade," she said and reached for the gearshift.

"You too," he rasped through the sudden dryness in his throat.

Get it together, man!

The outside of her truck was dirty, but the inside, not so much. A little dried mud on the floor, a colorful Navajo blanket covered the bench seat, and some tools and assorted items were stuffed in the console. Fairly typical for a farm truck. Several years newer than his rig, it seemed to run quite a bit better than his too, as she threw it into first and started down the road.

"Thanks for stopping," he said.

She glanced at him, flashing another quick grin. "It's the neighborly thing to do, right?"

He couldn't help but return her smile. Then he frowned. "Do you pick up strange men hitchhiking often?"

"You're my first," she said, sounding as chipper as before and his frown deepened.

Why did that bother him? Why should he care if she wanted to risk her life picking up men she didn't know? But he couldn't shake the discomfort her careless behavior churned up inside him.

"You with the rodeo?" she asked, interrupting his thoughts.

"Yeah," he grumbled, and she threw a nervous look his way, but was back to her chipper self a moment later.

"Leaving a little early, aren't you? Don't you have two more days?"

"Yep," he said. "Didn't make the first go-round and thought I'd get a jump on travel, but it doesn't look like I'm going anywhere for a while."

"'Cause of your truck?"

He nodded.

"Well, I'm sure you'll have that fixed in no time."

He was beginning to find her cheerfulness annoying. Or maybe it was just his moodiness and his unwanted attraction to her that made him cranky. Either way, he didn't reply.

"Were you headed home?" she asked after a short silence.

He glanced at her then out the windshield. "No, there are some other rodeos on the west side I was going to try, but now I'm going to have to find a job for a few months to pay for the new parts on the truck."

She nodded. "So you're stuck here for a while?"

"Looks that way," he answered, staring out at the road. "You from around here?"

"Yep, I'm a local," she said proudly. "Lucky you! You actually got to meet one who doesn't work in town. Most of us are a little scarce during rodeo weekend, but I don't mind the crowds as much as some of the others."

He chuckled. "Yeah, I noticed." He turned toward her. "Hey, may I ask you something? As a local?"

She glanced at him, again with a touch of trepidation. "Sure."

"Do you know of anyone looking for help? I mean, an auto garage or ranch or something like that, who are hiring?"

"You a good mechanic?"

"I get by."

"What do you know about ranching?"

"I grew up on one in Montana," he said. "It'd take less time to tell you

14

what I don't know."

"How about farming?"

"I'm a fair hand at that, too. We had to feed the stock and it's cheaper to grow your own when you can."

She nodded, but her brow was furrowed. "But you're not going home?"

Something in her voice seemed off, like she was suddenly concerned to be alone with him.

"It's not my home anymore and—" he said, about to go on about his parents, but he cut himself off. "Well, let's just say, there's nothing left to hold me there. I used to dream about the rodeo as a kid, so I thought I'd give it a go."

"How's that working out for you?"

He chuckled again, but with no humor this time. "Not so good, obviously."

That made her smile, and he couldn't help but admire her profile, or the way wisps of her hair twirled around her neck and face in the wind. His fingers twitched, wanting to rub the silky-looking strands between them to savor their softness.

"So, how long do you plan to hang around if you find work?" she asked and he heard a more serious note in her tone.

"Depends on the work and the pay," he said with a shrug and pushed his wayward thoughts about her hair out of his head. "I'd guess through October at least, maybe longer if the weather turns too bad."

"Hmm," she hummed, her delicate brows bunching over her nose.

"Is that a bad thing?"

"No, not really. I was just…thinking." She smiled again and a fuzzy warmth filled his chest.

"About anything in particular?" His nerves seemed to stretch. Why did he ask that? It felt like they were on the verge of flirting, but if that's true, it would be the oddest instance of it he'd ever been a part of.

"Do you have trouble taking orders from a woman?" she asked. "Taking orders and remaining professional?"

He frowned and straightened in the seat. *Well, that's direct.*

"No," he replied aloud. "No problems that I know of."

"Hmm."

He looked out the window, unsure where this was going. Did she know someone or not?

"You a good worker?"

Irritation buzzed in his head. She seemed to be grilling him, but she still hadn't given any indication that she knew of an available job.

"I've never had any complaints," he said. "I'll work from before sunup until after sundown as needed. Those have been my hours for years and it's not going to change now."

"I see." She glanced at him, but this time her smile seemed a little tenuous.

Is she afraid of me now?

Trying to appear as non-threatening as possible, he looked out the side window at the small businesses that lined his side of the road. They seemed to be on a backroad, but they were halfway through town already.

"I'm a decent guy," he said into the tense quiet of the cab and turned back to her. "I just need a job. I'm not looking to take advantage of or hurt anyone. I'll do any work needed, I'm not fussy. I just need to make some money."

"Thank you," she said. "I wasn't sure how to ask for that information."

"Ask whatever you need to know. If it has to do with a job, I've got no problem answering."

She nodded. "So, if I told you about a farm job—with lots of hard, dirty work—you'd take it?"

"What's it pay?"

"Enough to get your truck fixed and some for your pocket besides."

He thought about that for a minute. It was a good offer, but he wondered who the offer was coming from. Was it her or someone else? A friend, a husband, a neighbor? He glanced at her left hand—no ring. Something pulsed inside him and he locked it down before it could do anything else. No ring didn't mean much. Maybe she didn't wear it when working, or maybe it got lost, or they hadn't been able to afford one. Why did it matter anyway?

A husband or a neighbor would be great. Those two he could do, but if it was her, this attraction he'd been feeling from the minute he'd heard her voice and then met her eyes through the open window might be a problem.

He shook his head. Hell, no it won't. He'd worked around pretty women before and never had an issue. Why should this be any different?

Because she makes your stomach twist into knots with just a smile and your hand is still tingling from her touch.

He sighed. All that may be true, but he didn't have a whole lot of choices here.

"If that's not enough," she said, sounding cheery and cajoling at the same time, "since you're not from around here and you've got no money to go anywhere else, there'll be room and board as well. Homemade meals."

His empty stomach grumbled at the thought of food, and he found himself nodding. "I'll take it."

CHAPTER 3

The bell above the little coffee shop door jingled as Addie walked in. She had dropped Cade off at the auto shop and asked if he'd like a coffee and some lunch. His sad eyes had brightened a bit as he stood beside her truck's open passenger door, but when his stomach growled again—loudly—his face had clouded over.

"You don't have to do that," he'd said, his cheekbones turning pink.

"I don't mind," she said with a smile. "I'm hungry, too. Besides, the ladies who run the place are like family, so I get a discount." She hadn't wanted to shame him but was afraid she'd done just that.

He'd lowered his chin, the hat he'd put back on blocking his face, but when he lifted his head, he looked resigned. "Sure, I'd…like that."

"Great!" She beamed, glad that he'd allowed her to help him a little more. "Why don't you meet me over there when you're done here?" She pointed across the street. "It's a couple stores up."

He nodded. "Yeah, I know where it is. I'll be up in a few."

She wasn't sure now if he'd been upset or not when he swung the truck door closed and headed into the auto store. She'd shifted gears and started to roll the truck back out of the parking spot, but she couldn't help watching him stroll inside. Something seemed different, a little stiffer maybe.

I hope I didn't embarrass him, she thought for the second time as she got in line at the counter inside Sisters Café.

Her two friends were bustling around, one at the counter and the other in the kitchen with Veta's husband Ivan helping on the grill that weekend. They chatted with their customers as lively as ever, but when Addie stepped up to the counter, Lana's light blue eyes lit up, her face burst into a wide smile, and her vocal volume went up a notch.

"Addie!" she squealed as she skirted the counter. "Veta! Look who's here."

"Hi, Addie," Veta shouted from the grill, and Ivan waved as Lana enveloped Addie in an exuberant hug.

"Hi, Lana," Addie said into her friend's ear and waved at Veta and Ivan in the kitchen.

They were a cheerful family and luckily, for them and their business, the locals as well as the college students had welcomed their Ukrainian charm.

"You need to visit more often," Lana said as she held Addie at arm's length. "Two weeks is too long. Right, Veta?"

"Right," Veta said as she came out to the lobby and gave Addie a big hug.

"What's wrong?" Veta asked with a mischievous grin. "You find a man who keeps you too busy to visit us now?"

Addie laughed. "No, just a lot of farm work and writing deadlines."

The two other women chuckled as they got back to work. "You shouldn't be that busy," Lana said as she delivered a caramel mocha and a grilled sandwich to one of their customers, a big smile on her face and a sincere 'Thank you for coming in,' on her lips.

"You hired three strong men to help you," she continued as she returned to the counter. "You should have lots of time to come see us and go out once in a while."

Addie sighed. "Well, I had to fire those three strong men this morning. And when I checked, the work they were supposed to have finished was either half done or not done at all."

"Oh, no," Veta said as she brought another plate of yummy goodness to the front for Lana to deliver.

"That's no good," Lana said as she took the plate out to the customer.

Veta rested her elbows on the counter, concern in her pale blue eyes. "What are you going to do?"

"Well," Addie leaned on the counter across from her friend, "I was either going to do it all myself or take the long drive to Selah or Yakima, or even waste the four-hour trip down to Tri-Cities to see if I could find someone. *If* there was anyone still available. But I may not have to do any of that now."

"Oh!" Lana said as she returned and caught the last half of what Addie had said. "Did you find yourself a good man? Is he handsome? Is he smart? Does he have a brother?"

Addie chuckled at the younger woman's exuberance. Lana was a flirt and boy-crazy to boot, but Addie found her amusing rather than annoying. Maybe that was because of her genuinely sweet disposition.

"I did find a man," she answered, "but for the farm, not for me."

Lana pouted prettily in disappointment.

"Where did you find someone this late in the season?" Veta asked.

Knowing neither of them would like this, she chose her next words carefully. "I picked him up on the side of the road and gave him a ride to town."

"What!" the sisters said in unison, and Ivan looked over at her with narrowed eyes. Ivan wasn't much of a talker, but he was protective of his family, which she'd become when he married Veta two years ago.

"You picked up a stranger?" Veta asked, her eyes narrowed, looking every bit the protective older sister.

"Yes, I did, and a good thing, too—"

"He's one of the cowboys from the rodeo, isn't he?" Lana asked excitedly.

"Well, yes, he is. He's experienced, says he's a hard worker, and doesn't know any of the locals around here. Anyway, he's agreed to stay for a few months to help me out."

"And why did he do that?" Veta asked and Ivan nodded, both still suspicious and clearly expecting Cade to be dangerous.

"His truck broke down and he doesn't have the money to fix it."

When Veta tilted her head as if to say, "And how do you know that?" Addie recounted her experience and conversation with Cade.

"He's a better choice than Mark Harden," Addie said and her friends all nodded.

"That's true," Veta said.

The bell above the door jingled and Addie turned, hoping to see Cade ambling in, but it was only a couple of tourists. An odd sense of disappointment washed over her. She stepped back as Lana greeted the new customers and in a flash, had them telling her all they'd done and planned to do that weekend.

"We had a really handsome cowboy come in here this morning," Lana confided quietly once her customers had finished and gone to their seats. "One of the bronc riders."

Addie lifted her eyebrows and grinned. "Really?"

"Yes. Veta keeps telling me to slow down, but how can I when there are so many men in the world?" She smiled slyly. "Besides this one was..." She waved a hand in front of her face. "Oh, so hot, hot, hot! Had eyes you could drown in."

"Stop drooling, Svetlana," her sister said sternly as she brought two drinks to the counter for Lana to deliver. "I'm sure Addie has better things to think about than your endless crushes."

"No, she doesn't," Lana said with a wink that made Addie laugh as she sashayed across the cafe.

Veta shook her head as she eyed her sister. "I worry about her. She has no caution."

"She's still young," Addie said.

"Yes, young and silly."

"And so were you, once upon a time," Lana said as she returned to the counter.

Veta sighed and went back to the grill. "Are you going to get your regular, Addie?"

"I'm waiting for someone."

"Oh, the new man?" Lana's eyes sparkled with excitement. "Is it a date?"

Veta rolled her eyes behind her sister's back and Addie chuckled again.

"No, Lana, it's not a date. It's just time to eat and we're both here. Well, he should be here shortly."

"Ah, too bad," Lana said and then grinned broadly. "You need a date."

"No, I don't," Addie replied. She had enough to do as it was. "Don't start that again."

Lana's eyes widened in mock innocence. "I'm not starting anything."

"Leave her alone, Lana." Veta's voice snapped like a whip, but Lana waved off her sister's warning.

"I was just saying…"

Veta handed a bag of sandwiches to a customer and then turned back to her sister, her professional smile vanishing. "Well, stop."

It was Lana's turn to roll her eyes, but even her sister's scolding couldn't keep her down long.

"Oh, my gosh, Veta, it's him. The cowboy I was just talking about. It's him!" She grabbed Addie's hand and clutched it between both of hers while staring out the front windows. Then she released Addie and began smoothing her hair. "Do I look okay?"

"You're as adorable as ever," Addie said with a chuckle as she turned to see the cowboy her friend was so enamored with.

Her breath stuck in her throat.

Stepping up to the curb, headed for the front door of the shop was Cade Brody. She glanced at Lana's pretty, love-struck face and felt a twinge of something burning in her chest. Straightening her posture and pushing the unexpected sensation away, Addie turned back to Cade.

As soon as the door swung open, Cade glanced around the small shop with those startlingly blue eyes. The minute they landed on Addie and the corners of his mouth pulled up in a small grin, it seemed as if all the air had been sucked from the room.

Oh, boy, Addie thought. *Get ahold of yourself, girl.*

Despite her self-castigation, the moment he stepped up beside her and his scent—musky man with a touch of leather and wide-open spaces—washed over her, her whole body lit up like a Christmas tree.

"Hi," he said softly and she smiled back at him.

"Hello again," Lana said before Addie could reply. "Nice to see *you* again so soon. Couldn't get enough of our coffee, huh?"

He turned to look at the younger woman. "Hey," he replied with a friendly grin. "Yeah, the coffee's pretty good."

Lana's mouth curled up and Addie pressed her lips together. Why was she so annoyed by Lana's flirtation? She'd never had that problem before, and there'd been plenty of opportunities.

"So, Addie, are you going to introduce us?" Lana asked, her eyes glued to Cade. Veta, who was in the kitchen with her husband, cleared her throat loudly, but Lana ignored her.

"Sure," Addie replied and made the introductions. Ivan and Veta nodded from the back, but Lana's eyes lit up excitedly and that prickly feeling rose inside Addie once more.

"Well, what can I get for you this time, Cade?" Lana asked.

He glanced at Addie and she pushed back her irritation.

"I was waiting for you," she said with a small smile, nervous all of a sudden. "I forgot to ask what you wanted."

He nodded, glanced at the menu, and quickly placed an order for coffee and a hot pastrami sandwich with chips.

Addie ordered her regular BLT and chips. "To go, please."

Lana frowned slightly as she gave her sister the sandwich orders and began putting the rest together.

Addie shifted her feet and tried to swallow the guilt that thickened her throat. She usually stayed for her meal, but this time they'd have to eat in the truck. She told herself it had nothing to do with Lana and the sharp prickly feeling in Addie's chest when the younger woman smiled at Cade. It was only because there was so much to do on the farm and they didn't have time to waste. She needed to give Cade a tour and let him know everything that needed to be done and in what order. Plus, the animals needed feeding, she still had a few thousand words to type before the end of the day, and she would have to make a decent dinner for the both of them. She didn't have time to sit around here, and neither did Cade.

More customers entered, and Addie and Cade moved aside to wait for their order. He seemed nervous or self-conscious, but she couldn't understand why. Unless Lana's smiles and constant glances were the culprits, but she didn't think so.

"Miss Malory, I…" He shoved his hands in the front pockets of his jeans and shifted his feet. "I...need to ask a favor."

She tilted her head and frowned. "What kind of favor?"

He stared at his boots. "I need..." He paused, his shoulders hunched, but then he straightened his spine and pressed on. "I need to move my truck off the road," he said. "It's going to cost enough to fix without having to pay towing and impound fees, too."

She relaxed, though why she felt relieved she didn't know. "Sure, I can help you with that."

His eyes dropped again. "I don't mean for you to have to pay for it, but..."

"I don't either," she said, and he looked up. "If you're okay with it, I can tow your truck back to my place and you can work on it there. I've got lots of tools. I should have what you'll need."

Gratitude shone in his eyes once her words finally sunk in. "That'd be great. Thanks."

Warm tingles danced in her belly, swirling outward in ever-increasing waves, swelling her chest while the rest of her acknowledged just how attracted to him she was. *My goodness, he's like her most favorite candy, ever.*

She plastered her own awkward smile on her lips and reminded herself to breathe.

"No problem," she said, dropping her gaze and working to get her galloping heart under control. His eyes mesmerized her, spoke to her without words, saying things she longed to hear, drowning her in desire.

That's stupid, she told herself, squeezing her eyelids closed and hoping he didn't notice her discomfort. *You don't even know him.*

"You okay?" he asked, his long fingers gently gripping her arm. Goosebumps raced over her skin and warmth shot through her nerve endings like lightning.

Oh, my gosh!

Quickly getting herself in hand, she turned another big, neighborly smile his way. "Of course, I am. Why wouldn't I be?"

A wave of disappointment struck her when he dropped his hand and shrugged shyly. "Don't know. You seemed...annoyed."

"By what?" she asked, truly confused now.

"Not sure," he said, brushing the toe of his boot over the laminate flooring. "But I don't want you to have second thoughts about the job."

This time her smile was genuine. "That's not going to happen. As long as you're a good worker and don't disrespect me, you'll have a job."

"I won't...and thanks," he said, gratitude brightening his expression, making the excited woman inside her dance on her toes.

Calm down, she scolded. *He may not even be interested. Besides, he's your employee, not your boyfriend. You need his help, so don't screw this up!*

CHAPTER 4

As soon as he set the parking brake, Cade hopped out of his broken-down truck and jogged around the front to remove the towrope from the frame. Addie backed up about a foot to give him slack and, once he had the neon-yellow, nylon strap disconnected from both vehicles, he placed it in her truck's bed and she pulled off to the side to park near her house.

He took a moment to glance around the dooryard, and he could see right away that the place had been neglected for some time. Weeds clogged the flowerbeds by the house and the vegetable garden he'd spied out back on the way in seemed to need tending as well. The house and garage needed painting, as did the barn, which—by the shafts of light he could see through the open door—also needed to have the roof repaired.

She hadn't been kidding about needing help.

The engine of her truck cut off and he turned just in time to see her hop out of the four-by-four. She seemed so tiny beside the big truck, but her size wasn't what made his mouth go dry. Oh, no. Seeing how her ample breasts bounced inside her loose tank top as she landed on her booted feet did that. Once that vision met his eyes, he couldn't help but notice how her blue jeans hugged her hips and thighs as she approached him with a smile that struck him like a blow to the gut.

Damn, she's adorable. With the messy bun of blonde hair sagging off the back of her head and a blush of sun and fresh air on her cheeks, she looked downright kissable. Little wisps curled against the elegant line of her neck and longer strands brushed her shoulders. All that bare skin glowed in the afternoon sunlight and looked soft as silk. His fingers itched to test the smooth expanse and the rest of her supple curves, too. He could almost feel his hands dive into her hair and loosen it from its confines, could picture it unfurling down her back in a cascade of golden waves.

"Well, we made it," she said, stopping in front of him and lifting a hand to pull a stray curl from her cheek.

Damn if he hadn't wanted to do that for her. His hands clenched and he pushed them into his pockets to keep them to himself. But his mind stampeded into dangerous territory, envisioning this cute bundle of beautiful wearing nothing but her devastating smile.

"Yeah, we did," he said, stifling the groan of lust that flooded through his veins. "I'm impressed."

Her brows drew down. "How so?"

"Well," he said, rocking on his heels, "most women would've been nervous to do something like that, especially with a manual transmission. A lot wouldn't have even tried. But you jumped right in and were phenomenal. You're a natural."

His gut clenched when her face lit up at the compliment. He liked seeing her smile a little too much.

"I've done it a few times and it *is* a little nerve-wracking," she said, "but the truck wasn't going to move itself."

He chuckled. "Yeah, I suppose not."

"Now that we're here, though, I can give you the grand tour."

"Lead the way."

"All righty." She pointed at the large, round, squat metal structures across the wide dooryard from where they stood. "Those are conventional silos and hold corn and grain. They're about two-thirds full right now, and I plan to sell about half of each before winter."

She started strolling toward the barn and he joined her.

"Over there," she pointed at a Quonset hut to the right of the barn, "is the machine shed. That's where all the big equipment goes, like the tractor and the combine."

Stepping through the barn doors, she turned to face him.

"I'd like to keep more hay in here but, as you can see," she said, waving a hand at the shafts of sunlight streaming in through open holes, "the roof is less than sound. There are three covered areas in the fields near the cattle, but only one of those has a decent roof. The other two were supposed to be repaired by my last crew, but I checked earlier this morning and found only one had been half done. The other has the shingles torn off and some of the boards removed, but that's it. Except for the huge mess they left on the ground."

"How long have you been here?" he asked, glancing around the less than tidy barn.

"Only about three months," she said. "Why?"

"It looks like this place has been neglected for a lot longer than that." He frowned. "You said you have a harvest coming up. Did you do the planting?"

"No, the previous owner did that, but he was getting on in years and slowing down. I don't think he could keep up with everything anymore."

She strolled back out into the sunlight and Cade followed.

"When he had a heart attack, it was time to quit, but he'd already put in the crops." She turned to face Cade. "I offered to give him a percentage of the profits on hay and grain for the next three years, and he agreed to a discounted price."

"That's very generous of you."

"There's a little more to it than that." She tilted her head. "Remember the ladies at the coffee shop?"

He nodded, wondering what they had to do with anything.

"Well, Pete—the farmer who sold me this land—is a friend of theirs, and Veta's husband helped Pete out on occasion. They're the ones who told me about this place, and Pete left me detailed directions on how to proceed. He's a nice man and was in a bind financially, so I didn't feel right letting him sell so low. I wanted him to have something to live on."

Cade nodded but didn't voice his thoughts on how tenderhearted her actions were. It touched him that she'd be so concerned about a stranger.

But then, she'd picked him up off the side of the road and offered him better prospects than he'd had this morning.

"Plus," she added, "if I miss a payment, the farm will revert back to him, which is why I need to make as much profit as possible off the harvests. I'm arrogant enough to buy the place, but not enough to think that I can run it by myself. At least, not indefinitely."

"You ever worked a farm before?"

"No, not really." When his eyebrows went up, she continued, "I mean, I can grow things, but I've never done it on a large scale like this. That's why I was looking for reliable, knowledgeable help."

"I see."

Her chin went up obstinately and she glared at him. "I *could* do it if I had to."

Wow. All spit and fire all of a sudden. She was feisty. He liked it. And not just because she would need all that stubbornness and grit to run a farm.

He gave her his best smile—the one that always disarmed the ladies he met. "I didn't mean to imply that you couldn't."

"Well," she said, eyeing him askance, seeming both uncertain and feisty at the same time, "just remember I'm as capable as you. So keep me in the loop on everything. I want to learn."

"Yes, ma'am."

"And, please, call me Addie."

"Yes, ma'am."

She glared at him again.

His head dipped to hide the blush that heated his cheeks. "Addie."

She dropped her chin and her lips tugged up. "Thank you."

Kissable lips, he thought, then mentally shook himself. *She's your boss! And you're just a homeless loser who doesn't need another heartache. So, stop it!*

"May I call you Cade?" she asked.

Despite the familiarity of it, he hesitated only a moment. "Sure."

"Great," she said cheerily and headed toward the house. "This way, Cade."

Following her wouldn't have been so bad if his mind had cooperated with his previous command. But now, with the nice view of her perfect derriere swaying seductively in front of him, his thoughts turned dirty once more.

What's wrong with me? It's not as if he'd been celibate since he left home. There'd been plenty of buckle bunnies at the rodeos he'd attended over the last two years, but that had gotten old. He'd found himself turning down their invitations more often than not over the last few months.

At one time, he'd wanted so much more than that. He'd wanted the whole package—marriage, children—and was on the verge of getting it, too. At least, he'd thought he was.

Now, he was a drifter who just wanted some peace.

"So, you're growing corn and hay," he said, hoping to distract himself from the sexy roundness of Addie's rear end and how it would feel in his hands.

"Yep." Heading for the open garage, she grinned over her shoulder. The brightness and bit of tease in her expression made his cock jump in his jeans.

He swallowed, ignoring the heat flooding his nether regions and quickened his pace. "What kind of hay?"

She spun on her heel while still walking backward, her beautiful breast swaying as she moved—which didn't help the situation in his jeans at all.

"Timothy and alfalfa," she said and spun around again when he caught up to her.

He whistled. "That's some high-end feed."

"Yep, and it's almost ready to be cut again. At least, that's what I've been told. When we're done here, I'll take you on a tour of the fields. It's a little late to do much else today but get you settled."

He nodded again.

She rushed ahead a few steps and gestured expansively with her arms, clearly proud to be showing off her home, despite its shortcomings.

"The barn and machine shed have most of the tools, but in here," she moved forward, "you'll find my little car, lots of other things to help with your truck, and the door to the mud room." She pointed to an inside door behind her. "There's a sink in there and a place for dirty," her gaze drifted down his body and back up, a little too slowly to only be assessing his state of cleanliness, "boots," she finished and then averted her eyes.

That can't be what it looked like. It had happened so fast that he wondered if her seeming interest had only been a figment of his overactive imagination.

"There's cold water bottles and soda in the fridge beside the door if you need it. And over here——" She started to turn in the opposite direction as she entered the shade of the garage but never made it.

A surprised yelp escaped as her feet slipped out from under her and she started to fall. Cade rushed forward, putting himself between her and the fender of her sporty little car. His arms snaked around her as her head smacked into his breastbone instead of the metal, and he gathered her against his chest.

"Ow," she mumbled, pressing her hand to her head. She tried to stand, but her feet slid backward. He tightened his hold on her body to keep her from falling again and looked down. The concrete floor was covered in what looked like used engine oil. No wonder she'd lost her footing spinning around on that slick stuff.

"Hold on to me, I got you," he said as he stepped back onto the dirt driveway, taking her with him.

Safely back on her own feet again and with her hands on his shoulders, she looked up into his face. Her brown eyes were wide and the prettiest shade of pink crept over her bosom and cheeks. She felt so good in his arms, the soft pillows of her breasts crushed against his chest, straining upward in a lovely display, her nipples poking into him…

He inhaled sharply. *Oh, shit…*

He should let her go and move away, but he couldn't.

"Thank you," she murmured.

He barely heard her over the blood rushing in his ears. *You don't need this,* he told himself. *Let her go!*

Uncertainty flashed in her eyes and she bit her lower lip. His cock sprang to full attention. That got him moving. He released his hold and hastily stepped back.

"You're welcome," he said almost dismissively as he rounded her to get a better look at the mess on the garage floor. Anything to distract himself from her pretty face and hourglass figure.

Crouching, he ran a finger through the dark slime, rubbed it against his thumb, and then brought it to his nose. After a quick sniff to verify his suspicions, he wiped it on the ground.

"You always coat the garage floor with used motor oil?" he asked, glancing up at her frowning face.

"No," she said, looking unsure of herself. "Pete kept it in a barrel around the side." She pointed to the wall of the garage between them and the barn several yards away.

Studying the garage, he spotted the edge of a black fifty-gallon drum tipped on its side behind her car. He pointed at it. "Looks like it grew legs."

Addie stepped up beside him and squinted into the dimness.

"How'd that get in there?" she mumbled and shook her head.

"Got any enemies?"

"Just the ones I fired this morning," she said. "Ted's just petty enough to do something like this, too."

Cade turned and scanned the area. "You think he'd stick around for the show?"

"I doubt it. This is probably the only thing he did. Just wanted to let me know how much I need them and how pissed he is at me."

"Are you going to report this?"

Her shoulders stiffened and she shook her head again. "No."

He frowned. "You should. Someone was obviously trespassing and this vandalism could be considered malicious mischief."

"It's not worth the time," she said, strength returning to her voice, but she still seemed nervous. Even more so when he mentioned telling the authorities.

Now why would she not trust the sheriff?

He let it go. If she didn't want to report it, fine. It wasn't his problem.

"Okay then, let's get this cleaned up and check the other equipment for damage," Cade said softly, reaching out to sweep small, consoling circles on her back. "Then we can finish the tour and start getting this place back on track."

"Sure," she agreed.

He dropped his hand when she turned away, headed for the barn.

"The shovels are out here," she said. "We can use dirt from the side yard to soak it up."

She was all business once more, but Cade had seen her hands tremble as she'd stared at the black goo. Whoever had done this may have only intended to make a mess to inconvenience her, but they'd almost succeeded in doing so much worse. If he hadn't been there to catch her—or if he'd been a fraction slower—she would've hit her head on the car. It might've only knocked her out, but it could have caused a grave injury, too.

Something more was going on here than just a pretty woman looking for a farmhand. She'd told him about firing those men this morning, but when he asked, she hadn't thought they'd be an issue. This proved her wrong.

Cade turned to follow her to the barn. Whatever trouble they brought, he couldn't sit by and let some evil-minded asshole ruin or hurt her. It didn't matter if he was attracted to her, that she was kind and generous. He'd never taken kindly to bullies, and he wasn't about to start now.

CHAPTER 5

The sun sat low on the horizon, the sky filled with bright orange and pink clouds as the day began to fade. With dinner plates and utensils in hand, Addie pushed open the sliding glass door from her kitchen and stepped out into the warm, early evening air of her backyard. A cool breeze whipped at the skirt of her yellow cotton dress and caressed her bare legs—a reminder that Indian summer would soon be over. As usual, she'd tied her unruly hair into a messy bun on top of her head and—also as normal—little tendrils had escaped as she'd run around the kitchen making dinner. The annoyance of the wispy strands wasn't enough to spoil her mood, however. She loved the summertime, but she looked forward to the brisk air and changing colors of autumn, and the upcoming holiday season.

Almost two weeks had passed since Cade began working for her, and she was still getting used to her duty as the food service provider. Normally, she'd eat whenever her writing schedule allowed, but her employee needed the meals she'd promised at regular intervals, and on time. Not that he'd complained—not even when the food was late. But after seeing how hard he worked each day, she knew he'd be famished by lunch and again by dinnertime.

To avoid starving him, she'd begun planning ahead and setting herself a timer to make sure she got started cooking early, especially for breakfast. He'd said he was fine with cereal and toast in the morning, but after that first day, it had been clear, to her at least, that cereal and toast alone weren't enough. She'd gone to the grocery store that afternoon and stocked up on the basics for hot, hardy breakfasts.

When Cade stepped into the kitchen after his early chores the next morning, a wide smile had curled his handsome mouth and the appreciative look in his eyes had warmed her to her toes.

She smiled at the memory.

Crossing to the picnic table that sat a few yards from the house, Addie dismissed the dreamy image, though she was less successful with the warmth that swirled low in her belly. Shaking her head, she quickly set the table and returned to the house. Her bare feet made little noise as she stepped back inside to gather more items for the table.

Cade should be wrapping up his work any time now.

She'd been stunned by how many side jobs he'd completed in the short time he'd been there. He'd been more productive in a week than Ted and his two friends combined. Aside from helping with the animals and working on the hay harvest, Cade had repaired and re-shingled the roof of one of the hay storage sheds, cleaned up the mess left by the others, made a trip to the dump, and then started on the barn roof this morning.

Twenty minutes ago, she'd strolled across her lawn out front to let him know dinner was almost ready and gotten herself another more-than-pleasant surprise.

Cade had been shirtless, his tanned skin glistening in the setting sun with the wonderful display of flexing, bulging, and shifting muscles beneath. The combination had made her heart flutter wildly in her chest. A red-hot shot of lust had struck her low and deep inside and she froze in place.

Unsure how long she'd stood in the dooryard with her mouth hanging open, staring and forgetting to breathe, she'd maintained just enough self-control to keep from blurting out the first thing that came to her mind.

Oh, my God... I was right! He does have awesome abs... and arms, and shoulders, and... She'd sighed like a lovesick teenager.

More embarrassing was the twinkle in his eyes when he'd glanced over and caught her ogling him. Even at that distance, she had felt his gaze travel over her body, making her feel naked and aroused, and a little self-conscious. Increasing heat that had nothing to do with the sun or the warm, summer-like temperature had flooded her veins and crept into her cheeks when he grinned. But she'd refused to act like the young, shy girl she had once been or let the insecurities about her weight affect how she acted with Cade.

"Dinner will be ready shortly," she'd shouted to him and his smile warmed her further.

"I'll be down in a few, then," he'd replied but didn't move. He'd held her gaze from the barn roof, while she stood, her bare feet rooted to the sparse grass that dotted the edge of her front lawn. Electricity sparked between them, pulling at something inside her. She'd wanted to climb up the ladder, cross the roof, and pull him in for a long, hot kiss.

But that was crazy. She barely knew him. She may joke with her friends—and herself—about how she'd like to touch a man or fool around with one, but she really wasn't interested in a one—or two—night stand.

Was she?

Somehow breaking the spell he'd placed on her, she had smiled awkwardly and waved before heading back into the house to collect the dinnerware.

Now, she had the table set and had just wrapped a towel around the ceramic dish that held the warmed tortillas she'd heated for their chicken fajitas. Gathering it up, she headed back out the sliding glass door.

She'd taken several steps before acknowledging the sound of water running and splashing behind her. Glancing over her shoulder, she nearly tripped over her suddenly clumsy feet.

Cade stood at the end of the house. Still shirtless, he was bent at the waist, running cool water from the hose over his head and shoulders. Droplets sparkled like tiny diamonds in his short, coffee-colored hair as the clear liquid streamed through to splash onto the grass-covered ground, splattering his dusty boots.

As she took another step, the world around her slowed to a snail's pace. Cade straightened, flipping his head back, the water spilling from his head to his neck, over his broad shoulders and perfectly chiseled pecs in a cascade of shining glory. The water had crept down his flat abs to soak his faded jeans. The damp denim turned deep blue and was plastered to him from his hips to his knees, showing off the long muscles of his thighs and the perfect form of his cowboy ass. He was a vision of masculine beauty, and Addie's brain short-circuited.

Abruptly, the world jolted into normal motion. Her mouth went dry and a little squeak escaped her lips as she stumbled. Trying to keep from dropping the hot dish—or herself—onto the ground, she fumbled forward but only made things worse. Letting out a small cry, she landed on her knees, somehow managing to keep from sprawling face-first in the grass. As it was, her bare knees not only ached, but would be grass-stained as well. *A lovely greenish-brown to go with my pretty yellow sundress. Great...*

Footsteps came up beside her and her breath seized in her throat when Cade's big hand skated along her back. Her skin warmed and tingled everywhere he touched and she clenched the towel with the warm bowl still in her hands.

"Hey, are you okay?" he asked, his brows drawn together over his concerned blue eyes. "That looked painful."

She gave a little laugh, hoping it sounded less contrived to him than it did to her ears.

"I'm fine," she said, moving to get to her feet. "Just clumsy."

"Let me help," he said, wrapping a steadying arm around her waist, while his other hand gently gripped her elbow. "Are you sure you're okay?"

"Yeah," she mumbled as he assisted her to stand. She didn't even mind the moisture of his jeans dampening her dress.

When she was on her feet again, she glanced up at him, ready with a word of gratitude, but it disintegrated when their eyes locked and everything narrowed to just the two of them. That familiar tugging sensation inside her returned in spades and she was surprised not to see steam rising between them.

Nervously, she licked her lips.

His gaze dropped to her mouth, his face softened, and he leaned in a bit.

Oh God, is he going to kiss me?

Her heart rate went crazy, pounding in her ears so loudly, she was sure he would hear it. The air suddenly seemed too thin—she couldn't get her breath as she stared up at him, completely mesmerized, wondering if his lips were as firm and warm as they looked.

She shivered involuntarily and he pulled back, another frown marring his brow.

Disappointment tightened her chest, but she shoved it aside. *Of course, he wasn't going to kiss me. What the hell was I thinking?*

"Are you cold," he asked, interrupting her self-chastisement.

"A…little," she lied. She couldn't tell him it was his nearness that had her trembling.

"Why don't you grab a sweater while I run in and change?" He dropped his arm from her waist and stepped toward the house.

She instantly missed the warmth of his body beside hers, but smiled broadly, as if his suggestion was the greatest she'd ever heard.

"Yeah, I'll do that," she said as she set the bowl of tousled tortillas on the table and placed the lid—that she'd rescued from the ground after stumbling around—on top to keep them warm.

When she turned around, he stood just outside the sliding glass door, a look of concern on his face. "I don't mind if we eat inside."

This time her smile was genuine. "No, it's okay. I'd like to enjoy the pretty weather while we have it. Unless you'd rather…?"

He shook his head. "It's fine by me. I just wanted you to be comfortable." He stepped inside the open door. "Be right back."

Her heart melted a little more at his thoughtful concern.

He's just being kind, it doesn't mean *anything.*

She followed him into the kitchen to grab the rest of their dinner and take it out to the table, then she darted through the house to grab a light sweater. After all, the sun would set and she may need it before they finished the meal.

She made a quick stop in her bathroom to wipe the grass stains from her knees and then dashed back down the hall to the kitchen and out the back door.

Cade stood by the table in dry, faded blue jeans and a gray T-shirt that hugged the muscles of his back and shoulders—oddly, he hadn't tucked it in. His arms were crossed over his chest, staring at the sky as the sun sank toward the blueish-purple mountains in the distance.

She hustled forward, her bare feet rustling the longish grass. "You didn't need to wait for me."

He turned at the sound of her voice, a crooked grin on his lips. "What kind of gentleman would I be if I didn't wait for a lady?"

Her cheeks warmed and her chest felt light as a feather.

"Well, thank you," she said. "Please sit and help yourself."

They tucked into the meal and Addie was glad she'd made the extra chicken. This man could eat, and pride filled her watching him enjoy the meal she'd prepared.

"This is another great dinner," he said after a long drink of lemonade, poured into a glass from the pitcher on the table. "You're an awesome cook."

She inhaled deeply and smiled. "Well, that's quite a compliment. Thanks."

"It's more than deserved."

She took a bite of her tortilla-wrapped fajita as Cade built himself another one.

"How's the barn roof looking?" she asked after swallowing her mouthful.

He nodded, chewing rapidly and swallowing.

"Better than I thought," he said and sipped a little more lemonade. "The dry-rot hasn't spread far. I replaced four sheathing boards on the deck and I'm going to weave in some new felt and shingles. When I'm done, the whole thing should be good for a few more years."

"Oh," she widened her eyes in surprise, "that's great news."

He chuckled. "I thought you'd like that."

His laugh did odd things to her insides, made her warm, fuzzy, and shivery all at once.

"I do," she said in a low voice she didn't recognize.

He glanced at her mouth then met her gaze with a raised eyebrow.

She cleared her dry throat and took a drink of lemonade, anything to avoid his eyes.

"Um-hmm…" She waved her hand excitedly, remembering her phone conversation earlier that morning. "I have good news for you, too," she said once the lemonade was gone.

"Really?" he asked and she heard a low rumble of something hot and steamy in the single utterance.

That tugging sensation inside her was back and she bit her lip, drawing his attention.

"It's not a big deal," she said, backtracking a little.

"Please, do share." Now his voice sounded almost suggestive, and the look in his azure eyes ignited a burning tension between her thighs. She squirmed a little. *My God, he's got me turned on with just a look and the sound of his voice.*

"I'm… I…We…W-We're going to have company on Saturday."

"Okay," he said, seeming confused and…disappointed. "I'll be working all day, but I can fend for myself, eat in my room or in the barn—"

"Oh, no," she said hurriedly, followed by a nervous chuckle. "No, no, I didn't mean it like that. My friends from the coffee shop offered to help with the hay baling and stacking." She tilted her head. "You are going to start baling on Saturday, right?"

"Yeah, if it's dry by then. I may have to turn it to let the sun dry out all the internal moisture from the stalks for another day or two before baling."

"You think they won't be dried out by the weekend?"

"No, I think it will be if the forecast is correct, but anything can happen. The weather's supposed to cloud up next week, so we're going to have to get it up and stacked before any rain comes."

"That should be easy with the three of them," Addie said, "and Lana mentioned that she might bring a couple of friends, too."

He chuckled again. "I'll bet. Are you planning to join us?"

"Of course. I told you I'd be helping when I could. Besides, I need to learn."

He nodded and took another bite of his tortilla-wrapped fajita meat.

"How's the writing going?" he asked after swallowing.

Her chest warmed, gladdened by his curiosity in her work, though she wasn't sure why. "It's good. I finished one yesterday, I'm almost done with the story that's due on Monday, and I only need a little more research to finish the one I have to turn in tomorrow."

"What are they about?"

His interest made her smile. "Well, one is editing and fact-checking a piece on comparing the specs of the top-rated CPUs this year for a technical magazine. That one's pretty easy." She tilted her head and winked at him. "The other one has to do with immigration statistics and the effects of the system on families. That one's taken a lot of research."

"What kind of research?"

"You know, digging through statistics, talking to officials, and interviewing individuals and families, but I should be able to finish them both by tomorrow so I can help on Saturday."

He whistled. "Wow, I don't know how you can do that."

"What? I know they're very different writing styles, but…"

He shook his head. "No, I meant, write stories, period. I wouldn't know where to begin. I mean, give me a horse, a bull, a broken tractor any day, and I could do what was needed. But writing? Not my forte."

She chuckled. "Well, it's a good thing you can do those things, otherwise *I'd* be in big trouble."

He grinned. "I suppose so."

The hot tension that had sprung up between them lowered to a simmer, then became comfortable. As they finished the rest of their meal with sporadic conversation, Addie realized that Cade had become a friend over the last couple of weeks. She might be ridiculously attracted to him, but that didn't change that he was also kind and funny and—if his work was any indicator—extremely reliable. But there were times she sensed insecurity in him. Not in his abilities on the farm, but in his worth as a man. The way he would joke with her, laugh with her, and then his beautiful eyes would darken before he'd look away, or in how he refused to take a compliment.

"I really appreciate all the hard work you're doing," she'd commented at lunch a few days ago. "You're really good at all this ranch stuff."

He'd shrugged and avoided her eyes. "I'm not good for much else."

Her heart had squeezed tight at that comment and she wondered at his self-deprecation. She had disagreed, but he'd only shrugged again and they'd finished that meal in relative silence.

Surreptitiously studying him now, she wondered once more, what caused him to be so down on himself? But she didn't want to pry, so she kept her thoughts to herself.

When they'd finished eating their dinner, Cade helped her clear the table and clean the dishes.

"Thanks again for your help cleaning up," Addie said as she closed the dishwasher and wiped her hands on a dishtowel.

"You're welcome," he said, drying the now clean pan she'd used to cook the meat, onions, and peppers for their fajitas.

"You don't have to do that, you know."

"So you've said." He opened the drawer beneath the oven and set the pan inside and then pushed the drawer closed.

His willingness to help with the domestic duties each day had been a pleasant surprise. The fact that he'd learned where everything went in her kitchen so quickly—and that their conversations during meals and clean up seemed so easy—was also a happy wonder. All of it felt…special in an odd way Addie couldn't quite define.

"Well, I mean it," she replied.

Straightening, Cade folded the damp towel and hung it from the oven handle to dry. He chuckled, and Addie's insides twisted, then turned all soft and fuzzy.

"I know you do, but my mom taught us better than that."

"Us?" Addie arched a curious brow.

He froze. Only for a brief moment, but Addie saw it.

Turning toward her, he crossed his arms over his chest. "Yeah, my brother and me." He smiled sadly. "My mom made sure we knew how to take care of ourselves and the woman in our lives. She said it wasn't right to expect a woman who works to take care of everything in the house."

Her lips curled. "I think I'd like your mom."

His eyes darkened, turned dull, and his whole body seemed to fold inward. "She's dead. My dad, too."

Addie gasped. "Oh, Cade," she touched his arm consolingly, "I'm so sorry. I didn't know."

"Of course, you didn't." He shook his head and his sad half-grin broke her heart. "But thank you anyway."

"Do you want to...talk about it?" She had no idea why she'd asked that. He just seemed so upset, as if his parents' deaths had come recently and he was still grieving.

He stepped back away from her touch and leaned his hips against the kitchen counter, arms still crossed over his chest. "There's not much to talk about. My mom died while I was in school several years ago. It was sudden, a brain aneurysm, and my dad was never the same afterward. He passed about two years later. My brother and I worked the ranch for a while, but it was a little..." he shrugged, "crowded. I decided to head out on my own and I've been amblin' about ever since. End of story."

"When did you talk to your brother last?"

His frown deepened. "We don't talk much."

"You and your brother don't...get along?"

He sighed and his arms flexed against his chest. "You could say that."

A lot more lay behind that statement, but Addie got the impression it was off-limits.

"How long have you been amblin' around?" she asked instead, leaning her elbows on the end of the counter. This was the most he'd offered about himself since he arrived, and she was curious.

"Hmm," he murmured, looking up at the ceiling, apparently counting in his head. "Five-ish years altogether."

"Wow, that's a long time."

He nodded. "Yep..."

"Didn't you say you've only been in rodeo for a couple of years?"

"Yeah."

"So, why the delay?"

He shrugged. "I didn't think of trying it right away," he said, pushing away from the counter and dropping his arms. "I'm beat. If you don't mind, I think I'll grab a shower and turn in."

"Sure," she said, sensing a barrier had dropped between them, effectively ending that topic of discussion. "I'm going to turn in soon, too."

"I should be able to get the barn roof completed tomorrow," he said, moving toward the hall, his shoulders sagging a bit. "Then I'll check the machinery and make sure it's all ready for Saturday."

"Sounds good," Addie said. "Goodnight, Cade."

He stopped at the corner to the hall and glanced over his shoulder. Everything about him since she'd brought up his family seemed hard and resistant, but his face softened as he stared back at her. "Goodnight, Addie. Thanks again for dinner."

"All part of Addie's full-service kitchen," she said with a teasing grin and a mock curtsy. "Morning, noon, and night. Twenty-four, seven." She winked.

A smile spread across his face. "You're adorable." His eyes widened slightly as if shocked by his words, then his expression went blank.

"Thank you, Cade," she said quietly, meaning more than just for his compliment. Gratitude for him and his work, his company, his kindness were all mixed together in those three words. She lowered her gaze, feeling shy and uncertain all of a sudden.

When she peeked at him, she saw his slow, sexy grin soften the hard planes of his handsome face once more and he returned her wink, but his reply made her heart flutter.

"Any time, sweetheart. Any time."

CHAPTER 6

Cade lay naked on his double bed, a white sheet pulled to his waist, staring up at the dark ceiling trying not to think—but failing miserably. Thinking would get him into trouble, cause problems he didn't want to face, but his brain wouldn't shut off.

He'd been laying here for hours, trying to drift into unconsciousness, to ignore the heat and discomfort in his body, but had, so far, been unsuccessful at both.

I should just get up and take another shower. A really cold *one this time.*

He sighed and stayed where he was. He needed sleep.

He needed to get that woman out of his head.

Damn him if his first instincts about working for Addie Malory hadn't been correct. She was a huge distraction, one he'd sworn to avoid. Not that it mattered. Despite repeated and painful reminders of the last time he'd let his guard down, his body noticed, reacted to, and remembered Addie *vividly.*

She had gotten under his skin, wiggled down deep, and made him itch in the most erotic ways. And he couldn't seem to shake it.

Thanks to that pretty yellow dress and the erotically mouthwatering display she'd unknowingly given him when calling him for dinner, he'd sported wood throughout the meal and during his shower afterward. Talking about his family should have doused the inferno inside him, but it didn't. He'd been too aware of her and her subtle lavender scent. Hell, even now, his dick was hard as a rock and his balls ached from just his memories of her.

His fingers twitched, wanting to trace the generous curve of her hips, to grip the indent of her waist, and cup the heavy weight of her ample breasts. He could almost feel them swelling in his hands, spilling over his fingers, the hardened tips pushing into his calloused palms.

He groaned, gripping the fitted sheet in his fists, and cursed.

With the sun at her back, her golden hair had practically glowed like a halo as she gazed up at him from the dooryard, but the look on her face had been hungry. He bet if he had climbed down, taken her in his arms, and kissed her in that moment, she would have melted against him…and then gone off like a firecracker. Lord knows he would have. In fact, if he'd gotten that release, it would've solved his inability to sleep now.

He'd thought about taking himself in hand in the shower, and he'd tried, but none of his regular fantasies had been appealing. Addie kept popping into his head and wouldn't leave, which just didn't seem right somehow. She was his boss for God's sake, he had to work with her. But that didn't seem to make any difference to his body.

The minute he'd touched her after her fall, every nerve in his body buzzed to life. Awareness had swept through him like a tsunami. His mouth had gone dry and his heart—shredded and damned as it was—had fluttered in his chest.

Then she'd licked her lips. Those perfect, kissable lips.

He'd wanted to taste her so badly at that moment, it hurt. The past disappeared and his dismal, lonely future evaporated in the molten heat of the present. No thought of the consequences entered his head as he'd leaned toward her, desperate to feel her lips under his. His body at full attention, he'd longed for more of her heat, her softness, her lavender and sunshine scent. She was a breath of freshness in his dreary, solitary existence.

Then reality had suddenly slammed to the forefront. She deserved better than a broken cowboy with nothing to offer and no prospects. She deserved someone who'd commit to her and take care of her the way he never could. He couldn't do those things, not anymore.

He'd pulled away to protect them both. Not that his dick got the message.

Now, lying in bed alone, he couldn't stop thinking about her mouth. Those beautiful pink lips. He wondered how they would taste. *Would she open for me?*

His hand slid over his belly, moving downward as he imagined her mouth raining kisses along the same path, her tongue slipping out to tease him along the way.

His fingers wrapped around his hardened shaft and a shocked exhale escaped him as his hand squeezed and began to move slowly up and down while thinking of her.

"Oh, Addie," he moaned, his muscles tensing with expectation. His heart hammered in his chest, hot blood pounded in his ears, and his imagination ran away with him.

He pictured Addie's pretty lips stretched around his taut, over-sensitive flesh, her mouth hot and wet as she pleasured him, her fingers nimbly massaging his balls and driving him wild.

In his mind, she looked up at him, hungry lust burned in her chocolate eyes—just as they had earlier when she'd stared at him on the barn roof and when he'd looked into her eyes by the back door and been so tempted by her lips.

She needs to stop looking at me like that... The brief, wayward thought didn't break him out of the vision this time. He stroked himself, thinking of her until everything in him flexed, his back arched, and he growled out his pleasure as he finally found the release he'd needed so badly.

But, without her, it hadn't been enough.

Guilt and self-disgust crushed him into the mattress.

Addie was so sweet, innocent, and good. She was also his employer and he needed this job. Maybe he could find another somewhere else, but damn him if he wanted to.

In a few short days, he'd settled into this place like home, onto a farm and with a woman who didn't belong to him and never would. His heart was gone and had no capacity to open up or give again. That had been stolen from him by those who should've loved him. Who had said they did, even as they broke him into tiny pieces.

You're my brother, Cade, and I love you, but she doesn't want you. Not anymore.

Those words still stung.

Muttering a curse, Cade rolled over and sat on the edge of the bed. He snatched the gray T-shirt he'd worn earlier from the floor and wiped himself clean, then tossed it onto the small pile of clothes he needed to wash. He raked his hands through his hair then dropped them to his knees, cursing again. He had no business fantasizing about Addie Malory, especially when he had nothing to offer.

Pushing to his feet, he crossed to the door and opened it slowly. He stepped into the dark hallway and through it to his assigned bathroom. Addie's room was on the other side of the house, behind a locked door, so he wasn't worried about waking her. He needed another shower to wash away the sweat and self-loathing that coated his skin. A cold one.

Half an hour later, his body clean but his mind still seething, Cade crawled back into bed. He rubbed at his chest, trying to relieve the tightness and hurt that never seemed to leave.

Except when he was with her.

He shook his head. He barely knew Addie, for God's sake. Plus, he had no intention of staying once he got his truck running again and he knew she would be okay without his help. He shouldn't be feeling this insistent need to seek her out. But telling himself that didn't change anything. The turmoil in his soul calmed when he was with Addie. She soothed him and made him want things he could never have and had no right to desire.

He had nothing. He was nothing. There was no way a woman like Addie could care for a broken, unlovable man like him.

He'd learned that the hard way.

CHAPTER 7

Addie stepped out of her front door, and tucking her work gloves into her back pocket, she took a deep breath of the fresh September air. The sun's rays were only a hint on the horizon, leaving the dooryard still draped in shadows as she made her way to the barn. The chilly morning air reminded her again that summer was over. The fall winds would pick up any day now, and snow would soon follow.

Grateful they were finally getting to the last hay harvest of the year, she had a little bounce in her step. She'd done fairly well for herself with the farm. Despite her first questionable choices in employees, her stock of hay should earn a small profit and the corn would improve on that. At least, she hoped so.

With the way she'd been spending lately, her finances had taken a big hit and the harvest income would go a long way to diminishing the losses. Good thing she still had a day job. If she didn't, she would've been in a bind when Cade discovered the damaged equipment yesterday.

After breakfast the day before, she'd grabbed her laptop and set up at her dining room table to put the finishing touches on the three major articles she'd been working on for the last week and to write a couple of chapters in the new book she'd started. She'd been neck-deep in her writing when Cade had come through the garage door.

"Hey, it's a little early for lunch," she'd said with a friendly smile.

The way his mouth had been pressed into a hard line and he'd shaken his head alarmed her.

Frowning, she had sat up a little straighter. "What's wrong?"

"There's a problem with the tractor." He held up two cords. She looked at them, uncomprehending his point, but then saw that the cables he held in each hand were once one line.

Her chest tightened. "What about the other equipment? Were they damaged, too?"

"The baler trailer is okay, but the combine's engine belts are missing and one rear tire is flat."

She slumped back in her chair. They couldn't bring in the crops without the tractor or the combine, and she needed that harvest. "Was the tire damaged?"

He nodded. "I don't know how he did it—"

"He?"

"Yeah, that guy you fired, what was his name…?"

"Ted… But we can't be sure it was him."

"No, but it makes sense. He's got an axe to grind with you."

Addie nodded. "I suppose."

"In any case, I don't know how they accomplished it, whoever they were, but there's a big hole in the sidewall of the combine's tire."

"Damn," she murmured.

"There might be more wrong with the combine once I really get into it, but right now, the tractor seems to be the worst of it all."

"How many lines were cut?" she asked, calculating how much more of her savings she'd have to part with.

"All of them," he replied. "The tractor ain't going anywhere for a while."

She groaned and silently cursed. "Can you fix it?"

"With new parts? Yeah, I can fix it, no problem, but it'll take a while." He cocked his head. "Has anything like this happened before?"

She pressed her lips together and nodded. "One of the tractor's tires was deflated about three months ago, right before the last harvest. I thought it was just some kids messing around."

"That doesn't seem to be the case anymore," he said. "Whoever did this really didn't want you to use those machines."

"Yeah…but that's not the biggest issue right now."

"Maybe not, but I'd like to add some security lights and locks for the machine shed if that's okay with you?"

She nodded and reached into her coat that was hanging off the back of her chair to pull out her wallet. She tossed her credit card onto the table. "Whatever you think is necessary, but try to keep it under five hundred."

A frown pulled his eyebrows together, a stunned look in his eyes. "You trust me with this?"

"Shouldn't I?"

He grinned and reached for the card. "Me, yes. Not so sure about anyone else."

"Me neither," she said with a chuckle, a little thrilled by the protective note in his voice. "You can take my truck. The keys are on the counter by the garage door."

He had glanced at the keys and his frown returned. "What about the baling tomorrow? With the weather coming in, we need to get it off the ground. You know anyone with a tractor you could borrow?"

"Not really," she'd said, shaking her head. "Everyone's using theirs right now, but I can make a call."

She had called Veta on the off chance her husband knew someone with a machine they could borrow. Unfortunately, that hadn't been the case, but he'd had another suggestion, which they were about to implement this morning.

Shrugging into her quilted jacket and zipping it halfway, she smiled to herself. The memory of her conversation with Ivan filtered through her head as she crossed the darkened dooryard.

She could see the changes Cade had made to the machine shed off to the right of the barn. The door stood open, waiting for the others to arrive to help drag the baler trailer out. That wasn't unusual, but the floodlight at the peak of the roof that filled the area in front of the building with bright LED light was new. She also noticed a new silver latch fastened to the door with a thick, shiny lock hanging from it.

He'd said he made some changes, but she hadn't had the time yesterday to check them out. She'd needed to get her other work done in order to help him today, but she expected to see more lights and locks around. Sure enough, as she approached, another light near the barn roof temporarily blinded her with its brilliance. *The man certainly was a diligent worker.* She blinked and looked around, wondering where Cade had gone.

Just then, two trucks came down her drive, followed by a small car, kicking up a dust trail as they rolled into the dooryard. One truck pulled a long, white trailer with Ivan's suggested resolution for their lack of tractor inside it.

"Are you excited to do some old-fashioned baling?" Cade asked from behind her.

She glanced over her shoulder to see him exiting the barn. He looked so amazing in his boots, faded jeans, and black Carhartt jacket that her heart did a little dance in her chest. She had to stop this stupid attraction she felt whenever he was around before it became a more embarrassing problem. He was her employee, that's all. And she didn't want to scare him off by panting after him like a lovesick adolescent.

"Sure am," she said after working some moisture into her mouth.

Stopping beside her, he tipped his black felt hat back with one gloved finger then stood with his hands on his hips. "I'm glad one of us is."

"You think this won't work?" she asked, drawing his blue gaze.

"It'll work," he said, turning back to watch as one of the trucks parked by the house and the other maneuvered the trailer around and backed up between the barn and machine shed.

"You don't sound convinced."

He met her anxious gaze with a smile. "It's been a while for me, and I've never used horses to pull a baler."

"Well, it's a good thing we have help, then."

"Hey, Addie," Lana cried with a big smile on her face, but her eyes were glued to Cade and her voice dropped an octave when she greeted him. "Hi there, Cade."

Anger dropped into Addie's heart like a rock. She hated the hard edge of jealousy that struck when she realized the focus of Lana's attention and heard that seductive low tone.

Addie made a conscious effort to relax and breathe. Cade didn't belong to her, and Lana was welcome to look and flirt as much as she liked.

Unfortunately, telling herself that did little to alleviate her annoyance.

As Lana slipped out of the rear seat of the truck near the house, two young men—apparently from the car that had been following them, now parked next to Ivan's truck—vied for the chance to help her down. As soon as they appeared, Lana's attention focused on them and suddenly, Addie could breathe a little easier.

Knock it off, she scolded herself. *Lana is just young, and Cade is free to do as he likes.* Still, she was gratified to see from the corner of her eye that he wasn't paying any mind to Lana's antics.

Veta and Ivan exited the front of the truck at the same time as Lana, Veta flashing irritated looks at the scene with her sister. Shaking her head, Veta joined Ivan in strolling toward the second truck.

"Hi, guys," Addie replied with a smile and a wave. "Thank you all for coming."

"We're glad to help," Veta replied as she hugged Addie.

"I'm so excited to see the horses work," Lana said as she came forward to give her a hug and flick quick glances at Cade, with her two admirers following on her heels.

"Well, you'll soon get your chance," Addie replied, reminding herself again to let it go.

An older couple exited the second truck and introductions were made. From what Ivan had told her over the phone, Addie had a neighbor who raised horses to help with farm work and as show animals. Their draft horses had been showcased in the local rodeo for years, and they'd even been featured in a Hollywood movie or two.

"It's so nice to meet you, Dan and…Helga," Addie said, shaking hands with the older couple. "Thank you both so much for helping us out with this."

"It's no trouble," Dan said good-naturedly.

"Yes, no trouble at all," Helga said. "Farming ain't easy, especially for a young couple just starting out."

Addie frowned and glanced at Cade. Heat gathered around her coat collar as some of her fantasies danced through her mind.

"Oh," she said a little too breathlessly, "we're not... I mean...we... I..."

"I work for Addie," Cade said smoothly, coming to her rescue.

God, she really needed to work on her lack of grace under pressure. She usually wasn't so awkward, even when embarrassed.

"Oh, I see," Helga said, her eyes darting between them. "Well, no matter. We're glad to help either way."

The men went to unload the first two huge draft horses from the white horse trailer and walked them around the dooryard to stretch their legs while Helga made small talk.

"So you're new here. Bought out old Pete?" she asked.

Addie nodded. "Yep."

"Ever done any farming?"

"Just small gardening, but it's something I've always wanted to try."

"Hmm," Helga said, glancing over at Dan and Cade as they led the two horses back to the trailer and tied their leads to the side. They went back into the trailer and led out two more draft horses and repeated the process. "Well, it looks like you got yourself a good foreman to run the place."

A slow smile lifted the corners of Addie's mouth. "Yes, Cade's been wonderful."

Helga's eyebrows lifted and she glanced at Veta. "Hmm."

Addie's cheeks warmed. "I mean, he's so much more knowledgeable than I am, and he's willing to teach me what I need to know. I was lucky to find him."

"And where *did* you find him?" Helga asked. "Not around here, that's for sure."

Addie shook her head, but Lana answered.

"No, he was in the rodeo and Addie happened by when his truck broke down."

Veta and Helga exchanged another loaded glance that unnerved Addie. Was this woman judging her or did she just not approve of a woman running a farm?

"I see." Helga turned to Addie with a smile. "Well, you're a lucky girl to find such good help so late in the season." Her eyes drifted over Cade as he walked the second large horse back toward where Ivan and the other two younger men had been busy laying out harnesses by the trailer. Her eyes twinkled when she turned back to Addie. Leaning forward, she whispered, "And one so easy on the eyes, too." She winked. "A very lucky girl, indeed."

Addie's eyes widened and the warmth under her collar spread to her face.

"Well, I…" she stammered as the men walked by with the second set of horses, and her eyes were drawn to Cade. When she turned back to the other women, she grinned and chuckled self-consciously. "Well, I can't argue with that."

The other three women laughed.

"You're right, Veta," Helga said, still chuckling. "I like this one."

Addie's chest filled with pride and delight.

"I'm glad to hear it," Addie said. "I'd like to invite you both over for dinner so we can get better acquainted and to thank you for all this." She waved her hand toward the men and horses.

Helga beamed. "We'd love that!"

"We'll talk later," Addie said, still smiling. "What I'd like to hear about right now, though, is Lana's two friends."

Lana rolled her eyes. "They're just friends from school." She didn't seem overly interested in either of them.

"Yes," Veta said as if conveying secret information, "she says those boys are too young, but they're both older than *she* is."

"Oh stop, Veta. You just don't understand."

"Oh, I understand, little sister. You're too big for your britches."

That set off a sisterly squabble that luckily, Addie could avoid. "I'm going to go help with hitching up the team."

Helga nodded. "I'll take care of this."

Addie grinned her thanks and went over to where the men were arranging leather straps over the enormous horses' backs.

Cade saw her coming and his face lit up. "You want to try your hand at this?"

Addie returned his smile and nodded. "Absolutely."

"Okay then, come on over," he said with a smile and a wave of his arm. They had positioned the horses where they'd need to go, and Dan already had the closest two harnessed while Cade finished the last. As Addie crossed to the other side, Dan called to Ivan and the two younger men to help him drag the baler and its trailer out of the machine shed.

Cade tugged on a buckled strap and then looked at her. "You ever hitched up a team?" he asked as Addie rounded the big horse.

She shook her head, gazing up at the animal's huge head. Then her eyes traveled down to the long, feathery white hair that covered its lower legs and massive hooves, mesmerized by the equine's immense size.

This creature could squash her with one step.

She'd been around a horse or two before, but nothing like this. Her head didn't even top the animal's shoulder, making her feel tiny and vulnerable. From a distance, the horses had seemed very large, but up close…they were awe-inspiring and a little frightening.

The horse shifted and she stepped aside, her shoulder bumping into Cade's chest. Something in her expression must've hinted at the sudden burst of fear that shot through her because Cade's hand brushed across her back.

"Hey, it's okay. They won't hurt you," he said, patting the horse's chestnut-colored neck. "They're big, but they're gentle, and these guys are well trained."

The genuine smile and look of affection that filled his face caught Addie's attention and her whole body thrummed to life. Tingles danced across her skin, over her chest, and into her nipples, making them pucker and harden. Warmth swirled in her belly and pooled between her legs. All because he looked so damn handsome and…happy. And because he stood so close, she felt his body heat through her clothes, but when his sparkling eyes turned to her, everything else faded into nothing.

Every nerve in her body zapped with electricity, wholly attuned to him. The way his hand rested on her lower back, warming her and heightening her awareness. How his shoulders stretched the fabric of his quilted jacket and how his thigh muscles shifted under the faded denim of his jeans. She noted the whorls of dark brown chest hair that peeked out from the open V of his shirt and the clean line of his strong jaw. Then her eyes fell on his mouth. *So close. So sexy.*

Something pulled at her heart and the rest of her too, drawing her like an irresistible magnet. She leaned toward him, the scent of leather, and horse, and musky man filling her nose. She had fantasized about his mouth and how it would feel on hers. Would his kiss be soft and sweet, or would it be hard and possessive?

Would he pull her close?

Would he push her away?

She had to know and, in the blink of an eye, she was too far gone to care about anything else. All she could think about was his mouth and how much she wanted it on hers.

His head dipped as her fingers brushed the clean-shaven skin of his jaw, surprising her with its smoothness, and then slipped around his neck. His breath tickled her face and the tips of her breasts pressed into his chest.

Oh, God, please kiss me!

She went up on her toes to close the gap, to reach his beautifully chiseled lips, but she came up short. She'd come this far, and she wanted this—wanted him.

All or nothing, she thought as her fingers tightened on the back of his neck, pulling him in. He resisted. Doubt flickered in his gorgeous eyes for an agonizing instant before his mouth crashed down on hers. Hot and demanding, he nibbled at her lower lip, then his tongue traced the crease of her mouth and she opened immediately. His tongue darted inside and she tentatively greeted his invasion with an invitation for more. He groaned in his throat, soft but guttural, as his hands gripped her hips, pulling her tightly against him and then his arms wrapped around her.

Oh, God, he feels so damn good. All that hard heat crushing her, warming her, turning her on.

His fingers slipped into the braid she had fashioned her hair into this morning, dislodging several strands and tilting her head, capturing her completely. His mouth slanted over hers, taking control, diving deep. She moaned and melted into him, her fingers fisting in his shirt, wanting more, wanting him. More than anything, she wanted to grind against that hard shaft pressing against her stomach and—

"Addie!" Lana called and the world with all its distractions crashed into their little fairytale. "Do you have any extra gloves?"

Panting, Cade jerked back, his blue eyes dark with desire. Something tightened almost painfully inside Addie, leaving an ache that she suspected only Cade could ease.

With his eyes sparkling at her and the realization of what she'd done slamming home, Addie's cheeks turned hot.

"Oh, I…" she said, pulling her arms from around him and stepping back, feeling more than a little foolish, "I'm sorry."

"Don't be," he said in a breathless whisper, his arms falling to his sides.

She glanced toward him, but couldn't hold his gaze long enough to read the expression in his eyes. When she moved to go help her friend, Cade gently captured her chin between his thumb and finger, stopping her. She looked up at him, her eyes wide with fear of what he would say. Would he chastise her, express his disgust, or even quit the farm?

Oh, please, let the ground swallow me whole right now!

"We'll talk about this later. Okay?" His voice was low and deep and vibrated through her to settle in her core.

She bit her lip and her breath caught with the lump in her throat. Unable to find her voice, she nodded and stepped back. Hand dropping to his side, he grinned softly, reassuringly, and she could suddenly breathe again.

With a quick nod of his head, he turned and finished the hitching. She no longer wanted to see what he was doing or decipher the look in his eyes. All she wanted was to escape.

"Addie? Where are you?" Lana called again.

"Coming," Addie shouted, taking one last look at Cade. The soft turn of his mouth was still there when he glanced at her, and that odd internal tugging returned. It drew her to him, but she wasn't listening this time. Lips still tingling and her body still humming with desire, she spun on her heel, gave the large animals a wide berth, and headed toward her waiting friends.

Oh, God, what have I done?

CHAPTER 8

Closing the lid on the tractor's engine compartment, Cade grabbed a clean rag and wiped down his greasy hands and tools. Outside the machine shed, stars sparkled in the late-September sky and the air had turned chilly. It was late and he should've turned in hours ago, but he hadn't wanted to face Addie again. He knew it was cowardly, but something about her pulled at him and no matter how hard he tried, he couldn't shake it.

Despite all his best intentions and everything he'd told her after the hay harvest about not being the right guy for her, he still wanted to kiss her again. Wanted to see where it would lead, to give in to the desire in her eyes and the need burning through his veins.

That kiss they'd shared in the dooryard two weeks ago may have been short-lived, but he'd dreamt about it almost every night since. The kiss, the nervous way she'd scuttled away from him after, and the devastated look on her face when he'd said he wouldn't be staying. He found himself thinking about all of it and watching her when she wasn't looking, soaking in her sweet curves, remembering how good she'd felt against him, and basically driving himself crazy.

Cursing himself as a fool, he dropped the clean tools into the toolbox and rolled it over to its place by the wall.

He had no business thinking about Addie that way, especially when he had no plans to stay. He knew so little about her, yet he felt like he knew her well. She was smart, sassy, sexy, funny, and far more vulnerable than she let on. She made him laugh and sometimes, he even forgot the pain he'd been carrying around for the last five years. Almost as if his heart had begun to pull itself into one piece again. But all of that had faded away after their talk.

"I don't understand," she'd said, searching his face after he'd finally admitted nothing could happen between them. "You kissed me back. Did I do something wrong?"

He'd held in the groan that had wanted to rumble out of his chest. The sadness in her voice and the insecurity in her pretty brown eyes had nearly done him in. But he couldn't do the forever thing again. He was too screwed up, too shattered, and he didn't want her to get hurt.

No, to protect them both, he'd had to be strong. And so far, he had continued to be, but every time he caught her eyes, he was tempted. Every minute he spent with her, his resolve weakened just a little more.

"I did kiss you back," he'd said that Saturday after they'd finally returned home from the hay fields. "I am only human, Addie. You're a beautiful woman, and I do like you, but I can't be what you need."

Something like hope flickered in her eyes, but the last part of his comment dowsed it. He'd hated to see that. Hated to see her shoulders sag under the heavy weight of disappointment. He'd opened his mouth to say something, though he hadn't known what, but she had just shaken her head and looked away.

"Please understand, I don't want to hurt you."

Her eyes were shiny with unshed tears when she'd met his gaze again. "You think this feels good?"

That look had shredded him, but what could he say?

"No, I'm sure it doesn't, but if we crossed that line now, it'd be worse later."

Her shoulders had straightened and her brows had drawn down. "I'm a big girl, Cade. I can take care of myself. I don't need your protection."

He had merely nodded, but now he wondered, *Who's going to protect me?*

Pulling the shed doors closed, he fastened the lock in place and turned for the house.

Addie wasn't anything like the woman who'd torn his heart out and left him in pieces. And he wasn't the same man. He was far harder now than he had been at twenty-four. Nothing said things between him and Addie had to go south the way they had with him and Jenny, but he couldn't open himself up that way again.

Jenny had been beautiful, vivacious, and flashy, full of life and trouble. She'd stolen his heart the moment he saw her and had been way out of his league, but from the day they'd met in college, they'd been inseparable. He'd never known about the other men, had been too blinded by love to see—until his brother, Cord, had confronted him about six months after graduation. Cade had returned home with Jenny and had stupidly thought they'd make their life there together, but in a few short months, that had blown up in his face.

"She doesn't want you," Cord had said and Cade's heart dropped to his toes, even as he stood taller.

"You don't know what you're talking about," he'd shouted angrily.

"I know she came to my bed last night, saying she was looking for the better brother."

That had hollowed out his chest and left him struggling to breathe. He hadn't known how to respond. He'd wanted to punch his brother's face in. Instead, he'd walked away.

When he'd confronted Jenny later that night, she hadn't denied it.

"How can you do this?" he'd asked, his heart dying inside. "You said you loved me. We were going to spend our lives together."

She'd laughed at him. "You were fun, Cade, and I love fun, but now all you do is work. You don't pay attention to me and I'm bored. Your brother is just as handsome as you and the only other man around here for miles besides that old foreman of yours. Why wouldn't I look to Cord for a good time when you've turned into such a drag?"

"You wanted to come here," he'd reminded her. "You said you wanted to be with me."

"Yeah, well, that's when I thought you had a big place and lots of money."

That had been the final nail in the coffin of their relationship.

Let Cord have her, he'd thought as he packed his meager possessions. *He'll figure her out one day, too.*

He and Cord had been close at one time, as close as brothers could be. Maybe that's why the betrayal had hurt so much.

Shaking his head as he wiped his boots on the rug in Addie's garage, Cade shoved those thoughts back into a dark corner of his mind. He pushed open the door and stepped into the mudroom. Kicking his boots into the corner, he washed his hands, hung his jacket on a hook by the door, and then stepped into the kitchen. The lights were off, but a dim illumination came from the living room. He closed the door quietly and in his stocking feet, Cade made his way to the hallway off the front room.

The late news was playing on the television with Addie fast asleep on the couch. She looked lovely curled on her side in her pink terry cloth robe with one of the throw pillows positioned under her head. The soft contours of her face glowed in the low light, melting the wall around his heart a little more. He wanted nothing so much as to pick her up in his arms, carry her to his bed, and hold her tight all night.

His dick twitched at the thought.

After touching her, if only too briefly, he knew exactly how exquisitely supple her body was. But because he wanted to keep from hurting her worse, he wasn't going to test those waters again.

She must have been waiting for him. They hadn't talked much or easily since their chat. Everything between them after that had been stiff—even the meals that they sometimes still took together were awkward—and he hated it. He missed their easy conversations and her warmth. In truth, he just missed her.

He walked over to the couch, snagged the folded blanket off the back, and tucked it around her. She shifted slightly but didn't wake. A lock of her blonde hair had fallen across her face and, bending at the waist, he gently brushed it behind her ear. Then, for some reason he couldn't fathom, and without thought, he kissed her forehead. Thankfully, his stupid, impulsive move didn't rouse her. He straightened quickly, silently scolding himself, *What the* hell *are you doing?*

He grabbed the remote and switched off the TV, then headed to bed, determined not to dream about her again.

* * *

A heavy beating filled his dreams. At first, he'd thought it was his heart pounding or the lust powering through his veins at the gorgeous vision of Addie before him. But that didn't seem right.

When the noise abruptly stopped, it was almost like it had never been there.

He floated in a sea of warmth, images of Addie heating him in the most pleasant ways. Then voices interrupted his fantasy, coming from nowhere and everywhere at once. Whispers he couldn't quite make out, even when they grew in volume. Irritation colored his dream and he strained to get back to the pleasant sight and sense of Addie.

A scream and a loud thump yanked him from his slumber. He sat bolt upright and rubbed at his eyes, trying to orient himself. Sounds of a struggle came from the front room and then another scream had him on his feet and jumping into his jeans. With his heart in his throat and his stomach as hard and heavy as lead, Cade jerked open his bedroom door and dashed down the hall.

"No!" Addie screamed. "Get off me!"

A male chuckle followed. "I love it when you play hard to get."

Cade stopped just inside the living room, taking in the scene.

A man he'd never seen before had forced his way inside and now had Addie pinned against the wall. He'd somehow gotten her robe open and over her shoulders, which encumbered her movement, and he was now nibbling on her neck as she fought to get free.

"Get off!" Addie shouted as she tried to heave the stranger away with her whole body.

That was enough for Cade. Anger, hot and raw, filled his mind and tightened his fists. Pulse racing and the rush of blood pounding in his ears, he rounded the loveseat and approached the invader in three long strides. Snaking his arm around the stranger's neck and yanking one arm behind his back, Cade pulled him away from Addie. The man's free hand instantly clutched at Cade's arm rather than holding on to Addie, which was exactly what Cade had wanted. He stepped back, dragging the shouting man with him, putting space between them and the woman Cade wanted to protect. The man twisted beneath Cade's arm, trying to break free, but his movements were clumsy and Cade easily dragged him several feet, and then turned to shove him toward the partially open front door.

Cade glanced at Addie, touching her arm as she righted her robe. "Are you all right?"

His protective instincts surged even hotter when he saw the tears that filled her eyes and streamed down her reddened cheeks. She looked angry and terrified and flustered all at the same time. But she lifted her chin and cinched her robe's belt tight.

"I'll be fine," she said. "Thank you."

A little burst of pride warmed his chest at her display of inner strength. Sweet, kind, tender, *and* strong. This woman was amazing.

A growl from the stranger focused Cade's attention once more, and he turned as the man got to his feet. Older than Cade had first thought—at least fifteen years older than himself, if not more—years had left their lines on the stranger's face and gray tinted the hair at his temples. None of that diminished his appearance, however. At least as tall as Cade's six-foot frame, the man was leanly muscular and looked confident of his abilities. He had the look of a farmer in his jeans and flannel shirt, but Cade sensed power and danger emanating from him.

The stranger's gray eyes narrowed and instantly zeroed in on Addie, but Cade stepped over to put himself between her and the attacker.

"Well, what do we have here? Addie," the stranger said, drawing out her name, "are you cheating on me with this…*boy*?"

Cade frowned at the implied insult, but it was the reference to cheating that sparked a tiny flame of dread in his chest.

"We'd have to be a couple for me to cheat," Addie said, every word dripping with acid, and Cade breathed a little easier.

"Ah, when are you going to ssstop lying, little girl?"

Addie made a furious sound, something between a growl, a hiss, and a groan.

"You know this guy, Addie?" Cade asked, careful not to take his eyes from the other man.

"Yeah," Addie said with a sigh. "This is my neighbor, Mark Harden."

"I'm her *man*," Mark clarified.

"You are *not* my *anything!*"

"Oh, Addie, after all we've been through, how can you sssay that?"

Cade detected slurring in several of Mark's words, though at first glance, he'd appeared sober.

"We had two dates, Mark. Two! That's not a lifetime commitment."

"You waaantted me to come back," Mark said, taking a wobbling step forward.

Cade tensed. He wasn't sure exactly what was going on, but Addie definitely didn't want this guy around.

"You're drunk, Mark. I never asked you back," Addie said. "In fact, I asked you to leave. Now, I'm telling you. Go home and don't bother us like this again."

"Us, huh?" Mark's gaze shifted to Cade and darkened. "Who the hell *is* this, anyway?" His voice sounded hard and his eyes looked cold as they raked over Cade from head to foot, disdain curling his lips.

Cade widened his stance, preparing for violence.

"You trying to move in on my territory, boy?" A threat clearly rang in Mark's tone.

Cade shook his head. "The lady asked you to leave."

Mark chuckled. "You don't know who you're messing with, kid."

Cade bristled inside, but kept his face blank, though the tone of his voice could have cut granite. "Leave. Now."

Addie's small hand curled around his forearm, surprising him and warming him, too. "Don't let him bait you, Cade," she said, loud enough for only him to hear. "Please."

He glanced at her and saw a warning in her eyes. Curious, but knowing this wasn't the time to ask, Cade turned back to Mark.

Addie's hand tightened on his arm and he reached over to give her fingers a reassuring squeeze, keeping his attention on the intruder.

Mark smiled, though not in a friendly way. "I sssee," he slurred, staring at their joined hands.

"Just go, Mark," Addie pleaded. "You don't want to do this. Go home and sleep it off."

Mark's eyes lifted to Addie and he seemed to slump a bit and swayed. He blinked slowly and then refocused on Addie's hand gripping Cade's arm. When his gaze lifted to Cade's, he sneered, "This ain't over, kid."

Prickles of warning shot up Cade's spine as hate and a dark promise shot from Mark's gray eyes.

"Please, Mark," Addie said, and his drooping gaze shifted to her face as she peeked around Cade's shoulder. "Please, just go."

"We'll talk about thisss laaa-ter, Ad-dieee," Mark said, his slur growing more pronounced.

"No," Cade said softly, "you won't." He felt Addie's sharp glance but kept his attention on the other man, determined to let him know she wasn't unprotected.

"Go home, Mark," Addie said gently as if speaking to a sleepy, cranky child.

A crooked grin split the man's face. "Have it your way, but you'll be missing me later." Mark swayed as he turned for the door. Stepping outside without a backward glance, he stumbled toward his truck.

"He shouldn't be driving," Cade said, his hard eyes glaring out the empty doorway.

"No, he shouldn't." Addie stepped forward, but he caught her arm. "What're you doing?"

"Stopping him."

"After what he tried to do, you want to get in the cab with him?"

Her expression turned uncertain. "No, not really, but I don't want him hurting anyone else, either."

"Just report him."

Her shoulders slumped. "I can't."

"Why the hell not?" Irritation stiffened his back and sharpened his tone. "You do understand what that drunken bastard would've done if I hadn't been here, right?"

She lifted her chin and narrowed her eyes.

"Glaring at me won't change those facts, Addie. Stop being so tenderhearted and turn the guy in."

"It's not being tenderhearted," she replied, her defensive stance drooping. "It just won't do any good."

"You don't know that."

"Yes, I do."

"How?" he asked and when she stared up at him, tight-lipped and glaring, he got it. "This isn't the first time, is it?"

"No."

Heat surged through his veins and he growled low in his throat. "All the more reason to call the cops."

"It won't do any good."

"Why not?"

"Because he *is* the cops!"

CHAPTER 9

Addie took a deep breath, trying to still the runaway thudding of her heart. Anxiety riddled, her stomach hurt, but the rest of her body felt numb and cold as she watched understanding bloom on Cade's face.

"That jackass is a cop?" he asked incredulously, pointing toward the open front door.

"Deputy sheriff," Addie said with a nod, dropping her eyes. She appreciated Cade's help and that he was concerned about her, but she wasn't interested in going another ten rounds with the sheriff. The last time Mark had gotten drunk and pressed her too hard, she'd barely been able to fight him off on her own. Afterward, she'd gone straight to the sheriff's station and reported it. The long line of inquiry and suspicion directed at her had been grueling and she didn't want to go through that again. Besides, Mark had only gotten a verbal warning—a slap on the wrist—and was told to keep his distance. She still had to see him around town. Still had to put up with his longing looks and flirting smiles. He hadn't approached her since the last incident, but she'd always been careful to avoid him as much as possible.

"That's even more of a reason to report him," Cade said, interrupting her thoughts. "At least, tell them it happened."

"They won't believe me," she said, frustration tightening her fists. "They didn't last time and it was...awful. They said because we were alone it was my word against his, but none of them believed me."

A muscle twitched in his jaw before he answered, "Not this time. I saw what he tried to do. I'll stand with you. They'll have to listen."

She sighed and smiled tiredly. The anger and righteousness she read in his eyes over the unfairness of the situation warmed her heart. The fact that he cared and wanted to see to her safety warmed the rest of her, too. She tilted her head and her grin widened. "So protective."

He shifted his feet and shoved his hands into his jeans pockets. That's when Addie finally noticed his state of dress or lack thereof. He'd charged to her rescue with bare feet and a bare chest. The sight of all that warm masculine skin—all those ridges and valleys of muscle—made her mouth water. *How could a guy like him think so little of himself?*

"I just don't want you to get hurt," he mumbled.

Without thinking, she reached up and cupped his cheek. Awareness zapped down her arm, but the tickle of his stubble against her palm acted like its own kind of magnet. When he met her eyes, all those tingles in her hand swept through her whole body.

"I appreciate that, Cade, and everything else you've done for me," she murmured. "I really do. Thank you."

He stared back at her for what seemed like forever and she felt herself being drawn to him again, even as insecurity and doubt clouded his eyes—as it always did when this yearning sprung up between them. He'd said he wasn't the man for her, but she knew what he meant by that, and he was wrong. Everything he'd done in the short time he'd been with her had proved it. Time stretched as they gazed at each other, and Addie leaned toward him as he did the same.

A commotion outside snapped her out of the trance his eyes had locked her in. She turned as Cade stepped around her to look out the front door.

"He didn't make it very far," Cade said, glancing back at her. "Looks like he passed out in the flower bed. Took out the wind chime and a couple of weed-filled pots in the process."

Addie joined him at the door and shook her head. "We need to get him out of here. I don't want him knocking again. I don't want him here at all!"

Cade gave her a curious look that she interpreted as "Why did you open the door, then?" She ignored it. How could she explain? She was stupid to listen to Mark's drunken manipulations or to let herself feel sorry for him. Even though she told herself that it wouldn't happen again, she didn't want to test her resolve tonight. Right now, it was all she could do not to crumble into a small, blubbering heap.

"I'll take him home," she said as another flutter of nerves attacked her stomach and then began to spread. It was getting difficult to breathe. Determined to stay strong and not let the bundle of anxiety in her chest escape, she turned to grab her coat, but Cade stopped her.

"We've already discussed this," he said softly. "You don't want to be in that cab with him any more than I want you to be."

Her temper flared and she latched onto it to keep from thinking about what else might've happened. "Then what do you suggest?"

His hands curled around her shoulders then brushed up and down her arms in a consoling fashion. More warm tingles followed the path of his hands and she breathed a little easier.

"Will you let me help?"

She sniffed and rolled her lips together. "I thought you didn't want to get involved?" Okay, that was a cheap shot and she knew it, but she couldn't help herself. She'd been embarrassed and hurt by his unexpected rejection and his sudden need to spend more time alone, but she'd kept it mostly to herself…until now.

His lips pulled into an indulgent smile. "This is not the kind of involvement I meant, and you know it."

She dropped her eyes and shrugged.

He ducked his head and waited until she met his gaze before he spoke.

"I won't risk your safety," he said softly but in a tone so hard, it sent a shiver down her back. "If it were up to me, I'd leave the bastard where he lies, but since it's important to you and your safety for him to be gone, I'll help get him gone. But it's going to take both of us. So, if you feel up to driving, how about you get your keys and bring your truck around? I'll go stuff him in the cab of his rig and follow you to his place. Then we can both come back in your truck. How does that sound?"

Worry drew her brows together. "What if he wakes up? He won't be happy to see you."

Cade shook his head. "If he's drunk enough to pass out on the way to his truck, he's out for the night. But even if he does wake, I can handle him." His hand cupped her face and his thumb traced over her forehead and down her nose, easing the lines that had formed between her eyebrows. "Don't worry about me."

But she *was* worried about him, though she didn't see another way to get rid of Mark that didn't involve bringing in the authorities. Cade plainly didn't understand her aversion to that, and she was thankful when he didn't push it further.

"Okay, we'll do it your way," she said and stepped around him.

"All righty, then. I'll just grab a shirt and my boots and meet you out front."

She nodded as he headed for his room. The thick muscles of his back shifted as he walked and she couldn't help but watch.

"Cade?"

He turned, his eyebrows raised in question.

"Thank you."

He smiled. "Anytime, sweetheart."

Then he turned and rushed down the hall to his room, leaving Addie feeling lost, excited, and confused by it all. Her heart still beat way too fast, and not because of Cade's nearness or near-naked state. Fear gnawed at the edges of her resolve like a wild thing, threatening to break her down completely. Taking a deep breath and holding onto the emotional cliff she dangled from by her fingernails, Addie grabbed her jacket off the chair in the dining room where she'd left it, dug out her keys, and headed for the garage.

* * *

The drive to Mark's place had been uneventful. Cade had pulled up to the house, cut the engine, and hopped out, leaving Mark to sleep it off in his truck. She would've insisted on taking him inside if the weather had been colder, but it was only in the low sixties tonight, and the night was almost over.

Thankfully, when Cade approached her truck, he'd insisted on driving them home. Now that some time had passed, shock was beginning to overtake the adrenaline that had numbed her senses. Shivers rocked her as the truck rolled down her long driveway. By the time they pulled up to her garage a minute later, she was not only trembling but fighting back tears, too.

The engine shut off, but she couldn't move. She stared out the side window and tried to inhale, but she couldn't seem to get enough air through her constricted throat. Sweat broke out over her body and her heart pounded against her sternum. She felt faintly lightheaded and feared she might lose what was left of her dinner at any moment.

Ohmygosh. Ohmygosh. Ohmygosh! What the heck was wrong with her? *Am I going crazy now?*

"Hey," Cade said, gently brushing her shoulder.

She nearly jumped out of her skin and her trembling worsened.

He moved, but she wouldn't look at him.

"Addie," he murmured, "are you all right?"

She nodded at the window beside her, but a choked sob gave her away.

"Oh, honey," Cade crooned as he scooted across the bench seat. "You're okay." His arms wrapped around her.

The thought of pulling away, putting distance between them, floated through the chaos in her head, but she didn't listen. Instead, she squeezed her eyes shut as another sob escaped her lips.

His body curled around hers, blocking out the night, his breath warming her neck as he pulled her closer. "Shh," he whispered in her ear. "You're okay, I got you."

A tear trickled from her closed lids.

Oh, God, she felt sick!

But Cade felt warm, and strong, and solid all around her.

Losing more control of herself with every second he held her, she sobbed again and tried to break out of his embrace.

He didn't want to get "involved" with her, but every time something happened, he was right there to make things all right again. She needed to stand on her own, because…because…because if she let herself get too close, she'd be a wreck when he left. And he would leave, he had said he would.

But then why was he doing this? This wasn't in his job description.

Neither was kissing her, but he'd done that, too.

His arms tightened around her. "Sweetheart, don't run from me. Please..."

It was the "Please" that broke her. Her mouth opened and an incoherent wail ripped through the darkness.

Cade sat back and pulled her into his lap. The ease with which he'd handled her body spoke to his physical strength, but she hardly noticed. All she knew was that, right now, in his arms was the only place she wanted to be.

CHAPTER 10

Sitting in Addie's truck with her huddled in his lap, plastered against him and crying, was the last place Cade had thought to end up. But here he was and, oddly, he had no desire to leave. None of his normal urges to run for the hills when a woman got too close seemed to apply to Addie. No uncomfortable fidgeting on his part, no dry mouth, or planning how to get away. All he felt was a burning need to keep her close, make her happy, and protect her.

Addie had buried her face in the hollow between his neck and shoulder the moment he'd settled her against him. A heartbeat afterward, she'd sobbed and her whole body shook almost violently. Waves of heat poured off her, but when her fingers brushed his neck, they were ice cold.

He'd been surprised and impressed by her calm after the attack and during the short drive back to her house, but he knew it wouldn't last. She was a strong woman, but no one could go through something that traumatic and not be affected.

When it became clear that she was far from all right, his first instinct had been to touch her, to pull her close, and shelter her from the outside world. Moving her small form had been easy, but he had no idea what to do about her sobs or the shock that had quickly ravaged her, except to tighten his hold and let her know she was safe.

"I've got you, sweetheart," he murmured into her hair, his throat dry and his voice raspy. "He's not going to trouble you again."

She nodded, her face still pressed into his neck, tears still flowing, but the tenseness in her body eased a little.

"You're safe, baby. I promise."

What else could he say?

His heart pounded in his ears and everything in him screamed to make that bastard pay for this. If he could get his hands on the drunken fool right now, Cade would rip him apart. No woman should ever feel this way. No woman should be assaulted, period! And if he had any say in it, this woman never would be again.

How long he held her—soothing her with his hands and voice like a startled colt—he didn't know, but slowly, her sobs lessened to soft hiccups. She still trembled slightly, but he could feel her gathering strength.

"I-I'm..." she said, then sniffed, hiccupped, and continued, "I'm sorry... I c-cried all over you."

He shook his head and another surge of rage for the man who put that sad, vulnerable tone in her voice rocked him.

"You don't need to apologize to me, sweetheart," he said, gravel still rattling his words. "I just want you to be okay. Are you...okay?"

She sat back, her lovely, wild hair falling over her face, and nodded, but that wasn't good enough for Cade. He wanted to look into her eyes; he needed to know how much damage had been done. Brushing her hair back, he cupped her cheek and was again reminded of how small she was in comparison to him.

"Hey," he said, drawing her red-rimmed eyes to his. "Talk to me."

She shrugged, but kept her gaze locked on his. "He just scared me, that's all. I haven't seen him for weeks and then he shows up out of the blue, claiming—" Rolling her lips between her teeth, she shook her head and her words ceased as she looked away.

His muscles tightened. What did that asshole say to her?

"Go on," he encouraged, his thumb gently stroking her cheek.

Her mouth tightened. "He said he wanted to apologize, to make things right…"

"Is that why you opened the door?" He made sure to make that a question and not an accusation.

She grimaced and nodded. "I didn't know he was drunk until it was too late, but I should've known…" A little whimper sounded in her throat and her body convulsed as tears threatened again.

Cade pulled her against his chest. "Shh, it's all right now, I got you. He won't hurt you again."

"It's my own fault," she muttered into his chest.

"No," he said, pushing her back to cup her face again. He needed her to understand that he meant what he said next. "None of this is your fault."

"But I…"

He shook his head. "No, Addie, you are not to blame for any of it. Your only fault is you're too tenderhearted, but that isn't something I'd want to see change. I admire your kindness and strength."

Big, dark chocolate eyes stared back at him.

He could get lost in those eyes…

Whoa, cowboy…

He inhaled, her lavender scent infusing his brain, and dropped his hand from her cheek. "How about I get you inside and warmed up? Then, if you want, we can talk some more."

Her eyes shifted, seeming to search his face like she always did when unsure about him. His heart lurched and that tugging sensation was back, only this time he knew what it was. Not just attraction—he'd admitted that weeks ago. No, this was more, on a deeper, more emotional level. Addie was warm and kind, and he liked her. A lot. Part of him had known that for a long while. It explained why his protective instincts had risen to her defense so quickly, and why his body and all his senses were drawn to her like a bee to honey. She was the sweetest woman he'd ever known and, if he'd been on his feet, the desire to taste every soft and sexy piece of her would've dropped him to his knees.

Then she blinked and reality struck. He wasn't the one for her, wasn't good enough. Besides, she wasn't in any condition to even discuss the topic of them as a couple—not that they should discuss it at all. No, his only job right now was to make her feel safe and comfortable.

"You want to head inside?" he asked.

Her shoulders dropped and she nodded.

"Okay," he said, shifting her back to the seat. "You stay right here." Scooting over the bench seat to the driver's side, he exited the cab and rounded the front of the truck to open her door. Then he reached in, scooped her into his arms, and kicked the door closed.

Her nervous little laugh was music to his ears.

"You don't have to carry me," she said as he headed up the front porch steps, ignoring her protests as if she hadn't spoken at all.

"You mind?" he said with a grin, lifting an eyebrow and glancing at the doorknob.

She chuckled again and warmth filled his chest, puffing him up just a little.

"I *can* walk, ya know." Despite the slight irritation in her words she was smiling.

"Yes, I know," he replied as he once again used his boot heel to close the front door, "and I know you can take care of yourself. But sometimes we all need someone to take care of us for a little while. Right now is one of those times, and I really want to take care of you." He set her down on the cushy tan couch, but hovered near her, unable to look away from her eyes. "Will you let me care for you, Addie?"

CHAPTER 11

Staring up into Cade's stunning blue gaze, Addie's heart beat triple-time. Every nerve tingled where he had touched her, and every atom in her body was sharply attuned to him, his warmth, his size, his scent. After the scare she'd had less than an hour ago, she shouldn't be interested in any man. But Cade Brody wasn't just *any* man. He had risked himself to save her, had helped rid her of the man who'd assaulted her, and made her feel safe when all of her confidence and security had been ripped away.

A shudder rumbled through her and a frown darkened his brow.

"Addie?"

Oh, right, he's waiting for an answer.

Heat filled her veins, thawing the ice that had formed from the shock of being attacked in her own home. Thank God, Cade had been here. If Mark hadn't yanked her robe open and down over her arms the minute he forced his way inside, she could've fought him off. At least, she'd done it before. But she'd been defenseless this time. With her arms pinned, all that she'd learned had been useless. If Cade hadn't acted, her situation could've been so much worse.

"Yes," she whispered, but for a second she didn't know what she was agreeing to.

When he smiled, she remembered. He wanted to take care of her. Maybe that was a good idea. Her thoughts seemed to be muddled and sluggish at the moment, but there was no confusing the zing of awareness zapping through her body.

He hadn't moved. He still hovered over her, his face a few inches above hers. Those sexy lips curled into the sweetest crooked smile she'd ever seen.

He wants to take care of me.

Did that mean...?

I don't care.

Her hand reached out of its own accord, fingers brushing over his mouth. His lips parted and the smile slid off his face. His eyes flared with desire and her body responded. Heat spiraled downward from her chest, into her belly, settling between her thighs. Was she really thinking about kissing him again?

Then his eyes cooled and his fingers wrapped gently around her wrist, pulling her hand from his face.

"You don't want to do this now," he said, his voice rough as if he could barely speak. "Neither do I."

Breathless with anticipation and uncertainty, she whispered, "Why?"

He sighed, appearing hard and formidable, but his tone was gentle. "You were just attacked, Addie. I won't take advantage of you."

"It's not taking advantage if I want you, too." Her thoughts buzzed slowly through her brain, some agreeing with him, others demanding that she press her mouth to his. Mixed in with need and want was the shock and fear of Mark's attack, clouding everything and making the world feel fuzzy and far away. Every emotion seemed to battle against the other so furiously, she couldn't think straight. All she knew was she felt lost and forlorn, and she trusted Cade. He was so damn warm, so big and strong, and she didn't want to leave his side. At least, not tonight.

"Good to know," he replied with a lopsided smile, "but I think we should skip all that for tonight."

She nodded, giving in to his better judgment right now, but she couldn't look away from him, and he still held her hand.

"How about I help you get tucked in?"

She shook her head vehemently. "No, I don't want to be alone." The thought made her shiver and cold returned to her extremities.

"Okay," he murmured, tucking a strand of her messy hair behind her ear. "How about you get settled in here, I'll get you a blanket, and then make us some of your herbal tea? That sound good?"

She nodded. She could do that.

He squeezed her hand and then went to complete his self-appointed tasks.

By the time he returned with tea—for her but none for him—she'd wrapped the blanket from the couch over her legs and the new one he'd brought around her shoulders. She'd pulled her hair into a messy bun and then hunkered down in the warm cocoon she'd made.

"This should help you warm up," Cade said as he held out a steaming mug for her to take. She wrapped her cold hands around it and sighed as the heat began to bring life into her fingers again.

Cade sat beside her and stretched his arm along the back of the couch behind her.

She snuggled up close to his side and glanced up at him. "This is okay, right?"

Why did she feel so indecisive about everything right now? It's not as if anything really changed, but she couldn't shake the cloak of vulnerability that seemed to cling to her.

A small smile curled Cade's lips and he nodded. "Yes, honey, it's okay."

His hand brushed over her shoulders and pulled her more firmly against his side. His endearment and actions warmed her more than the tea he'd brought.

They sat quietly for several minutes while Addie sipped her tea. The slow swipe of Cade's fingers over her upper arm sent tingles through her body while comforting her at the same time. He seemed content to hold her, to lend his strength, and to help her recover from the shock of trauma.

But he'd said he didn't want to get involved, which to Addie had meant that he didn't want to get close.

If that's true, this was not the way to do it.

Addie finished her tea and set it down on the coffee table. Then she curled up against Cade's side and rested her head on his chest. His arm wrapped around her and he settled back into the cushions as if content to hold her as long as she needed.

She listened to his heart beating strong and even. The sound calmed her further, and warmed her, too.

She didn't think he was the kind of man who would lead a woman on. So did his sudden solicitousness mean that something had changed? Or was he just being a kind, attentive friend? She could call him that, a friend. They'd known each other for a little while now and they seemed to like each other's company. And she trusted him. Isn't that enough to call him a friend?

But she still knew so little about him and she wanted to know him better.

"Cade," she whispered, the flannel of his blue shirt tickling her lips.

"Hmm?" he replied.

"May I ask you a personal question?"

His body tensed, the slow sweep of his fingers on her arm ceased, and she feared she had read too much into his kindness…friendship…intentions.

"Sure," he said quietly as his fingers returned to swirling up and down her arm, but the tension in his muscles remained.

"Why don't you talk to your brother?" She'd been wondering about that since the first time he'd mentioned his family.

Beneath her ear, his heart stuttered and then picked up its regular beat. He sighed and some of the tension in his body eased.

"We had a falling out a few years back," he said quietly.

"What happened? If you don't mind my asking?"

He remained quiet for some time, but then he sighed again and started to speak.

"I met her in college and fell in love, but I didn't see the kind of woman she was…not until I brought her home after graduation. We had all these plans to improve the ranch, but I didn't find out until sometime later that she wasn't interested in hard work." He shifted slightly and his muscles hardened once more. "I hadn't known what she'd been doing behind my back with other men. That was, not until my brother told me she'd been in his bed."

Addie gasped. She couldn't help it. No wonder he was so gun-shy about getting involved. Draping her arm over his chest, she gave him a little squeeze of comfort and sympathy. "I'm so sorry, Cade."

His shoulders lifted in a shrug and his voice sounded gravelly when he spoke again. "I let myself be fooled. That's my fault, but I never expected my brother to stab me in the back like that. It was…painful."

"Were you two…close? Before, I mean."

"Yes." He seemed to choke on the word. "We were very close. I guess that happens when you share a womb."

"He's your twin?"

"Yes."

"That must have been so…hard on you."

He nodded. "Yeah."

"But I'm sure he still loves you, Cade."

"Doesn't matter."

"But it does." She sat up to look at him. "He's your brother. I'd give almost anything to have a sibling."

He frowned, but she didn't let that stop her.

"My parents had been older when I was conceived. A miracle baby, they'd called me, but they were never that lucky again. I grew up with lots of love and attention, but I'd been an independent, very lonely child. And now, I don't have any family left. I'm…alone."

"I'm sorry for you," Cade said stiffly, "but forgiving Cordell is beyond me." The way he said his brother's name sounded cold and indifferent with a sea of pent-up hostility brewing just beneath the surface.

"Is there any possibility that you misunderstood? That what you thought happened…didn't?"

His lips tightened and he shook his head. "Do you really think I'd leave my home and everything I knew if I had any doubt? She went to him and he fucked her. As far as I'm concerned, they both betrayed me."

His use of the vulgar term surprised Addie, but she refused to comment on it, knowing his anger wasn't directed at her.

"I never said they didn't. I'm just trying to understand how two brothers who were so close could not talk or find a way to forgive."

Cade chuckled dryly and brushed the back of his fingers over her cheek. "You are a way better person than I am, Addie Malory."

Warmth filled her chest and streaked along the path his fingers had traveled, but she wouldn't let herself be distracted. His happiness was too important.

"I'm not trying to be a good person. I'm saying that forgiveness is better than hate. You've been carrying this around for a long time…" She tilted her head. "How has that been working for you so far?"

His grin faded. "I can't do what you're asking."

"Can't or won't?"

He looked away. "Both."

Frustration and empathy clenched her heart in a hard fist. She hated seeing him like this, so full of anger and pain. He had never struck her as an angry person—he smiled too much for that, was too kind and considerate—but she could feel the negative emotions radiating off of him. His brother had hurt him, yes, but he was hurting himself more by carrying it around and not letting it go.

Addie turned his chin with her fingers until his impassioned eyes met hers.

"Just think about it, Cade. That's all I'm asking. And if you can't forgive your brother, try to at least let go of the anger. It'll eat you up inside, if you don't, make you into someone else, and I'd hate to lose the man I've come to know and…care for." She knew those last words might send him running, but they were true. She *did* care about him and she thought he felt the same but was too afraid to do anything about it.

Maybe it's time I tried again, she thought. But not tonight. He'd been right about that. Sometime soon, though, she might just have to kiss him again.

A little flame lit in his eyes at her words. Her mouth turned up slightly and she laid her head back on his chest. His heart was thumping faster than it had been and her smile grew.

"Just think about it," she murmured, snuggling up to him and closing her eyes, warm and content and safe in his embrace. Right now, this was enough for her.

She didn't expect him to reply, but when his quiet words rumbled through his chest, a burst of happiness and pride filled her chest.

"Okay, Addie. I'll try…"

She didn't know if he meant he'd try to forgive, to forget, or to just let go of the anger and hurt, but she didn't care. For now, it was enough that he would take the first step to try to heal himself.

"Thank you," she said, closing her eyes and listening to the regular steady beat of his heart. She felt his head nod in reply and smiled again. Whatever was going on between them had just changed. It had gotten…stronger.

Chapter 12

Flames leaped high into the air, lighting the darkening sky, the snap and crackle of old wood blended with the early evening birds' song and the buzz of quiet conversation. Cade shifted in the camp chair he'd borrowed, watching the dancing bonfire and nursing the one beer he'd allowed himself—he was driving, after all—while the rest of the partygoers mingled.

Before Addie's neighbors, Dan and Helga, had left after helping them with the hay harvest a few weeks ago, Helga had insisted that he and Addie both attend this bonfire and cookout at their place. Addie had been thrilled, and watching her now chatting with her friends, smiling and laughing, he couldn't regret attending. Even if he'd had to endure Lana's flirting for nearly twenty minutes before her sister took pity on him and led her away—clearly scolding Lana about leaving him alone once they were out of earshot. The two sisters now stood talking with Addie and some other ladies, but Lana still snuck a few glances his way. He could live with that; at least he didn't have to carry on a conversation with her—not that he hadn't spoken with anyone else at the party. Earlier, aside from evading Lana's suggestive comments, Cade had conversed with Dan and a few of the other men, but he wasn't much of a talker. Addie, on the other hand, was like a cute, little parakeet flitting here and there, jumping from one conversation to the next. She was so full of life, so cheerful, so sweet.

And so beautiful...

Lifting his beer, he finished off the last sip and his chair creaked as he shifted again.

It had been a week ago this morning that he'd awakened on the couch with Addie's warm, soft body snuggled up against him. How they'd gotten horizontal he didn't know, but they had and it had felt...wonderful. The way she fit against him, her lavender scent filling his nose, and her supple curves tantalizing every inch of his body through their clothes. It had been a revelation to have her there first thing, even though nothing but sleep had passed between them. He had always admired her strength and sweetness, but that morning he realized there was something more than mutual admiration, something too strong to ignore, between them. She excited him, challenged him, made him want to be a better man. And he wanted her. The need to protect her the night before had been too compelling to pretend anything different.

The temptation to claim her as his that morning had struck him hard and deep. The fact that his hand had found its way inside her robe to cup one of her bountiful breasts during the night hadn't helped any. Disappointed in himself, he'd guiltily removed it before she woke, but he could still feel the hard nipple digging into his palm through her nightshirt. And he couldn't forget how his almost painful erection had nestled perfectly between the round cheeks of her derriere.

Widening his knees, Cade once again shifted in his chair, trying to ease the increasing tightness in his jeans. That happened more and more frequently now when he thought about her. He hadn't wanted to feel this attraction whenever Addie was near or the charged zing of awareness whenever they happened to touch, but he did. Every. Single. Time. Denying it would be less than useless and he was done lying to himself. He'd been around her for almost two months, and in that time, she hadn't done or said anything that hinted at a red flag of warning.

No, all she does is look at me as if she wants to lick me all over like a popsicle. He smiled at the thought.

The heat in her eyes had seared right through his resolve more than once. In the last week, he'd barely kept from kissing her more times than he could count. He wanted her, but aside from some smiles and laughter—two things that had been absent from his life for far too long—he had kept his distance, giving her time to recover. She seemed to have bounced back rather quickly from the assault, but then, she was resilient that way and he respected her for it. It hadn't happened overnight, but day after day, her fear and doubt had slowly eked away and left the sweet, tempting woman he'd come to adore.

This desire he felt for her wasn't right. He had no intention of staying, and Addie deserved so much better than him, but refusing her because of his own fears didn't feel right, either. He saw the disappointment in her eyes whenever he figuratively dragged himself away, putting distance between them and temptation out of reach. But maybe she just wanted to feel needed for a while, wanted someone to make her feel loved. Maybe she wasn't ready for forever.

Then again, maybe that was all him.

"Food's ready," their host cried from where he stood in front of the huge grill on the deck of their house several yards to the north.

The groups of people who'd been chatting and laughing around the bonfire slowly moved toward the house, still conversing as they went. Cade waited, staring at the flames, lost in his thoughts and the lust that burned inside him.

He didn't know how long he sat there alone, but when a plate of food suddenly appeared in front of his eyes, he sat up a little startled. Following the hand that held the paper plate, to the arm, and then to the face of the woman who'd brought his meal, he couldn't help how his chest expanded or the frisson of heat that swirled inside him. A grin curled his lips as he met Addie's sparkling gaze.

"I thought you'd be hungry," she said. "I didn't want you to go without."

He chuckled as he took the plate from her hand. "I'm sure there's plenty. You didn't have to do this."

"I know," she said, plopping down in the chair beside him, her own plate of food in her lap. "But I wanted to."

A different kind of heat crawled up his neck. It had been a long time since anyone waited on him or since anyone had made him blush with pleasure by looking at him, but Addie did both all the time. And she made him want to return the favor.

He could get used to life with her.

They ate quietly for a few minutes, their silence a testament to either their hunger or how good the food really was.

"You're awfully quiet today," Addie said, after finishing most of her dinner.

He heard the question in her tone and shrugged. "Just not into big groups, I guess." No way would he admit that he was too turned on by her right now to carry on a decent conversation with anyone.

"Do you want to leave?" she asked without looking his way, but he heard the concern in her tone.

He frowned at his food and shook his head. "No."

"I don't want you to feel trapped here. I thought you'd enjoy the party."

He gently bumped his shoulder into hers and her head snapped toward him.

"I am enjoying myself," he said with a little wink that made her blush. He hadn't meant to make that comment sound so suggestive, but the deep pitch and gravelly quality of his voice more than hinted at the desire that had been rolling through him for the last week.

She lowered her chin and used her fork to fiddle with her food. "Are you?"

A lightning bolt zapped through him at the evocative heat that infused those two words. His jeans grew a little tighter and he held in the groan that wanted to break out. "Are you flirting with me, Addie?"

Her sweet, brown eyes were hooded and left no doubt about her meaning when she met his gaze. "Of course, I'm flirting with you, Cade. I think I've been trying to get your attention for weeks."

He grinned. "You didn't have to try. I noticed the day you picked me up on the side of the road."

"Really?" The bonfire had nothing on the blaze in her eyes.

He nodded once, his gaze locked with hers. "Would you like me to prove it?"

Her playful grin did something to his heart—it leaped and stuttered and shot electric tingles of heat through his veins.

"Yes, please."

The male part of him jumped with excitement, but he sobered and the smile slipped off his face. "Are you sure, Addie? My plans haven't changed, and I don't want to hurt you."

"Yes, Cade, I'm sure. I'm tired of feeling this…" she waved her hand between them, "whatever this is and not doing anything about it. It's making me crazy. We need to relieve the…pressure, but whatever we do, it doesn't have to mean forever."

Well, that made him feel good. At least, he wasn't the only one feeling the powerful emotion—lust or love, whatever it was—always zapping between them. Still, something about her last sentence squeezed his heart.

"What should we do about it?" he asked, a smile pulling at his lips again.

She glanced up at the sky, a darker gray than blue, then at the small groups eating and chatting. When she turned back to him, a gleam of internal fire burned in her eyes as she leaned in and whispered, "You want to get out of here?"

His heart thumped almost painfully in his chest and his sudden impatience to leave had his mouth as dry as the desert sand. But he couldn't keep the grin off his face. "Absolutely."

Apparently not needing any other encouragement, Addie grabbed his nearly empty plate and set it on top of hers. "Let me say our goodbyes and I'll meet you at the truck."

He nodded. "It'll be running."

She giggled as she walked away and Cade took the opportunity to admire her in her stiff new jeans and cowboy boots. He loved her curves, the softness of her skin, and the way she looked at him. The emotion in her eyes had frightened him at first, but now he hated to go a day without seeing it. She had changed something in him, or maybe he'd done it himself. Either way, when he was with Addie, he felt as if he could do anything—maybe even find forgiveness for the brother who had broken his heart.

Cade was just about to climb into the cab of her truck when he heard Helga shout, "Addie! Don't forget about the 'Fest next weekend. You promised to join us."

"I won't. I'll be there," Addie shouted back as she rounded the front of the truck.

Cade glanced out his window and saw Lana and Veta had joined Helga on the front deck. The two sisters smiled, but Lana's held more than a friendly invitation. He mentally reminded himself to thank Veta the next time he saw her for rescuing him from her sister earlier. With all the pent-up feelings swirling around inside him all night, if he'd heard Lana giggle or say "Oh, Cade" in that breathy way one more time, he didn't know what he would've said. Not that he disliked the girl, but she was too young for him. Besides, his interest lay in the woman sliding into the truck beside him.

"And bring that young man with you," Helga said, waving goodbye to Cade, who replied in kind, wondering what he was being dragged into now.

Addie glanced at him and chuckled. "I will, Helga. Thanks! See you soon."

Still giggling, Addie pulled her seatbelt around her.

"What was that about?" Cade asked as he put the truck into gear and maneuvered onto the driveway.

"Oh, nothing, really," Addie said, smiling at him, that hot flame of desire still bright in her eyes. "She wants us to join them at the Oktoberfest in town next Saturday. And she said that you might be more fun if you had a little more to drink."

He chuckled. "I see. I guess I'll need to apologize for my standoffishness the next time I see them."

"I don't think she was offended," Addie said. "It was more like she was worried about you."

He glanced at her and reached for her hand. "I'm fine. With you, I'm more than fine." He brought her hand to his mouth and kissed her knuckles, then flicked out his tongue to taste her skin—sweet and salty, just like her.

She gasped, so he did it again, and then lowered their hands to the seat.

He did not let go, even when he had to shift.

"I want to make you feel good, too, Addie. I want to touch and taste every inch of you, feel your body beneath me, and hear your sweet, little moans before I make you scream my name. I want it all."

Silence greeted his declaration and his heart slammed into his belly. Hot and cold swept over his skin, and he was afraid to look over at her, afraid of what he'd see, but he did it anyway. He had to.

She stared at him, her lips parted, rosiness riding high on her cheeks, and the spark of flame that had been in her eyes had turned into a roaring bonfire of need.

"I want that too, Cade," she said, her voice rasping in her throat. "I want all of that and more."

His already half-hard shaft swelled and fire surged through his veins. Too much sensation assaulted him as he tried to concentrate on the short drive back to the house. So much so, that he didn't think about what she might've meant by "all that and more." With her lavender scent driving him wild with lust and something else he couldn't quite discern, his foot pressed on the accelerator a little harder, willing to risk a ticket if it meant getting his hands on those soft, sexy curves of hers one second sooner.

"Tonight, sweetheart," he purred as they slowed to turn onto her driveway, "you'll get everything you want and," he lowered his voice, "maybe some things you didn't even know you needed."

Her hand tightened on his. "Oh, yes, *please!*"

CHAPTER 13

The truck came to a lurching halt in front of Addie's barn, the tires kicking up a cloud of dust that billowed outside the windows. Tiny bits of rock plinked on the truck's roof as the airborne soil began to settle back to earth. The new motion light Cade had installed had spotlighted the truck as they pulled up, chasing out the shadows and making Addie blink. But she couldn't fault Cade for his enthusiasm in getting home quickly. Excited anticipation pressed in on her, too.

Cade cut the engine and leaned over the steering wheel, his forehead pressed against its smooth leather cover. Their hands, still entwined, rested on the seat beside his felt cowboy hat. Addie sensed his hesitation and studied him, wondering if second thoughts now plagued him. They had certainly done a number on her too many times to count since Cade arrived in her life. Considering what he'd been through, she couldn't blame him for any qualms he might have.

His eyes were downcast and he seemed to be fighting an internal battle. The anxiety knotting her belly tightened a little more, waiting for him to speak.

The bright light on the barn went out just as he pushed back and turned toward her. She couldn't read his expression now that the illumination had disappeared, but she could see the hard planes of his handsome face. His azure eyes seemed to twinkle and a muscle flexed in his jaw.

"I've got to feed the other animals," he said, his voice low and raspy as if dying of thirst.

She nodded, knowing he was right—the animals must come first—but she wondered if this was his way of backing out. Or making it easy for her to do so. Frowning at their clasped hands, confusion and doubt assailing her, she found her voice. "I'll help you."

His hand tightened on hers and she looked up. A crooked smile stretched his splendid mouth and his expression softened.

Releasing her hand, he snagged his cowboy hat from where it rested between them and scooted across the seat. The hat disappeared behind him and then he was so close, she could feel the heat of his body through the layers of their clothes.

His hand skimmed up her arm, over her shoulder, and into her braided hair, holding her head steady as he leaned into her. Expectantly, she licked her lips. His eyes caught the small motion and he smiled, stopping inches from her face.

"You don't have to help," he murmured. "It won't take long." Hot breath caressed her waiting mouth and something hotter shot through her belly.

"I don't mind," she whispered, still confused about his intentions and so turned on, she would do almost anything to convince him to kiss her *right now*.

"I know you don't," he said, his eyes gliding over her face as if memorizing every line. "So sweet..." He brushed a stray strand of hair from her forehead.

This close, she could see the blue of his eyes, but the color seemed darker, dangerous even, and she swallowed her nervous giggle. Cade would never hurt her.

But he'll break your heart when he leaves.

Addie pushed that thought away. All that mattered was right now. She'd deal with anything else later. After he was gone.

"You seem...nervous," he said quietly, staring into her eyes.

She peered at him through her lashes and lifted a shoulder. "I guess I am, a little."

His brows drew together. "Why?"

She turned her head, but he wouldn't let her look away.

"Hey, sweetie, talk to me."

A sigh slipped from her and she met his concerned gaze. She opened her mouth, but nothing came out. How could she tell him she was afraid he would leave her wanting, burning so badly she'd never be able to sleep? That, if they did this, she would never get over his leaving.

God, I've never been this excited over a man before. And he hasn't even kissed me yet. She wasn't sure how to handle the abundance of emotion churning inside her.

"We don't have to do this," he said, his voice gentle, his eyes tender and caring. Concerned. For her.

A stuttered laugh escaped her and the uncertain grin that brightened his face squeezed her heart. Did he think *she* would reject *him*? "I was afraid you were…having second thoughts…about us."

A full, brilliant smile transformed his handsome face into a thing of unadulterated masculine beauty. Just looking at him made her chest tighten and her lady parts clench. Heat engulfed her and she found it hard to breathe.

"No chance of that, sweetheart," he said in a low, gravelly voice as he cupped her face in both hands. "I won't have you thinking I don't want you tonight. Right now. In this truck. So, let me ease your mind and give you proof of my intentions."

With that, he closed the meager distance between them.

Warm, firm lips brushed against hers, slowly at first, testing, teasing, promising her heaven. His tongue slowly swiped over her lower lip asking for entry, and she immediately opened for him. He delved inside like an invading army, plundering, conquering. And she loved it. She melted into him, offering everything—right there in her truck. With his mouth on hers and the hard heat of him so close, she didn't care where they were. All she wanted was this man holding her, touching her, kissing her. Everywhere.

He pulled back and rested his forehead against hers. Both of them breathing hard, each drawing in the other's breath and trembling with their mutual desire. Addie felt lightheaded, spinning out of control as if she would fall into empty blackness forever if he hadn't been there to hold onto.

"Does that leave any doubt in your mind as to what I want?"

She smiled. "It was…nice."

He sat back abruptly, a dark frown marring his brow. "Nice?"

She giggled. "Yeah. You know, in a hot, bone-melting sort of way."

His face softened with a slow, sexy grin. She'd clearly stroked his ego in just the right way. "That's better."

"I'm glad you approve, but you know if you have any doubts…" She raised her eyebrows and ran her hand down his thigh. "You could try again…"

A growl rumbled in his throat. "If you keep that up, we'll never get out of this truck."

She laughed and shifted to open her door. "Come on. The sooner we get the animals fed, the sooner we can get back to…" She gave him a flirty wink and he groaned again.

"You're going to kill me."

"Not tonight," she said, hopping out of the truck. "At least not yet." She giggled at his low groan and headed for the barn, certain that Cade would follow.

Feeding the animals didn't take long. Cade had taken care of the cattle before they left and as they entered the barn, she paused just inside to refill the feed bin for her tiny flock of chickens. A simple chore, but one that Cade made infinitely more difficult with his big hands gripping her hips and his wonderful lips nibbling her neck.

She sighed, loving the way his mouth felt against her skin. "You're making this harder, you know," she said with a smile, not that she wanted him to stop.

"I'm hungry," he whispered in her ear, and his hot breath pebbled her skin with goosebumps. "I had to have a little taste to tide me over."

Her already taut nipples grew harder and her insides clenched in anticipation.

"Well, you won't have to wait long," she said, grinning at him as she stepped out of his grasp and took the feed out to the chickens.

When she returned, Cade had already brought down a new bale of hay from the loft and had broken some off for Dreamer, the old, retired saddle horse she'd taken in when she bought the farm. He tossed the hay into the feed bin and paused as Dreamer pushed his nose in and began to eat. Running his hand over the chestnut gelding's sleek neck, Cade murmured encouraging words to the elderly horse.

Touched by his sweet gesture, Addie stopped and stared, her eyes traveling over as much of Cade's body as she could see. Aside from his handsome face, the man was well-proportioned—wide, muscular shoulders, lean hips, and she adored his sculpted ass in those tight-fitting, faded jeans. But he was so much more than just handsome. He was a valued friend, someone she knew she could trust. He might be a tad overprotective, but that, too, was part of his charm. The fact that he hadn't tried to force her to do what he thought was right with Mark told her he also respected her decisions, even when he didn't like them.

"If you keep staring at me like that," he said, as he lowered his hand and turned around, "I might not be able to do right by you." Brushing hay off his gray T-shirt, he met her gaze. His eyes were so intensely blue, so full of lust, her breath caught in her chest.

She blinked, unsure how she'd gotten so lucky. "And what does that mean?"

He stepped out of the stall, his burning gaze never leaving her as he shut the door behind him. The bulge at the front of his jeans made her mouth suddenly water and she wondered if she might not be able to wait until they got to the house.

"It means, sweetness, that you deserve better."

She tilted her head and frowned. *Did he change his mind?*

"I want our first time together to be in a warm, comfortable bed where you could moan and scream as loud as you want."

Air expelled from her lungs and stuttered back in. She wanted to say that she wanted him, too. That it didn't matter where they took their pleasure, but he didn't give her a chance.

"I don't want it to be in the barn," he said in that low gravelly voice that had liquid heat pooling between her legs. He strolled down the short aisle, keeping distance between them, but stalking her just the same. She mimicked his movement, only stepping farther into the barn, unable to break away from the hot need in his eyes. "But I don't think I can wait."

"What do you want, Cade?" Her voice, barely above a whisper, quivered. Thickness coated her throat making it hard to speak.

He took one step toward her, all the playful teasing gone from his eyes. "Isn't that obvious by now?"

"Tell me."

"I want to make you come, Addie," he said bluntly. "I want to bare your breasts and suck on them until I hear you cry out with pleasure, knowing that it's all because of me." He took another step forward.

She took one backward. She hadn't meant to, she just…did.

"You always look at me like a woman in need," he rasped. "Devouring me with your eyes. Like you *want* to devour me with your hands, your mouth, and your body." He stepped toward her, close enough to reach out and grab her.

She stepped back and bumped into the ladder that led to the loft.

"Are you in need, Addie? Do you want to devour *me* the way I want to devour *you*?"

Oh, God, yes!

She swallowed but didn't move as he closed the distance between them, his face and broad shoulders blocking out everything else. His fingers brushed over her cheek and along her jaw, down her neck and across her collarbone.

"You're so beautiful, Addie," he murmured as his fingers dove into the opening of her shirt. "Do you know how beautiful you are?"

"I'm not," she said, dropping her chin, even as she shivered from his touch, and a sliver of doubt dampened her mood. "I'm not beautiful. I'm short and fat with a passingly pretty face."

He frowned. "That's not true."

She shook her head, unable to look at him. She hated this. The time when she had to find out if he'd tell her the truth or if he would make up lies to flatter her into his bed the way so many others had tried to do.

Long, lean fingers sweeping around the outside of her breast startled her. When his hand changed direction and he cupped the heavy mound in his palm, her breath halted altogether. He gently lifted her face to his with a knuckle under her chin. "Look at me, Addie."

She did as he said, shaking, fearing what he would say, what she would read in his eyes.

"You *are* beautiful," he said.

She stared into his gaze, searching, but the lie she usually saw in a man's eyes at times like this wasn't there. The hesitation that said he held back part of his assessment. The part that said, *for a fat girl.*

"You're smart and funny, kind and generous. I could drown in your eyes. Your body is so damn tempting," his fingers swept over her cheek and down her neck once more, "and your skin is so soft. Softer than I imagined it would be, and now I want to touch it for days."

Tears welled in her eyes. No one had ever said anything like that to her. She'd always been the girl who had a pretty face, the cute, chubby girl with a great smile. Never this. Never beautiful. Not from any man, and not with so much honesty in his eyes.

He met her gaze. "You. Are. Gorgeous, Addie. Don't ever think anything different."

Something warm filled her chest, so intense and hot it felt like she might explode. She wanted to laugh. She wanted to cry. She wanted this man to do everything he'd said he would and then some, and she didn't care where.

"Kiss me, Cade…"

He smiled lazily. "Yes, ma'am."

Her eyelids fluttered closed as his mouth converged with hers. A gentle press of lips, petal-soft and so full of emotion, and Addie instantly leaned into him. Her hands skimmed over his chest, marveling at the hard planes and ridges beneath the soft cotton, and over his shoulders to curl into the dark hair at his nape.

Cade opened his mouth, his tongue inviting hers to play. When her lips parted, he tilted his head and deepened the kiss, overwhelming her with pent-up desire.

Her body burned like a furnace, low in her abdomen. She melted into him, molding herself to the hard muscles of his body. His hands slipped down from her waist to cup her buttocks and pulled her firmly against him. That hard bulge in his jeans nestled against her lower belly, and she instinctively bucked her hips, trying to grind her need against his. She wanted him there, to touch her there, but his hands remained on her butt.

She whimpered and a low chuckle rumbled through him.

"Don't worry, sweetheart," he said, punctuating the endearment with another soft kiss, "I'll get to the rest of you in a moment."

He didn't lie, but the slow, agonizing trail of kisses he left from her mouth, down her neck, and across her collarbone did nothing but make her more desperate. She lifted her leg and wrapped it around his hip, pressing the wet, throbbing part of her against his thigh. But she still couldn't get what she really wanted.

Somehow, while she shifted and twisted against him, he'd unbuttoned her shirt and pulled it from her jeans. He pushed the soft cotton down her arms as his mouth left a trail of fiery kisses over the gentle swell of her breasts. Her nipples longed for that mouth to kiss, lick, and suckle them, and the knot of need in her lower body pulled tighter. But he continued to take his time, caressing them with his fingers while he kissed along the lacy edge of her bra.

When the cool evening air finally caressed her naked breasts, she gasped in surprise.

"Oh, God, Addie," he said, sounding as if he were being strangled, but his eyes gleamed with blue fire as he stared at her freed bosom, the hard dusky nipples stabbing the air, dying for his touch. "You are the most beautiful thing I've ever seen."

He cupped her breasts in each hand almost reverently, measuring their weight, size, and circumference. His gaze burned her flesh and she shivered, waiting, wanting, needing…more.

"Cade…"

His eyes met hers and her heart clenched. So much passion blazed in his blue gaze, so much need etched his face.

He smiled. "I know, sweetness," he said as his thumbs brushed over her sensitive nipples.

She sucked in a breath and moaned as her eyes closed. An almost painful stab of desire shot downward from her breasts to the yearning, weeping flesh between her thighs.

He thrummed her nipples again and she gasped and jumped.

"So sensitive," he murmured, sounding pleased.

Addie barely heard him. Her whole focus was on the heat of his hands against her skin, how they, and not the chill air, sprung goosebumps all over her, and the constant pulse he'd created in her lower body.

"Please, Cade…"

"Patience, darlin'."

She groaned. He was making her crazy, kissing and touching her everywhere but where she desperately wanted him to. She squirmed, hoping to encourage his mouth where she wanted it, but whenever he got close, he would shift direction. It was maddening!

Just when she thought she couldn't take any more, scalding heat seared her right breast. She sucked air in through her mouth, unable to get enough.

His tongue flicked back and forth over her engorged nipple and she cried out with sheer sensual joy, even as the building tension within grew harder, heavier, more hot and needy.

He suckled her while the fingers of his other hand mimicked the movements of his mouth, tongue, and teeth. She wanted to reach for him, rake her fingers in his hair, and hold him, but the shirt around her wrists kept her hands at her sides.

Another moan slipped from her lips.

He hummed against her breast and the vibration sent another stab of pleasure downward.

The heat of his mouth and body disappeared. She whimpered at the sudden loss, but she needn't have worried.

Gently, he pulled her arms above her head, wrapping her loose shirt around her wrists and fastening it to a ladder rung. "What are you doing?" She didn't recognize her voice, which was too low, too breathy.

His eyes bored into hers, his hand sliding down her arms to her breasts once more. "Is this okay?" His voice was as low and as raspy as hers had been. "I know we didn't discuss it, but…"

She felt no fear, no internal warning that told her to escape the loose bonds of her shirt. All she felt was desire for this man and trust that he would give her everything she wanted. "Yes," she whispered. "Please,

Cade... *Please.*"

He stared at her breasts, swelling in his palms, and licked his lips. A shiver rocked through her, feeling that simple motion of his tongue all over.

His thumbs strummed her nipples, plucking her like a guitar string, and she whimpered once more. He kissed her hard and quick, and then pressed his body into hers. "Soon, baby," he murmured in her ear, his hot breath tantalizing her skin. "Soon I'll relieve that tension and then we can find a more comfortable spot to play a little more."

His words sent a lightning bolt to her core. All she could do was nod as his mouth traveled over her neck and down to her breasts once more. Licking, squeezing, kneading, all of it winding her tighter and tighter as her nipples grew more and more sensitive.

Like a drug, the more he touched her, the more she wanted, the more she ached and throbbed, the more she needed *him.* The thin cotton that covered her femininity was soaked with her desire, but all his attention stayed focused on her breasts.

Soft little moans filled the barn. Her moans, her passion.

Something about having her hands bound, about being so exposed and powerless, brought her to the edge. His tongue flicking over her nipple and then his teeth gently biting it while his fingers simultaneously pinched the other shoved her right into the abyss.

"Oh, Cade..." she screamed, and then screamed again when another jolt of pleasure rippled through her. He kept suckling her until her cries turned to pants and her body, once as taut as any piano wire, slumped against him in relief.

Slowly, he kissed his way up her body, over her jaw, to her mouth. Lips soft yet firm, she eagerly opened for him. Then he broke the gentle kiss and rested his forehead against hers. Both of them closed their eyes, his warm hands at her hips, thumbs tracing slow circles over her skin.

"Did you enjoy that?" he asked.

She huffed out a dry laugh. "You have to ask?"

He pulled back and met her gaze. "A man likes to hear a woman say it sometimes."

Something vulnerable danced in his eyes. "Yes, Cade, I enjoyed that very much. But I do hope we're not through."

He smiled that crooked, sly grin that always warmed her in all the right places. "Oh no, we are definitely not done." He tugged at her shirt, freeing her hands and pulling the garment from her wrists. He tucked it into his back pocket and before she knew what that was about, he'd slipped her bra down her arms and away from her body. It followed her shirt into his pocket.

"What are you up to now?" she asked.

"A little erotic dare," he replied.

She frowned. "What does that mean?"

"It means, I dare you to either walk to the house with your breasts bared to me and the world, or you let me carry you with your naked breasts tempting me the whole way."

Heat warmed her cheeks and spread over her chest. "I can't go walking around outside like this."

He crowded her against the wall, the hard planes of his chest crushing her breasts. He ground the thick rod in his jeans against her as his lips crashed down on hers. She moaned, the hot pulse between her legs building once more, and then, as suddenly as he'd started, he pulled back. He kept his erection pressed into her belly, its heat burning through the denim to scorch her tender flesh.

"Do you still want me inside you, Addie," he asked in a low, raspy voice that swept over her heated skin.

She stared up at him, her whole body alive with want once more. "Yes."

He stepped back, leaving her cold and still half-dressed. "Then let's go." He waved his hand toward the exit.

Glancing over at the barn doors, she shivered. Did he really want her to flaunt herself out there? Why? To prove how much she wanted him?

He must have seen her reticence. "No one's out there, Addie. I would've never suggested you do this if there was. This is for you and me. I want you to show off that beautiful body. I want to see you move with the confidence of the gorgeous woman you are... But if it's too much..." He reached for her shirt, but she shook her head and his eyebrows shot upward.

"No."

She could do this. He was right, she wasn't in the city anymore. No one was around for miles and it was fully dark out there now. There was no reason she couldn't do this. It was a little exhilarating to think of walking back to the house with her breasts free and Cade's eyes on her. She thought about telling him she'd do it if he walked back naked, but she wanted to be the one to remove his clothes, to have that beautiful bulge fall into her hands, but not here. She wanted to be inside, in her bed when she took him into her body. And what better way to turn him on—and get him back—than to tease him the whole way there? A plan quickly formed in her head.

I can't believe I'm going to do this.

Lifting her chin, she turned back to his questioning face. "Are you going to open the door for a lady?"

A smile split his face. "Of course." He darted over and pulled the sliding door aside.

Cold air rushed in, puckering her nipples. Excitement tingled through her breasts and arced down between her legs. She fought her automatic instinct to cover herself. Instead, she pressed her shoulders back and gripped her hands behind her. Standing a little straighter, she met Cade's eyes and smiled as she slowly strolled toward him, her breasts thrust forward, nipples stabbing the air. He liked her body and she wanted him to see it.

Standing at the entrance, the chill night air sweeping over her hot skin, she turned to him. "I'll do this," she said proudly, "but you will stay right here until I get to the door."

He frowned. "Are you sure? You don't have to prove anything. I didn't really mean for you to do this. I was just teasing you."

"Doesn't matter. You started it and I'll finish it. And if I do it right, you'll be more than ready to follow me inside."

"I'm ready now."

She grinned slyly, her plan coming together. "You will stay here."

He nodded. "Yes, ma'am, and..." his eyes dropped briefly to caress her breasts then returned to her face, "you're beautiful, Addie."

"So are you, Cade."

She stepped out into the darkness, her confidence swelling inside her. Then the brilliance of the spotlight fell on her and she cringed.

No one's out here, she reminded herself. She dropped her arms that had automatically crossed over her chest, straightened her shoulders, and continued.

Coyotes yipped in the distance and a gentle breeze soughed through the grass. Nervousness and pride swelled within her. Ten yards from the barn and halfway to the house, she spun to face Cade, her generous breasts swaying freely with the motion, but she didn't try to hide them.

His gaze burned her when she met his eyes. They slowly swept over her, lingering on her breasts before rising to her face once more.

"Like what you see?" she asked, dragging her hands over her hips and belly to cup her breasts.

"Yes," he choked out, "very much."

Her hands slipped down to the front of her jeans. "Would you like to see more?"

His mouth fell open as she popped the button on her jeans and slowly lowered the zipper. He nodded.

She kicked out of her boots. "You'll have to pick those up for me," she said, dancing backward a few steps, her breasts once again swaying with her movements. Then she turned and bent slightly, slowly sliding her jeans over her backside and down her legs to reveal the lacy white thong that matched the lacy white bra hanging from his back pocket. She stepped out of the jeans and looked back. "Grab those for me too, will you?"

She winked and he took a step out of the barn. His face flushed, his eyes blazing with desire.

"Uh-uh," she said, waving a finger at him like a naughty child, even though she was feeling a bit naughty herself. "No, you stay there until I reach the door." She was nearly there, but if she was going to walk naked then he was going to have to watch and wait. And she only needed a few more seconds to entice him.

He stopped and stood stone-still, like a statue of a Greek god. His chest heaved beneath his gray T-shirt and the thick bulge in his jeans seemed to have grown bigger in the short time since she'd left the barn.

Standing in the grass of her front lawn, she tucked her thumbs into the hip straps of her thong and tugged them outward. "You want to see what's under these?"

He nodded slowly, his mouth still hanging open.

God, this made her feel so powerful, so desired, and as beautiful as he'd said she was.

Smiling from ear to ear, she gradually, ever so deliberately, slipped the straps over her hips. Just as she was about to reveal it all, the motion light switched off and darkness encompassed them.

She let the straps snap back to her hips and giggled when he gasped with regret and maybe a little frustration.

"I guess you'll have to come and take them off yourself," she shouted as she ran for the door.

The light came on again as he crossed the yard, and she yelled a reminder about her clothes. "You'll get nothing from me without them."

He skidded to a halt and dashed back a few steps to grab her things.

Giggling and excited, she ran into her house and down the hall to her room, eager for his response to her little striptease in the yard.

CHAPTER 14

Cade hastened into the house, juggling Addie's jeans and boots in his hands and searching the front room for any sign of the temptress who'd just left him granite-hard and sweating in the yard. But she was nowhere in sight.

"Where the hell did she go so fast?" he muttered to himself.

One of her boots clattered to the floor. Startled by the unexpected thump, he looked down at the footwear and then dropped the other one next to its pair and tossed her jeans on the couch as he crossed to the hall at the center of the house.

She had to be in one of the back rooms, but was she in his room or hers? Did she run from him to get away…or to entice him to follow?

He hadn't expected her to take up his impetuous dare, but he'd been impressed and amazed by her audaciousness when she did. Addie was a strong woman, but he'd wanted her to know she was beautiful, too. That she could capture a man—capture *him*—with just a look.

The way she'd smiled at him when she slowly lowered the thong off her hips had been so damn hot. He could tell that she'd felt her power then, and his body had reacted to her display. Even now, standing in the front room, undecided about which way he should go, his cock strained against the zipper of jeans that had grown far too tight.

Guessing she'd be more comfortable in her own room, Cade turned down the hall away from his room.

Her door stood ajar and a shaft of light slashed through the hallway. She had to be inside.

Stepping up to the door, he peeked through the crack, but all he saw was a good-sized bed with its pale green comforter and white sheets pulled back. No sign of the woman he sought. But she had to be in there...

"Addie?" he called and knocked on her door. It swung open slightly to reveal more of her bed and her room.

"Come in, Cade," she said from somewhere inside. Something about her low voice dug inside him, warming his chest even as it ached with anticipation and something else that he refused to examine.

He pushed the door open and stepped inside, closing it behind him— an automatic action.

No one was in the room.

"Where are you?" he asked curiously, anxious to lay eyes on her once again.

"Take off your boots," she said from somewhere across the room. Another door stood there and he guessed it was the master bathroom. "I'll be right out. Make yourself comfortable, but...don't undress."

He frowned. *Okay. I guess we're not doing what I thought we were doing.* Cade slipped out of his boots and coat and left them by the door.

She'd been so responsive in the barn, determined to take the next step. Consternation squeezed his chest as he shook his head. Why invite him in here, and why the show outside, if she didn't intend more? Was she just playing with him?

He shoved his hands into his front pockets and stared at the well-worn beige carpet beneath his stocking feet, wild speculation running through his mind even as disappointment settled heavily on his chest.

"You could've sat on the bed to wait," Addie said with a touch of humor in her voice.

Cade's head came up and his mouth fell open. She stood six feet from him, naked and flushed. Her silky-soft hair unbound and brushed until it shined. It spilled over her shoulders in a golden cascade, the ends brushing over burgundy nipples that were taut from his touch. Her waist curved in below her ribs and then flared over her hips, giving her the most stunning hourglass figure he'd ever seen. She was more splendid than he'd imagined.

"You'll catch flies with your mouth hanging open like that."

His eyes met the sultry vixen and his jaw snapped closed with an audible click. He swallowed.

"Are you okay, Cade?" she asked with a frown, suddenly looking uncertain.

"Y-Yeah. Yes. I'm fine," he stuttered. "You…you're…just so beautiful."

"Yeah, you said that," she replied, her smile returning.

"Well," he said, raising his brows and perusing her body, "it needed saying again. Look at you."

"I'd rather look at you."

Her gaze heated the chill that had worked its way inside him only moments before. His body grew so hot, he thought his clothes might spontaneously combust, starting with his jeans.

"Why did you tell me not to undress?" He had no idea where that question came from. He hadn't been thinking about it right then, but he still wanted to know.

"Because," she said as she sauntered toward him, generous hips and ample breasts swaying seductively with each step, "*I* wanted to undress you."

"Oh, okay," he croaked through his suddenly dry throat. A grin tugged at his mouth as he dug out his wallet and the condom hidden inside.

She stopped inches away and stared into his face. Her chocolate eyes burned him, and he could almost feel the tips of her nipples taunting his chest.

He dropped his wallet and lifted a hand to touch her smooth skin.

"Uh-uh," she said, shaking her head. "Not until you're naked, too. I want to see you, Cade, feel you, skin on skin."

The condom wrapper crinkled in his hand. *Fuck! She's hot!*

Unable to speak, he nodded and lowered his hand.

"Better," she said, reaching for his shirt. Tugging the gray cotton free of his jeans, she slipped her hands inside. His ab muscles flexed with her touch and then rippled beneath her hands as she slid them along his sides. He lifted his arms over his head and her hands moved higher until his shirt pushed up over his head. Then he jerked it off and tossed it aside, not wanting anything to block his view of her.

"Are you a little…eager?" she asked, teasing him with another sultry smile as she popped the button on his jeans out of its hole.

"Mm-hmm," he murmured as she slowly lowered his zipper. His blood pumped a deep, needful yearning through his veins—it throbbed in his temples, his chest, his groin. To keep from touching her, his fingers fisted at his sides, the condom wrapper digging into his palm, and he closed his eyes. His legs, his arms, his *body* trembled…and he was so hard it *hurt*.

No one had ever unraveled him like this, not with his pants still on…*or off*. And the way she touched him, looked at him, it was almost as if she wanted to worship him, his body. Like she wanted to delve into his soul.

Oh, this is so dangerous, he thought, but it skittered away in a wake of hot blood and hotter desire. His skin was so sensitive to her movement, to her touch, to *her*, he tingled everywhere.

Denim slipped over his hips and down his legs in a raspy caress. Her fingers overwrote the sensation as they glided upward. They stopped at his waist and he clenched his jaw, breath stuttering through his teeth and parted lips. He swallowed the wash of moisture that filled his mouth.

"Addie. Please, hurry."

"Don't worry, handsome," she said as her hands dived inside his boxer briefs and over his ass, fingers clutching and kneading his back side, "I'm getting there."

He growled in reply, his ability to form coherent sentences slowly diminishing.

Her breasts pillowed his chest as she cupped his ass and squeezed, sending a bolt of heat straight to his balls. Fingers brushing little circles on his skin, they slowly moved inward to trace the dark seam between his cheeks. His breath halted, an audible cessation, as his eyes snapped open.

She giggled and the sound swept over him like a fist full of downy feathers, raising goosebumps all over his body.

"Addie," he groaned, afraid he might embarrass himself by exploding before she even touched him where he *needed* her to.

"Patience, darlin'," she said, using the same unflappable tone he'd used on her in the barn.

"You've got me so hot, I may not be able to be patient," he warned.

She giggled again and he opened his mouth to tell her he couldn't take any more.

The cold air that washed over his taut, hot skin startled him. His cotton boxer briefs were down his legs and around his ankles so fast, he'd barely processed it before her fingers closed around his shaft.

Head dropping back on his shoulders, he inhaled sharply.

"Oh, Cade. Your skin is so soft and you're so…hard and…hot…"

"Hard, yes," he said, lowering his chin to his chest.

He just got the words out when she abruptly bent at the waist and licked the weeping tip pulsing in her hand. Every muscle in his body had been pulled tight as piano wire by her agonizing foreplay, but that hot, wet flick of her tongue broke his tenuous hold on himself.

His fingers curled around her arms, trapping the condom against her satiny flesh. He pulled her up and then dragged her against his chest. Her eyes looked startled in the brief moment he saw them. Then he dropped his head and all thought left his mind, just as all resistance faded from her body. She melted into him, fitting perfectly against him, as her arms wrapped around his neck and her mouth opened for him.

Kissing her was like going home again. All the worries, pain, and disappointment he carried for the last five years fell away when she was in his arms. He felt new and better than he ever had in his life. Why he felt all those things, he didn't know. All he knew was that Addie made it happen.

Long fingers buried in her hair, the silky strands sliding easily over his calluses, while his other arm wrapped firmly around her supple waist and he pulled her closer, deepening the kiss. He wanted to feel every part of her, to kiss and touch and lick every inch of her. He wanted to hear her soft, little moans of pleasure before she screamed his name.

He wanted to be inside her.

In one quick motion, Cade swept her legs out from under her and lifted her against his chest. A surprised squeak escaped her and then a bubbling giggle that vibrated inside him. He liked her laugh.

Glancing at her passion-drugged eyes, he smiled and so did she. He kissed her again, putting one foot in front of the other, knowing where he was going without looking.

When his knees butted into the bed, he gently lowered her to it without breaking their kiss. Straightening, he fumbled with the condom, rolling it on by touch as he stared down at her, unable to look away. Her skin glowed in the low lamplight, a pale contrast to the dusky red of her nipples—still hard and puckered from his attentions in the barn—and the light brown patch of curls between her legs. She shifted her legs, rubbing her thighs together, clearly anxious for him, but it was her eyes that nearly brought him to his knees.

Heart thundering in his chest, for a moment, he couldn't draw breath. The longing he read in her gaze yanked at his insides—a hard tug that shifted something deep inside him. He couldn't explain it, but he felt it.

Somehow, everything had changed.

He let that almost-physical-pull draw him to her. Covering her body with his, he kissed her, slowly, reverently as his hips settled between her spread thighs. Again, their bodies meshed perfectly, and she did not hesitate to wrap herself around him, encouraging him.

Pulling back, he propped himself on his elbows and looked into her face. "You are sure about this, right?" He didn't want her to regret anything.

"Absolutely," she replied. "I want you, Cade. As long as you want me."

"How could I not?" he said, lowering his head. He kissed her again, a quick, light press of lips. "I think I've wanted you ever since you picked me up off the side of the road." His fingers toyed with a stray strand of her hair. "You were beautiful then…"

"And now?" she asked when words failed him.

"Now, you are so much more than just beautiful."

She smiled as her hands slid down to his ass. Fingers splayed over his backside, her legs wrapped around his waist, and she pulled him closer. "I want you," she said in a low voice as an inferno blazed in her eyes. "I'm ready. I want you inside me, now."

"Yes, ma'am," he murmured with a smile as he positioned himself, feeling the slick heat already coating her entrance. He rubbed his shaft through her essence, lubricating himself for entry. When he slowly pushed inside her hot, wet core, her body arched into him and her nails dug into his skin. He didn't care, just closed his eyes, savoring the way she gripped him, welcoming him inside.

A moan of pure pleasure emanated from her lips and his chest puffed and warmed. He wanted to hear more of those.

Slowly, he tilted his hips, pulled out, then slammed back in.

Her nails dug into his shoulders. "Yes! I love…it. More, please. *Please*"

Her hesitation registered, but only momentarily, and then it was swept out of his mind on a wave of heat, replaced by the driving need to give her more. To give her all he had, and, right now, all he had was his body and a battered heart that she had begun to heal.

Slowly, he pressed his hips forward, staring into her heart-melting brown eyes that seemed to hold a promise he was unworthy to receive. Using the same slow pace—memorizing her face, her body, how she felt around him—he repeated the motions and her eyelids fluttered closed.

"Oh God, Cade," she murmured. "You feel incredible."

"Just wait, sweetheart," he whispered in her ear and nipped her earlobe. "It'll only get better."

"I love your confidence," she said, kissing his cheek, his mouth.

That shifting feeling struck him again like a hard punch to the sternum. He hadn't had much confidence for the last five years—not with women or horses…or anything else. But being with Addie had changed that. His old self peeked through the cracks she had made in the protective ramparts he'd built around his heart. Maybe he still had a shot at becoming the man he'd always wanted to be.

Her arms snaked around his shoulders, pulling him closer.

Grinning stupidly, he increased his tempo, holding nothing back now, building to a rapid rhythm that had them both panting and moaning. Out, in. Out, in. Her hips crashing into his with each thrust. His muscles tightened and bulged. Heat swept up the back of his legs to tingle in his lower back, tightening his balls.

"Yes!" she screamed. "God, Cade! Yes!"

Her body gripped him, hard, and then rippled over his shaft. One more thrust and he groaned, his release joining with hers. He continued to pump, in and out, in and out, helping her ride the last vestige of her orgasm until she lay still but trembling beneath him.

Dropping his head and nuzzling his face against her neck, he breathed in the subtle scent of lavender in her hair. He pictured warm, sunny days making love to Addie in a meadow, hearing that low, sexy voice of hers scream his name again and again.

God, he wanted that!

An instant later, walls of fear and doubt slammed into place.

He had nothing to offer.

She deserved better.

What if this meant more to me than it did to her?

He pushed the thought away and hugged her closer.

He would deal with whatever happened next. But until then, he wanted to enjoy the comfort of a woman who wanted him. Wanted to see where it would lead—if it would lead anywhere.

And if he really could love again.

CHAPTER 15

Addie breathed in Cade's warm, musky scent and reveled in the heavy weight of his body pressing her into the mattress, his arms wrapped around her and his hot breath scalding her neck—his turgid flesh still part of her. God, she'd missed this! Having a man rest on her, replete in the aftermath of great sex. More than great. Sharing that intimacy with Cade had been…something she'd never experienced before. The swell of emotions inside her still threatened to bubble over and stumble out of her mouth in some gushy froth of girly feelings.

No one, not even Jared—the man she'd once thought she wanted to marry—had ever made her feel that way.

When Cade looked at her, she felt every bit as beautiful as he told her she was; and in his arms, she felt safe and cared for. Something else was also mixed in with all of that. Something that promised so much more than just one night, more than just a seasonal fling.

Her heart ballooned with every emotion she'd experienced since he'd arrived. It threatened to explode, and she couldn't help the giddy giggle that bubbled out of her chest.

"What?" Cade asked, pushing up onto his elbows. Addie silently thanked him for not rolling away.

She smiled. "Nothing. Just…happy."

His curious frown bloomed into a gorgeous smile that locked up her lungs.

"I'm glad to hear it," he said, his blue eyes almost glowing.

She tilted her head and remembered to breathe. "Something's different…"

Cade's brows snapped together. "Don't know what you mean."

"You seem…" She paused, considering her words. "You seem happy. Are you happy, Cade?"

His grin returned, but with a bit more sizzle than the last one. "Of course, I am. What man wouldn't be if he got to hold you like this?"

She rolled her eyes. "You really need to stop exaggerating."

"I'm not." His gaze turned serious. "Addie, you need to believe me. You are a catch and so much more than a guy like me deserves."

It was her turn to frown. "And what kind of guy are you, Cade, that you don't deserve to be loved?"

He blinked at her choice of words and Addie wanted to kick herself. She hadn't meant to say it like that. She didn't really love him—did she? It seemed too fast. Thankfully, she'd stopped herself from saying, "I love you," while he was rocking her world. Maybe the words had simply slipped onto her tongue because of the glorious things he'd done to her body.

But that didn't seem right, either.

Something dark swirled in his eyes—sadness, pain, doubt—and she cursed silently.

"Everyone needs to be touched, Cade, to feel affection from another human being," she said, trying to reel back the implication in her last statement. "Why wouldn't you deserve that?"

He shrugged, rolled away from her, and got up to discard the condom. She mourned the loss of his heat and the weight of his body, and wondered if he would leave her there waiting. Thankfully, he returned moments later and plopped down on the mattress beside her, seemingly comfortable in his nakedness.

Unwilling to let the distance between them grow or lose the closeness they'd shared, she wiggled up to his side. He smiled and wrapped his arm around her to pull her close.

They lay quietly together, and as much as she loved listening to the calm, steady beat of his heart beneath her ear, Addie wished he would speak. When he didn't, she tried to reach him again. "I'll make a deal with you."

He chuckled. "Okay. What kind of deal?"

"I'll stop questioning my beauty, if you stop beating yourself up all the time and believe me when I tell you, you're a good man who deserves the best in everything."

He laughed again, and the sound rumbling through his chest made her smile.

"Only you, Addie," he said through his chuckles.

She tilted her head so she could look up at him. "Only me, what?"

"You're the only one who's made me think I can believe you."

"That's a good thing, isn't it?"

He kissed her forehead. "Yes, it is."

"So, does that mean we have a deal?"

Looking up at the ceiling, he pulled in a deep breath. "Sure, I'll give it a try."

"Good," she said and returned his smile as she cuddled up against him again.

"I can't believe you're still single," he muttered as if talking to himself.

She looked up at him. "What does that mean?"

He met her frown with a grin. "How is it that a woman like you is still single? I mean, why hasn't some lucky guy snatched you up and put a ring on your finger?"

Addie sighed and settled her head back on his chest. She didn't want to talk about that when she felt this good, but she owed him that, especially after sharing his pain with her just last week.

"I was engaged once," she said quietly, her fingers absently tracing circles on his chest.

"And?" he asked when her words fizzled out.

"He died."

Cade's body tensed before he shifted onto his side and rolled her to face him. Concern filled his gaze as he brushed her hair back. "I'm sorry. I didn't know…"

She shrugged. "Not very many people do. And you don't need to be sorry. It was a while ago now. I've healed, moved on."

"But you haven't dated." Something curious filled his tone, a question that he didn't articulate.

"I have, a little," she replied, "but my choices haven't been the best of late. There were a couple others before I moved here, but they didn't really interest me, and Mark—You remember him…the cop?" Cade nodded, his eyes darkening with memory. "I think I was just going through the motions at first, trying to find my feet again. You know?"

He nodded, but something like doubt shimmered in his eyes. "So…have you? Found your feet again, I mean?"

She cupped his face in her hands. "You are not just a fling to me, Cade. There's something important between us and I've long since gotten over Jared's death."

His eyes changed, brightened, grew less wary. "Jared. Was that his name?"

"Yes." She dropped her hands to his chest.

"What happened to him, if you don't mind me asking."

She smiled sadly. "He loved danger and would do anything to chase that rush. At least, in the end, that's how it was. In the beginning, it was just skiing or snowboarding off the main slopes. That quickly grew into other things. Scuba diving, boxing, hunting, surfing, skydiving, base jumping… He even said he wanted to try bull riding."

"Is that what killed him?"

She looked up at Cade's quiet question and then remembered that he had been bronc riding for the last couple of years. She shook her head. "No, he ended up street racing with motorcycles. Said he eventually wanted to do it professionally, win that crazy 300 mile-an-hour race on the Isle of Man.

"He'd been riding all his life. He was good at it, but he pushed too hard too fast and made one little mistake that ended up with him slamming into a brick wall. He died instantly."

"Oh God, Addie, I'm so sorry," Cade said again, pulling her against him and wrapping his arms around her.

She hugged him back, sadness banding her chest. "I'm okay, Cade. It's just a sad ending. Jared was a great person, full of life and energy. I think that's what attracted me to him, at least, at first. Part of me wishes I'd have been more adamant about him letting go of his daredevil side. Maybe he'd still be alive."

Cade pulled back and caught her eyes. "He wouldn't have it let go. From what you've said, he loved the thrill too much to stop. It wasn't your fault, Addie. He made his decision."

"I know," she said softly, mourning the loss of such a vibrant life, but not the relationship that would have never lasted. She knew that now. "It's just…sad."

"Yes," Cade replied, "it is."

He cupped her face and she turned into his palm, enjoying the rough scrape of his calloused hand on her cheek.

"I'm not like that, you know," Cade said and her eyes sought his.

She smiled. That he'd want to separate his jaunt into rodeo from the kind of life Jared had chosen for himself touched her heart. "I know that, too."

The tightness around his eyes eased a little bit.

"Do you miss him?" Cade's voice held a strangled note.

"Sometimes."

Cade dropped his gaze and nodded. She lifted his chin with her fingers and looked into his eyes.

"But not the way you think," she said. "Jared and I wouldn't have worked. He wanted things I didn't. We argued about his insane thrill-seeking more than once, but, like you said, he didn't want to give it up. I wouldn't have been able to live like that for long. I miss my friend Jared, but I don't know that I ever really loved him. Not the way he deserved to be loved." She chuckled sadly. "He needed someone much stronger than me."

"You are strong, Addie," Cade said. "Stronger than most everyone I've ever met. I've known guys who loved to live on the edge, just like Jared. Bull riders and the like. It takes a special kind of crazy to do those things…and another kind to put up with them." He grinned and threaded his fingers through her hair before brushing his thumb over her cheek.

"You're not crazy, just smart."

"There you go with the compliments again."

"And you promised to believe me."

"I did, didn't I? Well, you know what that means."

His grin brought light back into his eyes. "No, what does that mean?"

Her lips curled impishly and she gave him her most sultry look while sliding her hand down his chest and over his belly. Her fingers found the velvet flesh of his manhood and stroked him gently. "You need to accept a little more affection, and I'll have to show you just how much you deserve."

Smile broadening, he closed his eyes, inhaled deeply, and allowed her to push him onto his back. By the time she'd kissed her way down his strong body to tease his belly and thighs with her tongue, he was hard and panting and ready. Addie was more than happy to oblige. She took him into her mouth and he moaned, hips flexing as his fingers slid into her hair. Savoring his salty flavor and the soft texture of his skin, wanting to make this as good for him as she possibly could, she bobbed her head, took him deep, and proceeded to show him how much affection he truly deserved.

CHAPTER 16

Two days later, Cade put the last of the dry goods into the truck bed and closed the tailgate. Thanking the clerk who'd helped him ferry the items out of the store, he rounded the truck to climb into the cab and settle on the squeaky bench seat. He hadn't driven his truck since it had broken down last August—almost four months ago—but when he turned the key, it started right up.

Since things had slowed down a bit on the farm—and since he'd been getting a regular paycheck—he'd finally had the time and money to fix all the issues with the old vehicle. He'd spent the better part of that afternoon replacing the plugs and wires and then flushing the system, getting it ready for the winter weather that threatened to arrive sooner than normal. Surprisingly, Addie had been a big help with that, too.

In the middle of reconnecting hoses after replacing the dead water pump, Cade had paused when he saw Addie sauntering across the dooryard toward him. A smile had pulled at his mouth as memories of the night before flitted through his mind. She was amazing and beautiful, but right then, she'd been about to build upon his already soaring opinion of her.

"Hi," she'd said with a big smile that lit up her gorgeous brown eyes, brightening the dreary October morning.

"Hi back," he'd replied as he rolled out from under his truck, wiping his hands on an old rag that he'd tugged from his back pocket. "What's up?"

"You said we needed supplies. I need to run into town for some paper and a few other things. You want to come along? Kill two trips with one ride?"

He glanced at the old engine and the work he still needed to do. With freezing temperatures threatening, he needed to get the truck back together and ready for the winter. "I've got a bit left to do here. Should only take me another couple of hours to finish, if you don't mind waiting."

"What all do you need to do?"

"Well, I've got to replace the plugs and wires, finish connecting the hoses, connect the new battery, flush the system, and then add the antifreeze."

"I can help with that," she'd said, stunning him. He hadn't expected she'd want to get greasy under the hood.

"Are you sure?"

A frown wrinkled her brow as her hands landed on her hips. "What? You don't think a girl can work on an engine?"

He grinned at the fire in her eyes. "No, that's not it at all. I just meant that this truck is old and very dirty."

Her scowl disappeared and her cheeks pinked a little. "Oh, well, no worries. I'll just change real quick and come back to help. Together we should be able to finish all that in an hour or less." She smiled as she skipped back to the house. "I'll be back in a few," she called over her shoulder.

Sure enough, she'd been as good as her word and more knowledgeable about engines than he'd thought. She'd grabbed a socket wrench and started removing the plugs without any instruction. She'd even known to remove the wires one at a time to keep from messing up the engine's firing order, and how to check the plugs' gap before installing them.

To say that he'd been impressed was an understatement. Most of the women he'd known wouldn't have gone near the sludgy mess under the hood of his old truck. But Addie had jumped right in, and she'd been correct. With her help, they'd finished the job in less than an hour and, a half-hour after that, they were both cleaned up and in his rig as it rumbled down the road.

Grinning as he thought back on how well they'd worked together, he tightened his hands on the steering wheel, but one small thought wiped the smile from his face.

The fields had been cleared and once they were planted with the winter wheat crops, he could help her hire a new worker, and then there'd be nothing left to keep him here. He could get back to his lonely life on the road.

But that's not what he wanted.

He shook his head as he stared out the windshield at other local customers as they loaded their purchases into their vehicles.

He could've left after the harvest, let Addie do the work she claimed she could on her own, but he didn't. Something was keeping him here, something stronger than the pain he'd been running from. Something… Some*one* he couldn't ignore.

He had worried that the day after they'd made love would be awkward, but thanks to Addie's sweet boldness, they'd gotten through it easily and had grown closer. To him, she was more than just a boss, more than a friend, but he didn't know exactly where he stood on that scale with her.

The part of him that still stung from his last relationship wanted him to run. Not only to keep his heart from feeling too much but to save Addie from himself. Then a little voice inside that sounded just like Addie, reminded him that he'd promised to stop beating himself up. That was proving to be harder than he'd thought it would be. Considering all the mistakes he'd made in the past, he didn't want any poor choices he may make now to come back on her. But then again, didn't his vow include learning to trust himself again, too?

He shook his head and put the truck into gear, his mind still turning as he left the parking lot and headed to the Sisters Coffee Shop Café where he and Addie had agreed to meet. His mind, only half on his driving, returned to what was growing between them.

Addie was as attracted to him as he was to her, and, like him, she had thoroughly enjoyed their night together. She'd awoken him yesterday morning with kisses and a clear intent to pick up where they'd left off the night before, and, with no objections from him, they had enjoyed each other thoroughly.

He smiled, remembering her breathless words once they'd both been satiated.

"That…was…fantastic!" she'd breathed in his ear, nibbling on his lobe and humming happily. "Can we do that again soon? Like tonight? Or maybe this afternoon?"

He'd chuckled. "Whatever you want, sweetheart. I'm willing whenever you are."

"Hmm…in that case," her hands slid down his back to grip his ass, "I can't wait to see what you do to me tonight."

Her invitation and praise had filled his chest with warmth and more than a little pride. There'd been no questions about taking her up on her offer last night—not that he'd had much choice. The sexy, red summer dress she'd been wearing for dinner had his blood heating from the minute he saw her.

Their third time around had been as fantastic as the first two, and the feelings inside him grew with each encounter and every exchange. The closeness they shared frightened him, but he also longed to hold her again. If he was honest with himself, he liked her too much, and that's why he stayed. He wanted to find out what would happen next.

A few minutes later, Cade pulled into a parking spot beside the coffee shop, and, killing the engine, he hopped out of the truck. A little surprised by the small thrill that jabbed him in the gut at the thought of seeing Addie again, he took a deep breath and told his body to calm down.

Jerking open the glass door, Cade stepped inside. That's when he heard the raucous laughter.

The coffee shop was packed with patrons and several in the far corner were laughing as if at something hilarious. Addie's friends were busy helping their other customers, but Cade caught Veta's eyes as she glanced toward the door. She signaled him with a frown and a tilt of her head toward the front counter. Glancing across the room, he saw Addie, standing beside the long front counter, her shoulders hunched, head down, and deep pink infusing her cheeks. She had her arms wrapped around her purchases from the office supply store he'd dropped her off at earlier, holding it against her chest like a shield.

Cade's hands fisted at his sides and he turned narrowed eyes on the crowd. Whoever put that look on her face would soon learn what a mistake they'd made.

"Yeah," a short but broad, dark-haired man near the corner booth stood, and pointed at Addie, "she wants to be a rancher, but she can't even farm her own land."

More chuckles floated around the packed café and several of the older men, apparently local ranchers themselves, hid their amused smiles behind cups of coffee.

"She had to ask how to start the tractor!"

Addie shook her head, studiously ignoring the heckler in the corner, but anger straightened Cade's spine. No one would talk about her like that when he was around.

As he hurried to her side, the heckler spoke again. "Makes you wonder what else she doesn't know."

"She knows plenty." Cade came to her defense, his tone low and hard as he glared at the speaker. Placing a gentle hand on Addie's back, he whispered, "Are you okay?"

She looked up at him with so much relief and gratefulness that it made his heart clench.

How dare they make fun of her!

"How the hell would you know?" the taunting man asked, and Cade's narrowed eyes swung toward him, but the guy didn't take the hint. "She's just a rich city girl who moved here to steal land from the locals. We all know it. We've seen it happen more than once, but this one..." he shook his head and laughed, "she takes the ignorance cake."

More chuckles ensued.

"I'm fine, Cade," Addie murmured, tugging lightly on his shirt. "Just ignore them."

"I don't think so." He turned and sauntered toward the shorter man. "You shouldn't talk about things you know nothing about."

"I know enough about her," the man said, once again pointing at

Addie. "I used to work for her."

"Ah, so you're the one who half-assed all those jobs around her place," Cade said and grinned along with several of the others sitting nearby.

The dark-haired man glowered at him. "You don't know anything about it."

"I know it took you and two other men a month to strip the shingles off one building and half of another, and then you left the pieces all over the ground. I know you couldn't drive a straight line with the tractor while planting a cornfield. And I know you couldn't fix a fence or plant a post that would stay upright to save your life."

Everyone laughed at each of Cade's comments and he gave the other man a challenging grin. His shoulders tensed, waiting for the man to attack. *Come on, you bastard. Give me your best shot!* He looked forward to bloodying the asshole's nose.

The other man's dark eyes glanced at the chuckling ranchers before focusing on Cade again. "I don't have to listen to this bullshit," he growled. "Come on, JR, Jorje, the rest of you, let's get out of this shithole." A tall, blond-haired man about Cade's size immediately got to his feet, rubbing at his nose while his eyes were constantly on the move.

He must be JR, Cade guessed. *Twitchy looking dude.*

Giving Cade a narrow-eyed assessment that clearly found him wanting, JR grinned tauntingly as he sauntered by, followed closely by three more of their little gang—all of whom looked almost as disreputable as JR. They only made it two steps toward the door when the loud mouth turned back. His Latino friend—Jorje, no doubt, and the only one in the group who hadn't laughed at Addie—stayed where he was, shaking his head and sipping his coffee.

"Jorje…?" Loud mouth called, though he kept pronouncing the Latino's name in the English fashion of George. "Come on!"

Jorje shook his head again. "No, Ted, I'm staying. I haven't gotten my order yet, and I want to eat. You deserved what he said after all your mouthing off." Jorje inclined his head toward Cade. "Go, if you want, but I'm staying to eat my meal."

Ted stared at his friend as if flabbergasted by his refusal to follow along. Or maybe it was Jorje's mild castigation for taunting Addie.

Whatever the reason, Ted was stunned. Snapping his hanging jaw closed, he turned hard eyes on Cade once more. "Fine," he muttered, "the food in this place sucks anyway."

Belying his words, Ted grabbed his previously forgotten coffee and half-eaten homemade Danish, and strode slowly past Cade, glaring the whole way. And just to prove he wasn't intimidated, Ted slammed Cade's shoulder with his own and grinned as if he'd won some major coup before ambling to the door with his chuckling buddy JR and the rest of his pack right behind him.

The whole place seemed to sigh when the door swung closed behind them.

"Thank you, Cade," Veta said from behind the counter. "We'd told him to leave earlier, but he wouldn't go."

Cade shrugged as he returned to Addie's side. "No problem." He looked down at Addie and found her watching him with her eyes so full of gratitude that flames of awkward embarrassment heated his cheeks.

"My hero," she teased and he felt his ears burn, even as his chest filled with delight at her approval.

"It's no big deal," he said with another shrug, wishing someone would change the subject.

She smiled and her dark eyes sparkled. "It is to me."

"Wow, Cade, you were amazing," Lana swooned from her register as she handed the last customer in line their change. "Coming to Addie's defense like that was *so exciting* to watch."

"Yeah, Cade," Addie murmured and gently elbowed his ribs.

He didn't mind Addie's teasing, but he was getting tired of Lana's not-so-veiled hints. Ignoring the younger woman's adoring eyes, he focused on Addie.

"Are you okay?" he asked again, brushing her arm consolingly, and Lana walked off with a huff when her sister told her to take care of the dishes in the lobby.

"Yes, I'm fine," Addie answered. "Ted's just upset that I rebuffed him before I fired him."

Cade's eyebrows climbed toward his hairline. "He came on to you?"

"Yeah, he kissed me once," she said, shrugging it off, but she couldn't hide the shiver of revulsion that made her shoulders twitch. "My reaction wasn't what he'd expected. I don't think he could walk straight for a few days afterward."

Cade chuckled and gave her a quick, one-armed hug around the shoulders. "That's my girl."

She smiled and turned such a pretty shade of pink that he almost kissed her, but someone clearing their throat behind them had stopped him.

"Ma'am," an older gentleman with darkly tanned skin and liberal streaks of gray in his black hair said. "I wanted to apologize for all that nonsense. It was uncalled for and we shouldn't have encouraged Ted's bad behavior by laughing. I'm very sorry."

Cade glanced down at the woman beside him. A part of him wanted her to tell the old guy off, but seeing her soft smile, he knew she wouldn't.

"Thank you…?" she said, drawing out the last word and holding out her hand in greeting.

"Frank. Frank Griffith," the old guy said, shaking her offered hand. "I live out Robinson Canyon way on the bluff before the elbow turn. Feel free to stop by and meet the missus any time. We'd be happy to help if you have any ranching questions."

"Thank you, Frank. I'm Addie and this," she pointed at Cade, "is Cade. I appreciate the offer and I'll be sure to do that." Addie's smile broadened at making a new friend, though Cade wasn't quite so forgiving.

Frank's hazel eyes turned to Cade and he held out his gnarled hand. "And thank you, son."

"For what?" Cade asked, begrudgingly taking Frank's hand.

"For doing what one of us should've done before the situation got out of hand. Ted had no call to act that way, even if she did fire him."

Cade's opinion of Frank went up a notch, but that feeling of embarrassment swept over him again. He could feel the eyes of everyone there boring into him as heads bobbed in agreement with Frank's comment. The unwanted attention made him want to squirm a little, but he straightened his back instead.

"Thanks. I…" he glanced down at Addie, still tucked against his side, and then back to the man's age-faded eyes. "We appreciate that."

Frank nodded. "You come visit with your lady, son. We'd love to have you both."

Addie tensed beside him, but he gave her a little squeeze.

"We'll do that," Cade said before she could speak, not bothering to correct Frank's thinking.

"And if I could give you a word of warning…?"

Cade's shoulders tensed again, but he nodded.

"Be careful of Ted Ballinger and his friends, especially that blond one," Frank said, more to Cade than Addie as he nodded toward the door. "Ted's mean as a snake and twice as dangerous. He won't forget this and he's known to retaliate with a vengeance. There's a reason he's not working for any of us."

"I'll do that," Cade replied with a nod. "Thanks for the tip."

A crash came from the back of the café, drawing everyone's gaze. Veta rolled her eyes and hurried to the back, calling her sister's name. An angry string of Ukrainian followed.

"That's my cue," Frank said and headed for the door. "Good to meet you, folks."

"You too," Addie said and then turned her head aside and giggled.

Cade frowned. "What's so funny?"

Addie lifted her laughing eyes to his. "You didn't notice Lana?"

His frown deepened and he shook his head.

"She was stomping around the café, slamming dishes into her bus tub. I don't think she likes it when you ignore her."

He snorted. "Too bad. I've already got a girl. Lana will just have to get used to it."

Addie's eyes widened slightly and her cheeks grew pink again. She twined her fingers with his and gently squeezed his hand. The look on her face made his heart speed up.

"Here's your order, Addie," Veta said as she pushed two drinks and the rest of their order across the off-white counter. "I'm sorry it took so long."

"Don't worry about it," she said as she grabbed her drink and Cade reached for the rest. Addie inclined her head toward the kitchen. "Is everything okay?"

Veta smiled at Addie as she glanced over her shoulder, then rolled her eyes in a way that only an annoyed sister could.

"Lana's just a little jealous of you. She'll get over it."

"Of me?" Addie's voice rose in question.

Veta glanced at Cade and guilt tugged at his gut, though he didn't know why.

"I never encouraged her," he blurted out.

Veta shook her head. "I know that, Cade. Lana's just looking for someone to appreciate her, someone to love. The problem is, she keeps looking in the wrong places. That worries me. You do not." She smiled.

He nodded, not knowing what else to say.

"He's a good one, Addie," she said in a conspiratorial whisper that wasn't quiet at all. "You should hang on to him. You two are good together and it's obvious you like each other..."

"Yeah, I've gotten kind of used to him being around," Addie said, her gaze full of heat as she looked at him.

Cade's heart slammed into his breastbone and he tried to swallow. He recognized that look; the one that said he could have her all to himself forever if he wanted. All he had to do was say yes, but he didn't know if he could take that first step. He could stand up to guys like Ted every day, but letting another woman into his heart, allowing her to have the power to drive him to his knees and destroy him all over again...? He didn't know if he was ready for that. Didn't know if he ever would be. And Addie deserved to be happy. He needed to figure his shit out before he broke her heart, as well as his own.

CHAPTER 17

The drive back home was quiet, but not uncomfortably so. The only sounds were the rumble of the engine and hum of the tires on pavement as the headlights cut a swath through the dark evening. Cade seemed to be lost in thought. He'd hardly said a word since they'd gotten into the cab. Not that Addie minded; she'd been distracted too, thinking over everything that had happened and dwelling on the anxiety that had taken root inside her.

They'd eaten at the café, which, apparently, had given a couple of other local ranchers the incentive to stop by their table to apologize and caution them about Ted and his friends. Not that Addie needed the warning; she'd been worried about Ted since she'd fired him. He was mostly all talk, but what Frank had said about retaliation was probably true, which was why it stuck with her. Though, she wasn't concerned for her sake—no, she feared for Cade.

"You need to be careful," she blurted into the quiet cab.

Cade glanced at her. "Why?"

"Ted," she said, staring at Cade's profile. "I don't want you to get hurt."

"I won't," he said, flashing her a cocky grin. "I'm not worried about him, and you shouldn't be, either. I can take care of myself if I need to."

Addie didn't argue as he turned onto her driveway, dust spinning up in a whirlwind behind them. Still, she did have a bad feeling about the whole thing. She knew Cade was a strong man, a smart man, but she didn't trust Ted to be an honorable one. He wouldn't forget the embarrassment Cade caused him today. She couldn't see Ted facing Cade head-on if he wasn't sure he'd win nor, she suspected, was Ted above underhanded tactics.

"What the *hell?*" Cade said in a hard tone that sent a shiver down her spine as the truck skidded to a halt.

Addie had been lost in thought again, trusting Cade to get them home. At the sudden stop, she glanced at his fierce profile before she turned her head to see what had upset him.

The first thing she saw made her gut clench with fear.

The aluminum garage door was bent on one side as if it had been forced open, and the words *"Go Home, Bitch!"* were spray-painted in red on the white panel.

Her breath caught in her throat and a tremor of fear fluttered in her stomach.

"Stay here," Cade said as he pushed open his door.

"No way," Addie replied. "I'm coming with you."

Cade stepped out of the truck then turned to face her, one arm resting on the roof of the cab. "Addie," he said softly, "someone may still be inside."

She glanced at her home and noticed that the front door was wide open—something she hadn't noticed at first. Turning back to Cade's serious expression, she tried to keep her voice level and to quiet her riotous nerves. "I don't want to sit out here. Besides, it's my house; you shouldn't have to face a possible intruder alone. What if they have a gun or something?"

"I could deal with it more easily if you're not there distracting me."

A frown pulled her eyebrows down. "I'm not going to distract you."

"If you go in there, I'll be worried about you the whole time. I won't be focused on what I need to be. Please, Addie, just wait here. I'll come back for you if it's empty."

She stared into his concerned blue gaze and, though she didn't like it, she knew he was right. "Okay, but please, be careful."

"I will. If anything happens out here, if you need me, honk the horn."

She nodded and swallowed the lump in her throat as Cade quietly closed the door and slowly crossed her front yard. Her heart pounded when he disappeared inside and she sent up a silent prayer that whoever did this had left long ago.

With Cade no longer in sight, cold suddenly settled into her bones and she shivered. Rubbing at her arms and darting glances all around, she did her best to remain calm, but she felt like someone was watching her.

Minutes ticked by, three, five, but still no Cade.

What if he can't come back? she thought. *What if someone hit him or stabbed him, and he's lying in there bleeding to death?* Her mind conjured all kinds of horrible scenarios that might have kept Cade from returning, terrifying herself until her fear for his life outweighed any possible danger for her own. She couldn't take it anymore. She had to know if he was all right. Grabbing the door handle, preparing to exit the truck, she took one last look at the house and sucked in a lungful of relief when Cade appeared at the front door. The look on his face as he approached the truck, however, twisted her stomach into knots. Sweat prickled her skin and she absently wiped her palms on her jeans.

"How bad is it?" she asked when he opened his door.

"Bad. We need to call the sheriff."

Addie's heart clenched. She must have turned very pale because Cade's angry expression softened and he reached for her hand as he slid onto the seat.

"I know you don't want to deal with them, but this is serious, Addie. You can't handle this on your own, even with me here. You're going to need a police report for your insurance as well. You do *have* insurance, right?"

She nodded, unable to speak.

"Good, 'cause we'll have to call them, too."

His words hit her like a punch to the gut. Her eyes burned and a small tremor rolled through her body. *Insurance? Police report? What all did they do?*

"How bad *is* it?" she repeated. "Tell me."

Cade sighed and pulled her into his arms. She didn't fight him; she wanted his strength and the sense of security he gave her, but she also wanted the truth.

Pulling back a little, she looked into his beautiful eyes and saw concern for her and anger for what had been done. "Please, Cade. Just tell me."

He lowered his chin, inhaled and exhaled, then met her gaze. "It's bad. The garage door is just the beginning and not the worst of the damage."

The lump in Addie's throat returned.

"Your little sports car has a shattered windshield and all the lights have been broken."

A little whimper escaped her lips and Cade stopped, his eyes searching hers. "Do you want to hear the rest?"

"There's *more?*" Her voice, barely above a whisper, cracked on the last word.

He nodded. "That's probably the worst, but yes, there's more."

She took a steadying breath and straightened her spine. "Tell me."

"The kitchen is a disaster. Everything from the cupboards was tossed around the room. I don't think any breakable stuff survived. The drawers were pulled out and upended. The food from the fridge is..." he shrugged, "everywhere. The living room was tossed as well and the TV is busted. They did the same thing to your room. It's not livable in there right now and... Addie, they destroyed your laptop."

She felt her lips tremble and knew that the tears she'd tried to hold back had spilled onto her cheeks. What was she going to do now? She had some money and the insurance would help pay for the damage, but she still had other bills to pay as well. After taking care of all of that, would she have anything left to pay Cade? Would he leave if she couldn't pay for his time and effort? He'd planned to leave anyway, but she had hoped that maybe he would change his mind. Over the last few days, it had seemed as if he might be willing to stay. But would her monetary shortcomings cause him to hit the road sooner? With his truck running again and the extra money he had now...

Damn it! I'm not ready for this to end! Not yet.

"Hey," Cade murmured as he cupped her face and wiped her tears away with his thumbs. "It's not that bad. We'll get it cleaned up and good as new in no time, don't worry."

"I may not be able to pay you," she whispered and wanted to bite her tongue. Why did she say that?

A sob bubble up from her chest and the tears she'd bottled up sprung free. All her fear for their safety, her financial situation, and his leaving shattered the hold she'd had on her emotions. "What am I...g-going to do?" she cried, staring back at him.

Cade's jaw clenched and she didn't fight when he tugged her into his lap. Holding her close, he rocked her gently.

"Don't worry about that," he said and kissed the top of her head. "I'm not going anywhere. Right now, we need to get the sheriff out here. Do you think you can handle that? Calling them, I mean. Or do you want me to do it? Either way, it needs to be done."

She sniffed, sat back, and wiped her face with her hands. "I'll do it."

* * *

Thirty minutes later, they were sitting on the tailgate of Cade's truck, watching the sheriff's deputies trail in and out of her house, recording the damage done to her home and property. She and Cade had already given their statements but had been asked to hang around a little longer in case there were any additional questions.

When they had asked if she knew of anyone who would want to do this to her or if she had any enemies, her first thought had been Ted. But for some reason, she hadn't been able to say so.

Cade, however, had not been so limited.

"Ted Ballinger," he'd said with more conviction than Addie could muster. "We just had a run-in with him in town a couple of hours ago, and one of your deputies, Mark Harden, has been harassing her, too."

Addie closed her eyes and moaned. She hadn't wanted to bring Mark up with his coworkers, but the woman taking their statement simply nodded, her pen scratching away on her pad. When she stopped writing, the deputy had glanced up at Addie and smiled as if she understood Addie's hesitation and the situation.

Maybe she's been on the receiving end of Mark's unwanted attention, too.

"We've had a few complaints about him in the past," the deputy said quietly, "but recently, he's been...better. Do you really think Deputy Harden would do this?"

"Yes," Cade replied, but Addie shook her head.

Flicking a guilty glance at Cade, she finally found her voice. "I don't think so. I mean, he drinks and gets pushy, but he's never struck me as being vengeful or destructive. He was always just...overly...friendly."

"That doesn't mean he had nothing to do with this," Cade countered. "He may just be more frustrated than before, even angry, now that I'm here."

Addie sighed but didn't argue.

The deputy had nodded and made another note on her pad, then went on with her questions.

Thinking back on it, Addie still didn't think Mark was responsible for the damage to her house. It seemed too vicious and vindictive, too...personal. That, coupled with all the cut wires, punctured tires, and other damaged equipment around her farm over the last six months—which Cade had made sure to mention to the deputy taking their statements—had seemed to be aimed at ruining her financially. The thought had frightened her.

Thankful, Cade hadn't left her side since this all began and now, with him sitting beside her, a protective arm wrapped around her, and the deputies everywhere, she felt a little less terrified. That feeling of being watched had dissipated as well. Fear still whispered at the back of her mind, but it wasn't overwhelming her any longer.

"How are you doing?" Cade asked. His low voice brushed along her skin, enveloping her in a layer of warm concern.

"I'm okay," she said, staring into the deep blue well of his eyes. "It's just a lot to take in."

"I'll be right here," he said, giving her hand a little squeeze. "You won't have to deal with all this alone."

Appreciation swelled her heart and she thought she might cry again, but she forced a smile. "Thanks..."

Someone cleared their throat nearby and they both looked up. Addie almost groaned when she saw who was facing them.

"Hi, Addie," Mark Harden—her neighbor, deputy sheriff, and her one-time stalker—said.

Cade's body stiffened beside her. "What the hell do you want?"

She patted his knee. "It's okay, Cade. This is part of his job." She turned to the deputy. "Hello, Mark."

He gave her a grateful smile. "Thank you, and I'm sorry this happened." He waved his hand toward her house and the other deputies who were wrapping up their investigation.

"Me too," Addie replied.

Mark nodded, looked down at the ground, and kicked at a tuft of crabgrass. He looked nervous, but aside from Cade's death-glare, she didn't know why Mark would be anxious.

"Is there something you need, Mark?" she asked and Cade grumbled beside her.

"Don't be so nice, Addie. It was just over a month ago that this guy showed up drunk and attacked you in your own house."

Mark quickly glanced around to see if anyone had heard Cade's less-than-discreet comment. Then he turned back to them and met Cade's angry glare.

"You're right. I don't deserve her kindness," he said in a firm tone, but then he dropped his head as if it was too heavy for his neck and his voice lowered to nearly a whisper, "but if you'll let me, I-I'd like to...apologize."

Addie blinked in surprise. She hadn't thought Mark would ever admit to any wrongdoing, and an actual apology had seemed remote at best. She opened her mouth to ask what he was apologizing for, but Cade beat her to it.

"And which thing exactly are you sorry for?" he said in a low, dangerous tone. "For hurting her, trying to rape her, or for this shit tonight?"

Mark had flinched at the first two comments, but the last one snapped his head up. "I didn't do this." His startled eyes darted between them and settled on Addie. "Please, believe me. I didn't do this, Addie."

Addie nodded. Mark was a drunk and a womanizer, but he wasn't vindictive. Not like this, anyway.

"I believe you," she said and felt Cade's heated glare land on her, but she ignored him.

Mark sighed in relief. "I wanted to apologize for all the rest. I know

I'm an alcoholic, have known it for a long time. I don't remember exactly what happened the night I came here last, only that I was here. Then I woke up in my truck at home with a broken nose and blood all over my shirt."

He glanced at Cade, who grinned wickedly, but Mark didn't question how his injury had happened.

"From what he said," Mark nodded at Cade, "it sounds like I deserved that and more."

"Damn right you did," Cade muttered and Addie gave him a sharp glance. His lips thinned but he let it go.

"I've been thinking a lot about that and the things you've said, Addie. Like being someone for the town to look to for help and support, and that I couldn't be that if I drowned myself in a bottle." He looked up and gave Addie a sheepish smile. "I know why I started. I know I can't stop on my own. And I knew I needed to do something before I ended up hurting someone beyond forgiving. So, I...got help."

"You did?" Addie said, pleased, and surprised to hear it.

"Yeah, the very next day," Mark said, rubbing the back of his neck. "And part of my responsibility in the healing process is to make amends with those I've wronged." He met her gaze. "And I've wronged you a great deal, Addie. I had no right to demand anything from you. I had no right to push you farther than you were willing, and for that, I'm truly sorry. That's not who I am, or who I want to be. From now on, I will be a better man, a better deputy, and a better neighbor. I just hope you can forgive me."

"Well," Addie began and Cade's muscles tense around her, "I think I might need a while for that to happen, but I do accept your apology."

Mark nodded. "I understand, and I don't blame you." He turned to Cade and held out his hand. "I'd like to offer you an apology, too."

Addie looked up at the kind, caring man she'd come to know. A muscle in his jaw twitched and he eyed Mark's outstretched hand as if it might turn into a snake and bite him. She gave Cade a little nudge and he met her gaze. She lifted her brows, tilted her head, and shifted her eyes to Mark's hand and back as if to say, *Go on, take it.*

Cade's lips thinned in obvious irritation, but he took Mark's hand.

"Fine, I accept," he ground out, "but only because Addie wants me to. I don't trust you and I don't want you anywhere near her. Understand?"

Mark grimaced and Addie saw that Cade had gripped Mark's hand so tightly that his fingers had turned dark red. She opened her mouth to tell him to stop, but he released Mark before she could speak.

She gave Cade an annoyed look, but he merely grinned and shrugged.

"I don't blame you, either," Mark said, "and don't worry, I'll keep my distance. But if either of you need anything, don't hesitate to call us because of me, especially after something like this tonight. It's our job to help. It's why I took this job in the first place."

"Thank you, Mark," Addie said, while she gently elbowed Cade to keep him from replying. "We'll do that."

Mark nodded.

Another younger deputy approached. "We're wrapping things up," he said. "If you two want, you can go now."

"Can we go inside?" Addie asked.

The young man glanced at Cade and from the corner of her eye, Addie saw his head barely indicate that they shouldn't be allowed to enter the house.

"It's a mess in there, ma'am," the deputy said, his gaze once again focused on her. "I'd find somewhere else to stay tonight and take care of it tomorrow."

As much as she wanted her house put back in order, she was exhausted from the ordeal. All she wanted right now was to lay down in Cade's arms and go to sleep. She sighed. That's probably what he would want, too.

"That sounds like a good idea. Thank you."

Cade helped her down from the truck bed and walked her to the passenger side, his arm still around her shoulders. As he assisted her into the cab and closed the door to hurry to the driver's door, Addie wanted to let it go, to forget about everything until morning, but more tears filled her eyes and molten rage bubbled to the surface. Staring at the open door of her house, her blurry vision unable to make out the faces of those going in and out, Addie's hands balled into fists and a high-pitched squeal spilled from her lips. It increased in intensity until it became a frustrated scream.

How dare someone do this to her? She'd never thought Ted would be so destructive as to destroy her home. How could anyone do something like this?

"Hey, sweetie," Cade said, sliding across the truck's bench seat to pull her into his arms. "It's okay, I got you."

She'd been holding back the defeat and shock as best she could, but the minute he wrapped her in his strong embrace and she was engulfed by his warmth and manly scent, all her defenses crumbled. She slumped against him and the tears came as he rocked her gently and whispered words of comfort.

Arms wrapped around Cade's middle, Addie's fingers gripped his shirt, desperately holding on to him to keep from spiraling into a dark hole of despair. *What am I going to do?*

"*We* are going to get everything cleaned up and fixed," Cade said, pushing her back so he could clutch her tear-streaked face in calloused hands and look into her eyes. "You are not alone, Addie. I'll help you, and I'm sure your friends will, too."

She tried to swallow the lump in her throat as she nodded, but it didn't work. The constriction was too tight to dislodge.

"You're trembling," Cade murmured as he brushed her hair away from her face. "Are you okay, sweetheart?"

She gave him a shaky smile, then sat back and wiped the tears from her cheeks. His blue eyes searched her face and she shook her head. "No, I'm not okay, but I will be. You're right, I'm not alone." She cupped his cheek in her hand. "I'm glad I have you. You can't know how glad I am to have you beside me right now."

Cade pulled her into his arms again. "I'm right here, baby, and we'll get through this. I promise."

She didn't miss the 'we'll' in that statement and his encouragement, not to mention his kindness, burrowed deep inside her and a warm calm emanated outward.

"Thank you," she said and when he sat back with confusion in his eyes, she elaborated. "Thank you for being here, Cade. For checking the house, for holding my hand, for this," she waved her hand between them, "for holding me. I feel better—still sad and a little shocked, but better…and that's all because of you."

He smiled and rested his forehead against hers. "Good."

They stayed like that for several seconds before he ducked his head to look into her face. "Let's get out of here."

She glanced at the house. Fear, anger, and frustration battled inside her, but she straightened her back and gave him a grin, nodding her assent. "Yeah," she muttered, "let's get out of here."

"I think I know just the place."

"There's a motel in town," she offered.

"Good enough for tonight, but I think we can do better."

She nodded, though she didn't know what he meant and didn't reply as they headed to town. Except for the rumble of the tires and the occasional rattle of Cade's old truck, silence filled the cab until they turned into the motel parking lot.

"Are you really okay?" Cade asked after he'd parked the truck and shut off the engine.

"Yeah," she said and sighed. She looked over at his concerned expression. "Will you stay with me tonight? Hold me? Please?"

His lips curled into a slow, indulgent grin. "Of course, I will."

She nodded as her emotions tumbled over each other inside her.

"Hey," he said as he scooted over the seat and tugged her closer. "I'll take care of you. You're safe. And we'll get the house fixed up good as new."

"I know," she said, patting his thigh. "I'm just really tired. All I want is to curl up with you and sleep for a week."

He chuckled. "All right. I'll get us a room and then we'll see about getting some rest." His eyebrows lifted. "Sound okay to you?"

"Sounds perfect."

"Be right back," Cade said as he hopped out of the truck to secure their room for the evening. She watched him walk away, relieved to know he'd be coming back, that she'd have him a little longer.

But for how *much* longer?

CHAPTER 18

The walls of the huge, colorful tent undulated with the cold breeze outside, making the infused-ink-printed Bavarian village shimmy unnaturally. The polka band played loudly, but at times, the surrounding chatter and laughter nearly drowned out the music. The long rows of tables lined up end to end were jammed full of merrymakers enjoying everything the festival had to offer.

The two huge tents had been set up in a large meadow on the outskirts of town to celebrate Oktoberfest, and large heaters in the corners kept them warm. Blue and white streamers lined the roof and—along with the faux village on the tent walls—gave the whole place an outdoorsy look. Servers in traditional Bavarian dirndls and lederhosen bustled between the guests, and the beer was plentiful.

Cade and Addie had arrived earlier in the evening to meet up with Veta, her husband Ivan, Lana, and their friends. Dan and Helga had run hayrides pulled by two teams of their draft horses during the day, but now the couple sat at the table with the rest of them, enjoying the festivities.

Picking up his nearly full bier-stein, Cade took a long draught. They'd finished their dinner of grilled chicken, pork ribs, bratwurst, coleslaw, and beans hours ago, but had stayed to drink and relish a well-deserved night off.

They sat at the far end of the tents where a large dance floor bustled with numerous couples—including Addie and Ivan—dancing to the accordion-infused melody of the Beer Barrel Polka. Though it appeared neither of them was adept at the polka, they were giving it their best.

Cade grinned. He couldn't say that he liked seeing Addie in the arms of another man—even if Ivan was several years older and married to Addie's friend—but she looked so happy and cheerful as they stumbled through the steps that he couldn't help but smile.

It was a relief to see her so carefree after the last few days of misery. He hadn't wanted her to see the mess the vandals had made of her home, and thanks to her friends—both old and new—she hadn't seen the worst of it.

The first night, he and Addie had stayed in the local motel. She'd tried so hard to be strong and, after that first burst of shocked and angry tears, had refused to cry in front of him. Five minutes after their arrival, she'd gone into the bathroom to take a shower, but he'd heard her crying through the door. Luckily, she hadn't locked him out.

When he slowly pulled back the shower curtain, she'd been sitting under the warm spray with her arms wrapped around her bent legs and her head on her knees. Soft sobs echoed in the small space as he'd quickly shucked his clothes and stepped inside.

He wrapped himself around her small, shivering form, giving her his strength and vowing his protection. "We can fix what's broken, but no matter what, no one will hurt you, Addie. I promise you that."

She'd only nodded and clung to him.

When the water grew cold, he'd shut it off, picked her up, and set her on her feet on the thin bath mat. Still shivering—from cold, shock, or fear of the future, he didn't know—Cade dried them both off and led her to the bed. Without a sound, she'd crawled under the covers and curled into herself. His chest constricted at how tiny, fragile, and alone she looked in the queen-sized bed. An urgent need to ensure her security and happiness welled up inside him, so deep and wide he thought it would break him. Instead, he took a deep breath and silently promised her that he'd make everything right. How he intended to do that exactly, he hadn't known at the time, but it didn't matter.

She's not alone anymore, he'd thought as he crawled in behind her. He pulled her into his body, whispered soothing words he couldn't recall now, but he'd meant every one.

With a sob, she'd turned in his arms and cried against his chest as he held her tighter, murmuring to her, stroking her hair, her back. "Don't worry, Addie," he'd said. "Everything will be all right."

She'd only nodded and eventually quieted right before she fell asleep in his arms.

They'd stopped at Sisters Café the next morning for breakfast. As soon as Veta saw Addie's pale, tired face, she'd known something was wrong.

Leaving the kitchen, Veta pulled him and Addie into her office. "What happened?"

Addie shook her head. "It's okay, Veta. Really, it's—" She'd choked on a quiet sob and turned to bury her face in Cade's chest. Veta's worried gaze lifted to his and he'd quickly explained.

Upon hearing the news, an angry yet determined expression filled Veta's round face. "I'm so sorry, sweetie." She rubbed Addie's back, but Addie only nodded against his chest. "You take care of her, Cade. We'll take care of everything else."

Thirty minutes later, they were ushered into Veta's home with breakfast from the café, shown where to find the guest room, and told to make themselves at home.

"I'll pick up some clothes for both of you and call when everything is settled at the house," Veta said to Cade after asking for Addie's house key and Cade's phone number. He'd gotten a new cell phone a few weeks back, thinking it prudent after the incident with Mark Harden. He'd wanted to be available if Addie needed him. Now, he was glad he'd done it.

"Try to get her to eat something," Veta said with a nod toward Addie.

He nodded, but that had been harder to do than it sounded. He managed to convince her to take a few bites, but she'd been too upset to eat much.

They'd ended up staying with Veta and her family for three days.

Strangely, he hadn't been bothered by Lana and her flirting once the whole time, but then, he'd been too distracted by a listless Addie to notice much else. She seemed overwrought and defeated, and he hated it. He did everything he could to make her smile, and though he'd succeeded a few times, her halfhearted grins never reached her eyes.

When Veta had finally told them it was okay to go home, Addie had been less than enthusiastic.

"I'm afraid of what I'll see," she'd admitted when he asked, "and how much it's going to cost me."

"Don't worry about that now," he'd said, pulling her in for a consoling hug. "It's just stuff. As long as you're all right, we can fix the rest."

"Can we?" she'd said with an odd look in her eyes and her tone struck a chord in him that he didn't understand. He'd been about to ask what she meant, but she shook her head. "Come on. Let's get this over with."

Her attitude brightened considerably when she saw what her friends had done. The inside of the house looked almost brand-new when they stepped through the front door. Addie's mouth had dropped open in shock. "How did you do all this?"

Veta blushed, but Lana was more than happy to fill them in. "We called in a contractor to fix the cupboards, the doors, and the holes in the wall, but had some friends help clean everything up and paint, too."

"Your other car is still at the shop," Veta added, "but it should be back next week."

"How much do I owe you?" Addie asked.

"Not a thing," Veta said with a big grin. "The contractor is Ivan's cousin and the shop belongs to a friend. They may have to charge for parts, but they both assured us that won't be much." She glanced at her sister. "Lana's friends worked for free meals from the café while they helped, and the paint was nothing. We just threw that in."

Considering the amount of damage he'd seen, their generosity and the speed at which they'd pulled everything together had stunned Cade. After some argument from Addie about the costs and payment, the smile that lit her watery eyes had warmed him, filling him with so much gratitude that he grinned as well.

Last night—their first night back in her home—Addie had been more sexually aggressive than normal—leading him to the bedroom, pulling his shirt off, and pushing him down on the bed. Not that he'd complained, nor would he. He'd never forget the way she'd stripped him and teased his body to attention with gentle hands and her hot, voracious mouth. More than that, the way she'd straddled his hips and taken control, riding him with abandon like a golden-haired goddess, had been so erotic that he'd had to struggle to hold back his release. When she'd finally clenched around him and screamed out his name, he'd been right there with her.

"Thank you," she'd murmured after collapsing on his chest.

"You don't have to thank me for anything, sweetheart."

"I do," she'd said, sitting back to gaze into his eyes. "I don't know how I would've gotten through this without you. So, thank you for taking care of me."

Those soft words and the look in her eyes had pierced his heart.

Even as he watched her now, dancing and laughing with Ivan, he felt her inside, a soft, warm tingle that sometimes made it hard to breathe. But he wouldn't have it any other way.

The song ended and Cade suddenly realized that everyone in the place had been singing along while he'd stared at Addie. The band started another, slower song as Ivan led her back to their table. Without thinking, Cade stood and met them halfway.

"This is my dance," he said as he took her hand and a jolt of awareness shot straight to his groin.

"About time," Ivan joked as he slapped Cade's shoulder good-naturedly before returning to their table.

Cade barely heard as he stared into Addie's face. "You mind dancing with me?"

Her eyes widened and she shook her head. "I'd love to dance with you, Cade."

Taking her in his arms felt so natural, so *right*, that he couldn't help pulling her closer than technically necessary. They swayed slowly to the rhythm, neither needing to speak, but Addie's gaze said more than words. A lump formed in the back of his throat. She was so beautiful and so damn amazing, she took his breath away.

The song ended sooner than seemed possible—he hadn't noticed time passing—but the other couples had broken up and were shuffling past them.

Addie stepped back. "Thanks for the dance."

He smiled. "You want to get out of here?"

That sweet, sexy mouth of hers curled up in the corners and her eyes held a spark of mischievousness. "Yes."

"Cade?" someone nearby called. "Caden Brody, is that you?"

Cade turned toward the familiar voice and grinned at the tall, brown-haired, bearded man that approached. "Zack? What the heck are you doing here?" He took Zack's offered hand and pulled him in for a brotherly hug.

"Just passing through," Zack replied, slapping Cade's shoulder before stepping back. "Where the hell ya been, man? I haven't seen you for…years."

Cade cringed inwardly. He hadn't seen or spoken to anyone from back home since he left. Seeing his old friend now made him realize again just how much he'd lost when he walked away. "Ah, you know, here and there."

"Well, shit, it's good to see you alive and breathin'. I've been wondering what happened to ya. Cord hasn't been very forthcoming about why you left."

Of course not, Cade thought, the resentment he still felt toward his brother brewing in his chest.

"We had a disagreement," Cade said and couldn't keep the bitterness from his tone.

"Yeah," Zack said, eyeing Cade askance, "that's what your brother said, too."

Cade braced himself for the next obvious question, but thankfully, it never came. Instead, Zack glanced down at the woman Cade held close to his side.

"Well, I can see what's been distracting you," Zack said with his too-charming, white-toothed smile and an appreciative sparkle in his amber-brown eyes. "Howdy, ma'am."

Cade nearly growled at his old friend to back off, but he bit it back just in time.

"Hi," Addie replied, taking Zack's offered hand and glancing at Cade. "It's nice to meet one of Cade's friends."

Cade made the introduction. "Zack's a family friend from way back."

"Yeah," Zack said, holding Addie's hand longer than Cade liked. "This guy, his brother, and I used to cause trouble and break hearts back home in Montana, and not all that long ago, either." He glanced at Cade and his grin widened. "Well, not that long ago for me, anyway."

"I'm sure Addie doesn't want to hear about our glory days," Cade said dismissively. He certainly didn't want to relive them.

"Actually, I'd love to hear more about Cade," Addie said with a smile.

Cade wanted to groan. *Don't encourage him, Addie.*

Predictably, Zack's brown eyes twinkled and he tossed a loaded look at Cade before he stepped to her other side. "Well, I could tell you a couple of wild tales about good ol' Cade." He chuckled and winked at Cade as he led her toward their table with his hand resting on the small of her back. "One of them might even make you blush."

He'd forgotten what a flirt Zack was and how much the man loved to tease his friends. It appeared he hadn't changed much in the long years since Cade had last seen him.

"I'm going to run to the restroom," he said to Addie. "If you don't mind hanging out with Zack for a few?"

She was smiling when she looked back at him, but when their eyes met, she frowned. "Everything okay?"

"Yeah." He tried to smile. "Call of nature, you know."

"Sure." She smiled again, but her eyes held a question she didn't ask. "See you in a few."

"While I have you alone," Zack said, as he placed a guiding hand against her back, drawing her toward the tables.

Cade didn't hear the rest of Zack's comment, but it was probably for the best. He didn't like seeing another man touch her, *any* other man, but for some reason, Zack was worse. He stifled the sudden urge to go after them and tear his friend away from Addie. He had no right to be possessive. He'd made no promises and neither had she. Still, Zack's too familiar behavior toward her stirred up feelings he would've rather left dormant.

He turned and headed for the door. *Damn him,* Cade thought but without malice. Zack was a good-looking guy, but he'd never been one to stab a friend in the back. *But then, I'd never thought Cord would, either.* That thought stopped him in his tracks. He glanced back and saw Addie in her seat at their table, introducing Zack—who had taken Cade's seat beside her—to her friends.

Addie is not Jenny, he told himself as he continued out the side door and toward the portable toilets around back. He wanted to believe that, but he wasn't sure if he actually did.

CHAPTER 19

Addie laughed with her friends at another one of Zack's wild stories about him and the Brody brothers. Cade's brother actually sounded like a great guy...just like Cade. If it weren't for the terrible things he'd done and said to Cade, she'd be thrilled to meet Cord Brody. As close as Cade had said they were—and as Zack's stories had indicated—it didn't seem right for them to be at odds. For Cade's sake, she hoped the brothers could somehow find their way back to each other, but considering what had happened between them, she wasn't sure that was possible.

The band was playing another polka tune and several other festivalgoers were dancing, while Zack kept their table laughing.

"Did Cade and his brother ever get you back for that?" Lana asked after Zack finished another funny tale. Her wide eyes were so focused on Zack, it was obvious she was taken with their new tablemate.

"Oh, yeah," Zack said as he brushed his fingers along the closely trimmed beard covering his jaw. "And I learned my lesson, too."

Lana frowned. "You mean that was the end of the practical jokes?" She sounded disappointed.

Zack's charming grin split his face and he chuckled. "Nah, I just learned not to prank them both at the same time. They were quite a pair and stuck together, always. Having them both after me was nerve-wracking."

"How long have you known Cade and his family?" Helga asked after exchanging a glance with Veta. Addie recognized Veta's protective sister look. It didn't take a lot of thought to understand they were looking out for her.

"Oh," Zack said in reply to Helga's question, "I've known them my whole life. We're neighbors, and our families worked together, helped each other out. We were inseparable for most of our lives. I remember this one time…"

He launched into another story, but Addie only partially listened. She glanced over her shoulder toward the side door where Cade had exited. He'd been gone for some time—longer than seemed normal—and she wondered if something was wrong. The look on his face when he'd left troubled her, but she hadn't wanted to ask about it in front of Zack.

She turned back to the table as Zack rounded out another story of teen pranksters and more laughing broke out.

The band had announced a short break about five minutes before, and the chatter around the table was much easier to follow.

"Sounds like a bunch of hooligans," Pete, the older man across from Addie, said.

Pete O'Brien was quite spry for being in his seventies and had been the owner of her farm before she bought it. He was gruff but caring in his own cranky sort of way, and Addie liked him despite his grumpy exterior.

"They were just kids, Pete," Helga said from Addie's other side. "Can't fault them for that. Zack seems like he turned out okay, and Cade's been a big help to Addie."

"Yeah, well," Pete grumbled, his eyes on the half-full mug of coffee on the table before him. "Some don't always turn out so good."

Ivan patted the older man's shoulder. "Don't dwell on the past, old friend. There's still time, things may change."

Pete's lips thinned but he nodded and Ivan turned. "Don't mind him, Zack. He's just a bit old-fashioned and he's forgotten what it was like to be young."

Pete huffed, as if Ivan's comment annoyed him, and his voice was clear and strong when he spoke. "I haven't forgotten anything. And there's nothing wrong with being old-fashioned."

"Damn right," Zack chimed in. "My father was a hard one—as well as a little old-fashioned—but a good man. I couldn't have asked for a better father and I think he'd like you, Mr. O'Brian."

Addie smiled. Zack had figured the old man out quickly enough. His show of respect by not using Pete's given name, as well as off-handedly comparing him to someone Zack obviously admired, had smoothed Pete's ruffled feathers.

Pete turned shrewd, old eyes toward the younger man and seemed to rethink his previous assessment. Addie knew Pete appeared to be the epitome of a grumpy, old man, but he was also intelligent and fair, and had a quick-wit that not everyone got to see.

Pete looked Zack up and down before he nodded. "I might at that, young man. Your daddy seems to have done right with you, despite your shenanigans as a youngster."

Zack's expression turned humble and gracious. "Thank you, sir. That means a lot."

"Well," Pete muttered and shifted as if uncomfortable with Zack's gratitude, "you turned out better than my boy did. A damn sight better, I'd say. At least, you and your friend seem to understand how to work and ain't afraid of it."

"No, sir," Zack replied. "I ain't afraid of hard work, and neither is Cade, or his brother."

Pete's chin jutted before he nodded his approval. "What kind of place you got in Montana?" Pete asked, apparently willing to forgive Zack's past mischievousness. Zack's broad grin lit up his handsome face as he happily explained their horse and cattle ranch setup.

"What was that about?" Addie whispered to Helga who sat on her other side.

Helga leaned toward her. "After his mother died, Pete Jr. got into a lot of trouble, and it only got worse as he got older," she said quietly. "Not the innocent jokes like Zack's been talking about, but other, more damaging things like drugs and breaking and entering. He's been arrested a couple of times that I know of, cost his father a lot of money, and heartache, too."

"Oh, that's too bad. I'm so sorry to hear that,'" Addie said, glancing at Pete, who now seemed enthralled by Zack's conversation. After hearing about Pete's troubles, she was even happier that they'd worked out a deal for the farm that had benefited them both.

"Yeah," Helga said with a sigh. "They were like oil and water. Pete Jr. was nothing like his father—always looking for the easy way to do everything, trying every get-rich-quick scheme he came across." Helga shook her head sadly. "They finally had a falling out about three years ago." She leaned a little closer and lowered her voice even more. "If you ask me, Pete's heart attack was because of all the stress his son had caused him over the years."

"Is his son still around?"

Helga nodded. "We've seen him around town once in a while. He hangs out with Ted Ballinger's group, but I have no idea where he's living."

"That's awful."

"Yes, but what about you?" Helga asked. "How are you doing?"

Addie lowered her eyes. "Better now."

"That boy taking care of you?"

Her eyes snapped to Helga's, but all she saw was concern. "Yes, Cade's been wonderful. I don't know what I would've done without him the last few days."

That was truer than Addie could say. She still felt insecure in her own home. Nightmares of dark shapes laughing and chasing her had awakened her several times over the last few nights. Cade had always been there though, pulling her into his arms, murmuring softly that she was safe, that he wouldn't let anything happen to her. She didn't know what she would've done without him.

Helga smiled and rubbed circles on Addie's back. "I thought he'd make sure you were all right, but I'm still glad to hear it." Her hand stilled and Addie braced herself for another question. "How about the house? How'd everything look when you got back yesterday?"

Addie smiled as warmth flooded her chest. "It was fantastic," she said, feeling her cheeks heat as she remembered what she'd done with Cade in her newly cleaned and painted room last night. "You all did such a wonderful job. The whole inside looks brand-new. I don't know how I'll ever repay everyone."

Helga grinned and gave her a one-armed hug. "Nonsense. It was our pleasure. That's what friends are for, right?"

"Sure," Addie replied," and if you ever need anything…"

Helga chuckled and dropped her arm. "You'll be the first one I call."

The band returned to the stage and after checking their instruments, began another polka tune. Several partygoers flooded the dance floor and once again, Addie glanced at the exit, looking for Cade. She'd lost count of how many times her eyes had ventured that way. It had been almost twenty minutes and he still hadn't returned. She hoped he was okay and that he hadn't climbed into his truck and run as far from her as he could get. She'd been a bit of a basket case after the vandalism to her house, but he'd treated her with such kindness and had made her feel safe. She wanted more of that, more of him. Maybe too much more. Maybe she'd spooked him. She didn't want to believe that, but she wasn't going to lie to herself, either. She cared about him—a lot. Might even be falling for him…

Oh, who am I kidding? She'd already fallen for him—hard, fast, and irrevocably. She wanted him to stay, be more than just a hired hand, and far more than just a friend with benefits. What she didn't know was if he wanted that, too.

"I'll go find him for ya, if you'd like."

Addie spun her head toward Zack. "Oh, I…"

"You like him, don't you?"

She hesitated, but there was no reason to deny it. "I do."

Zack grinned. "Cade's a good guy. He deserves to be happy."

"I feel the same way."

"I'm glad to hear that." His eyes drifted off to stare into the distance. "I wish I knew what happened between him and Cord. It's not right, the two of them being at odds like they are."

"You're close to both of them, aren't you," Addie said.

He nodded. "I have two older sisters, but those boys are the only brothers I've ever had. I've missed Cade and I know Cord has too, but he won't talk about it. Says it's between him and his brother. I'm getting the same vibe from Cade."

Addie nodded but didn't offer any insight.

"Do you know why Cade left?"

She shook her head. "I'm sorry, Zack, even if I do, it's not for me to tell."

"Yeah, I thought you might say that."

"He seemed genuinely pleased to see you, though."

"Of course," Zack said, sitting up a little taller and raising his eyebrows smugly. "Who wouldn't miss me?"

She laughed at his outrageousness.

"Seriously, though, he's been gone awhile. I'm going to go check on him," Zack said. "Do you want me to tell him he needs to get his butt back here?"

Addie shook her head and chuckled. "No, just tell him…" She wasn't sure what she should say. They'd been on their way out the door when Zack showed up, and not because they were tired, either. She sighed. "Just tell him we can go whenever he's ready."

"Ah," Zack said with a speculative lift of one eyebrow. "That's how it is, is it?"

Heat crept up her neck and into her cheeks. "I don't know what you mean."

Zack's grin didn't falter. "Sure, sure. I'll let him know." With that, he unfolded his tall frame and headed toward the exit.

Addie only hoped Cade was still somewhere to be found.

CHAPTER 20

It only took Cade a few minutes to locate the portable toilets and do his business, but his mind had been running a thousand miles a minute and in nearly as many directions the whole time.

Zack was one complication he hadn't expected. Seeing him again brought up memories of home and his brother that Cade would've rather left forgotten. The last thing he wanted was to hear from Cordell. *What if Zack tells Cord where to find me?* Cade shook his head. *If Cord wanted to find me, he'd have done it long before now.*

He had considered telling his friend to keep his mouth shut, but now he wondered, why bother?

Then there was Addie. He didn't know what to do with all his feelings for her or all the fear they dredged up. Yet, his normal need to run when things got too personal hadn't been an issue with her. In fact, he found himself wanting more—more of her smile, more laughter, more kisses— but he couldn't do that to her. She had so much going for her and he was just a homeless drifter with trust issues.

Maybe I should tell her to hook up with Zack.

He frowned. That idea did not sit well with him. Not only was it disrespectful and dismissive of her feelings—not to mention hurtful and crude—but he hated the thought of any other man touching her.

He shook his head at his stupid thoughts. It wasn't like him to be this indecisive. He should just thank her for her kindness, get in his truck, and go. He had everything he needed to move on. His truck was better than it had been when he arrived in town, and he still had plenty saved from the months he'd worked for her. But every time he thought about leaving, everything in him seized up and he felt sick to his stomach.

He knew Addie wanted him to stay and a big part of him wanted that, too. But taking that last step—agreeing that what was between them was real, saying it all out loud—didn't seem possible. He still had nothing to offer her, but damn it, if he did, he'd give her everything. She deserved that and more.

Staring at the ground, his brain still whirling, he headed back toward the tents, something inside tugging at him to hurry back to Addie.

"Well, look-ee who we have here," an unfriendly voice said from in front of him.

Cade's eyes snapped up and met Ted Ballinger's dark, cocky gaze. Movement off to the side caught his eye. Ted was not alone. His friends quickly spread out, encircling Cade. He eyed them all and gauged his chances—of either escaping their trap or winning the approaching fistfight alone—as slim to none. His jaw clenched and he turned back to Ted.

"What the hell do *you* want?" he growled between his teeth.

"Oh, I thought I'd pay you back for those lies you were spouting about me at the coffee shop the other day," Ted said as he slowly strolled forward.

"So you needed to bring all your friends to talk about what I said?"

"I didn't say anything about talking," Ted said as he continued forward, as did his friends.

Cade's shoulders tensed and he readied himself for attack. "Fine. Let's get this over with."

Ted stopped and grinned.

A shiver of apprehension danced along Cade's spine. His hands curled into fists at his side and the irritation inside him grew. "What?"

Ted chuckled. "It's just funny that you think I'm going to fight you."

Cade frowned. "Aren't you?"

"I wasn't the only one you offended," Ted said, but before Cade could reply, something hard hit the back of his head and shattered over his neck—a bottle he thought. His hat tumbled to the ground and everything went black.

He didn't remember falling, but he couldn't have been out long. He blinked away the darkness that threatened to wash over him again and pushed onto his hands and knees. He shook his head, but that only made the pain worse and he groaned.

"Get him up," Ted said, excitement tinging his voice.

Polka music echoed loudly around them as hands grabbed Cade's arms and hauled him to his feet. He tried to pull away, but without success.

"I am going to enjoy this," Ted said and landed a right cross that would have spun Cade around if Ted's goons hadn't been holding him.

Stars twinkled before Cade's eyes as his captors pulled him back to face Ted once more. He took a breath, about to berate Ted for his cowardice, but a hard punch to his gut stole his voice. Cade coughed and struggled against the hands holding him, but he was far outnumbered. The blows kept coming hard and fast. He tasted blood in his mouth and could feel more oozing down the side of his neck from the bottle they'd hit him with earlier.

Someone grabbed him by the hair and jerked his head back. Ted's smug face filled Cade's vision. "You need to get out of town," the other man growled. "Get in your truck and leave. Tonight."

"Ted…" another voice said quietly, but Cade couldn't see who it was. "Ted, that's enough."

Ted ignored whoever it was and glared into Cade's face. "You understand me, cowboy?"

Cade spit the blood from his mouth, most of it landing on Ted's face and shirt. "That all you got, asshole?" He laughed at the look of surprise on Ted's face. "I ain't going *anywhere*."

Ted's eyes narrowed and Cade knew it was coming before the next blow landed on his cheekbone. Several more strikes to his body doubled him over and weakened his knees.

"*Ay, dios mios,*" the soft voice from earlier muttered before it grew to a shout, "Damn it, Ted."

Suddenly, Cade was free. He collapsed to his knees in the travel-muddied meadow grass and tried to get his bearings before someone grabbed him again.

"Get out of my way, Jorje," Ted shouted.

"No," that voice said, though it was filled with iron this time. "He's had enough. You said you were just going to talk to him, not beat him to death."

"That's my business," Ted replied hotly. "Now, get out of my way before you join him."

"Can you stand, *señor?*"

It took Cade a moment to realize Jorje was speaking to him. "Yeah," he groaned as he pushed to his feet. "I'm good."

Jorje turned back to his one-time friend. "I'm tired of your bullying, Ted, and the way you hurt people. I won't let you do this."

Ted laughed. "You won't, huh? Hey, JR, you hearing this?"

"Yeah," Ted's tall, blond friend—the one who'd laughed when Ted had been taunting Addie at the café—stepped forward, "I heard."

"This ain't right," Jorje said. "None of it is, and I don't want any part of it or you, anymore."

"Then leave," JR growled.

"I'm not leaving him behind." Jorje inclined his head toward Cade.

Cade was grateful for the intervention, but unless this guy was some kind of super fighter, they were still outnumbered six to two.

JR shrugged. "Suit yourself." He exchanged a glance with Ted.

"Be ready," Jorje whispered to Cade. The warning was unnecessary. Cade could feel the tension coming off the other men and knew another attack was imminent.

Ted and his crew assailed them as one with flying fists and kicking feet, but this time, Cade was ready and so was his new friend. Back to back, they held their own for a while. Knocking down one opponent after the other, but never getting a reprieve. It didn't take long for Cade's injuries to get the better of him, and he began to fade. When one of them came at him with a two-by-four, Cade lifted his arm to keep the board from striking his head, but he went down from the slanting blow. His arm ached, but he didn't think it was broken. That wasn't his biggest problem, though. His biggest problem was the fact that the moment he hit the ground, someone had begun to kick him repeatedly and he couldn't get back up. He could hear Jorje's shouts, but he couldn't do anything to help.

Cade curled his body, protecting his head, doing everything he could to keep from losing consciousness or being kicked to death, but he was afraid he was going to fail. Not just himself, but Addie, too. He didn't want to leave her alone...

"Cade!" a familiar voice shouted, but he was too light-headed to place it. The boot that had been assaulting him vanished and Cade finally got a chance to catch his breath.

"Hey!" another shout drifted toward him, bursting through the grunts and scuffling sounds that surrounded him. "What's going on back here?"

"Five-O," someone shouted before six sets of feet thundered by, one tripping over Cade in their haste. He grunted, but no further harm was done.

"Cade? Are you all right?" Zack's familiar voice asked as his hand curled around Cade's arm and helped him to his feet.

"Fine," Cade muttered, rubbing at the lump forming on his forearm from the two-by-four.

"Oh, man," Zack said when he got a look at Cade's bloody face. "What the hell happened?"

Cade shook his head and regretted it immediately as pain shot through his skull. He hissed through his teeth and squeezed his eyes shut. Lifting a hand to his head, he muttered, "I'm fine, Zack."

Zack grabbed Cade's chin and gently turned his head. "You ain't fine," he said, gingerly touching the huge lump forming on the back of Cade's head.

Cade ducked away from his friend's fingers, but the quick movement made him groan.

"Yeah, you're just grand," Zack said, sarcasm heavily lacing his words. "You'd better sit before you fall down." Zack slowly pulled Cade toward the bumper of a nearby truck, and with his hands on Cade's shoulders, forced him to sit.

Cade didn't complain. His head was pounding, he felt a little nauseous, and his ears were ringing.

A bright light flashed over them and stopped. Cade averted his eyes as the light came closer.

"Everything okay, here?"

Cade caught a glimpse of a uniform and a badge, and realized why the man's voice sounded familiar.

"I'll be fine, Deputy Harden," Cade said. "You mind lowering your flashlight?"

The light dimmed and Cade opened his eyes.

"What happened?" Mark Harden asked and tugged a handcuffed man forward. The wobbly image settled into Jorje's familiar face after Cade blinked a couple of times. "I caught this one trying to take off, but I know there were more."

"No, he…" Cade made the mistake of moving too fast when he stood and groaned at the pain that assaulted him. His head swam and he swayed on his feet.

"Sit," Zack ordered and pushed him back down on the truck's bumper.

Cade groaned, lifting a hand to his pounding head, but didn't fight.

"You were saying?" Mark asked when Cade's hand dropped again.

"Jorje was trying to help me," Cade said, frowning up at the deputy. He still didn't like the guy, but right now, Mark had the law on his side.

Mark glanced at Zack, who nodded, then turned to Jorje. "Is that true?"

"Si," Jorje said, looking both glum and resigned.

"Why?"

"*El hombre…*" Jorje nodded toward Cade. "He was outnumbered."

"So it wasn't your friends who took off into the night?" Mark asked.

Jorje's lips thinned and a muscle bunched in his jaw, but he didn't say another word.

Understanding Jorje's reluctance to name his so-called friends, Cade tried to draw Mark's attention. "I'd be in a lot worse shape if he hadn't stepped in, deputy."

Mark nodded before he turned to Zack. "And who are you?"

"A friend of Cade's," Zack replied.

"And you were a witness?"

Zack shrugged. "Kinda. Cade had been gone a long time, so I came looking for him. Found him and this one," he nodded to Jorje, "in the middle of six other guys, getting their butts kicked." He explained what he saw and how the attackers took off when Mark shouted.

"Well," Mark said as he reached for his keys and turned to Jorje, "I guess that means you're free to go, Rivera. If you'll take my advice though," he removed the cuffs from Jorje's wrists and tucked them into his belt, "you'll find some better friends than Ted and his group."

Jorje nodded, but he didn't look happy about it.

Another man walked up in a blue uniform, holding what looked like a tackle box. "You call for the aid car?"

"Yes." Mark nodded toward Cade. "He needs to be checked out."

"I'll be fine," Cade insisted.

"Don't be stubborn, Brody," Zack admonished. "Let him check you out."

"You willing to press charges?" Mark asked Cade once the EMTs had finished their examination and told Cade he needed to go to the hospital for a concussion.

"Against the others? Oh, yeah."

"Cade?" Addie's voice sounded hesitant as she pushed her way between the other men, Veta, her sister, and the others stood right behind her. "Oh, my God. What happened?" She touched his cheek and, even though her soft, warm fingers were gentle, he winced at the minor discomfort she caused.

"Long story," Cade replied, "but I'm okay." He glanced at Lana as she stepped forward, for once not ogling him, while simpering and vying for his attention. Instead, she had locked eyes with Jorje, who looked both interested in the young woman and terrified of her, too. But Cade didn't get much chance to ponder that situation.

"He has a concussion," Zack said, replying to Addie's question, while giving Cade a disapproving look.

"It's only minor." Cade tried to sooth Addie's worried expression.

"I knew something was wrong," she mumbled then glanced at the

EMT who was packing up his supplies. "Are you taking him to the hospital?"

"I don't need a doctor," Cade said.

At the same time, the EMT replied, "He said he didn't want to go."

"He's going," Addie said.

"Addie—""

"No, Cade, you need to go. You can't see yourself right now. You need to let a doctor look at you...your head, at least."

His jaw tightened. The last thing he wanted was to sit around an emergency room all night.

"Please, Cade. If you don't go, I'll worry. Please, just let them see how bad it is. Then we'll go home and I'll take care of you." She smiled and her eyes twinkled at him suggestively.

He couldn't help himself. "All right, but I don't want any company when we get home." He glanced pointedly at Zack, who laughed.

"Hey," he said, still chuckling, "I told you, I'm just passing through."

Cade   glared   at   his   friend,   but   didn't   reply.

CHAPTER 21

Addie rolled over in bed and sighed, her exhaustion weighing her down. Her eyes felt gritty, her lids heavy, but she couldn't seem to drift off. Images of Cade, bloody and swaying on his feet, kept popping into her head, and the 'what-ifs' would not stop swirling through her thoughts. *What if they'd hit him harder? What if they'd kicked him one more time? What if he'd died?*

"I'm too ornery and stubborn to die," he'd joked that night in the emergency room. She hadn't argued, it wasn't the time for it, but her silent reply had been, *Jared thought he was, too.*

She sucked in a cleansing breath and shook her head. "Stop it," she told herself. "Cade is going to be fine."

She just had to make herself believe it.

The doctor had said Cade would recover with rest and time, but Addie couldn't help the worry and fear that kept her awake. Memories of how Jared had looked after the accident that killed him—pale and limp, all life and animation gone forever—rolled over and over in her mind. Her long-dead fiancé's fate kept her anxiety over Cade's condition—and the situation that caused it—running on high. The human body was frailer than anyone wanted to believe, including Cade.

He'd been discharged after only one night of observation in the hospital, which was supposed to be a good thing, and she was glad to have him home, but Cade was a terrible patient.

Despite being weak and in pain, he hated being in bed all the time. Thankfully, the doctor prescribed something to help him sleep, as well as something for his headaches. Though, that didn't mean Addie got much sleep.

Cade had been home for four days and, though the temptation to have him close was strong, she'd insisted he use the bed in his room where he was more likely to get the rest he needed. And he had slept a lot, but she'd caught him more than once attempting to get up to help with chores.

"You need to stay in bed," she had scolded the second morning since he'd returned.

He had glared at her with slightly unfocused eyes. "The animals need to be fed."

"And they will be," she told him as she maneuvered him back into his bed. "Zack's already left to take care of it."

Cade's lips had thinned, but he didn't argue further as she pulled the blanket back over him.

Thankfully—despite his assertions of not staying long—Zack had hung around to help Addie with the farm chores and to make sure Cade was okay. She appreciated his help with the farm, and with Cade.

"I thought I told you not to be here when I got home," Cade had said to Zack later on the second day.

Zack's eyebrows had shot up in faux surprise, but his tone was dripping with sarcastic humor. "What? And miss out on all your friendly conversation?"

Nothing Cade did or said seemed to phase his old friend, which worked out well for Addie. When Cade was awake and grumpy, and Zack was back from chores, he would wander into Cade's room to catch up and give her a break, but she never went far. Somehow, Zack's good-natured comradery eventually softened Cade's mood and they'd end up talking and joking for hours—well, at least as long as Cade could stay awake. She loved to hear them bicker like brothers and how their voices turned soft and low when they'd talk about home. It sounded like a wonderful, beautiful place and her heart had ached at how much Cade missed it. She heard the hurt in his voice when he'd said he would probably never go back. She wished he could, at least to work things out with his brother.

Zack being with them also seemed to heal something inside Cade. Though he was cranky because of his injury and the bedrest situation, Cade also seemed happier, calmer, and more confident than before. Not that he didn't already have a measure of those things, but this was deeper, more personal, and she was glad to see it.

She was also thankful for Zack's company when Mark stopped by the morning after Cade returned home. A female deputy accompanied Mark—the woman they'd talked to after Addie's house had been vandalized—to get their statements about what had happened at the festival.

"Miss Malory, if he's able, we'd like to get Mr. Brody's statement." Mark's formality had surprised her, but considering the situation, it had been totally appropriate. "Mr. MacEntier? We'd also like to speak with you as well."

Addie had glanced over her shoulder to find Zack standing in the dining room entry, his thick arms folded over his brawny chest.

She'd played the good hostess—invited them in and offered coffee—while they all sat in her dining room and Zack recounted what he remembered. By the time he'd finished, Cade had been awake and, though he was a little groggy, he had no trouble recounting the events that led to his injuries.

The two deputies hadn't been her only visitors over the last few days. Jorje Rivera stopped by yesterday afternoon. Another surprise, but not a bad one.

"*Hola, señorita,*" he'd said quietly when she opened the door, his dark head bowed and his soft brown eyes looking unsure.

"Hello, Jorje," she replied. "What can I do for you?"

"I..." he shuffled his feet then straightened his shoulders, "I came to check on *Señor* Brody and to speak with you both."

Her eyebrows climbed upward. "May I ask what about?" Jorje didn't frighten her; in fact, the handsome young man had been the only one of the three who used to work for her that didn't make her uncomfortable.

"I would prefer to tell you both at the same time. Is he able to talk?"

"Well, yes, he is, and he's awake right now. Come in," she said, stepping back to allow him entry. "I'll take you to see him."

Cade had smiled when he saw Jorje and once they'd all settled down—Addie on the bed beside Cade and Jorje in a chair at the end of the bed—Jorje finally spoke. "I'd like to apologize for my part in everything that happened the other night and…to thank you, *Señor* Brody, for standing up for me with the police."

"I'm the one who should be thanking you," Cade replied. "Things would've gone a lot worse for me if you hadn't stopped them when you did."

"*Mierda*…I shouldn't have even been there," Jorje murmured.

"I'm glad you were," Addie said and he looked up. "No matter how you got there." She smiled to let him know she meant what she said.

He shifted, looking uncomfortable.

"You're not like them, Jorje," Addie said. "Why do you hang out with them?"

Jorje shrugged. "I don't know. When I first moved here, Ted said he'd help me find work and he did, but it was never…good."

"You mean you did all the work while he screwed around," Cade said.

"Him and JR," Addie added.

Jorje nodded. "I never approved of what they did or how Ted treated you, *señorita,* but I needed the work. I didn't know how to disagree with Ted without losing my job…but then, I lost it anyway." He gave her a halfway grin that spoke volumes about the shame he felt.

"I never blamed you, Jorje. Ted made his own decisions. I'd thought you'd stay the day I fired him, though."

Jorje nodded. "I wanted to, but I was too afraid and…stupid."

"Are you still out of work?" she asked.

"*Sí.* Most places have let their seasonal helpers go and there's not much to choose from…but that's not why I'm here." He straightened his spine and met their eyes directly. "I wanted to offer my help on the farm."

Addie frowned, unsure if she had enough to pay Cade let alone another worker. She glanced at Cade, who smiled as if to say, "Sounds good to me."

Jorje must have seen her doubt because he hurried on, "You won't have to pay me. I'll be looking for other work, but I wanted to make up for my part in everything that's happened, too."

"You can't work for free," Addie said, an idea already forming in her head.

"I've already been paid for more than I was able to finish," Jorje said.

Addie smiled. "Well, I have a counter offer." She turned to Cade. "If you're okay with him helping out?"

"I don't mind, but it's your place. I'll do whatever *you* want."

Addie smiled and turned back to their guest. "I'll allow you to help out for one month without pay, but," she said, raising one finger as if to keep him from interrupting, "after that, if you still want to work here and if it's at all possible, I'll find a way to pay you. It won't be much, but until then, you'll take your meals with us as my thank you for helping Cade. Does that sound all right?"

Jorje's smile had been wide and instantaneous as he nodded his agreement. "*Sí, eso es muy bueno.* That would be wonderful."

"What would be wonderful?" Zack had asked as he stepped into the room.

Addie hadn't heard him enter the house, though she wasn't surprised to see him. It was nearly dinnertime.

"You're going to have some help while I'm laid up," Cade had told him.

"Oh, really?" Zack said with a teasing grin that Addie had come to know over the last few days. "That'll be great... Addie's a real slave driver, I'm telling you." He shook his head and Addie chuckled.

"Sure, sure," she replied. "A good thing too, with all the food you eat."

"Hey," he said with a hand pressed to his chest and an exaggeratedly wounded look, "I can't help it if you're a good cook."

Addie had laughed with the rest of them. Leave it to Zack to lighten the mood.

Lying in bed now, thinking back on that conversation from yesterday, another grin pulled at her lips. Feeding all three of those men today and cleaning up, on top of taking care of Cade all day while still getting two stories outlined and a rough draft finished, had exhausted her. But she couldn't sleep.

She closed her eyes again and tried to relax, concentrating on her breathing. After a while, she felt as if she were floating, slowly drifting into unconsciousness.

Bang!

Addie eyes snapped open. She lay motionless, listening. She'd been hearing odd noises ever since they'd gotten back from the hospital. Strange sounds that were out of place on her normally quiet farm. She'd looked out the window and even stepped outside more than once, but she never found anything. That heavy thump against the wall near her window was new, though.

Every muscle inside her tensed as she laid there, stretching her hearing for any sound from outside. When she heard nothing after minutes had ticked by, her lids slid closed. As tired as she was, she wasn't about to go on another wild goose chase. Whatever it was would be gone by now and she could relax.

She didn't know how much time had passed, only that she had started to float slowly into unconsciousness, when another loud bang dragged her back. She bolted upright and wiped at her eyes. Looking around the empty room, she cocked her head to listen. Something scraped against the house near her window, then tapped lightly against the glass.

"What the hell is that?" she whispered to the empty room.

The sound suddenly stopped and her breath caught when she saw what looked like a man's shadow pass by her window. It was too dark to tell exactly what moved, but *something* definitely did.

Rolling out of bed, Addie slipped on some jeans over her night shorts and tossed one of Cade's heavy flannels over the baggy T-shirt she wore. Whatever was making that noise, it was still there, and it had to go. She thought about waking Zack, but he'd been working since before sunup and he was leaving early in the morning to head back home. He needed his rest. The last thing she wanted was for Cade to lose someone else he cared for in a senseless accident because she thought she saw a shadow. Besides, it's her home and her responsibility.

Stuffing her bare feet into her muck boots in the mudroom, Addie grabbed a flashlight off the shelf by the door before she hurried to the sliding glass door and slipped out into the cold, quiet night.

The overcast sky allowed for little natural light as she made her way around the whole house. At any minute, she expected to run into a man or animal, or whatever it was that had made those sounds, but she found nothing. The only unusual thing was that the light Cade had installed over her garage didn't turn on when she stepped in front of it. Making a note to check on it in the morning, Addie turned and swept her flashlight over the dooryard and then, even though it barely illuminated them, the other buildings. Nothing seemed out of place.

Slowly, she crossed to the barn and machine shed to check the doors. Both were still locked, but something didn't feel right.

Pulling the quilted flannel more tightly around her, she looked up. It was then she realized neither of the motion lights over the barn or machine shed had turned on when she approached. She'd been so used to having no light in the yard that she hadn't noticed at first.

That's not right, she thought. *Even if they were all installed at the same time, it's too convenient for them all to have gone out at once.*

The back of her neck tingled and the sensation quickly crept down her arms. Shivering, and not just from the cold, she panned her light around the yard, but the tool slipped in her suddenly damp grip. Swiftly wiping her palms against her thighs, she took up the flashlight and started again, noting that the beam quivered ever so slightly.

Something was wrong and because of the uncomfortable tingles racing along her back, she'd swear she was being watched.

Gravel crunched somewhere to her left and she spun toward the sound. Her light arced over the driveway and she squinted into the darkness beyond its reach, but she saw nothing.

Another sound came from behind her and she swung around again. She dashed to the open strip between the barn and machine shed, her flashlight revealing assorted piles of old wood, metal, and other items she couldn't name. But she saw nothing to explain the noise she'd heard.

Something rustled in the grass on the far side of the machine shed. Determined to discover the cause, she jogged over and again, she found nothing.

Standing in the center of the dooryard, peering into shadows, she clamped down on her quivering insides. She didn't believe in ghosts or monsters—other than the human kind—but she'd heard *something*.

It could have been anything, she thought, feeling foolish for the jittery panic that threatened her calm, logical thought. *Deer might be out here walking through the grass, for all I know. Or maybe coyotes...* That thought didn't make her feel any better.

A metallic sound bounced along the drive to her yard.

She whirled toward it.

Nothing.

Her eyes darted from one dark shadow to another as she wrapped her free arm around her middle. A sinking feeling settled over her and the need to run was almost overwhelming.

"There's nothing there," she whispered to herself, willing her trembling limbs to steady. "It's just the wind...or an animal. Nothing to fear."

But there was no wind. The fall storms had come and gone already, and the air was quiet and still tonight.

Another soft sound came from the far side of the barn. Then another from the other side of the machine shed. A flash of something shiny glinted along the drive, something else rustled loudly in the grass, gravel crackled, what sounded like a metal can skipped toward her over the dirt.

Her heart thudded loudly in her ears and her knees went weak. Someone had thrown that can at her. It didn't roll like a breeze had caught it or an animal had tripped over it. The small, rusty can had sailed out of the darkness to come to a stop no more than three feet from her.

All of the sounds stopped as she glanced up, flashing her light back and forth.

"Whoever is out there, you need to go home before I call the police," she said, surprised that her voice had remained steady.

Silence.

"I mean what I say," she said, though her voice faltered. The words barely slipped past the knot of fear in her throat. "Go home and don't come back. This is not funny."

Silence.

Good, she thought, then waited a few more seconds before she returned to the house. Her legs felt a little shaky, but she was proud to have stood her ground on her own. But still, that itchy feeling of being watched hadn't left, making her want to look over her shoulder.

A loud thump emanated from the barn. Her breath halted as did her feet, and she glanced back. Something moved in the shadows. Nothing she could see clearly, but she definitely sensed danger.

"Go home, bitch..." a voice whispered out of the darkness.

"Get out..." another echoed from her other side.

"You don't belong..." a third murmured from behind her.

They grated along her taut nerve endings, scraping away her last semblance of strength. The animosity in those voices was palpable.

All at once, the noises started up again and she jumped. The flashlight dropped from her suddenly nerveless fingers and she forced her trembling legs to run back to the house. She rushed inside and slammed the door behind her. Throwing the little used bolt lock, she leaned back against it and slid to the floor.

A moment later, she rushed to her feet, flipped on the porch light, and went to the window to peek outside.

Nothing.

She could just barely see her flashlight on the ground where she'd dropped it, but nothing else. No animals milling in the yard. No people threatening to break down her door. Nothing.

She heaved a sigh and flopped onto the couch. Maybe she'd just been hearing things. Though that metal can soaring toward her had been real enough. Still, it didn't make any sense. She'd never had anything like this happen before.

It's over now, she told herself. Whatever it was, whatever she'd thought she heard, was gone.

As her adrenaline faded, her shaking abated and exhaustion returned. She could barely keep her eyes open, and the longer she sat there, the more unreal the experience had seemed.

"I'll call them in the morning," she mumbled, too tired to think about talking to the police tonight. Cade was still recovering, but Zack slept in her other guest room. If anything else happened, she'd wake him.

Getting to her feet, she shuffled to her room, tossed off her extra clothes, and climbed into bed. She didn't think she could sleep, but she had to try. Tomorrow would be another long day, even without talking to the police, and she was so damn tired. Yawning, she turned onto her side and stared at the wall for some time, expecting the worst, until her lids grew too heavy to keep open. Slowly, she drifted into dreams of a monster chasing after her and Cade coming to her rescue.

CHAPTER 22

Addie stood, staring dumbfounded at the shelf beside the door to the mudroom. Her body flushed hot and cold as her mind swirled with confusion and doubt. There, on the shelf, sat the standard black flashlight that she'd left on the ground in the middle of her dooryard last night. Not even a speck of dirt marred its shiny surface, and she couldn't figure out how it had gotten there.

Somehow, she'd fallen asleep after the scare she'd had last night. Though, now she wasn't so sure that the whole scene had even happened.

Bad dreams had plagued her while she'd slept and woke her before anyone else had risen. It had still been dark outside when she'd rolled out of bed, but as she'd started breakfast for everyone, the sun slowly woke the day. By the third time she'd wandered into the front room to look out the window, she'd been able to see nearly all of the dooryard. Her eyes had widened when she noted that the flashlight was gone and a cold shiver swept through her. Flicking a nervous glance over the surroundings, she had decided to step out and have another look around.

"What'chya looking at?" Zack's voice had startled her. She'd glance over her shoulder to find him standing beside the couch, his dark, chestnut-brown hair slightly mussed and his small duffle bag in his hand.

"Nothing," she said, feeling foolish for her nervousness. "I just thought I heard something last night."

"Really?" Zack had sounded serious and intrigued as he tossed his bag onto the couch and moved toward the front door. "Well, let's take a look around, then."

At the time, Addie had been glad for the company, but as they'd searched through the yard, it had become clear that they would find nothing amiss. Not only had the flashlight been missing, but the small can that had come to rest on a section of gravel in her driveway last night was no longer there, either. Zack had found a couple of spots where the longer grass had been trampled near the machine shed and barn, but said it could've been flattened by an animal. And the frozen November ground had ensured that there were no footprints to be found, not even her own. To top it all off, the motion lights were working normally again.

Now, as she stared at the flashlight that was mysteriously back on its shelf, doubt cracked through her certainty that something dangerous had occurred last night. After all, hadn't she noticed that the clothes she'd worn outside were not on the floor where she'd thought she left them before crawling into bed? The flannel was on a hook behind the door and her jeans had been hung on a hanger in her closet—just as they had been before she grabbed them last night. She didn't remember putting them away, but then again, she couldn't prove anything else, either.

Zack chuckled softly from behind her and his big hand patted her shoulder. "Don't worry," he said consolingly, as if trying not to cause her embarrassment, "it happens to the best of us. Country life can be fairly isolated, so it's not unusual that we sometimes hear weird things at night."

Addie shook her head as she listened to his boots take him to the kitchen counter to pour a cup of the coffee she'd made earlier.

"What things?" Cade slowly walked into the kitchen.

Addie glanced between him and Zack, and shook her head again. "I'm not sure."

"Sit," Zack said, nodding his head to indicate the small kitchen table. "I'll pour you some coffee and we'll talk." He pulled another mug from the cupboard and poured two more as Cade turned to her.

"Addie…?"

She didn't want to worry him—he was still recovering from a concussion after all—so she flashed him a small smile. "Yes, sit and I'll tell you."

"I don't need you two babying me just because I got a little banged up," Cade said defensively.

"You're a little more than banged up," Addie said, turning toward the kitchen and letting the mudroom door close behind her. "Besides, it's not about you. I'm hungry." She smiled again to cover the lie and headed for the table. Apparently accepting her excuse, Cade followed.

Once they were all gathered at the table, a plate of pancakes, scrambled eggs, and sausage in front of each of them, Addie repeated the story that she'd already told Zack when they'd searched the yard earlier.

"Why didn't you wake me?" Cade asked, concern hardening his tone. "You shouldn't have gone out there alone."

Addie sat up a little straighter. Despite the fact that she had been frightened and alone last night, she didn't like the implication that his words and their delivery conveyed. "I am perfectly capable of taking care of myself, and you need your rest."

"You could've woken up, Zack…"

"Hey," Zack said as if perturbed by the suggestion, "I need my beauty sleep."

Cade tossed a glare at his friend before meeting Addie's eyes once more. "Regardless of whether you can take care of yourself or not, that wasn't the smartest move. What if someone or something had been out there? If you had disappeared, I'd have—"

Addie's frown deepened. "You'd have what?"

His eyes shifted to Zack before they returned to her and then dropped to his more than half-full plate. He pushed the eggs around with his fork and shrugged. "I don't know."

"He means to say, he'd have been lost without you," Zack said with a mischievous wink.

"Knock it off, Zack," Cade growled and then rubbed at this temple. "This is serious."

Zack stood to grab the coffee pot and refilled their mugs. "Yeah, it is, but if you can't tell the whole truth, someone has to." He grinned at Cade, who glared in return.

"The truth about what?" Addie asked, exasperated with the both of them.

"I'd have been worried," Cade said quietly, his stunning blue eyes more serious than she'd ever seen them. "Please, don't take unnecessary chances alone. I...I don't want anything to happen to you."

He sounded so sincere yet contrite that she forgot to be annoyed with him.

"It's okay, Cade," she murmured. "I'm beginning to think it was all a bad dream."

"Well, I hope so, but if it happens again, wake me." He glanced at her sternly, but then his face softened. "Please."

She inhaled, intending to call him on his bossy attitude, but that heartfelt "please" stopped her. Instead, her lips curled up and warmth suffused her insides. She liked that he worried about her—as long as he didn't try to control her.

"I will," she said, "but like I said, I think it was just a very vivid dream. We didn't find anything outside. Right, Zack?"

"Right," he replied around a mouthful of food, the only one of them who seemed to be eating.

"See?" Addie said, turning back to Cade. "Nothing to worry about."

Cade stared at her and sighed, but he let the argument go.

"Well, good," Zack said and took a swallow of his coffee. "Now that that's settled... As much as I'd like to hang around, I gotta get going. I've got a ton of work and animals waiting on me at home."

"Thanks for staying so long," Addie said.

"I'm sure you'll miss me," Zack replied with an audacious wink.

"Yeah, thanks," Cade grumbled, narrowing his eyes at his friend's flirtatiousness.

Zack grinned. "No problem. I figured you'll have plenty of help now with Jorje."

Uninterested in more food, Addie set down her fork. "Yes, I'm glad he decided to return."

"Yeah, and I think you may see more of your other friend, too."

Addie frowned. "What other friend?"

"The little sister who's always making eyes at Cade when you're not looking."

"Zack..." Cade's low voice held a note of warning, but Addie wasn't concerned about Cade and Lana.

She kept her gaze on Zack. "Why do you say that?"

"Because, the night of the fight, she was staring at Jorje."

"Really?" She smiled at the thought of Lana's interest in the quiet young man.

"Yep," Zack replied, "and she seemed real interested, too."

"Thank God," Cade muttered with a roll of his eyes.

Zack laughed.

"I think they might be good for each other," Addie said with a smile.

"Maybe..." Zack grinned as he pushed away from the table and stood. "But, I gotta get going. I expect y'all to come visit me really soon, though. I could use another hand with tagging and vaccinations in the spring."

Addie grinned. "We'd love to come for a visit."

But Cade shook his head. "I don't know. We've got a lot going on here. Not sure we'll be able to leave for that long."

"I'm sure you can find a neighbor who'd feed for you for a few days." Zack's face turned serious as his eyes pleaded with Cade. "At least visit for a couple of days. I don't want to lose touch with you again." The poignant note in his friend's voice tugged at Addie's heart and by the softening of Cade's expression, she knew it touched him, too.

"You won't," Cade told him as he also stood. "You've got my number. Call me any time."

"Yeah, I do." Zack patted his breast pocket where the lump of his cell phone pushed against the material. "And I do know how to use it."

Addie chuckled as she followed the men outside, but her thoughts kept returning to what had happened the previous evening. Had she imagined the whole thing or had her mind just run wild with dreams of mysterious, stalking monsters?

CHAPTER 23

Cade slowly made his way to his room, being careful not to disturb Addie, who was hard at work on her new laptop in the dining room. She looked to be deep in thought, her fingers flying over the keys. He'd become used to seeing her there, writing or researching her next literary work. When she was slightly bent forward—as she was now—with the ticking of the keys sounding something like rain on a barn roof, she was in her own little world. Unless he spoke up or made some noise to pull her out of it, she'd stay that way for hours.

Just looking at her brought a smile to his face.

It had been a little over a week since Zack left and aside from a slight, recurring headache, Cade was well on the mend. Still, Addie had insisted—to his utter annoyance—that he take it easy for at least another week. Jorje had been a great help, taking on the more strenuous jobs, but Cade was feeling antsy and chaffing a bit at her mothering.

But he'd do what she wanted just to see that brilliant smile of hers. Even if it bored him to tears to do the less interesting jobs—like feeding the chickens or checking fences—he'd do it for another week to please her. He might slip in a few hay bale tosses or feed bag moves here and there, but he knew his limitations and that he could handle the strenuous chores now.

Watching her work, the familiar warmth of desire pumped through his system. He'd like nothing more than to walk up behind her and kiss the soft arc of her neck, right below her ear. With her lustrous hair fastened into a messy bun on top of her head, her satiny pale skin called to him, but he knew it would lead nowhere. She'd made that clear two days ago when he hinted at taking her to bed.

"No, Cade, not yet," she'd told him, her eyes wide with concern. "You're still healing, remember. 'No strenuous activity,' the doctor said. You shouldn't even be doing the light chores around here, but you're too stubborn to listen."

"Addie, I'm fine. I know how much I can take, and I'm careful," he'd replied. "You worry too much."

"I have my reasons and the doctor's directions."

He'd rolled his eyes, but he couldn't blame her. After what she'd told him about her long-dead fiancé and his recklessness, he couldn't criticize overmuch.

Then she'd walked up to him, her eyes soft and sweet as she ran her hands up his chest and behind his neck. She'd leaned into him and, going up on her bare toes, she tugged him down for a gentle kiss.

When they parted, her chocolate eyes had been filled with so much emotion, so much love, that the last semblance of the walls surrounding his heart dissolved into dust.

"I'm not saying forever," she'd whispered while her fingers caressed his jaw. "I miss having you close too, but I won't risk your health, Cade, not for anything."

He'd given in. How could he not? She'd looked so vulnerable gazing up at him, her eyes pleading for him to understand. But he still yearned for the day she'd let him back into her bed.

Taking in the small wisps of hair that had escaped her bun to brush against her neck and the intent frown on her face as she stared at the screen, clearly intent on her work, his smile broadened. He loved her tenacity, perseverance and strength—her desire to live on a farm to fulfill a dream when she hadn't known the first thing about farming or ranching was an indicator of all three, not to mention how she'd bounced back after being attacked. He knew that event still bothered her at times. The supposed incident outside last week that she'd described as a vivid dream was proof of that—especially if it had never happened, which she'd almost convinced him was the case. Still, he couldn't deny his strong need to keep her safe. The fight in town, his concussion, and his healing were unimportant. To him, Addie was everything.

Quietly, he turned down the hall, heading to his room. He tossed his hat on the bedside table and pulled off his boots, then grabbed a clean pair of sweats he'd bought in town a few weeks back, and headed for the bathroom across the hall. A hot shower would ease the sore muscles in his neck and maybe relieve the slight throb in his head, too.

He turned on the taps to let the water heat up, then stripped out of his clothes and stepped into the steaming tub. The warm water felt wonderful as he braced his hands against the wall and dropped his head under the gentle stream. It sluiced down his body, washing the dust and sweat from his skin. The heat and rhythm of the water lulled him and tiredness washed over him. Eyes closed, he stayed that way for some time, breathing slowly and allowing himself to fall into a fantasy that Addie had joined him. Imagining her soft hands working soap into suds that she ran up and down his spine, sweeping wide circles over his back and shoulders, working her way downward. He was so lost in the daydream that when a gentle pressure slid over his ribs and another pressed against his back he hadn't, at first, thought anything of it. But then reality rushed in and he snapped his head up, right into the shower's spray. He spluttered as he turned around, wiping the water from his eyes.

When he could finally see again, he couldn't believe his eyes. Addie stood not more than an arm's breadth from him, soap bubbles dripping from her hands and an uncertain smile on her face.

"I'm sorry if I startled you," she said, moving as if to exit the tub.

He reached for her hand. "No, wait. Don't go."

She turned back to him with a warm smile. "Okay."

He couldn't help but look her over. It seemed like years since he'd last seen her naked, and the gorgeous sight nearly dropped him to his knees.

"My God, you're beautiful," he murmured, trapped in her spell.

She rewarded him with a brilliant smile that dimpled her cheeks and flashed her straight, white teeth. "You don't mind?"

He laughed. "Of course not."

She reached out to slide her finger down his chest and belly. "So, it's okay if I touch you?"

He didn't know what game she was playing, but he liked where it was going for sure. "Absolutely."

When her small hand wrapped around his manhood, he closed his eyes and sucked in a harsh breath. Her touch sent bolts of heat and awareness through his whole body, coming to rest in his balls. The ache was exquisite.

When his lids lifted, he found her staring up at him, a mischievous curve to her mouth.

"Were you thinking about me?" she asked as her soapy hand slid along his already hardened shaft.

"Would you believe me if I said no?"

The corners of her mouth tugged upward as her second hand cupped his tight, achy balls, kneading them as she stroked him. "No, I wouldn't."

He reached out to touch her in return, but she pushed his hand back to his side and shook her head.

He frowned. "What...?"

"I want to take care of you," she said, her hands still rubbing and washing his body. "Let me do this for you. I've been fantasizing about it for days."

He chuckled. "All right, but only if you let me touch you after."

"Touch me where?"

"Everywhere."

She smiled. "We'll see about that."

His frustrated growl made her giggle, but he made no move to touch her. If she wanted it this way, he'd take it for as long as she was willing.

She soaped him up from head to toe, making him sit and rest against her spread thighs while she sat on the edge of the tub and worked shampoo into his hair. She massaged his neck and shoulders, his scalp and temples, easing the pain that had been there only a few minutes before. Then she told him to stand and rinse.

He'd nearly finished following her directive when he felt her body slide between his legs and then she took him in her hands again. Intense heat engulfed the head of his cock, so hot and inviting he groaned. Locking his trembling knees and bracing his hands against the wall once again, he sheltered her from the falling water. When he opened his eyes, the sight of her pretty pink lips wrapped around him almost put him over the edge. Her eyes were soft and loving as she stared up at him, bobbing her head.

"God, Addie," he muttered, "that feels...so good..."

She took him deep into her throat and hummed. The vibration drove his pleasure to the next level and his hands fisted against the wall to keep from touching her. His hips flexed—he couldn't help it—and as she increased her pace and slid forward, she kept humming, her eyes never leaving his, telling him things, making him feel things he had no right to feel.

He cried out at his release, his heart pounding in his chest. Words pushed into his mouth. Sweet words, possessive words, words that would change his life and break his heart all over again. Three little words were ready to fall off his tongue, but fear and insecurity pushed them back down his throat.

Instead, he reached down and pulled her up, crushing her against his chest. He wanted her for more than just the physical pleasure she gave him. He wanted her smile, her laugh, that sweet, loving looking in her eyes. He wanted it all, every day.

She wiggled and he loosened his hold. He thought she would pull away, but she surprised him once again by pushing up on her toes to kiss him. Not the slow, gentle kisses she'd given him for the last week, but a hot, needful, demanding kiss that had his body heating again.

She broke the kiss to stare into his eyes, her chest rapidly rising and falling against his. "Is it too soon?"

"Hell no," Cade growled, pulling her to him and this time, he was the one devouring her lips.

CHAPTER 24

The gray, overcast sky outside the sliding glass door looked ominous as Addie closed her laptop with a smile. The clouds looked heavy with the promise of snow. The evening temperatures had been well below freezing for the last week, and the daytime highs had been almost as cold. Not that she had minded; she looked forward to the change in weather. And even though the house might be a little colder at night, Cade had made sure to keep her warm.

Ever since that hot scene with him in the shower and the even hotter sex in her bed right after, Addie hadn't spent another night alone. Even if their evenings weren't always filled with ardent kisses and passionate lovemaking, she couldn't get enough of Cade. He was sweet and funny and caring, and she had fallen for him…hard. She hadn't meant to let her heart get this attached, but it was too late now.

He had never said that he'd changed his mind about staying, but she had high hopes that he would. After all, he seemed as interested in her as she was in him.

Still, doubt sometimes squeezed her heart, but she wouldn't listen. Cade could have left weeks ago, but he hadn't. That had to mean *something*. Right?

Addie pushed back from the table where she'd spent her morning finishing her most recent literary work and stood to stretch a little. Then, pulling her quilted flannel a little closer, she walked to the glass door and stared out at the dreary landscape. The vegetable garden had long since been cleaned out and covered, ready for next year's crop, and the grass that had once been overgrown and weed-filled was now trimmed and green. By the look of the sky—and the early morning forecast—heavy snow would cover everything by nightfall.

I hope Cade and Jorje get back before it gets too deep, she thought. They were fixing a downed fence on the far end of her acreage today. Some of her cattle had pushed through a weak spot and invaded Mark Harden's property during the night. His call had come as they were about to have breakfast and had ruined her thoughts about convincing Cade to stay home with long, lingering kisses.

"Sweetheart," Cade had said, his voice low and raspy after her first kiss, "I've got work to do."

"It can wait," she'd replied as she kissed his neck. His hands had pressed into her back, holding her a little closer, and she heard a needful sigh escape his lips.

"Jorje is already here," he murmured halfheartedly as she nibbled at his ear in the hallway.

"I'll send him home," she said, undeterred. "I'm sure he'd love a day off."

"There's snow coming."

"I know…"

"Addie…" He grabbed her arms and gently pushed her back. His vivid blue eyes were dark with desire, but he shook his head. "We can't do this today. I have to feed the animals and make sure everything's ready for the snow coming in."

"Maybe I should help…?"

He'd smiled. "It won't take too long. I'll be back early, and then we can pick this up where we left off… Okay?"

That was when the phone had rung and all her hopes of a morning tryst had died.

She smiled as she thought back on the promise in his eyes. A little shiver of anticipation made her giggle like a schoolgirl with her first crush.

What was it about him that made her so giddy? He was handsome for sure, but that wasn't the whole reason. It was how he made her *feel*.

They'd grown closer over the last several days. Talking late into the night, Cade had opened up even more—telling her about his home for the first time—and she'd fallen even farther under his spell.

"When we were young, my brother and I used to sneak out early on summer mornings to go swimming in the river not far from our house," he'd told her a few nights ago as she lay comfortably in his arms. "We built a treehouse out there with our dad and had hung a long, thick rope from a sturdy branch that we used to swing out and drop into the middle of the water."

"Sounds wonderful," she murmured, her fingers tracing lazily along the arm he had thrown over her middle, holding her to him.

He sighed. "It was." He remained silent for so long after that, Addie had started to drift off. But she hadn't wanted to miss out on anything else he might share.

"A treehouse, huh?" she said. "I always wanted one of those."

Cade chuckled and his arm tightened briefly. "Well, maybe I'll build you one here."

"I'd like that."

He'd smiled. "Maybe we'll camp out there, too. Cord and I used to do that when we got older."

"You mean you had girls out there." She laughed.

A crooked grin played on his lips. "Yeah, we did, but most times it was just Cord and me. We'd talk about the future and how we'd run the ranch together. We'd both wanted big families, to have them all know each other, and to be as close as we were." He huffed a cynical laugh. "Didn't really turn out that way, though."

The heartache that filled that last statement and the forlorn note in his voice had tightened her throat and made her eyes sting. But he wouldn't have appreciated her sympathy.

"Maybe things aren't as bad as all that."

He shook his head. "They're bad enough that I'll never go back."

She cupped his cheek in the low light. "I'm sorry, Cade."

He shrugged. "No need to be."

"You obviously miss it…*and* you brother."

"Yeah, well, that was all a long time ago. Things have changed. Our parents are gone and there's no reason for both of us to stay. Besides, the way things went, those old, childish dreams would've never come true anyway."

Tears had filled her eyes, but she didn't let him see them. His hurt had been palpable, radiating outward. She'd felt the heavy pressure of it and for her, it had been unbearable.

All that pain must be crushing him.

Even now as she turned away from the glass door and headed into the kitchen to make some tea, she fought the burn of unshed tears.

The container where she kept the tea bags was empty so she opened the cupboard where she normally kept a backup, but the two boxes she'd thought she bought weren't there. The bright yellow of her favorite tea brand would've been hard to miss among the other duller shades that lined the shelves.

She frowned and searched again, moving a few other items to ensure that the tea hadn't gotten shuffled behind something, but to no avail. Stepping back with her hands on her hips, she glanced around the room but the missing tea boxes were nowhere to be seen. Shaking her head, she went to the garage to grab a secondary backup from the shelves out there.

That had been happening a lot lately—her forgetting things or misplacing them and then not remembering where. Like her jacket the other day. She'd thought she left it slung over a chair in the dining room one night, only to find it hanging from the hook by the front door the next morning. Or her muck boots—which she always left in the mudroom—that she found outside the front door last week. She'd found her hair brush on her bedside table rather than in her bathroom drawer one day and that same morning she found the coffee grounds that she always kept in the freezer, in the refrigerator instead.

"I must be losing it," she muttered to herself as she refilled the tea container, put the box with the remaining sealed bags in its regular place, and returned to pour her tea.

She'd attributed most of the missing or moved items to her

absentmindedness, but some hadn't made sense, even with her distraction over Cade. Thinking that he may have moved a few things too, she'd asked him about it, but he'd denied it and she believed him. She had wracked her brain, trying to remember moving those items or placing them there temporarily and just forgetting to return them to their rightful places—which she assumed she'd done—but she couldn't clearly recall how any item had gotten to where she'd found it.

Taking up her tea mug and chocking up all the oddities to her own forgetfulness, Addie headed toward the front room, intending to spend an hour or two with a good book. She just pulled one from the bookshelf when she heard a knock at her front door. She had thought she heard something from the kitchen earlier, but when no one entered, she'd assumed she'd been so eager for Cade to return that she'd imagined it.

It was too soon yet for Cade or Jorje to be back and she wasn't expecting any visitors today. A jolt of alarm shot through her, but then she pushed it aside. If someone wanted to hurt her, they wouldn't knock politely at the front door. It wasn't locked after all. But even though she'd never had to lock it before, maybe she should start remembering to do that.

Shaking her head, she set her tea on the coffee table and went to see who had stopped by.

When she opened the door, her eyes widened and her heart stuttered in her chest. Sweeping his snowflake-dotted black cowboy hat from his head, the good-looking man on her doorstep awarded her with such a charming smile that she felt her body begin to heat. Yet, something wasn't quite right. She opened her mouth to ask why he had knocked instead of coming in, but he didn't give her a chance.

"Howdy, ma'am," he said politely. "I'm looking for Caden Brody. I heard he might be working out here?"

At first, all Addie could do was stare. Everything was the same—the brilliant blue eyes, the coffee-brown hair, even the way he grinned was reminiscent of Cade—but something about his eyes was different, the length of his hair, even the way he stood. All of a sudden, realization hit her. "You must be…Cordell?"

His smile grew and his earnest expression filled with hope. "Cord, please, and yes, I am. That must mean I have the right place…?"

"Yes, you do," she said and noted the look of relief that crossed his face, "but Cade's not here right now. He won't be back for a while. Would you…like to come in for some tea…or coffee?" she amended, remembering how Cade had cringed at tea. "He should be back in an hour or two."

"Sure," he replied slowly. "I don't want to put you out, ma'am, but that would be great."

She stepped back and held open the door. "It's no problem, and please, call me Addie."

He stepped inside. "Nice to meet you, Addie."

She wasn't sure how Cade would respond to his brother showing up out of the blue, but she had some questions for Cordell Brody. And, depending on his answers, he may not be around when Cade returned.

CHAPTER 25

A thick layer of snow covered the roads by the time Cade and Jorje had finished herding Addie's cattle back onto her land and had crawled back into Cade's truck. Thanks to Dan and Helga lending Cade a couple of their quarter horses and a trailer to move them with, rounding up the stragglers only took a few hours rather than all day.

Thankfully, Mark hadn't hung around for more than a quick greeting and easy directions to where the animals had wandered before he left for work. Cade had growled a quick word of thanks before turning away to unload the horses from their trailer. His curt behavior might have been rude, but he couldn't help it. No matter how reformed the man claimed to be or how friendly and personable he seemed when sober, Cade couldn't like him. He didn't trust Mark's sudden reformation and he couldn't forgive what Mark had done to Addie. Maybe the man was regretful, maybe he would stay sober now, but Cade wasn't ready to believe it.

Jorje had proven himself a good horseman as they rounded up the wayward cattle.

"You're really good at this," Cade had shouted after they'd been at it for a while.

Jorje had grinned happily. "I love horses."

"Where'd you learn to ride?" Cade had asked when they took a short break for coffee from his thermos.

"*Mi abuelo*, my grandfather, was a cowboy, *un vaquero*. *Un muy buen vaquero*. He worked for *un rancho grande* in Mexico most of his life and taught my father when he was small, but *mi padre* didn't like the life. When I was old enough to ride, I went to work with my grandfather for many years."

"Your grandfather sounds like a good man," Cade said as he screwed the top onto his thermos and tucked it into his saddlebag. "He certainly taught you well."

Jorje nodded and smiled. "*Sí*, he did. I am much like him. I love the openness and the freedom." He waved his arm to indicate the empty rolling hills surrounding them. "I want something like this one day."

Cade grinned. "I'm sure you'll get it. You're a good man, Jorje, and a hard worker."

Jorje hadn't responded, only glanced at Cade with an unreadable expression. Maybe he'd thought Cade was only shining him on, but he'd meant what he said.

The snow had started while they were repairing the fence and started falling in earnest before they'd gotten back to the truck. They'd loaded the horses before crawling into Cade's truck and turning the thermostat to high. Unfortunately, being an old truck, it took a little while before warm air pushed through the vents to give them some relief. They'd both been shivering on the drive to Dan and Helga's to drop off the horses and trailer. Only the hint of warmth had touched them when they'd needed to exit to unload the horses and disconnect the trailer.

"You don't have to come with me, Jorje," Cade had said before exiting. "I can unload them. You stay and warm up."

"No, *señor*, it will go faster with both of us."

He had been right, of course. They'd quickly moved the horses, unhitched the trailer, and thanked Dan for their use before getting back into the truck and heading home. The drive back had been slow due to the freezing temperatures and the six inches of accumulated snow, which made the road home like an ice rink.

Home, Cade thought as he turned onto Addie's long drive. It was funny how in such a short time he'd grown attached to a place. *No, not a place. Addie...* He wanted so much more with her than he had a right to hope for, and he still had nothing to offer...nothing but himself.

"Someone's here," Jorje said, interrupting his thoughts. "I don't recognize the rig. Must be from out of town."

Cade glanced at the other truck parked beside Jorje's in front of Addie's garage. Mud covered the tires and had splattered the navy-blue quarter panels. It had been parked there long enough for several inches of snow to accumulate on its upper surfaces, but none of that was what made Cade's hands tighten on the steering wheel or put the icy knot of dread in his belly.

He recognized that truck. It was nearly identical to the one he'd traded-in to get some extra cash a few months after leaving home. He hoped he was wrong—it had been years since he'd seen it—but the sinking feeling in his gut said otherwise.

"Is something wrong, Cade?" Jorje asked, his dark brows gathered over his nose and his voice filled with concern—like everyone else, Jorje had heard about the vandalism of Addie's house. "Do you think *Señorita* Addie is all right?"

Damn small towns, Cade silently seethed as he pulled up behind the familiar truck to park. He knew his whole body had tensed as recognition had settled over him, but he didn't want to alarm Jorje or start a line of questions he didn't want to answer.

Switching off the engine, Cade glanced at his friend and tried to grin. "No, it's fine. I'm sure it's just a delivery or something. No need to worry."

But he was worried. Anxiety pumped through his system, making him nauseous and slightly lightheaded. He tried to loosen his stiff posture but wasn't too sure he'd succeeded.

Jorje's frown deepened as he glanced from Cade to Addie's front door and back. "Are you sure?"

He chuckled, but it sounded forced to his ears. "Yeah, I'm sure." He held out his hand for the other man to shake. "Thanks for your help today, Jorje."

Jorje slowly took his hand as if a little leery. "You don't need help with anything else?"

"Nah," Cade said as he cracked his door, preparing to step out, "we've got enough done today. It's cold and wet, and I want to warm up before the evening feeding. I can do that myself, so you can head home and wait out the storm." He glanced out the windshield. "Looks like it's just getting started out there. I expect we'll see another foot or more before it stops. Wouldn't want you getting stuck out here."

Jorje nodded. "All right, if you're sure you don't need any more help…"

"I don't." Cade said and pushed open the door. "You head on home…and don't worry about coming in tomorrow if it's still coming down like this. I'll call you if we need you."

He hopped out of the truck and slammed the door behind him.

Jorje did the same, then climbed into his truck, backed up, and turned for the drive. *"Adiós,"* he shouted as he drove away, his hand waving from the half-open driver's side window.

Cade returned the wave. *"Hasta luego!"*

When he turned away, the smile dropped from his face and the tension in his shoulder grew. He didn't want to go inside. Didn't want to face what he might find. Didn't want to deal with anger that was, even now, burning inside him.

But this was his home and he wasn't going to have his backstabbing brother run him off this time.

But what if Addie figured out what Jenny had? That Cade wasn't worth the love she had to give? What if she found Cord more interesting, more…desirable?

A growl rumbled up from his chest. *No! Not this time.* He would not give Addie up without a fight. He would not let his brother win a second time. Last time, he'd been too shocked, hurt, and devastated to do anything but run. This time, he would stand his ground. Addie belonged with him. His brother, whatever his business here, would have to go.

With long, purposeful strides, Cade headed for the front door, not caring that he was wet and his boots were covered in snow. He would not give any advantage in this battle. This war, he intended to win.

CHAPTER 26

Addie's sparkling laughter was the first thing Cade heard as he reached for the doorknob. His heart clenched and then fury rushed through him, heating his skin as if he was on fire. *How could she sit and laugh with Cord after what I've told her?* How could she betray him like that?

Turning the knob and pushing the door open with more force that necessary, Cade stormed into the room, ready to fight. Addie sat on one end of the couch, a mug of coffee in her hand. Cord sat on the loveseat a few feet away, sipping from his own mug.

Pain lanced through Cade's chest seeing them together, and Addie's wide-eyed expression said that he wasn't doing a very good job of hiding his feelings. A welcoming smile lit up her face, but he wasn't ready to hear what she would say. He'd deal with her later.

He turned to his brother, his eyes narrowing. Staring into the face that looked so much like his own, Cade felt the familiar sting of disappointment. At one time, Cord had been his best friend, the one person he could always count on, who understood him better than anyone else ever could—his other half.

Now, Cord's was the face of his worst enemy.

"How did you find me?" he growled, uncaring that he sounded aggressive.

Cord swallowed the coffee he'd just sipped and then set the mug on the coffee table. He stood and faced Cade. A muscle in Cord's jaw twitched and determination filled his expression. Then he uttered one word, "Zack."

Cade cursed. "I knew I should've told him to keep his big yap shut."

Cord frowned. "Don't blame him. You could've picked up a phone."

"For what?" Cade shouted, his whole body shaking with rage. "To hear how my ex-fiancée and my brother are getting on? Like I'd want to know."

His brother recoiled, but straightened his shoulders and his determined look returned. "That's why I came."

Cade barked a derisive laugh. "Why? To rub it in?"

Cord shook his head and his shoulders drooped. "No."

"Then why are you here?"

"To explain…about Jenny."

Another bitter laugh bubbled up from Cade's aching chest. "There's nothing to explain. It's over…and good riddance. You two deserve each other."

Pain filled his brother's blue eyes. "You don't understand—"

"What's to understand?" Cade asked, ignoring the hurt on his brother's face. "You fucked her and she left me for you."

Cord sighed and shook his head. "No…I didn't."

"You should listen to him, Cade," Addie said, breaking the heavy silence.

Her soft voice came as a surprise. For a moment, he'd forgotten she was there. Her eyes pleaded with him and he almost caved. His gaze darted between them and then renewed fury hardened his heart as suspicion weighed on his chest.

"You too?" His voice cracked.

Sadness and worry filled her beautiful eyes. "No, I—"

"Forget it," Cade said harshly, unable to stomach what she would say. He'd heard it before. He wasn't worth it. He wasn't enough. He'd known it would come, but it wasn't until now that he realized how much he'd hoped to be wrong.

Unable to face either of them without losing the meager control he had on his anger, Cade turned and walked out.

"Cade…wait!" Cord said as he grabbed Cade's arm.

Unthinking or caring what happened, Cade tightened his fist and turned, putting all his weight behind a right cross that sent his brother flying back to the couch.

"Cade!" Addie shouted as she stepped over to check on Cord.

His chest tightened again as she placed a hand on his brother's shoulder and asked if he was okay. Another wave of raging heat swept through Cade and he spoke out of anger and heartache. "Do you want to sleep with him, too? You want to compare the twins in bed, like everyone else?"

Addie straightened and slowly turned to face him. Anger filled her eyes, but there was pain there, too. "You have no right to say something like that to me."

"I have good reason."

"Not from me you don't!"

"You don't—" He never got to finish that statement, because the next words his brother said cut him off cold.

"I never slept with Jenny, Cade."

Silence.

Addie crossed her arms and glared at him, but he ignored her smug look. His eyes drifted to Cord, who was sitting on the edge of the couch, rubbing his jaw.

This was too much. Now, Cord had Addie believing his bullshit.

Suddenly, the air inside the house became thick and it was too hard to breathe. He had to get out before it and his emotions crushed him.

He made it to his truck before he stopped. No, he wasn't running. He just needed to cool down before he put his fist through the wall. Footsteps followed him all the way to the side of his truck, where Cade stood with his arms folded over the bedrail. From the corner of his eye, he saw Cord's arms mimic his own.

"I'm really glad to see you, Caden," Cord said quietly. "I've been searching...for a long time."

Cade frowned, staring at the truck bed in front of him. "Why?"

"You're my brother. Why wouldn't I look for you?"

"That didn't seem to matter to you before."

"It always mattered to me." The forlorn note in his twin's voice struck a chord in Cade.

"What was I supposed to do?" Cade asked, turning to glare at Cord. "Hang around and watch my fiancée with my brother?"

Cord shook his head. "I didn't sleep with Jenny. I never touched her. I didn't want to, but she wouldn't take no for an answer."

"You told me you slept with her."

"I never said I slept with her. I thought you'd confront her and kick her out. I never expected you to leave instead."

Cade stared at his twin. "But you..." He shook his head. "I don't understand."

"We were never together, Cade. That's what I'm trying to get through that thick head of yours."

"But you said—"

"I said she came to my bed and she did, claiming all kinds of things, but I didn't let her stay. I'd never do that to you."

"But you'd let me think it?"

"If you hadn't been so bullheaded, I wouldn't have had to. I planned to let you cool off and then tell you the next day—once Jenny was gone— but you just took off...in the middle of the night. I practically had to have Jenny arrested to get her off the property..."

"I didn't want to face either of you," Cade muttered.

"If you had, I would've explained. I knew you were pissed and needed time to think. I just never considered that you'd run and leave your whole life behind—the land, your inheritance, everything."

"You should've known me better than that."

Cord nodded. "Yeah, well, after thinking on it for a bit, I guess I would've done the same thing. But I'd like to think I also would've called or at least wondered if something else was up. I mean, how many times did I ever backstab you, Cade? And how many times was I right there with you in a fight? I always had your back. *Always*. Why couldn't you at least give me the benefit of the doubt and call or...something?"

Cade hung his head as a new ache crushed his heart. Heat suffused his cheeks and he couldn't meet his brother's gaze. He'd been so willing to believe the worst, he hadn't even questioned Cord when he'd said Jenny came to him. He hadn't asked for details or clarification. He'd just...left.

I am an idiot, he thought as he wracked his brain, trying to uncover the lie in Cord's words.

The day he'd left, Jenny had smugly told him about all the other men, including his brother. She'd happily revealed the others she'd taken to her bed in college; she'd even slept with a couple of the migrant workers they'd had at the ranch. So when she'd admitted to going to Cord, he'd just assumed the same had happened with him.

Jenny had smiled at the hurt she caused and then flipped her blonde hair over her shoulder. "You're a sap, Cade. Besides, you lied to me, too. I thought you were fun, sexy, strong, and rich. Imagine my disappointment to discover you never really were any of those things? Why shouldn't I look for something better?"

She'd messed with his head...and he'd let her. He'd allowed her to alienate him from his brother and his home by believing her lies.

Another wave of shame heated his skin and he found it hard to breathe. Cord was right. Cade should've trusted him, or at the very least, questioned what his brother had said. Instead, he'd run like a coward, cutting off all connection to the people and places he'd loved the most.

The fury that had consumed him dissipated, and now all he felt was self-loathing. If it hadn't been for his pig-headedness and Cord's courage to come after him, Cade would have gone on believing that his twin had betrayed him.

He hung his head, too ashamed to meet his brother's eyes.

"You never slept with her?" His words were soft, but Cord heard him.

"No, never."

Cade sighed. Jenny had made a fool of him again.

The big flakes of snow continued to fall, coming faster now and the wind had picked up a bit as they both stood in the white silence.

"I'm sorry," Cade whispered and lifted his head to meet those eyes that were so much like his own. He'd expected anger and disappointment to be reflected there, but all he saw was sadness and love.

"Me, too," Cord said. "I should've handled it better, not let you think..."

Cade shook his head. "After everything, *I* should've known better... I was stupid. It won't happen again."

Cord's mouth quirked up on one side and Cade felt his do the same.

"I've missed you, Cade. More than I can say. I've missed my brother."

Cade inhaled deeply and his eyes burned. The sudden thickness in his throat wouldn't let him speak. Instead, he stepped forward and wrapped Cord in a bear hug that was eagerly returned.

"Me, too," he croaked, blinking back tears.

A moment later, they pulled apart, grinning like the happy fools they were.

"Let's not do anything like that again," Cord said, humor mixed with a hint of somberness.

Cade nodded. "Yeah, let's not."

Cord chuckled as he crossed his arms over his chest and shivered. That was when Cade realized Cord hadn't even grabbed a jacket when he came out after him.

"We should head back in," he said and Cord nodded as they turned as one toward the house.

Cade felt that familiar unity that had always been between them return. He felt whole again in a way he hadn't known in years. But there was more to it now. Addie was in that mix and made it stronger, made him stronger. He wanted to be better... For her.

"So, it may be too soon to ask this," Cord said, "but...will you come home?"

Cade stopped and Cord turned to face him.

"To Montana?"

"Yeah, back to the ranch. Half of it is yours, you know, and we've been doing well over the last few years."

Cade glanced around the dooryard, taking in the barn and the roof he'd repaired, and the machine shed that held all the equipment he'd worked so hard to fix and maintain. Did he want to leave?

No, I don't... I don't want to leave Addie.

"Bring her with you," Cord said, apparently reading Cade's mind. "There's plenty of room and she's... She's a nice girl, Cade."

Cade's surprised gaze fell on his brother, but then he realized he'd said that last part out loud. "I don't know..."

"You're not still worried about me, are you? I mean, 'cause if you are, you don't need to be."

Cade shook his head. He'd been stupid over a woman once. He wouldn't make the same mistake twice, but he also wanted no doubt about his feelings for Addie, either. "No, I'm not worried about you, but you should know that I care about her...very much."

Cord nodded. "I figured. She's adorable, very sweet, and," he tilted his head as if searching for the right word, "loyal. You're a lucky guy, Caden. Wish I could find a girl like that."

Pride inflated his chest. Addie must have said something to Cord before he had a chance to explain himself. She'd obviously been convinced that a major misunderstanding had happened between Cordell and himself since she'd told him to listen to his brother. "You have no idea." He smiled. "She's a firecracker, but I don't know if she'll want to leave here. It's all she has."

"She has you," his brother pointed out gently. "Besides, this place needs a ton of work."

Cade nodded. The house, barn, and machine shed still needed paint, not to mention several repairs, and that didn't include the cattle or the spring plowing and planting that would have to be done in a few months, nor the machine maintenance he still needed to finish to keep the equipment in working order.

"I know," Cade replied, "but this was her dream and it's hers, I don't want to take it away from her."

"So you...don't want to come home?"

His heart thudded a couple of times at the thought of finally returning to the home he'd longed for over the years, but the thought of leaving Addie made him ache. "It's not that," he said.

Cord nodded. "It's her. You don't want to leave her. I can't blame you." There was no accusation or jealousy in Cord's tone, just the surety of his guess.

"No, I don't," Cade said. "But I'd also be lying if I said I didn't want to go home too."

Cord rubbed his arms, clearly chilled from the cold air. "Well, t-think about it," he said with a slight stutter. "Talk to her and see what she says. We can always figure something out."

Cade nodded, then inclined his head toward the house. "Let's get back inside before you freeze. I just got you back, I don't want to lose you again now."

Cord nodded, his boots making tracks toward the house. Cade was right behind with his mind turning. Despite what he said, his fear hadn't completely left him. He knew Cordell had told him the truth—he'd always been able to tell when his twin was lying. The only time he'd ever fooled Cade had stolen almost six years from them.

"Cord?" he called and his brother turned back to him. "No more lies, all right? Even if the truth'll hurt, no more secrets, okay?"

"For either of us."

Cade inclined his head. "For either of us."

"Absolutely," Cord replied, "but we have to listen, too. I tried to tell you several times that Jenny was no good. You just never heard me."

"I know," Cade said softly. "That won't happen again."

A small smile pulled at Cord's mouth. "Glad to hear that, brother, but I've got to say, I don't think we'll have the same issue with Addie. You've done good for yourself this time."

Cade grinned in reply. "Yeah, she's something special, and far too good for me."

A frown replaced Cordell's smile. "You deserve to be happy, Cade, and she seems to have chosen you. At least, she's very…protective of you."

Cade didn't reply. He couldn't seem to make himself believe his worth, especially to her.

"Come on," he said instead, patting Cordell on the back and turning him toward the house once more. "Let's get you inside."

His brother chuckled and shivered. "Yeah, I could use some more of that coffee if I'm going to make it back home tonight."

Cade looked around. Nearly a foot of snow covered the ground and the wind had increased as well. "I don't think you should drive in this. Looks like this storm is just getting started. Why don't you stay for a while? At least until it stops and the roads are cleared."

"Will Addie mind?"

"I doubt it, but we'll ask her." He gently pushed Cord toward the front steps and they hurried inside. Cade had no doubt Addie would invite

Cord to stay herself, especially once it became clear that they'd cleared the air between them. But how was he going to tell her that he wanted to go home? That he wanted to get back everything he'd stupidly left behind. Seeing his brother again and learning that he'd always been true made Cade's homesickness so much more acute. But the last thing he wanted was to leave Addie. Anxiousness twisted in his stomach. Maybe she'd understand, maybe she'd even join him, but then again, maybe she'd tell him to hit the road, too. After all, he'd never said he wanted to stay and she hadn't asked. Maybe she didn't want him to.

One thing was for sure, he'd never know if he didn't ask. But with Cord there, it would have to wait until he could talk to her in private. Maybe he could convince her with kisses. He smiled to himself at that thought as they stepped through the front door. Even if she didn't want to go with him, they'd have a lot of fun while he tried to change her mind.

But it would break his heart if she said no.

CHAPTER 27

Pulling her hand-knitted shawl more closely around her, Addie watched as Cade and his brother floundered through the four-plus feet of snow to Addie's truck. Snow still floated down from the low gray clouds, but only in light, sporadic flakes, leaving small, white dots on their felt cowboy hats. The first storm had passed, but the forecast threatened more. For now, however, Cade's plan was to drive her truck to the machine shed to hook up the snowplow and then use it to clear the dooryard and driveway.

She could've done all that herself, but Cade had insisted and Cord agreed. Though Cord's reasons had nothing to do with the job and everything to do with annoying his brother.

"You're paying him to do a job," Cord had said with a playful wink. "Make him earn it."

The teasing grin he'd thrown Cade's way had made her chuckle.

"Right," Cade had growled in return, "and you're helping me. Come on." He'd hooked his hand around Cord's bicep and hauled him out of his chair at the dining table where they'd just finished breakfast.

"I'm not the hired hand here," Cord had complained, but Addie could tell the joke was still playing out. "I'm not the one getting paid."

Cade wrapped his arm around his brother's broad shoulders as they crossed through the front room, headed for the front door. "You'll have my unending gratitude," he said, his voice heavy with sarcasm.

"That's not much of a consolation prize," Cord grumbled as Cade tossed his jacket to him.

"What? My eternal gratitude isn't enough for you anymore?" Cade asked as he pulled on the insulated farm coat he'd bought a few weeks ago. "You've gotten selfish in your old age."

"No, not selfish," Cord replied as he opened the front door and stepped outside. "I just don't want to show you up in front of Addie." The half-grin he couldn't quite hide had made her chuckle softly once more.

Cade had glanced at her over his shoulder. "We'll be back in a while."

She nodded and he turned back to his brother. "I'll show you who's going to out-work who."

"Are you sure about that?" Cord inquired with a doubtfully raised eyebrow. "It's been a while since you've worked a ranch…"

"Right," Cade's voice dripped with sarcasm, "I remember a time, Cordell, that—"

The closing door cut off the rest of Cade's reply, but as she came to stand by the window, she saw them still bickering as they forged a path to her truck.

Sibling squabbling and teasing aside, the obvious affection between them had warmed her heart. The way they often spoke with a look and no words made her a little jealous of their connection. What would it have been like to have a brother or sister? What would it have been like to have a twin? She could only imagine the emptiness and loss they'd felt through the long years of their separation. Thankfully, the rift that had torn them apart hadn't been too much to overcome.

Addie had been leery when Cord first appeared on her doorstep, a charming smile on his face and hope in his beautiful eyes.

"I'm not sure Cade will be happy to see you," she had said after they settled onto her couch with their drinks. They'd been chatting politely for a few minutes and their conversation had waned.

Cord had nodded and his shoulders seemed to sag a little more. "I'm sure he won't be," he'd replied. "He thinks I betrayed him."

His honesty surprised her, but she quickly recovered. "Did you?" She'd tried to keep the accusation out of her tone, but she hadn't succeeded very well.

Cord's bowed head had snapped up and his eyes turned sharp. "No, I didn't."

For Cade's sake, she'd been skeptical, though she'd read the truth in Cord's eyes.

"Then why did you tell him you did?" she'd asked, determined to protect Cade if she had to.

"He told you?"

"Yes, he did."

He canted his head and stared at her as if stunned and confused. "Huh…"

"You think he shouldn't have?"

"No, it's not that. I'm glad he did. I would've needed someone to talk to, if it'd been me. I'm just surprised. We're both…private and don't share our feelings easily."

"I see." The honor of Cade's trust swirled in her chest, making her feel lighter somehow. She had known the importance of it then, but Cord's comment made it all that much sweeter.

They sat quietly as a minute ticked by, Cord staring at the mug in his hands as it rested on his knee while Addie studied him.

"You didn't answer my question," she said.

He frowned and glanced at her. "Why did I tell him I slept with his fiancée?"

She sat a little straighter. "Yes."

Cord's gaze dropped and his posture sagged again. He shook his head. "That was a mistake, but not a total lie." He went on to explain how Jenny had flirted with him whenever Cade wasn't around, how she'd tried to kiss him more than once, and then finally showed up naked in his room in the middle of the night to slip into his bed. "I tried to tell Cade she was no good *before* that night, but he wouldn't listen. It got to the point where hurting him was the only way to open his eyes…" He shook his head again. "I should've never left him alone after what I said. That's my only regret."

She frowned. "What about Cade hating you and all those years apart?"

He met her eyes and his heart was in them when he said, "Yeah, that was awful and I wish it had been different, but I could take Cade hating me until I could make him see the truth—however long that took. What I couldn't stomach was my brother wasting his future and his life on a woman who didn't love him and never would."

The remorse in his voice had been palpable. She had felt it crash into her chest and pound against her ribs, and the ache of it brought tears to her eyes.

A small fear had bloomed inside her at that moment. She'd believed Cordell, and Cade would, too. How long would it be before Cade decided to leave for home? His real home in Montana. How long before he left her?

She hadn't dwelt on it long, but the tightness lodged behind her sternum hadn't left.

When Cade had walked through the front door, she'd been so happy to see him—and for the inevitable reconciliation she sensed would soon follow—that she'd smiled. It had never occurred to her that Cade would think she'd turned on him, too. Though she'd quickly discerned that the accusation had come from a deep seeded belief that he wasn't worthy of her affection.

"You know nothing happened between Cord and me, right?" she'd asked later that night as they lay side by side.

"Yeah, I know..." His voice had been low and ashamed.

"And you know I'd never do that to you? That I'm not like...*her*."

He turned to her with hard eyes that softened the instant they met hers. "You're nothing like Jenny." He shook his head. "I shouldn't have said that. I was just angry and...confused. I never wanted to hurt you. I'm sorry. It won't happen again."

She found his hand beneath the sheet and threaded her fingers through his. "Thank you. I do understand, though. Seeing Cord again must've been a shock."

He huffed a short laugh and looked away. "Yeah."

They'd lain quietly, gazing at the ceiling as the snow continued to fall outside and all her fears had come flooding back. Would he stay or would he go? How long before she'd be lying here alone? Before she'd be on her own again, longing for his touch? She wanted to spend every moment she could with Cade, to make memories she could drag out and run through her mind after he was gone. But then, she knew more time with him would only make her hurt worse when he did decide to leave. Her heart clenched with that thought. His departure would break her, but she couldn't help wanting to be with the man she loved.

Loved? she'd thought, but it was the truth. She could've taken him being with her without saying he felt the same, but leaving her? The seesawing of her thoughts—of the not knowing—abraded her nerves and weighed on her heart, and that moment hadn't been any different.

"So," she'd said nervously, unsure how else to ask what she wanted to know, "are you...going back to Montana when Cord leaves?"

She felt him stiffen, not just his hand but his whole body. The slight vibration rattled through the bed and told her the question unnerved him.

Trepidation filled her heart.

"Well..." he began, "I've been thinking about that."

"And what have you been thinking?"

He turned his head to meet her gaze and his hand tightened around hers. "I do want to go home, but I want you to come with me."

Her heart clenched. "I see," she said and turned away, hiding the sudden burn in her eyes.

He must've sensed her distress because he rushed on, "You'll love it there, I know you will, and there's so much I want to show you."

She swallowed through the ache in her throat, but her voice still sounded raspy when she asked, "What about the farm? *My* farm?" She turned her head, hoping to see...what, exactly? His sudden desire not to go home? She didn't know.

"You can sell it and get some of your money out of it," he said. "It's a bit of a money pit and would take forever for you to get all the repairs done. If you can still afford them...?"

Turning away again, she tried not to grimace. He'd left that last part open-ended, waiting for her to confirm his suspicions, but she couldn't do that. She wasn't ready to give it up for someone who'd never intended to stay with her in the first place.

She shook her head and waved her hand. "This is mine. My dream. I worked hard for it and hard times are part of the package. I don't want to give it up now. I just got started."

The dejected look that flashed across his face expanded the achy tension in her chest. *How could he ask me to leave? This is my home.*

She had said as much, but his reply only sunk the knife deeper into her heart.

"We can build a new home. Our own home, our way."

We? Our? When did they become an item? The last she remembered, he had never meant to stay with her and had planned to hit the road as soon as it was convenient. Their little tryst was just that, a temporary sharing of affection and physical ease. What happened when he got tired of her? If she went with him now and sold the farm, she'd have nothing.

"I don't think so, Cade. I'm sorry, but this is my home. It's the one I dreamed of my whole life. I don't care about the extra work. It's my land and I want to keep it." She'd left out the other half of that dream—having someone to share it with.

Hurt filled the crystal blue depths of his eyes. She saw the internal battle play out there. Finally, he said, "Will you, at least...think about it?"

No promises, no profession of love, or anything else. Just his request that she give up everything she'd worked for to follow him. If he'd given her more—said he loved her, that he wanted to take care of her, and didn't want to be without her—she would have agreed. After all, that's what she wanted to do for him, what she wanted from him. If she had his love, they could've made their home anywhere. But none of those things left his lips and her heart had shrunk as disappointment crushed her into the mattress. Her arms and legs had turned to lead weights, but she couldn't be angry with him. He'd never made a secret about his plans to leave. She had just built up this image in her head of them together on her farm.

Now, as she watched Cade and his brother swipe the last of the snow from the windshield and then climb into her truck, it became clear how fragile that fantasy had been. She couldn't compete with his home, his brother, or the memories both held for Cade. She couldn't give up on her own dreams either, at least not without something more concrete from him. That left her with only one option.

Let him go.

* * *

Cade chuckled as he stripped out of his wet clothes and tossed them into the washer. Addie had met him at the front door with a towel and the garage door opener. She'd clicked the button to start the metal door opening and shoved the towel at him.

"Not this way," she'd said sternly. "Your brother already dripped all over my floor. Use the mudroom to strip off before heading for the shower."

"But Addie…" he'd whined, shivering on the doorstep. He should've gone in with Cord rather than running to the barn to feed the horse and check on the chickens first.

She shook her head. "I know you're cold, but you should've thought of that before rolling around in the snow. I've just mopped up Cord's mess, and I'm sure my truck's going to need a cleaning, too. You and your brother will take care of that, *after* you get warmed up." She pointed toward the garage. "Mudroom. Now."

He'd grinned at her, unable to be upset, especially if Cord had already dragged the mud and snow he'd been covered in into the house. Cade wasn't much better off.

Darkness had fallen by the time he and Cord had finished feeding the cattle, and they'd been on their way back to the truck to head home when Cord had thrown the first snowball. It had splattered against the back of Cade's head with a cold, wet slap, knocking his hat askew and raining bits of icy snow down his collar.

"Hey!" he'd shouted as he turned to berate his brother, but Cord had been waiting and two more snowballs hit Cade in the chest.

He'd looked down at the wet spots on his farm jacket, then slowly lifted his head. Cord had a fourth snowball in hand and a challenging grin on his face while he waited for Cade's response. It had been another opening, another chance to heal what had broken between them, and Cade eagerly took it.

"So, it's like that, is it?" Cade had said, pretending exasperation.

"You know it is," Cordell replied, grinning like a madman and daring him to do something about it.

Adrenaline had shot through his limbs as he'd stared at Cordell while his mind rapidly formed a plan of attack. Some of the snowdrifts over the open fields had reached six feet or more, but not near where he'd stood. His only cover had been the truck, unless he wanted to drop into the snow and quickly form a fort.

Cade had stared at his brother, remembering all the other times they'd done this very same thing back home on their Montana ranch. Every winter growing up they'd had at least one massive snowball fight that left them both soaking wet and freezing, but laughing all the same.

Uncertainty and insecurity had crossed Cordell's face as they'd stood facing each other in Addie's field, and Cade knew he'd been staring too long.

"Last man standing wins," he'd said as he reached for a handful of snow, even as he ducked behind the truck bed.

Cord's next strike caught Cade in the thigh and the one he'd launched in reply had splashed over Cordell's shoulder. Back and forth they went, slipping and falling in the icy mud of the field, while leaping out of the way of each other's volleys, getting wetter and dirtier as the battle raged. Cade finally tackled his brother several minutes later, and they'd both fallen onto the cold, frozen earth. They'd wrestled around, both laughing as they tried to dampen each other more.

By the time they'd climbed into the cab of Addie's truck, they were soaked through and muddy to boot.

They'd all been stuck at the house for three days, only venturing out to feed the animals. Cade had feared that the fragile truce he'd established with Cordell would break under the strain of the forced confinement, but that hadn't been the case. If anything, they'd grown closer again, become like the brothers they once were. He was thankful for that, which was fitting considering the season—Thanksgiving was only two days away.

Throwing the remainder of his wet clothes into the washer, along with what he assumed were his brother's soaked things and others that needed cleaning, Cade started the wash. Then he rubbed the dry towel Addie had given him over his cold-prickled flesh before he wrapped it around his hips and headed into the cozy warmth of the house.

He heard the guest shower shut off as he walked through the dark kitchen, but Addie was nowhere in sight. One lamp burned in the living room, but she wasn't there, either. Grinning, he turned toward her bedroom and the master bath. If she was annoyed with him, he was going to enjoy cheering her up later tonight.

Then he remembered their earlier conversation about her moving to Montana with him and the smile slid off his face. His feet stuttered to a halt a short distance from her door.

"I don't know, Cade." Pain had lanced through his chest at her words. He hadn't expected her to be overly excited about leaving the home she'd worked so hard for, but he hadn't expected her to flat-out refuse, either. *"This is my home... I don't want to give it up now..."*

But you don't mind giving me up? Cade had thought and it had hurt far more to realize that. It still did. Absently, he rubbed at the throbbing ache in his chest that began that night and had never ceased.

What was he doing? He had no business thinking of continuing their physical relationship, knowing it would go nowhere, knowing how she felt. He had to go back home, at least for a little while, but she didn't seem willing to do even that much. Instead of planning to deepen their connection—of investing his heart even more—he should be encouraging her and himself to let it go. He should turn around, shower in the guest bath, and then sleep in the other bedroom.

It was the right thing to do. *But, damn it, I don't want to do that. I want her...*

Addie's bedroom door opened unexpectedly as he stood debating himself in the hallway. His head snapped up and he met her gaze. She smiled and his heart fluttered as she started toward him.

"Well," she said as her eyes swept over his nearly naked body, "you look all warmed up."

He grinned. "Yeah, mostly."

The moment she understood his real meaning—that there were parts of him that only she could warm—her smile broadened.

"Well, in that case," she said as she reached him. Her hands were warm as they slid up his chest and around his neck, "let's see what I can do about the rest of you."

She tugged his head downward as she rose up on her toes and pressed her mouth to his. He went willingly, forgetting everything except how much he wanted this woman—*only* this woman.

His arms encircled her. One hand gripped her ass, pulling her closer, as the other dived into the silky glory of her hair. *God, I'm going to miss this...*

Her tongue slipped over his and then she pulled back.

Again, his heart stuttered. "Why did you stop?"

She brushed her fingers along his jaw. "We have company."

"We could lock the door...?"

A soft smile curled her lips and heat burned in her eyes. "As nice as that sounds...we have *company.*"

"Cord won't mind. And even if he did, I don't care."

Eyes clouding over, her brow suddenly furrowed and she stepped back, her nose wrinkling. "What's that smell?"

He frowned. "What? I'm going to take a shower..."

"Not you." She sniffed the air. "Don't you smell that?"

Confused, he inhaled deeply. "I don't smell anything."

She lifted her nose and tested the air more thoroughly. "Something's burning."

Before he could reply or grab her, Addie slipped by him, jogged down the hall, and around the corner into the living room. Cade was only a few steps behind her. She swung opened the front door and started coughing as smoke lazily curled through the opening.

Alarm shot through Cade's body and he stopped in his tracks, watching black smoke pool against the white ceiling.

Cord's door opened down the hall and the brothers' eyes met as he entered the living room fully dressed. That same internal dialogue passed between them—the same understanding of each other's wants and needs, joys and fears. Cord's posture changed instantly, his eyes searching for the cause of Cade's distress and came to rest on the smoke sweeping into the front room.

Addie's eyes were wide as she glanced at Cade over her shoulder from the doorway. "The barn's on fire," she said in a panicked voice while trying to suppress her smoke-induced cough. "The animals..." She ran out before Cade could stop her.

"Addie, wait!" He moved to go after her then stopped and looked down. All he had on was a towel. The nakedness didn't faze him, but running out there unprepared could leave them both dead. He had to at least cover his skin and stomp into his boots. Still, the urge to run outside kept him rooted in place—indecisive—for longer than he would've liked.

A second that felt like a lifetime later, his eyes met Cordell's. His brother nodded, instantly understanding Cade's thoughts. Dread welled in Cade's throat. He couldn't lose Cord. Not now. But even if Addie didn't feel for him the way he did for her, he didn't want her to get hurt. He didn't want to risk either of them, but he didn't have a choice. The fear that Addie would rush in and do something rash that could injure or kill her spurred his decision.

"Go," Cade said before he turned for the bedroom, and as he raced for his clothes, Cord ran for the front door. His brother would keep Addie safe until Cade could do it himself. He only hoped he got there in time to protect them both.

CHAPTER 28

Two short but excruciating minutes later, a hastily dressed Cade raced out the front door and down the steps. The thick stench of smoke hit him as he crossed the night-darkened dooryard and his lungs rebelled, doubling him over with coughing, while his watery eyes searched for Cord and Addie. He didn't know what he'd been expecting to find, but what he saw as he got closer to the fiery barn hadn't even been on his radar.

Black smoke billowed high into the cloudy evening sky, flowing from the barn's hayloft doors like a chimney. Everywhere he looked, yellow flames licked at the old wood and cracked paint. Soon, the whole building would be one giant pyre, but that wasn't what had captured his attention.

The chickens that littered the dooryard scurried out of his way as he broke into a run. There was no sign of Addie, but Cord lay sprawled on the ground a few yards from the barn door. He wasn't moving.

Fear clenched Cade's chest, making it even harder to breathe. Pulling a red bandana from his pocket, he tied it around his head, covering his nose and mouth as he dashed toward his brother's body. The cloth wouldn't stop much, but it would help.

Kneeling beside Cord—a knot of pain and dread forming in his throat—Cade pressed trembling fingers against his brother's neck. A long heartbeat later, the breath he'd been holding whooshed out when he felt a pulse. Partially relieved, Cade glanced around for the cause of Cord's condition but found no reason for him to be laying there unconscious. Off to the right, half covered in soft snow, Cade saw his brother's phone, the silver case glinting in the glow of the fire. Cord must have been calling for help when he fell. He could think of no other reason for it to be out of his brother's pocket.

But where was Addie?

Shrill neighing echoed out of the barn, followed by the loud bang of hooves on wood. Addie must have gone in for Dreamer, but it sounded as if the horse was still in his stall.

"Addie!" he shouted. "Addie, where are you?"

No reply.

Fear banded his chest as his gaze lingered on the gapping barn door. Flames shot out of its black mouth and the heat emanating from the conflagration had him sweating yards away.

Could something have happened to Addie inside? Would she have gone in alone to get Dreamer out?

Cade's muscles tensed and anger, fiery and sharp, pumped through him. *Of course, she would.* She was in there all right. And if she'd been able to release the horse, she'd have done it by now.

His body went hot then cold and a shiver of trepidation shot up and down his spine. He had to get her out, had to make sure Addie was safe. She had no more business running into a burning building than he did, but he was going to do it because she needed him. He felt it in his bones, in the sinking of his rapidly thudding heart, and in the knotting of his stomach.

Cord moaned and rolled to his side.

Only a few seconds had passed since Cade had knelt beside his brother, but it seemed a lot longer.

"Cord?" he said in a rough voice, dread over what he must do, what he may find, prickling the back of his neck. "Are you all right?"

"Yeah," Cord groaned and sat up with another pain-filled moan. Grabbing his head in both hands, he rested his elbows on his bent knees and cursed. "Who hit me?"

"Someone *hit* you?"

Cord gingerly tested the back of his skull and winced. "Yeah."

"I'll be back to check on you," Cade said, urgency tugging at him to move. "I've got to find Addie."

"Go," Cord replied without lifting his head. "I'll be fine."

Cade stood, tucking the loose end of the bandana inside the white T-shirt he'd thrown on. "Are you sure?"

"Yes." Cord glared up at him from between his hands. "Get going."

Cade ran for the barn door and dashed inside. The heat was unbearable, and he instantly wished he'd grabbed something other than a thin T-shirt to protect his skin from the falling cinders.

Too late now.

"Addie!" he called, blinking at the black smoke that burned his eyes and made him cough. The darkness inside the burning building was almost complete. He squinted as he inched forward, his arms held over his head to fend off the blazing heat and to keep the red-glowing cinders falling from above out of his face. "Addie!"

Dreamer screamed in his stall, kicking madly at the walls as Cade approached. Reaching the stall, he threw the latch that held the door closed and stood back as the sturdy old horse ran for the dooryard. One less thing to worry about.

"Addie!" His throat felt raw from the smoke and his cough. His lungs burned and he could barely see, but he kept going, moving farther into the inferno.

Timbers that supported the hayloft cracked and a hail of red embers rained over him. He brushed the burning pieces from his head and bare arms and kept moving. Somewhere to his right he heard a loud snap and part of the ceiling tumbled into the stall beside him. Flaming hay bales crashed to the ground and caught the wall ablaze. As it streaked upward, the flames lit the interior. It was still smoky and his eyes still watered, but he could see a little better with the terrifying new light.

He didn't have much time before the rest of the ceiling collapsed. The crackling above his head had increased and a constant blanket of heat and licking flame emanated from the loft.

Had the bales somehow smoldered and caught fire? And if so, how?

He'd been so careful to make sure they were dry and well stacked.

No time to think about it now.

Hacking uncontrollably, his skin so hot it throbbed as if burnt, he took another look around. Nothing. Had the fire just been a distraction? Maybe Addie wasn't even in the barn. *Maybe someone had hurt her and taken her away.* That thought chilled him.

He'd think about it later. Now, he needed to get out before the whole thing collapsed on his head.

Another crack came from behind him and he spun around in time to see part of a beam fall across the aisle where he'd stood only moments ago. Hurrying back the way he'd come, Cade jumped over the burning beam, and that's when he saw her. Or better, when he saw her boots.

Yanking open Dreamer's stall door, Cade rushed inside and found Addie on her side. She had blood on her face and she moaned softly when he lifted her against his chest.

"Hang on, baby," Cade rasped. "I'll have you out of here in a minute."

"Cade?" Her voice was weak, but she was awake. Then she started coughing and Cade started running.

Pieces of burning hay rained down on them in thick clumps and Cade ignored the intense heat on his back as he sprinted for the door. Fear spurred him on as another loud crack split the night, followed by a second, and a third, and then a deafening roar as the heavy weight of the hay broke through the burning second floor and crashed onto the lower level.

Cade fell to his knees, skidded in the snow, and tumbled over with Addie on top of him. They'd only just made it out in time.

Coughing, Addie slowly scrambled to her feet, her eyes on the blazing heap that had once been her barn.

"Are you both okay?" Cord asked as he came to stand beside Addie.

She nodded and coughed, but didn't take her eyes off the disaster before them.

Cade stood and ushered them all farther from the flames. "Come on, let's back up a bit." He kept his raspy voice even, but fury brewed just below the surface.

They made it ten feet farther away when Addie spun around.

"Dreamer!" she shouted as she tried to dash back the way they'd come.

Cade grabbed her arm and pulled her around to face him. She tried to break free, but he took hold of both of her arms and wouldn't let go.

"Addie, he's okay," he shouted, trying to gain her attention, but she was too busy fighting to listen.

"Let me go! I've got to get him out."

"Addie." He shook her as gently as he could and her dark eyes burned with ire when they landed on his. She was pissed.

Well, that's fine, he was, too.

"Let me go, Cade," she said. "I won't let an animal die like that."

"That's what I'm trying to tell you," Cade growled. "Dreamer's fine. I freed him before I found you. Even if he wasn't, I wouldn't let you go back in there."

Some of her fight had faded from her eyes as he spoke, but his last statement kicked up the flames once more.

She yanked her arms out of his grasp. "You wouldn't *let* me?"

It didn't appear as if she intended to endanger herself further, so he let her go.

"It's not your place to *let* me do *anything*."

"Oh, so I should've just left you and the stupid horse in there?" he asked, pointing at the burning remains of the barn.

"Stupid…?"

"Yes. Stupid. How stupid do you have to be to run into a burning, dilapidated barn? You almost got yourself killed. And me along with you. What the *hell* were you thinking?"

From the corner of his eye, he saw Cord back away, plainly wanting to stay clear of the new sparks that were flying.

Cade had no idea why he was shouting or why his body trembled with rage. Maybe it was the harshness of her words or the rebuke he read in her eyes. Whatever the reason, he couldn't seem to stop himself.

"You didn't need to come after me," she shouted, seemingly as angry as he was. "This is my place, my responsibility. Not yours."

"So I was just supposed to sit out here and wait for you to appear?"

"I just slipped and hit my head. I was awake when you walked in. I would've been fine."

Cade snorted. "No, you wouldn't."

"Oh, so now I'm just the poor, helpless woman who needs a man to do everything for me?"

He blinked. *Where did that come from?*

"That's not what I said."

"Stop being a Neanderthal, Cade. I can take care of myself!"

Oh, *that* comment made his blood boil. "Maybe if you didn't act like a reckless child, I wouldn't have to be so protective."

"You don't need to be protective at all. You've made your decision. I'm not part of your future. Why are you even still here? You and your brother should go home."

His heart clenched. "Is that what you want?"

"It's what's going to happen anyway, so why not?"

"It doesn't have to be that way."

"Just go, Cade. You'll be happier there. Maybe you'll even *want* to stay."

Sirens blared from the driveway as Addie turned her back on him and folded her arms across her chest. He stared at the back of her head, stunned into silence.

This was *not* what he wanted. What did he have to do to get her to see that he cared about her, wanted to be with her?

Apparently, that didn't matter. The fact that he'd risked his life to help her didn't matter. *He* didn't matter. Just as he'd always known.

It was like suffering through Jenny's betrayal all over again, only this time there were no other men to take his place. She just didn't need him, didn't *want* him. *Just like Jenny...*

Addie had told him to go. No more discussion, no compromise, nothing. Just a dismissal.

It took a lot of effort to swallow the lump of disappointment in his throat and to straighten his sagging shoulders. Part of him wanted to shuffle over to his truck and take off—to get as far from her and his feelings as he could—but he wasn't going to do that.

She'd told him to go, and he would, but on his own terms. He wouldn't run like a beaten dog this time. No, this time, when he left, it would be with pride and self-respect. She'd helped him when he needed it.

He'd help her through the next few days of cleanup, of prepping Jorje to take over for him, and then he'd say his goodbyes with his head held high and his dignity intact.

CHAPTER 29

Though Cade kept his speed down, his old truck handled the newly cleared roads with ease. The high hills of plowed snow that lined either side of the road, filled the irrigation ditches, and hid the flat open fields beyond as they slowly rolled by. They'd briefly stopped to check on her cattle and to throw out some hay for them for the night. It had been a brief reprieve to get out of the truck, even to go out into the frigid air, but the rest of their trip inside the cab had felt like a pressure cooker. Addie hadn't realized how stressed she'd been until they bumped over the large mound of snow at the head of her long driveway and she sighed in relief.

Placed in the middle between the two brothers, she'd kept her back ridged and her hands in her lap. The last thing she wanted was to lean on either of them. She didn't want to start trouble between them if she showed too much favor to Cord, and she definitely didn't want Cade to think she was trying to seduce him into staying. As far as she was concerned, if he didn't want her, she wouldn't beg him to stay. And all the tension that stretched between them had made for a very stiff and uncomfortable drive.

The whole evening had been that way, difficult and awkward to say the least. The only good part of it was that her new friends and neighbors,

Dan and Helga, had invited them all to join their family in celebrating the holiday. Addie hadn't felt like doing anything, and she was feeling far from thankful at the moment, but she'd always loved the holidays. *Besides,* she'd told herself, *it would be better than sitting around alone again tonight.* At least with company, there had been more distraction, though Helga had quickly picked up on the strain between Cade and Addie. She'd been kind enough not to bring it up at dinner, but as everyone helped clean up, she'd pulled Addie into their den and got straight to the point.

"What's going on with you and that young man out there?" she'd asked, irritation and consternation in her eyes. "Something's been wrong between you two since the night of the fire."

Helga and Dan had been there that night. They'd arrived right behind the fire truck, ambulance, and sheriff's vehicles. Cade had stomped off to check on Cord, who sat on the aid car's bumper while an EMT examined the large knot on the back of his head. Soon, Cade had sat beside him, getting the burns on his arms and back treated, leaving her alone to stare at her sorry excuse for a barn as it went up in flames.

"Nothing's wrong, Helga," she'd said softly, avoiding her friend's gaze.

"The hell it's not. The two of you have barely said three words to each other. The last time we saw you, you could barely keep your eyes off each other."

At Oktoberfest... Addie couldn't help the sad grin that had pulled at her lips. Had that only been a few weeks ago? It seemed like years since Cade had held her in his arms.

She'd shaken her head and given Helga a soft smile. "We had a disagreement," she told her friend, "but it's all right. Nothing is wrong, everything's as it should be."

Helga had frowned at that, her lips pressed into a thin line, as she eyed Addie critically. "I know we don't know you well yet, Addie, but I think it's safe to say that you're full of shit."

Addie had chuckled softly, blinking back the tears that had burned her eyes. There was no point in talking about it. Cade didn't want to stay and she'd had no reason to think or hope that he would.

Instead, she'd wrapped her arms around her friend for a quick hug. "It's fine, really," Addie had said as she stepped back. "I'm just worried about…well, everything. I'm sorry to be such a downer, I'm just not really in the holiday mood."

"Well," Helga had said as she pulled back, leaving her hands on Addie's shoulders, "as long as you're okay. Things may look bad now, but just remember, you're not alone." Helga had looked so earnest in that moment that Addie's heart clenched.

"Yes, I know. Thank you."

The problem was that she would be alone sooner or later, and somehow, this time—with Cade gone and all her new financial worries— it would be so much harder to bear.

"That young man cares about you," Helga had said, dipping her head to catch Addie's gaze. "Men can be block-headed and aggravating at times, but it'll all work out. Just wait and see."

Addie had nodded, but she no longer had any faith that things would work out the way she'd hoped.

The night of the fire, after Cord had left her to check on his brother, she'd refused to think about Cade or their argument. Instead, she'd thought about how much this new disaster was going to cost. All the money still left in her account would need to go into building a new barn and replacing all the tools she'd lost. Thankfully, the snow had protected the machine shed from more damage, but as it was, the building would still need some repairs, and she would have no funds left. Fear and loss had filled her, bringing new tears of sadness and frustration. She had stood alone and used her anger to burn out the hurt in her heart.

Cade had none of the tender feelings for her that she held for him. He hadn't wanted her to die and had saved her, but the façade of the sweet man she'd known had disappeared. The angry, distant man he'd become since that night was no one she wanted to spend time with, and he'd made no attempt to change her mind since.

Cord, on the other hand, had spoken with her a lot. While Cade did everything he could to avoid her company over the last two days, Cord had sought her out and done his best to repair the damage—and tonight was no exception.

"I'm going to check on Dreamer and feed the animals," Cade said as they rolled up to her house and he threw the truck into park. He hadn't looked her way or asked either of them to accompany him. Still sensing the vast, icy wall between them, she'd nodded without a word. She'd like to see how Dreamer was doing in the little lean-to the brothers had quickly built for him in the pasture behind the barn's charred skeleton to keep him out of the weather, but she was tired of the tightness in her chest. She wanted to breathe and, she suspected, Cade needed his space, too.

His door slammed shut and Addie's tense nerves jumped at the sound. Her gloved hands tightened into fists in her lap and she fought the need to weep.

"Are you all right?" Cord's soft voice startled her.

She turned to meet his concerned gaze and felt a pang in her chest. They were so different and so much alike, these two men, and seeing Cord's handsome face only made her long for Cade even more.

She nodded and swallowed the knot of despair that had lodged in her throat, but her voice cracked when she said, "Yeah, I'm fine."

He stared at her for a long few seconds not moving, his eyes impossibly blue under the black cowboy hat he wore.

Her mind dredged up an image of Cade's beautiful eyes, staring down at her as they made love. She shook her head and shoved those memories away.

"How about you? Is your head doing okay?"

The EMTs had insisted he go to the hospital for X-rays two nights ago. Luckily, all they revealed was that he had a hard head—no concussion and no other issues other than a giant lump and a bad headache.

"Yeah, it's fine. Yours?"

She touched the spot just above her hairline where a one-inch gash had opened above her temple when she'd fallen that same night. She could feel the two stitches it had taken to stop the bleeding, but she still couldn't recall what had caused her to fall. "Yeah, it's much better. I hardly even remember it's there. Are your headaches doing better, too?"

He nodded, his gaze lingering on her face, still looking concerned.

"Are you going to get out?" she asked with raised brows. "It's getting cold in here." With the truck shut off and the heat of Cade's body no longer beside her, she was definitely feeling the winter cold.

"Sure," he muttered and slid out of the truck. As much of a gentleman as Cade had once been, he helped her down from the cab and walked her into the house.

Addie pulled off her layers and hung them on the hook by the door. Shivering, she dashed over to the thermostat and cranked up the heat.

"Would you like me to build a fire?" Cord asked as he hung his jacket beside the door.

"Yes, please," she said. "I think I'd like some hot chocolate, too. Would you like a cup?"

Pausing in his task at the mantle, he smiled at her over his shoulder. "That'd be great."

"I'll be right back."

Knowing Cade wouldn't come in for at least an hour, Addie hadn't bothered to make a third mug. Pushing down the pain that constricted her chest, she quickly heated the milk, added the chocolate, and picked up the mugs. She headed into the living room, where she found Cord lounging on the couch staring at the flames in the hearth.

He looked so forlorn and sad sitting there alone that she stopped to study him. She wondered what he was thinking to put that look on his face. Was there someone he was missing? Did he regret being here, dealing with her and his brother's fall out?

The conversations she had with him since he'd arrived, and especially over the last few days, had given her a better understanding of Cord Brody and his relationship with Cade. The two of them were so similar, yet they were each their own man.

Still, it had been almost comical the way they'd finished each other's sentences and had so sweetly thanked Dan and Helga for the meal and company tonight. It made her smile, even now.

The memory also brought the reminder that those pleasant moments would soon be over. Sighing softly, she straightened her back and stepped into the living room.

"Here you go," she said with a smile as she handed the hot mug to Cord.

He took it with a grin and a word of thanks before she plopped down on the couch and pulled the blanket from its back over her legs. A comfortable silence fell over Addie as they sipped the chocolate, but Cord seemed edgy.

"Is something wrong, Cord?"

He glanced at her, a frown marring his brow. "You tell me." He set the mug on the coffee table and clasped his hands together between his knees. His blue eyes were piercing when they turned toward her again.

"I...I don't know what you mean."

"Yes, you do."

She looked away, unable to meet his penetrating gaze. She'd already admitted how sorry she was for her argument with Cade, that she wanted things to be better again, but there was no point.

"Why are you bringing this up again?"

"Because," he said gently, "you're hurting and so is my brother. It's killing me to see, and there's no reason for it."

She shook her head. "I know you don't understand, Cord, but Cade made his plans very clear, and I won't beg or manipulate him into staying."

He sighed, clearly frustrated, and raked his fingers through his short brown hair. The movement so much like Cade's frustrated actions, she smiled, but it quickly slipped away.

Cradling her mug between her hands, she dropped her eyes and sipped her drink.

"He doesn't want to leave," Cord said to the fire before turning to look at her again. "Not without you."

"He told you that?"

A muscle twitched in his jaw. "No, not in so many words, but I know my brother. He cares for you, Addie, and you're good for him. He'd be a damn fool to let you go." He turned to the fire. "And I've told him that...more than a few times."

"He's never implied any of that to me, and I can only go by what he's told me."

He stood suddenly and began to pace in front of the hearth. "He's such an idiot sometimes," he mumbled to himself and then turned to her. "Why do you think he ran into that burning barn? What does that tell you about how he feels?"

Addie sighed. "I never said he wasn't a kind and caring person. I know he doesn't want me to get hurt. I know he'd probably do it again, but it doesn't mean anything more than that. I can't let it. Besides," she said as she set her mug on the table, "I have a ton of baggage he doesn't need and no money to pay him anymore." That was truer than she wanted to think about right now. Based on the short conversation she'd had with her banker yesterday, it was likely she would have to sell her dream just to survive, and she dreaded going back to the cramped and busy life of Seattle. Not to mention the heavy responsibility she felt toward Pete and their agreement about the harvests.

"Cade doesn't care about the money," Cord replied. "He cares about you."

She didn't reply, only looked at him with a raised eyebrow, unwilling to continue the circular argument.

Apparently getting the point of her annoyed stare, his lips thinned. They'd argued that topic half a dozen times already. A moment later, he sighed and crossed to the couch. He sat, resting his head back on the cushion behind him. His eyes were closed, his arms hanging limply at his side, but she could see worry etched on his face. And he looked...defeated.

"I'm sorry," he said, so quietly she almost didn't hear him.

"What for?"

"I thought coming here would be a good thing. That I'd get my brother back, whether he came home or not." He lifted his head and she saw pain in his eyes. "I never meant to become a wedge between you or an excuse for Cade to leave."

Her breath stuck in her throat. How could he think that?

"Oh, Cord, it's not your fault," Addie said sadly. "This was going to happen at some point. I'm just glad he's going home with you and not meandering the road with strangers."

"True," Cord replied, "but I honestly don't think he wants to leave."

"He's never wanted to stay."

"I'm not so sure about that."

Addie shrugged. "He's leaving, isn't he? His bags are packed and he's distanced himself from me. I may not like it, but it *is* for the best…" she reached over and took his hand, "for both of us."

"I think you're wrong about that," Cord said, giving her hand a little squeeze and a sad smile that broke her heart. "I think he needs you."

"Maybe, but it's up to him to realize that. Not for me to change his mind."

He turned toward her and leaned forward. Taking her hand in both of his, he looked at her with grave honesty. "Look, us Brodys, we're a stubborn bunch, and sometimes it takes a while for us to come around, but we're not dumb." He grinned. "At least, not all the time. Cade will figure himself out, and I have no doubt he'll choose you when he does."

Addie pulled her hand from between his warm, calloused palms and tugged the blanket up to her shoulders. Her eyes burned, but she refused to cry again.

"I want to believe that, Cord. I really, really do. But given everything I know, I can't hope for it. I just…can't."

CHAPTER 30

Addie splashed cold water onto her face, hoping to ease her gritty eyes and hot cheeks, but when she looked at herself in the mirror, she could see it did no good. Her nose and cheeks were still red and her eyes were visibly puffy. The fact that she'd been crying uncontrollably for the last half hour was obvious, but there was nothing more she could do about it.

Grabbing a towel off the rack, she dried her hands and face before going back to her bed. She fell back onto her quilt and stared at the ceiling.

What are you doing? she asked herself. *Cade is gone, and you have work to do.* So much work that would never lead anywhere.

Her insurance would cover some of the costs for rebuilding the barn, but not nearly enough to keep her out of debt. And her honest, responsible side said she would still owe Pete, the previous owner, for the profits of the hay that had burned. At least half of the crop had been stored in that hayloft, and she had no idea how she would make up the difference.

Jorje had said that he would still help, even without the promise of a paying job at the end of the month, but she couldn't let him do that. He needed to pay his rent, too. She would have to find some way to do it herself. It's not like this was the first time she'd been all on her own. It was just…

Tears welled in her eyes again. *Maybe I should've gone with him…*

"The offer's still open, Addie," Cade had murmured as he sat behind the wheel of his running truck, letting the engine warm up. "You can still come with me."

It had been less than an hour ago that Cordell had made himself scarce, telling Cade he'd meet him at the gas station in town. She almost wished he hadn't given them the short moments of privacy.

She had shaken her head at Cade's words, unwilling to rehash everything again. "No, Cade. I can't. My place is here and you need to go home and get your life back. You *should* go."

His eyes had narrowed and he opened his mouth as if to argue, but when she'd lifted a challenging brow, he sighed and nodded sadly. The defeated look on his face nearly did her in. She could see it hurt him to go, but he was still leaving. Besides, if he wanted her to give up everything she'd ever worked for to follow him, he'd have to offer something more than just the opportunity to warm his bed. She wanted his heart, but he'd have to say it. She was not going to guess or assume anything.

"Okay," he'd said, throwing the truck into gear after a long, uncomfortable pause. "You have my number. Call if you need anything. I'll be here."

"Thank you, but that won't be necessary." Pride had made her say that. She'd always been able to take care of her own problems, but this time, he was the problem and she wasn't sure she'd ever recover.

"Please, Addie…" his blue gaze begged her even more than his voice, "I'd feel better if you'd let me know how you're doing with…" he glanced over at the charred remains of her barn then returned to her, "…everything."

She couldn't deny him that much. "Okay, Cade. I'll let you know what happens."

"Do you know if you'll be able to stay yet?"

She had hoped he wouldn't ask that question. "No, not yet," she lied.

"But you'll let me know, right?"

She nodded, but made no promises.

He stared at his hands that had a white-knuckled grip around the steering wheel. Suddenly, he turned back to her. "Addie, I—"

She held up a hand and shook her head again. "Don't. Don't say anymore. You don't owe me anything. I'll be fine, and I hope your homecoming is everything you want it to be. You deserve it, Cade. I know how much you've missed your ranch *and* your brother. Now, you have both. You're finally going home."

His sad smile had returned, but his hands hadn't ceased their stranglehold on the steering wheel, almost as if to keep him from reaching out to her.

"All right, Addie," he had said as the truck began to roll backward. "Thank you for helping me. Take care of yourself."

More tears coursed down the side of her face, dropping on the quilt beneath her head. Watching him drive away had been the hardest thing she'd ever done—harder than attending her dead fiancé's funeral had been. She had waited until Cade's truck was out of sight before she went back inside. The tears had started before she made it to the front steps. Once inside, she'd fallen against the door and slid to the floor, sobbing and so distraught that she couldn't move. She'd lain there for a long time, her tears making little puddles on the entry floor.

She'd finally dragged herself to her feet, gone to her room, and into the master bath to splash water on her face and cool down. Now, she lay on her bed, her arms wrapped protectively around her middle with more hot tears leaking from her eyes.

"I can't do this," she said to the empty room. But she had no choice. He didn't make her any promises, no profession of love or anything else. He'd been honest, which is more than she could say for herself.

"Whatever we do, it doesn't have to mean forever..." That's what she had told him the night of the bonfire at Helga and Dan's place. But even then, it had been a lie. Drawn to him from the moment she saw him, she had wanted so much more. Maybe that first twinge had been lust, but as she'd spent time with him and had gotten to know him, it had blossomed into something sweeter and stronger than anything she'd ever known.

But she'd gotten too close, and the heat of that flame had scorched her in the end. Just as she had known it would.

Reaching out, she grabbed the pillow he hadn't used since their argument outside her burning barn and held it over her face. His scent had grown so faint she could barely detect it anymore. Which, of course, made her cry a little harder. She screamed into the pillow, releasing the heavy ache in her chest with the power of her voice. It did little good to ease her suffering, but some of the tension lessened a bit.

That wouldn't last for long.

She threw the pillow aside. Part of her wanted to run to the second guest room where Cade had spent his last few nights, drape herself in his scent, close her eyes, and pretend she was once again wrapped in his arms. But that was next to useless.

"Get yourself together, girl," she said, giving herself a pep talk. "You can do this. You've survived worse than a man walking away."

Cade wasn't just any man, though. He was—

A loud knock at the front door startled her out of her misery. She lifted her head from the mattress. *Who could that be?*

Her first thought was that Cade had come back and a little thrill of joy flashed through her. She got to her feet and hurried out to the front room. She peeked through the front window and saw a familiar truck in the drive, but it wasn't Cade's. She looked toward the front steps and saw JR, her ex-farmhand and Ted Ballinger's best buddy.

"What the hell is JR doing here?" she muttered. If he was around, it was a sure bet Ted wasn't far away. How convenient that they should arrive *after* Cade and Cord left for home.

She debated about answering, but her truck was outside and there was still too much snow on the ground for anyone to think she'd gone for a walk or out to the fields. Besides, it would be better to find out what he wanted and quickly send him on his way, than to wait and wonder until he returned, which she knew he would.

Wiping her sore eyes with the sleeve of her shirt, she crossed to the door. She quickly checked to make sure all her buttons were buttoned and straightened the collar before reaching for the doorknob.

"Hello, JR," she said as cheerily as she could, opening the door wide and not so secretly looking for Ted. "What can I do for you?"

In a flash, his hand fisted in her shirt and he jerked her forward. A loud rip sounded as the cloth gave way and several buttons flew through the air. She came to a jarring halt when her chest slammed into his and he glared down at her. "You can get the *hell* out of *my* house, you bitch!" JR snarled into her face, his eyes wild and dangerous.

She'd never seen him like that. His actions and expression seemed almost feral in their ferocity. Apparently, the man she'd known as her farmhand was not the real man. This crazed-looking lunatic with the strung-out eyes and bad breath had been hiding beneath that other façade. Maybe it had been an act just to get closer to her…and what he called *his* house.

His hostility stunned her, but only for a moment. The hatred in his eyes sparked terror inside her, so much so that when she tried to scream, only a breathy wheeze came out as she pushed at his chest, trying to escape.

He laughed, a frighteningly manic sound. "Go ahead and scream. No one's going to hear you. Your boyfriend's gone. I saw him in town, and heard him say he was leaving. So, I figured now was the right time to have us a little conversation." He licked his lower lip as he eyed the creamy flesh her torn shirt had exposed. "And maybe a little fun, too. I was just gonna kill ya, but now… Hmm, nice undies." He traced a finger along the lacey edge of her bra and she slapped his hand away.

"Keep your hands off me!"

He chuckled again, still staring at her breasts. "You know, I always wondered what these big tits of yours would look like without your clothes. I think we got time for me to find out…" he said as if she hadn't said a word.

She had managed to put some distance between them, but he still had a hold of her torn shirt. Understanding how much danger she was in, she clawed at his hand and jerked against his hold. Her shirt ripped a little more, but she didn't care; she wasn't free yet. She tried to spin away and out of his grasp, but he twisted his wrist and yanked her back around by the ragged edge of her shirt. It slipped over her shoulder, imprisoning her arm, but she wasn't giving up yet. Drawing on her defense training, she flattened her free hand and jabbed the heel of it into his face. She heard the crunch of bone as blood poured from his nose. His grip loosened slightly and she jerked away, but only gained a few more precious inches before his fingers tightened again.

JR brushed at his nose and then stared at the blood on his fingers. His gaze, when it crashed into hers once more, was darker than before and more menacing. A shiver of all-encompassing terror bubbled out of her chest, culminating in a long, piercing scream.

"You should've left when you had the chance," he growled right before his fist collided with her face and the whole world went black.

CHAPTER 31

By the time Cade reached the gas station in town, Cord had already texted to meet him at Sisters Café. Apparently, Cade had taken too long talking with Addie and his brother had decided an early morning snack and more coffee would be a great way to pass the time.

Pulling the fuel nozzle from his truck, Cade hung it back on the pump with a little more force than necessary. *Why couldn't he just wait?* They'd already had breakfast and Addie had filled their thermoses as well, but still, Cord had headed to the coffee shop. He could've just headed out of town—it wasn't as if Cade didn't know how to get back home.

Shaking his head, he sauntered inside the station to get his change and then returned to his truck.

He had no idea why Cord's modification of their plans annoyed him so much. His brother wasn't his problem. It was the ache in his chest that wouldn't go away that had him feeling like a grizzly with a thorn in his paw. Why did it seem like he was making a monumental mistake?

Because you don't want to leave her. You want to stay...

Cade shook his head again at that thought. Addie had broken his heart when she'd told him to go. She was done with him, but it still hurt, even if it was for the best. She'd dismissed him like the farmhand he'd been, told him to go home and get his life back. And that's exactly what he intended to do.

But the doubt still stuck in his mind as he climbed into his truck's cab. He started the engine and then sat without moving. That familiar tug around his heart was as strong as ever—pulling at him, demanding that he return to Addie. He'd been arguing with himself about leaving for the last two days and, staring at his hands as they gripped the steering wheel now, the things he should've done and said tumbled over each other in his head yet again. *Maybe I should've tried harder to stay. I could've fought harder to convince her to come with me or to let me stay. I should've shown her how much I want her, how much I want to be with her. I should've told her I'd take care of her, love her, that she'd never be alone again...*

Then her words from that morning sliced through the noise in his brain and pierced his heart. "My place is here and you need to go home and get your life back. You *should* go."

She didn't care about him, didn't want him, wouldn't even bother to consider it. She'd refused him without a second thought and then treated him with so much indifference, he'd had no choice but to go. He'd let one woman tear his heart apart, he refused to let it happen again. Besides, if running into a burning building to save her life didn't convince Addie of his feelings for her, nothing would.

Putting the truck into gear, he aimed his rig for Main Street. It took a moment for his eyes to adjust from the bright lights above the gas pumps to the darkness-draped road, but he quickly traversed the half a mile to the café with very little traffic in sight. He parked the truck behind the coffee shop and with heavy feet, he went inside.

Cord sat in one of the front booths, deep in conversation with Veta's husband Ivan, and Mark Harden in his sheriff's uniform stood beside their table.

"What's going on?" Cade asked as he stepped up beside Mark. He thought of sliding into the booth beside his brother, but Mark still made him uneasy and that kept him on his feet.

"Deputy Harden was just telling us about Addie's vandalism case and the men who attacked you," Ivan said in his heavily accented voice.

"Seems they might be the same perps," Cord added and Mark nodded when Cade looked his way.

"So, you think the guys who attacked me are the same ones who trashed Addie's house?"

"That's the theory," Mark answered. "Only problem is, we can't find the ringleaders. Ted and his two best buddies are nowhere to be found."

The line of tension between Cade's shoulders pulled a little harder. "That's not good news."

"Don't worry," Mark said, "we won't stop looking for them."

"I'm more worried about Addie being out there alone."

"Yeah," Mark nodded toward the table, "your brother said you're leaving town for a while."

Cade narrowed his eyes and his hands curled into fists at his side. "Don't get any ideas about that, Harden. She's off limits to you."

Mark shook his head. "I told you before, neither you nor Addie have to worry about me anymore. I'm just a deputy to her, and that's all."

"If I find out any different," Cade said in a dangerously low tone as he stepped into the other man's space, "that uniform won't save you."

Mark's eyebrows rose as if surprised. "You know it's not a good idea to threaten a deputy, right?"

"It's not a threat, Harden. If you hurt her, I *will* make sure you pay."

Mark's shoulders slumped and he shook his head. "I won't. You have my word on that."

Cade glared into the other man's eyes and saw something he didn't expect—the truth. Mark was telling the truth. At least he believed it to be the truth. And he hadn't backed down when Cade crowded him. The man had backbone, if nothing else, but that little glint of honesty brought Cade's opinion of him up a notch or two.

"I'll hold you to that."

"I'd expect nothing less."

Giving Mark one last hard look, Cade nodded and stepped back.

"So, none of you have had any other run-ins with Ted or Pete Jr.?" Mark asked as Cade slipped into the booth beside Cord.

"Pete Jr.?" Cade asked.

"Peter Larsen Jr.," Mark clarified. "Most people call him JR."

"Yeah," Ivan added, "because he hates his father too much to use his name."

"Pete? As in, old man Pete, who sold his place to Addie?" Cade questioned, a sinking feeling churning in his gut.

Ivan nodded. "The same. They haven't been on good terms for years."

"Has JR been in here at all over the last couple of weeks," Mark asked.

"No," Ivan replied, shaking his head, "not since that day Cade put Ted in his place for mocking Addie. But Pete Sr. was in the other day. He said JR had been out to visit him a couple of weeks ago."

"Did he say why?"

"JR asked a bunch of questions about selling the farm and was really interested in the particulars of the arrangement with Addie. I guess JR was pretty upset that his dad didn't offer it to him."

"Why would he?" Cade asked. "It didn't look like the old man had much help over the last several years. At least, not by the condition the farm was in when I got here."

"JR never had any interest in farming or ranching or anything else that required hard work," Ivan said. "He always took the easy way. Landed him in jail a couple of times that I know of. Last I heard, he'd gotten into drugs—selling, smuggling, *and* using."

Mark nodded. "That tracks with what we know as well. Did Mr. Larsen say anything else? Like where his son may have gone or where he's staying?"

"Nah, just that JR wanted money. Said he owed some bad people a lot of money, but when Pete wouldn't give it to him, JR threw such a fit that the building security had to remove him. Shook Pete up pretty good. Security told him they thought JR had been high and not in his right mind, but that hadn't been the first time he'd disrespected his father like that."

Cade shook his head. That was no way to treat your father, let alone an elder, but that wasn't what had bothered him. "What about Ted?" he asked. "Has anyone seen him?"

"Some of his buddies," Mark replied, "but none of them are exactly what you'd call reliable or helpful. They're all involved in the same mess, but from what we've been able to determine, Ted's a lot of talk. JR's the dangerous one. We might have a line on Ted Ballinger though, and I expect to hear about it soon."

Cade frowned. *JR's the dangerous one…* floated through his head as he thought back to the first of the two times he'd seen the man. JR had been sitting with Ted's gang the day Cade had walked into the café to find everyone laughing at Addie. He hadn't thought much of the cocky bastard at the time, but now something about the other man nagged at Cade.

"Thanks for the info, Ivan," Mark said as he tucked his notepad back into his pocket. "I'll head over to the senior apartments and talk with Mr. Larsen. Maybe he's heard from his son since then."

"Good luck, deputy," Cord said as Mark turned for the door.

Cade barely heard as he stared into space and rummaged through his mind, trying to locate the cause of his new agitation. What was it about their information that seemed so important? It was right there, he knew it, but couldn't quite bring whatever was bothering him forward.

JR was Pete's son. He wanted Addie's farm. He'd—

"Earth to Cade?" Cord joked. "You with me, bro?"

Cade blinked and turned to his brother. "What?"

"I said, 'Are you ready to get out of here?'"

Cade sighed, but didn't hesitate further. "Yeah, let's go."

Whatever was bugging him would come in time. Right now, he had a long drive ahead of him and they needed to get on the road before the full force of the next snowstorm hit.

Saying their goodbyes to Ivan, Cade stopped at the counter to do the same for Veta and Lana—who, surprisingly, showed little interest in flirting with him or his brother.

"Have a safe trip," was all she said, and Cade couldn't have been happier to have lost the girl's interest.

"You remember how to get there, right?" Cord asked with a grin as they walked to their vehicles. "Or do you want to follow me?"

Cade gave his brother a dark look. "You can follow me… If you can keep up."

Cord laughed. "I'll keep up, just keep it between the lines."

* * *

As they pulled onto the eastbound interstate, Cade's mind drifted back to his thoughts from the café. Something about Ted and JR and Pete and

Addie... What was it that she'd told him about her arrangement with Pete?

"I offered to give him a percentage of the profits on hay and grain for the next three years and he agreed to a discounted price..."

He remembered thinking she'd been awfully generous in that deal. Her tender heart had convinced her to give an old man something to live on, but what was it she'd said after that? Something about the hay payments...

The tires hummed along the snowy, sand-treated asphalt as Cade's truck propelled him farther and farther from the woman who occupied his mind.

Addie's smiling face flashed into his thoughts. She winked at him, flirted with him, made him feel like he was ten-feet tall. Addie's eyes staring up at him with heat and so much more as they made love. Despite everything he'd done to protect himself, she'd reached inside him, broke down his walls, and touched his lonely heart in ways no one ever had. No other woman had troubled his mind the way this one did, nor did they stay with him as he was leaving them behind.

"She pushed me away and told me to leave," he mumbled to himself, but the reminder of that fact didn't alleviate the ache in his chest. *I should've done something...more...* He shook his head and distracted himself by turning his thoughts back to what he'd heard in the café and the elusive something that kept pecking at the back of his mind. "Something about the payments..."

A chill ran down his back as Addie's words came back to him... *"If I miss a payment, the farm will revert back to him..."*

He glanced in his rearview and saw that his brother's truck was right behind him. Turning his eyes forward, he searched for a place to pull over.

He had to go back, he just hoped Cord understood.

Spying an emergency vehicle turnaround, Cade signaled his intention and turned onto the snow-packed gravel. After coming to a halt, he stepped out of the cab as Cord pulled up behind him. He too hopped out of his truck and hustled over to where Cade waited.

"What's up?" Cord asked as he stuffed his hands into his pockets.

White plumes of steam floated out of his mouth as he spoke and in the early morning darkness, it looked eerie.

"I can't do it," Cade said. "I can't leave her. She needs me."

Cord smiled. "I thought you might change your mind. She's a great girl."

"She is, but I screwed this up royally."

"I don't think she'll hold that against you. Not for long, anyway."

Cade's brows drew down in confusion and suspicion. "What do you know?"

"I know she's in love with you."

His head snapped back in surprise. "What? No...she's..."

"Yes," Cord replied. "She's in love with you, and you're in love with her."

Cade blinked but didn't argue.

"Go, brother, tell her how you feel and don't hold back. Do what you need to do to *get* her back. She's worth it. We can work out what to do with the land at home later."

"I don't know..." Cade muttered, lowering his head and kicking at a hard clot of icy snow.

"If you don't go back now, you'll regret it for the rest of your life." Cord huffed a short chuckle. "Don't get me wrong, I want you to come home, but I don't want to live with grumpy Cade. I want you to be happy and she makes you happy. Don't let her go and don't let her push you away. That's not what she wants."

Cade grinned. "I don't intend to."

Cord's return smile was broad as he slapped Cade's shoulder. "Then go get her, brother." His grin faltered. "But don't be a stranger, okay?"

"No way," Cade said, as he held out his hand. When Cord took it, Cade pulled him in for a brotherly hug. "I'm not losing track of you again."

"You'd better not," Cord replied as he pulled back and headed for his truck. "Come out for Christmas if you can," he said over his shoulder. "We'd love to have you...and Addie."

"We'll see." He waved as Cord climbed back into his truck.

Rolling down his window, Cord shouted, "No worries. I'll call you next week about your inheritance and the income from the ranch. We'll talk more then." With a wave, he rolled up his window and pulled back onto the interstate.

Cade got back in his truck, wondering about Cord's parting words. *We'd* love to have you? His inheritance? And what income? It's not as if he'd been there to do any of the work. He shook his head as he put the truck into gear and turned onto the westbound side of the interstate. There'd be plenty of time to think about that later. Right now, he had an apology to make and a woman to convince of his love. Then they'd figure out how to save her farm. Even if that wasn't a possibility, he didn't care. All he wanted was Addie, and if he had to follow her back to Seattle, he would, because he wasn't going to ever let her go again.

CHAPTER 32

The sun had barely crested the horizon by the time Cade turned down Addie's drive. An intense, internal urge had him driving a little faster than was safe on his return trip. Something tugged at him, screaming in his head that he needed to hurry, though he had no idea why. Still, the feeling was strong and insistent, and after hearing about Ted and his friends, Cade wasn't willing to risk being wrong.

"She's safe," he muttered hoping to convince that inner voice telling him to go faster that everything would be all right. He murmured the same words as he repeatedly told himself to slow down. But somehow, he ended up going faster and worry weighed on him more and more as the miles passed slowly by.

The house looked empty and dead when Cade finally pulled up beside Addie's truck. Though the only thing that hinted at something being amiss was the front door that stood wide open. In the early light, he could just make out the TV stand and part of the couch through the doorway. Fear tickled the back of his neck and his heart thudded a heavy warning. Something was very wrong. None of the lights were on, as if she'd gone back to bed after he left, but that open door said otherwise. As did her cold truck, covered with snow and still parked where it had been when he left only a couple of hours before.

Sliding out of the cab, he quietly shut the door and carefully approached the entryway. If anyone was inside, they'd probably already heard him drive up and part of him wanted to rush inside without delay, but he held back. No need to make a possibly bad situation worse by being rash.

He reached the doorway and looked inside. Nothing looked too out of place, except for a scrap of cloth that lay on the hardwood floor just inside the door. Bending, he snatched it up and turned it over in his hands. Cold swept through him and his legs turned weak when he realized the material had come from the shirt Addie had been wearing when he left earlier that morning. His hands trembled slightly as he turned it over, his mind going to all the horrible reasons such a large piece of her shirt had been torn from her body. Why did she drop it by the door? And why did she leave the door open?

"Addie!" he shouted into the house. "Addie? Are you here?" He listened intently, but no sound emanated from inside. Stepping through the doorway, he slowly, carefully searched through every room, trepidation crushing him with every minute that passed without finding her. All he found as he hunted through every room was some of her things from her closet strewn on the floor in her bedroom, her purse upended on the dining room table along with her empty wallet, and the canister of tea bags she kept in the cupboard open and spread across the counter. Though Cade found those things odd, they didn't seem overly alarming, but still…

Why would she dump this stuff all over the place?

Standing in the kitchen, he pulled out his phone and dialed Addie's number. It rang until it went to voice mail. He dialed two more times, praying she would answer, but each one ended the same as the first. He tried to slow his racing heart and banish the terrible thoughts of the worst possible reasons for her absence that kept crowding his mind. He couldn't think clearly if he panicked. And if he panicked, he would let her down.

"I shouldn't have left her," he mumbled and shook his head, but self-blame wasn't going to help her, either.

Ted had to be behind this. He had a good motive, but then, so did

Pete's son. The question was, which one? Or was it both? That was possible, especially since the police hadn't managed to locate either of them. *Maybe they'd teamed up to get what they wanted. Damn...* That thought scared the crap out of him. "How the hell am I going to find her?"

Staring around the tidy kitchen, Cade wasn't sure what to do next. The fear that something horrible had happened to Addie kept jumbling his thoughts. He was debating his next act when he heard a vehicle pull up outside.

Maybe she'd gotten a ride with someone. His heart leaped at the possibility even as his hand clamped around the torn piece of her shirt. He dashed through the front room and onto the front steps, hoping to see Addie's blonde hair swirling around her shoulders as she exited a friend's car.

Instead, he found Jorje, just showing up for work.

Cade's heart sunk to his toes, but he wasn't about to give up.

"*Buenos dios,* Cade," Jorje said with a friendly wave, but Cade wasn't in the mood for pleasantries.

"Jorje, have you heard from Addie this morning?"

Jorje frowned. "No. I haven't."

"Did she say anything to you about being gone this morning?"

He shook his head. "No, señor, she did not. Is something wrong?"

Cade swallowed hard and glanced around before his eyes settled on his friend's face. "She's missing."

"Missing?" Jorje's eyebrows shot up in surprise and then lowered in concern. "How long?"

"I left her here, in front of the house, about two hours ago. She's not in the house, there's no note inside, and, as far as I know, she had no plans to leave." He rubbed the back of his neck and looked back at the front door. "Plus," he added as he waved back at the house, "the front door was open when I got here, and I found this on the floor." He held out the piece of her torn shirt.

Jorje's frown deepened when he recognized it.

"Do you have any idea where Ted might've taken her?" He hated saying those words out loud. It somehow made the impossible so scarily possible.

His heart fluttered rapidly in his chest as he waited for Jorje's reply, hoping for a break that would lead him to Addie.

Jorje shook his head. "Ted wouldn't take her. He's a...*un matón*...a bully, but that's all he is. Kidnapping doesn't seem like something he'd do. He'd be more likely to do things he wouldn't get caught doing, like scare her or something."

Addie's depictions of the noises she'd heard in the middle of the night several days ago and the voices that had told her to leave popped into Cade's mind. *I guess she hadn't been dreaming after all.*

"JR," Jorje continued, nodding to himself. "I can see him taking someone, especially a woman."

"Why would he take her?"

"JR's a...bully too, but he's also mean as a snake and doesn't care what others think. Plus, he had a thing for her. Not sure if it was that he liked her or hated her, but he used to stare at her a lot when we were all working together and he talked—"

"You worked together? He worked here, with Addie?"

Jorje tilted his head. "Yeah, I thought you knew that."

"No," Cade said. "I didn't. I mean, I knew Addie had another farmhand working here with you and Ted, but I didn't know his name until just now—or maybe I just didn't remember it."

"Well, he'd be my bet if something bad has happened. *El hombre* está *loco.*"

Cade nodded. He'd gotten the impression JR was a little unhinged himself. He stared toward the hills, the adrenaline in his veins urging him to hurry up and start looking, his brain running so fast he felt a little out of control. But he had no idea where to start.

"Where would he take her?" Cade asked as he turned to Jorje and pinned him with his gaze. "JR, if he took her, where would he hold up?"

Jorje tilted his head. He stood silently thinking for so long, Cade wanted to shake him.

"The Mouse House," Jorje blurted out a couple of heartbeats later.

Cade frowned. "The *what?*"

"The Mouse House," Jorje said, his eyes grew wider as he warmed to his guess. "Yeah, he's got a dumpy, mouse-infested trailer up on the Manastash." He pointed over Cade's shoulder to the northwest at the long ridge of hills in the distance. "But why would he even be angry at Addie? He never seemed to care that she fired him."

"He's Pete Larsen's son, and he wants this farm. I think he's the one who's been harassing Addie, trying to run her off so the farm would revert back to his father. Then, he'd coerce the old man into either giving it to him or selling it again. Only this time, JR would be around to collect the share he thinks he deserves, all so he can pay off debts he owes to bad people. And now Addie's missing and not answering her phone."

Jorje's face turned white under his naturally tan skin. "*Dios mios,*" he muttered.

Cade's stomach dropped like a stone at his friend's dismay. "What?"

"I'll show you where to look." Jorje turned and headed for his truck.

"Wait," Cade called, reaching out to tug on Jorje's arm. "Tell me what you're thinking."

"JR's not a good guy," Jorje said. "He's the only one Ted will back down from, and Ted doesn't pull punches. If JR took her..." He shook his head. "We need to hurry...and we're going to need help."

"What kind of help?" Cade asked as he started for his rig.

"The official kind of help," Jorje said as he pulled open his truck's door. "We should call the sheriff. JR's got weapons up there and God knows what else."

Cade hesitated as he opened his driver's side door. Addie didn't trust the sheriff and he had his own misgivings about the department. But was he willing to risk her life with a man who might kill her out of spite or for his own profit...or for fun?

He remembered the honesty in Mark Harden's eyes when he'd said all he was to Addie was a deputy. The man had clearly not touched alcohol for over two months and showed every indication that he had nothing but remorse for the way he'd treated Addie. But did that make him trustworthy?

Not necessarily, Cade thought, but then again, if JR had guns, they wouldn't stand a chance without Mark and his fellow deputy's help. And he *knew* Addie was in danger. He'd felt it the moment he decided to come back, and it had only gotten worse since.

"Do you have their number?" he asked Jorje.

"*Sí.*"

"Call 'em," Cade said. "Tell them where to meet us, 'cause I'm not waiting for them."

Jorje's jaw tightened and he nodded. "I'll call them on the way."

Cade climbed behind the wheel and started his truck. One leg bounced anxiously while he waited for Jorje to back up and pull out of the way. Then he watched as the other man hopped out of his rig and jogged over to Cade's. He yanked open the passenger door and crawled in.

"Makes sense to go together," he said.

"Yeah," Cade muttered as he threw his vehicle into reverse and headed for the driveway.

Hang on, Addie, he thought. *I'm coming…*

CHAPTER 33

The icy air in the small, messy living room prickled Addie's skin. Not that the lower temperature had anything to do with her shivers or chattering teeth, or the cold ball of dread that sat inside her like a lump of lead. That was entirely the fault of the man who manically stuffed wood into an old stove, attempting to start a fire. His erratic movements and agitated mumbling sent chills up and down her spine.

JR grumbled a string of curses, and Addie pushed a little farther into the corner where she sat on her knees.

After carrying her kicking and screaming from the truck, JR's fetid breath had made her gag when he'd dropped her to her knees and licked at her parched lips. She'd pulled back and slammed her forehead into his already injured nose. Then he'd slapped her, twice, before her ragged shirt had finally torn free of her body and he shoved her onto the dirty linoleum floor.

"Damn bitch thinks she can do whatever she wants," he muttered to himself as his dirty fingers gingerly examined his swollen nose.

With her hands and feet bound together and gasping through her gag, she'd done her best to push herself into the corner away from him. He'd watched her, glaring down at her for several seconds after she'd bumped against the wall. The fevered look in his rapidly shifting eyes had made her heart slam painfully against her ribs, fear of what he would do next chilling her bones. But then he'd suddenly turned and started filling the stove.

He had tried something similar before he'd dragged her from her house. She'd awoken on the floor in her hallway, cold air rushing in from the open front door and her face throbbing from his first punch. She'd lost consciousness for a minute or two and as she came to, she'd heard JR in her bedroom mumbling to himself as he rummaged around.

The next thing she knew, he'd grabbed her shirt again and hauled her to her feet.

"Where's your money?" he'd shouted in her face, his horrible breath nearly making her retch as she pushed at his chest. "I know you've got some cash around here. Where do you keep it? Tell me!" He'd grabbed her arms in a bruising grip and shook her so hard her teeth rattled.

"I-In my p-purse," she said, still pushing away from him.

"Where!" he shouted.

"Di-Dining room," she stuttered, as tears of fear and pain rolled down her cheeks.

She cried out when he grabbed a fistful of her hair and towed her into the other room. Finding her purse hanging from the back of a chair, he'd dumped the contents on the scratched, wooden tabletop and snatched her wallet from amongst the clutter.

"Forty bucks? That's all you got?" he said with another hard shake that nearly tore her hair out by the roots.

"K-Kit-Kitchen," she sobbed as her hands gripped his wrist in an attempt to lessen the wrenching on her scalp.

"Please," she begged, "just take it and go. You don't have to hurt me."

He stuffed the bills from her wallet into the front pocket of his jeans and tugged her into the kitchen.

"Me and you's got unfinished business," he said, pulling her up and pressing her back against the counter. His hand was still tangled in her hair as he bent her backward and pressed his lips to hers. She had tried to turn her head, tried to escape his disgusting probing tongue, but he held her firm and forced his way inside. Too shocked and afraid to respond, her body went still while he ravaged her mouth.

His free hand had slid up her side and closed over her breast, squeezing it tight and pinching her nipple until she sobbed and squirmed to get away. He jerked her bra strap over her shoulder and uncovered the tormented bud. Pulling back, his frantic eyes glared at her, then lowered to her bared breast. The look on his face turned her mouth dry and her heart raced faster than before.

"N-n-no," she pleaded through her tears. "P-Please, no, don't."

His gaze met hers and the evil smile that crossed his face had made her shudder.

"Oh, yes," he'd said and, dropping his head, his mouth landed on her breast. He proceeded to savage the sensitive tip, licking, sucking, biting, and showed no sign of slowing his attack as his hand pushed between her legs. "Shit, this is better than I'd thought it would be."

At first, shock had kept her immobile, but then anger and desperation snapped her out of it and she fought back. She screamed as she threw her first punch and kept on screaming as she hit, and scratched, and kicked him until he stopped.

He stepped back and slapped her. She cried out as her head bounced off the cupboard and she tried to pull away, but his hand was in her hair again, too tangled to break free.

"Please," she sobbed, "s-someone will be here s-s-soon. If you don't w-want to go to jail, you s-should let me g-go and leave."

"Your boyfriend's gone. No one's gonna save you this time, sweetheart."

She gulped and forced her trembling knees to stay straight, hating the way he used the endearment that Cade had so often said to her.

"But, just in case," he'd said as he cupped her breast and squeezed again, "I've got a better place where no one will disturb us." His fevered eyes flashed with lust and eagerness. "Don't worry, you'll get used to my touch."

Bile bubbled into her throat, choking and burning the already raw flesh and keeping her from screaming again.

"No." It was barely a whisper.

"Oh, yes," JR said with a nasty smile. "Now, where's the rest of your money?"

She'd been too afraid to do anything but tell him. Once he dug the five twenties out of her tea bin, he'd pocketed the cash and then grabbed a serrated knife from her kitchen drawer.

"No!" she screeched as he dragged her to the garage door. "Don't hurt me. I won't say anything. You don't have to hurt me."

He'd only laughed and tugged her into the darkened room.

She'd fought him, given everything she had in a last ditch effort to escape, but he'd been too strong. Before she knew what he was about to do, he'd shoved her face down on the cold floor and had bound her hands and feet. Then he ripped off another large piece of her torn shirt and shoved it into her mouth. She tried to spit it out, but another section of the rope he'd tied her with slipped between her teeth to hold it in.

He'd hauled her up over his shoulder and carried her back into the house, only to dump her unceremoniously onto her bed. More tears spilled from her eyes as she squirmed away from him, but he'd only laughed and raked his gaze over her.

"This is kinda fun," he said, more to himself than to her. "I like you better this way, tied up and muzzled. When I get you home, I'm gonna enjoy stripping you bare and stretching you out for my pleasure. Now…" he clapped his hands together and headed for her closet, "don't you move. I'll be right back." He stepped into her closet and began rummaging again.

Glancing around her room, sweat had trickled down her face and her heart had raced so hard that her chest hurt, but she'd frantically searched for a weapon. Something, anything that she could use to either get herself free or hurt him, or both. Whatever she had to do to stop him.

Panic swirled inside and kept her senses on high alert. He was crazy. He meant to rape her, to eventually kill her, and she couldn't allow that to happen. She had too many things to live for.

I should've gone with Cade, she'd thought miserably. *Why did I let him go without telling him how I feel?* If she'd been smart, she would've taken him however she could get him because…because she loved him. If all it had meant was spending days and nights with him until he tired of her, she should've taken them and never looked back.

Instead, she'd let him leave, thinking she didn't want him.

If I can just slow JR down, stall him just long enough for Jorje to arrive... At least then, someone would know and could call the police.

Unfortunately, that's not what had happened.

"Ah-ha!" he'd shouted before she got a chance to do more than roll to the end of the bed. "There it is." He'd come out of the closet waving a set of papers in his hands. She hadn't needed him to tell her that it was the deed to her property as he smiled triumphantly and pocketed it.

How did he know my business papers were in the closet? Has he been in the house when I wasn't around? Or even when I was? That thought terrified her even more. Then his crazy eyes had taken her in at a glance and a deeper chill froze her bones.

"Where do you think you're going?" he'd said with a twisted grin. "I've got plans for you."

And then he'd come for her. She'd tried to fight him off, but it had been useless. He'd hit her again, punched her in the stomach so hard she couldn't breathe for a few seconds.

While she struggled to regain her breath, he'd flipped her over his shoulder and lugged her out to his truck, where he'd tossed her onto the front seat and pulled a pillowcase over her head.

"Be a good girl and I won't have to hurt you so much next time," he said as he slammed the passenger side door.

He'd forced her to lie on her back with her head in his lap while he drove. When he'd fondled her breasts again, she'd tried to roll and kicked at the door.

"Stop it," he'd hissed as he pinched her nipple, but she only fought harder until he pulled over and tied her wrists to her ankles.

Now, she huddled in the corner of JR's ramshackled house, still bound and gagged, wearing nothing but her underwear and jeans as her kidnapper coaxed the fire to life inside the stove.

Slamming the door on the licking flames, JR turned to stare at her. His leg bounced incessantly while his eyes moved over her. The lust still flickered in his eyes, but something else was there now, too. Fear?

"Bitch," he mumbled as he turned away and almost ran to the kitchen. As he fumbled through items in his tiny kitchen, Addie's gaze travelled to the front door.

Could she get out before he realized she was gone? She wouldn't make it far, tied as she was, and the last thing she needed was for him to hit her again. Her face hurt from the blows he'd already landed and her stomach still ached from the punches he'd aimed there earlier. Still, if she rolled quietly, she might be able to turn the doorknob with her chin and fall out onto the deck.

Working up the courage to try, she jumped when JR let out a screeching "Whew, yeah!" from the kitchen. A moment later, he sniffed loudly several times and then appeared at the doorway, rubbing at his nose, though a dusting of white still edged his upper lip.

He's high, she thought, the idea scaring her stiff. If he was crazy enough to kidnap and threaten her, what else would he do with a narcotic in his system? Or maybe he'd already had it in his system and this little booster was just to fuel his bravado.

He smiled at her, his leg still bouncing rapidly, as he held up a pair of scissors.

Her eyes widened in fear and her chest squeezed tight.

Snapping the blades open and closed, JR stalked her as she frantically looked around for something to save herself. Her eyes landed on a poker that sat beside the stove, but JR was already between it and her. She looked up, trembling, tears once again flooding her eyes, just before she dived for the poker.

He caught her easily and pushed her onto her back. Holding her down with a chokehold around her throat, he grinned wider as he slipped one blade of the scissors between her jeans and her skin. A long snip followed and she began to scream as the blades made quick work of the denim.

JR lifted the blades in front of her face and cackled. He lowered them, the cold metal caressing the skin of her chest. Then, with a quick clench of his hand, he cut through her bra strap. It snapped open, the cup barely clinging to her breast, as his eyes grew even more fevered.

She struggled against his hold, but she couldn't break away, until she was suddenly rolled onto her belly. The cut he'd made in her pant leg flapped open and he pulled it aside to expose one of her cheeks covered only by a thin nylon panty. Pausing, he grasped her cringing flesh, kneading it. "Nice ass," he muttered as he pulled up on the rope connecting her hands and feet.

Fighting against his hold, she tried to scream, but the way he held her, she was practically laying on her chin. All that came out was a rasping squeak.

Something tugged at the rope and then she fell flat on the floor. She groaned at the soothing feeling of being able to straighten her legs, but her relief was short-lived. A minute later, JR had untied her ankles and yanked her cut-up jeans off her leg. Tossing them aside, he rolled her onto her back and dropped to his knees between her thighs, forcing her legs open wide. She screamed again, knowing what he planned next, but it sounded more like a gargle.

"I had planned to tie you to my bed," he said as he grabbed her by the neck to stop her from wiggling away, "but I don't think I can wait that long." His eyes drifted over her body as he blatantly adjusted himself. Apparently liking what he saw, his mouth curled upward and he met her frightened eyes. "I've been waiting a long time for this," he said and, once again wielding the scissors, he cut through the center of her bra. Using the metal tips, he flicked the cup away, baring both generous breasts and grinning wider as she continued to struggle, screaming through her gag.

Holding the scissors up, his lips parted, showing his yellowing teeth. "Only two more little snips and we'll have a lot of fun." He cocked his head. "Well, at least, I'll have a lot of fun. Soon you'll be screaming for me not to stop," he said, dragging the dull side of the scissors over each rosy tip of her breasts and then down over her belly and between her thighs.

Addie's scream sounded feeble with his hand digging into her windpipe, but she bucked and writhed wildly, trying to knock him off of her. With her legs free she could run now, move faster than the wind if she had to, but he had her crammed into the corner with a strangling hand around her neck. There was no escaping him and his plans, no second chance for her to make things right with Cade. She'd never see him again.

A sob of regret broke from her lips. JR would rape her as many times as he liked. She would scream and fight until she couldn't any longer, but out here, in the middle of nowhere—judging by how long they drove and his cavalier attitude about the noise she made—no one would hear her or stop him.

More tears filled her eyes, blurring his hated face as the cold blade of the scissors slid between her hip and panties. She released another garbled scream, bucking like a wild mustang, but she knew it was no use. He had her, and would have his way with her, would most likely force her to sign over her land, her home, and then kill her.

I'm sorry, Cade, she thought and a pang struck her heart even as she fought against her attacker, making him work hard to complete his plans.

She wanted to hope she'd survive, find some way to escape, and see Cade again, but after what JR intended to do to her, would Cade still want her?

Of course, he would, she told herself, though she wasn't sure if she believed it.

"Stop squirming or I'll hurt you more," JR threatened, but she didn't listen. She was running on autopilot, in full fight mode. Blood pounding in her ears, her mind focused on survival and escape. She couldn't hear anything else, couldn't form sentences. All she could do was fight for her life and scream through her gag until she couldn't any more. And hope against hope that someone happened by. Maybe they would help. They might just call the police, but that was better than nothing.

"Stop wiggling," JR ordered and released her neck to slap her hard.

The stinging pain made her pause. Then she realized he wasn't holding her down and tried to roll aside and kick him, but it was no good. She didn't even get to her side before his hand was around her neck again, pushing her down and squeezing off her air.

"I said, hold still," JR shouted inches from her face, his nasty breath making her gag. He held her that way for endless seconds until blackness began to creep into her vision. She wanted to claw at his hand, but her hands were still tied—her arms and legs were growing too heavy to move anyway. His eyes locked with hers as her struggles slowed and then he loosened his hold. "That's better."

She coughed, and he picked up the scissors where they lay on her belly. He slid them back into place on her hip and she screamed as she heard them slowly cut through the thin material. She screamed through her gag, so loud people in town should've heard it, until it felt as if something tore free in her throat, and then she screamed again and again and again...

CHAPTER 34

The snow had started falling again by the time Cade and Jorje reached Manastash Ridge. The windshield wipers, slapped back and forth, removing the white veneer, but more snowflakes rapidly replaced them, making it difficult to see in the early morning darkness. Cade had slowed his old truck as it bounced over the uneven dirt track Jorje had directed him to. Their progress along the pothole-infested road thus far had been agonizingly slow, but Jorje said JR's place was close.

Cade prayed his friend was right. He had a sinking feeling that Addie needed him worse than he'd first thought. That driving need urged him to slam the accelerator to the floor once more, and the consequences be damned. But if he lost control and slid into one of the tall, sturdy trees that lined this narrow, rutted road, they may be too late to help her.

"Pull over up there," Jorje said, pointing at a wider area ahead of them where they could park the truck and not block the road.

Cade glanced at his friend. "Are you sure?"

Jorje nodded. "*Si*. JR's place is just on the other side of those trees," he said, pointing again, "maybe half a mile. If we drive any closer, he'll know we're coming. I think it would be better if our arrival was a surprise."

Cade agreed. He pulled off the road, making sure to leave enough room for the sheriff's cars to make it through. Jorje had called the sheriff's office with a rundown on the situation as they left Addie's driveway, and told them how to find JR's place. They should be arriving soon, but Cade couldn't wait to find out. He needed to find Addie and ensure her safety.

He slammed on the brakes, then shifted into park, and reached for his door handle.

"Shouldn't we wait for the sheriff?" Jorje asked.

"The sheriff won't be here for another twenty minutes, if we're lucky. You can wait and direct them," Cade said as his door swung open. "I'm going in."

Jorje's forehead furrowed. "You can't go in alone. JR has weapons in there. He'll shoot you as soon as look at you." He opened his door and hopped out of the cab.

"What do you suggest?" Cade asked as he quietly shut his door and rounded the front of the truck.

"We stay on the road as long as we can and watch for traps in the brush."

Cade lifted an eyebrow at that and Jorje sighed.

"JR's very paranoid. He's got booby-traps and warning signals all over the place."

"Cameras?" Cade asked, worried that the man would see them coming and hurt Addie.

"No, nothing like that. He's got nylon strings stretched over open areas with cans attached that'll make a huge racket if you trip them."

Cade frowned. *What kind of guy was this JR?*

"Anything else?"

"Holes to catch prowlers," Jorje replied as he started down the rutted path with Cade right beside him. "JR once said that he'd dug several around here. He may have put stakes in the bottom, but I'm not sure about that."

Cade stared. *Stakes?*

"I know," Jorje said, seeing Cade's questioning look. "Like I said, he's paranoid. Always worried someone will break in and steal his drugs or guns or whatever else he's got hidden away up here. He's also afraid of getting raided by the sheriff. I think he sees himself as some kind of gangster."

Cade nodded, remembering how twitchy JR had seemed at the café. His thoughts turned to Addie. What would a man like that do to her? Especially if Jorje was right about JR's interest in her. And what about his interest in her farm? From everything he'd heard, the man seemed determined to get it back, no matter the cost.

"Do you know if JR had caused any problems for Addie before now?"

Jorje shook his head. "No, but I wouldn't be surprised to find out he did. Like I said, he was interested in her, but she never paid him any mind. She barely acknowledged his existence. Ted was the one who always held her attention."

Ted. He was another problem Cade couldn't afford to ignore. "Do you think they may have done this together?"

"I doubt it. Ted wouldn't have come out here. He hates JR's place."

"It'd be the perfect place for him to lie low," Cade replied. "No one would think to look for him out here, if he hated it that much."

Jorje's brow furrowed and he nodded. "Maybe…but I still doubt it."

"We should expect it anyway."

"*Si,*" Jorje agreed and grabbed Cade's arm to stop him. "We should also be quieter. The house is on the other side of these trees."

Cade nodded and followed as Jorje led the way into the forest and to the edge of the brush, careful where they placed their feet. They crouched behind the low-hanging boughs of an evergreen and scoped out the ramshackled mobile home in the small, junk-littered clearing beyond.

They were looking at the front of the house at a slight angle and could just see part of the front room through the awkwardly hanging shades. A single light seemed to illuminate the front room, but little else was visible.

"That's JR's truck," Jorje whispered and pointed at the rundown-looking red pickup in front of the house. "It's the only vehicle he has, so he's definitely here."

Cade nodded. Movement through the partially uncovered window caught his eye. JR was moving around inside. He had something in his hand, waving it back and forth in front of his face as if taunting someone.

Addie…

JR dropped to his knees and appeared to be struggling with

something…or someone.

She must be fighting him. Good. At least, that meant she was still alive.

They could hear scuffling going on inside and then a ringing slap that thrust Cade to his feet and toward the front door. He had no idea if Jorje followed and no thought about Ted entered his mind, nor did he hear the distant rush of tires speeding over the muddy road behind them. The only thing that burned in his mind was that JR had hurt Addie, probably planned to do far more, and he would not allow that to happen.

A terrified, slightly muffled scream halted his breath. A long heartbeat later, Cade was running toward the house and up the rickety stairs. He yanked open the front door and rushed inside.

The front room was mostly empty, a card table littered with used, unwashed dishes and one chair sat across from Cade, and to its left, a ratty old couch had been pushed against the far wall. A small TV had been perched on a box across from the couch and a tiny coffee table was also covered with dishes and garbage. In the far corner, on the other side of the couch, were two people. A naked woman lay on her back with a much bigger man hovering over her. Cade reacted on instinct. Yes, he was there for Addie, but he would have done the same for any woman. The fact that this was Addie made him far more reckless.

Because his emotions were already running on high, the hot, blinding fury that crashed over him at seeing JR assaulting her propelled him across the room. The other man glanced over his shoulder as Cade approached, but it didn't matter. Cade grabbed JR by the hair and the back of his jeans and tossed him to the side.

Addie squirmed backward until her back was pressed against the wall. Her eyes were wide and terrified, and she didn't seem to recognize him, at least not at first.

The bruises on her face registered and he muttered an angry curse.

"Addie?" he said gently, wanting to pull her trembling form into his arms, but he didn't get the chance.

JR had gotten back to his feet and was coming for him. "You son of a bitch," he shouted as he lunged at Cade with something metallic in his hand. Cade tried to avoid it, but he refused to step aside. Addie was right behind him and he didn't want this lunatic anywhere near her.

He barely glimpsed the long, sharp blade before it plunged deep into his side. The pain was instantaneous as JR buried it to the hilt and twisted. Warmth streamed down Cade's side, but he didn't have time to check it. Groaning, he pushed his attacker back and threw an upper cut at JR's chin that had him stumbling backward and upending the box and TV as he smashed into the wall, the bloody scissors still in his hand. He shook his head as if stunned and Cade went on the offensive.

He threw another punch at JR that sent him sprawling into the narrow hallway to Cade's right. Just as JR hit the ground, movement to Cade's left distracted him. Turning his head, he breathed a quick sigh of relief at seeing Jorge in the doorway.

"Get her out of here," Cade shouted, nodding his head to indicate Addie.

Jorje nodded and dashed to the couch, where he snagged a ragged afghan off its cushions to wrap around Addie's nakedness.

Addie's eyes met Cade's. He read fear and something else flickering in the coffee-colored depths. Then her eyes widened in alarm and she screamed, "Look out!"

Cade returned his full attention to JR, who had gotten back to his feet and was barreling toward him. Like a battering ram, JR's shoulder slammed into Cade's middle, launching them backward several feet, blocking the exit.

Cade landed on his back with JR on top of him. He groaned as all the wind rushed from his lungs. JR immediately straddled his chest, making getting his breath back almost impossible. Then pain exploded along the side of Cade's head, one side and then the other, disorienting him. He put his arms up to block the blows but a few more fell before they ceased.

"You just wait right there, *George*," JR said smugly as he glanced over his shoulder at Jorje. "You've got something there that belongs to me."

He leaned to his left, reaching for something, and Cade took advantage. Heaving up with his hips and pushing with his arms, he shoved JR to the side and rolled out from under him.

"Come on, you bastard," he taunted JR, "is that all you got?" He needed to distract the wild-eyed man so Jorje could get Addie to safety.

"Hell no, *cowboy*," JR smirked, his head twitching to the side and back as he sniffed and wiped at his nose. "I've got more than enough to take you down." He lifted the bloody scissors again and dove at Cade.

He heard Addie's scream as if from far away, but he didn't have time to think about it as JR tackled him into the wall. The sharp, open blade sliced over his left bicep as he shifted to avoid it, and JR knocked him to the side with a punch to his chin. He stumbled to his knees, shaking his head to clear the darkness that threatened, a bout of weakness zapping his strength. He looked up to see JR's face twisted with hate as he roared and lunged at Cade with the crimson-coated blade lifted above his head.

Everything seemed to slow.

Somewhere, Addie cried out again and a deep voice said, "Get her out of here."

A shuffling noise followed with Addie's cries not to leave him, and then that same deep voice shouted, "Sheriff's office. Stop or I'll shoot."

Cade threw up his arms to ward off the blade aimed at his chest and ducked his head as JR hurtled toward him.

The loud bang made Cade jump and he cringed at the sharp pain that lanced through his forearm. The next instant, JR slammed into him, crushing his body against the inside wall, and Cade felt himself falling. His head rebounded off the floor, his sight flicked and blurred. Someone approached where Cade lay with a heavy burden strewn over him, crushing him into the cold floor. The person held something long and black in their outstretched hands, but he couldn't see it clearly. He tried to move, to get up, but the weight on top of him kept him in place.

Suddenly more exhausted than he remembered being moments before, a deep ache in his side, and more warmth soaking his skin, Cade closed his eyes and sighed. He'd done his best. He only hoped it was enough to save Addie.

His eyes popped open. "Addie," he croaked.

"She's all right, Cade," that deep voice said.

Cade squinted at the dark-haired man who crouched beside him. The gray eyes that smiled at him seemed familiar. "Mark...?"

The crushing weight rolled off him and he moaned at the intense pain in his side. The threat seemed to have disappeared as Cade's eyelids blinked closed.

I'll just rest here a moment, he thought as his mind drifted and the world faded away.

CHAPTER 35

Semi-darkness surrounded Addie as she adjusted the thin, white hospital blanket around her shoulders and pulled a second more tightly over her legs. She glanced into the empty blackness outside the room's large windows and huddled a little farther into her blankets. Unable to see much else but the night beyond the glass, she could clearly see that snow was falling. The minuscule flakes fell slowly through the pale shafts of the hospital's sign several yards away. The bleak and lonely image made her heart speed up and for some reason, a flutter of fear danced in her chest.

Averting her gaze, she shifted on the vinyl visitor's chair. Tucking the blanket's edges in around her body to keep the chill out of her makeshift cocoon, she settled back into the chair's thin cushion once again. It wasn't exactly the most comfortable place she'd ever reclined, but she wasn't ready to go back to her bed in the small room down the hall, nor did she wish to be alone. At least, she had Cade's presence here, even if he was still unconscious.

Beneath her blankets, a chill prickled her skin, her breath halted, and the cold dread she'd been fighting all day made her check the machines that monitored Cade's heart rate and respiratory system. All the colored lines looked the same as they had the last time she'd looked at them only minutes ago. He was still alive.

A sigh of relief started her breathing again and she returned her gaze to Cade's still form.

She'd spent most of the day answering all sorts of questions by the sheriff and the doctors, and then lying in bed, anxiously waiting to discover if Cade would survive the awful damage JR had inflicted with those horrid scissors. The waiting had been tortuous—and still was since he hadn't awakened from surgery yet, at least not enough to be coherent. The staff hadn't wanted her in the room, but she'd finally convinced them. In her fragile state of mind, she hadn't been able to bear not being near Cade. When they'd told her she couldn't see him, she'd panicked and thrown such a childish tantrum that they'd finally relented.

Humiliation burned her cheeks. Thinking back on the scene now, she regretted acting like a spoiled, angry child. She hadn't meant to, but she couldn't have stopped it, either.

Mentally and emotionally, she was a total mess.

The only thing—besides seeing Cade alive—that kept her from slamming the door closed and barricading herself in this room was the fact that JR was dead.

"I had to shoot," Mark had said when he and the same female deputy Addie had given a statement to after the fire had arrived.

"I'm glad you did," Addie had said with a little shiver. "I have no doubt he would've killed us all if he could have."

Mark nodded. "Mr. Rivera told us about JR Larsen's arsenal. He hadn't exaggerated. We found several handguns and other firearms in the house. It's a good thing he didn't have any of them handy, for you and Mr. Brody's sake, at least."

She'd smiled and thanked him again for coming to their rescue, but knowing that the situation could've turned out so much worse hadn't made her feel any better, or any safer.

She hated being happy that JR was dead. It wasn't like her to wish ill on another person, but after bruised ribs, a black eye, a swollen lip, and assorted other cuts, scrapes, and bruises, Addie wasn't feeling all that forgiving. Especially not once she realized how badly Cade had been hurt.

She glanced at the bed, where his long body lay so still. A white sheet and blankets covered him to his chest and his hands rested on top. His head, on the thin pillow, was turned slightly, but even in the dim light, she could see the discoloration on his handsome face. The beating he'd taken had been almost as bad as hers, but it wasn't the reason he lay unconscious on that bed.

The doctors had joined the edges of the long slice that had been gouged through his left bicep with three butterfly bandages, and gauze covered his right forearm to keep the two wounds beneath them—that had needed ten stitches to close—clean. JR had been vicious with the blades, but he'd inflicted the most damage with his first strike—when he drove the six-inch shears into Cade's abdomen. Cade had refused to step out of the way when JR had run toward him with the scissors in his hand. He'd stood his ground to protect her—she had no doubt about that—and it had cost him in blood and pain.

The hospital blankets now concealed the large swath of white that wrapped about Cade's middle, but Addie had seen it. Earlier, Addie had watched when a nurse pulled back the blankets to examine the area. A little blood had seeped through—not enough to cause the nurse any concern, but it worried Addie. She repeatedly had to fight the urge to check it again herself. To touch him to make sure his skin wasn't too hot—or too cold—and that his chest still moved.

"What about infection?" she'd asked the doctor when he came to talk to her after Cade's surgery. "I know an abdominal wound can be very dangerous."

"Yes, it can," the doctor had replied as he stood beside her bed, "but the surgery went well and I see no reason to think Mr. Brody won't make a full and uneventful recovery." He smiled. "Try not to worry, Miss Malory, he's in good hands here."

She had nodded, but Addie was still paranoid. Sepsis could kill him, and the idea of losing Cade now made her chest so tight, it felt as if she were being strangled.

A soft sob escaped her and tears threatened again as a flash of JR grinning gleefully with his hand around her neck, squeezing tighter and tighter, came to life in her mind. Another reason she didn't want to be alone or go to sleep. The doctor had encouraged her to rest and she'd tried, but she kept seeing JR's hated face, reliving the terror he'd wreaked on her, and waking with strangled screams covered in sweat.

She tightened her arms around her middle. "Get a grip," she muttered to herself for the hundredth time. *Be strong, you're not a victim.*

The on-call therapist she'd talked with earlier that afternoon had said her unreasonable fear and feelings of vulnerability were normal, considering what she'd been through.

"But he didn't rape me," she'd argued. "A few punches and some pain shouldn't make me feel so…so…so out of control!"

"Trauma can make us feel all kinds of things," the doctor had said with a shake of her head. "The experience you had *was* traumatic, whether you think so or not. And you *should* expect your emotions to be a little unpredictable for a while. It's normal. With time, some support, and therapy, you can get past it and live a normal life."

Normal? Ha! she thought with a derisive chuckle. *I doubt I'll ever feel normal again.*

* * *

Afternoon sunlight streamed through the double windows of Cade's hospital room, bathing every corner in light or shadow. The machines were all turned off and he'd kicked the blankets to the side so he could sit on the edge of the bed to pull on his clothes.

The doctor had cleared him an hour ago and the paperwork for his release had finally come through.

Thank God, he thought as he pulled on a pair of jeans someone had brought him from the duffle in his truck. He didn't want to spend another second in this place. Not that he had any particular aversion to hospitals, he just disliked laying around doing nothing.

A sharp pain lanced through his abdomen as he reached back for the sleeve of his shirt. He grunted, but gritting his teeth, he reached back again, determined to be dressed before the nurse or Addie returned. The last thing he wanted was for one of them to start waiting on him again.

He'd awoken the day before, disoriented by the strange surroundings and wondering where he was. Something heavy rested against his thigh and he'd felt a warm hand grip his. When he'd looked down, he found Addie asleep with her head propped against his leg and her hand in his.

The bruises on her face had made him flinch and stirred a vengeful rage inside him as memories of his fight with JR had crashed into his mind. Unwilling to disturb Addie's slumber, however, he hadn't moved. She'd looked so small and tired and frail, and all he'd wanted to do since that moment was hold her.

When she awoke a short time later, there had been something different about her...something in her eyes. He hadn't been able to determine exactly what, but he knew it had something to do with what had happened.

"Damn him," Cade muttered to himself as he buttoned his shirt and reached for a pair of socks. He had no sympathy for JR. The man deserved worse than a bullet in the back for what he'd done to Addie, and after his conversation with Mark Harden, his opinion had only strengthened.

"It appears JR had acted alone when he kidnapped Miss Malory," Mark had told him this morning when he came to get Cade's statement.

Call him over-protective or even jealous, but Cade had liked the way the deputy had distanced himself from Addie, even in his speech. "How do you know?"

"Ted Ballinger," Mark replied. "He was hiding out with a new girlfriend in Kittitas when we found him, which was the same morning I saw you at Sisters Café.

"He and his girlfriend stated that Ballinger hadn't left for several days. He did admit to participating in some vandalism at Miss Malory's place over the last few months and in helping JR spook her by sneaking around her place at night making noise to scare her a week or so back, but he says he never went inside her home."

Cade frowned and shifted in his hospital bed. "But JR did?"

Mark nodded. "Yes. Ted claims he didn't do anything harmful, just moved stuff around to frighten Miss Malory."

Cade's frown deepened. Except for that one morning, when she'd told him and Zack that someone had been outside trying to rattle her the night before—but then later convinced him it had all been a vivid dream— Addie had never mentioned anything about things moving inside the house. He'd ask her about that later. "So, they were responsible for the damaged equipment and trying to scare her?"

"Yes." Mark's jaw flexed, clearly agitated by that bit of news.

"What about the fire?"

The deputy shook his head. "According to Ted Ballinger, he didn't know anything about it and repeatedly claimed JR must've done that on his own."

"Do you believe him?"

"About that, yes, but we're still investigating."

"Is Ballinger still in jail?"

"Yes. His lawyer will petition for bail, but, luckily, not until next week."

"Will he get it?"

Mark shrugged. "Hard to tell. I doubt he could afford it on his own, but his new girlfriend may put up the money. I'm not sure."

That hadn't been great news.

Cade jerked on his socks, still thinking about that conversation and his awkward thanks that had followed.

"I don't remember much about how the fight ended," Cade had said, plucking at the white blanket that covered him, "but I hear I've got you to thank for saving my life."

"No need," Mark replied. "I was just doing my job." He shook his head. "First time I've had to fire my weapon."

"I'm sorry to have been the cause."

"I don't regret it. I'd do it again, it's just…" Mark hesitated, shuffling his feet and then meeting Cade's eyes again. "Taking a life is never easy and it's something I hope to never do again."

Cade had nodded, unsure how to reply to that. "Well," he'd said a moment later, "I'm grateful just the same."

The deputy had stayed a few more minutes and then said his farewell, leaving Cade to rest.

Cade pulled on his boots and stood. Looking around the room for any stray items and finding none, he grabbed his clean Carhartt off the end of the bed and headed for the door, his discharge papers stuffed in his coat pocket. He wanted to see Addie. He had smiled at her this morning when she woke, looking sleepy and adorable. She'd seemed happy to see him, but distant too, and had returned to her room soon after. Was her odd reluctance to meet his eyes or to stay near him due to their argument, his leaving, or what JR had done to her? Maybe it was a little of each, but he was determined to discover the truth.

Stopping at the nurses' station to ask where to find her, he learned that Addie wasn't in her room any longer.

"Where is she then?" he asked, agitated and more than a little worried.

"She'd asked where to find the therapist's office when she checked out," one of the nurses told him.

He got directions to that office and hurried down the hall to knock on the doctor's door.

"Come in," a woman's voice called from inside.

The therapist seemed surprised to see him. Her blue eyes regarded him dispassionately, but she smiled a greeting. "How may I help you?"

"I'm looking for Addie Malory."

"Ah, you must be Cade," she said as she stood and rounded her desk to shake his hand. "She's told me a lot about you."

Cade grinned, but he felt uncomfortable with the woman's assessing eyes as he took her hand. "Yeah, that's me. Do you know where I could find her?"

"She's in the chapel," the doctor told him. "But I wonder if I might have a quick word with you?"

Dread prickled the back of his neck. What did she want with him? Was she going to ask him a bunch of questions he didn't want to answer? Or tell him he should stay away from Addie? He wasn't sure he wanted to hear anything she had to say, but it might be important for Addie. Still, he couldn't keep the suspicion out of his voice. "I suppose so. What can I do for you?"

She smiled at him like she was looking at a five-year-old. "It's not like that," she said with a wave of her hand, clearly sensing his apprehension. "I just wanted to ask you to take things slow with Addie. She's very vulnerable right now and might react in strange and uncharacteristic ways for a while, but she needs your support."

"She has it," he said without hesitation.

"I'm glad to hear that. Do you plan to stay here then?"

His brow furrowed. "Why do you ask?"

The doctor sighed and went back around her desk to sit in her chair. "Addie said that you had left to return to your home in Montana."

"Yes, because she told me to go."

"Did you want to?"

Cade snorted. "No, but I don't see how that's any of your business."

"It's not, not directly," the doctor said as she laced her fingers together and placed them on her desk. "I'm concerned about Addie feeling safe and secure once she leaves the hospital."

"She *will* be safe and secure. I won't let anything else happen to her."

"So you're staying, then?"

Heat gathered around his neck and he clenched his jaw tight. He didn't want to have this conversation with a stranger, especially not before he spoke with Addie about it. But he could read the accusation in the woman's blue eyes, *If you had stuck around in the first place, this never would've happened.*

"I'm not blaming you," the doctor said, "and you shouldn't blame yourself, either."

Surprise lifted Cade's eyebrows. Had he said that out loud?

"Even if you had been there when the man showed up at her door," the doctor continued, "there's a very good chance something terrible would've happened anyway. Addie needs stability and security right now. I know she cares about you a great deal. If you feel the same, you should tell her or, at least, *show* her. She needs to know she's not alone."

He stood a little taller. "She's *not* alone."

"Good," the doctor said. "Just be gentle with her and be conscious of the trauma she's been through."

"I plan to."

She smiled again. "Great. I thought you might." She tilted her head and he sensed a 'but' coming. "Just don't forget to take care of yourself, too. You're no good to her if you run yourself down."

Cade had nodded at that, but couldn't help thinking, *I'll do whatever I have to do to make her smile and remove that haunted look from her eyes.*

That was his mission now, his only mission, and he intended to succeed.

CHAPTER 36

Scooting across the leather backseat of Helga's SUV, Addie stepped out onto her snow-covered, gravel driveway. Cade went to the back to collect their bags and then to the driver's side door to convey their thanks for the ride from the hospital. Addie barely heard as she wandered into her yard, staring at the front door. *That's where JR first grabbed me.*

Shoulders hunched forward, she wrapped her arms protectively around her middle. *I will not cry,* she told herself. *I can do this. I'm fine, he's gone, and this is* my *house.*

Unfortunately, the pep talk did little good. An icy ball of dread sat in her stomach, growing larger and heavier with every inch closer to the front door she came. Could she go inside? Could she stand to see all the places JR had hurt her?

Cade had asked her about objects in the house moving on their own before they left the hospital. When she told him what she had seen, he'd shaken his head and explained that JR had entered through her unlocked doors and moved those items to spook her, to make her think she was losing her mind.

Well, he'd almost succeeded. It had unnerved her, but apparently, not fast enough for JR.

Addie shivered. *He'd been in my room while I was sleeping!* The skin on her arms prickled as she hugged herself a little tighter. That thought terrified her. He could've taken her then—when Cade had been in the guest room after they'd beaten him and broken his ribs. JR could've done several things to her in her bed and no one would have known until it was too late.

A sob pushed into her achy throat, but she swallowed it down. She could do this. It was her home and she wasn't going to let JR take it away from her.

"Are you ready to go in?" Cade's soft voice startled her, but his hand on her back nearly made her scream. She hadn't even noticed that Helga had backed up and driven away.

Get a grip, girl!

She smiled at Cade, ashamed of her automatic reaction. She'd pulled away but stepped back to his side. "Yeah, I…I guess so."

"Okay, then," Cade said, but to her dismay, his hand did not return to her back. "Helga said the door's open."

Addie stiffened. *Anyone could be inside.*

Cade glanced back at her, a crease between his brows. "Do you want me to check it out first?"

A sigh escaped her. She was being ridiculous. JR was dead, and his buddies were still in jail. No one else would care about her.

"Yes, please." Her cheeks burned. Those words had just slipped out without her knowing she would say them.

Cade grinned and she felt slightly better. "Sure thing," he said as he turned the knob and stepped inside.

Her chest squeezed tight as he disappeared through the doorway. Cade had been hurt, too. How could she ask him to step into danger for her? Again. What if JR had left traps inside? What if one of his other friends— or enemies, like the ones he had owed money to—were waiting inside, thinking to get whatever they could from her? What if…? Her mind thrashed through so many horrible scenarios, ramping up her anxiety, and the longer Cade was gone, the worse it got. *I will never forgive myself if I get him hurt again…or worse.*

But no matter how much she berated herself, she couldn't force her feet to move.

A wave of dizziness swept over her as Cade reappeared. "Nothing to worry about," he said with a reassuring grin, but even with his strong presence waiting for her, she was reluctant to take another step closer.

She must not have done a very good job of hiding her fear because Cade rushed down the steps toward her.

"Hey," he said, looking down into her eyes and rubbing his palms up and down her arms. "It's okay. You're safe with me. I promise you that."

She tried to smile, but it felt forced. Still, she was determined not to let what happened ruin her home for her. She swallowed, took a few deep breaths, and straightened her spine. "I know, and thank you, Cade. You don't have to stay. I know how much you wanted to go home."

"I am home," he said with a soft smile that melted something inside her. "Wherever *you* are, Addie, is home for me."

Her breath stuttered and her gaze darted around the yard, looking anywhere but into his deep blue eyes. The emotions his words stirred up were almost too much. She had wanted to hear something like that before, and hearing those words now made her heart swell with love and gratitude, but she couldn't help wondering if he only said them because he thought she needed him—not because he really meant them.

"You want to head inside?" he asked. "It's a little cold out here."

Addie realized then that her shivers were caused by more than just dread. The snow was quite deep now and the sneakers that Helga had brought along with their changes of clothes weren't exactly made for snow. Her fingers were starting to freeze and her toes felt a bit numb. The jacket she wore should've been adequate for the low temperature, but the icy wind still knifed through it and her.

Forcing another smile, she nodded and Cade's arm slipped protectively around her.

"Okay," he said cheerily, "let's go in and get you warmed up."

She let him usher her forward and, before she knew it, they were up the steps and through the front door. Cade set the bags of clothes from the hospital beside the door, shut it behind them, and then helped her out of her jacket.

Glancing around the room, it didn't look any different than it had before, but it was different. Her heart sped up and beat so hard, she thought her ribs might break.

"Are you hungry?" Cade asked as he turned from hanging up his quilted coat.

She shook her head and, hugging her middle again as something cold slithered around inside her, tried to ignore the sudden churning in her stomach.

"How about some hot chocolate?"

Her mouth felt dry and some of the chocolaty goodness would go a long way to warming her and cheering her mood. She nodded and he grinned.

"Okay, then, follow me," he said, rubbing his big hands together as he headed for the kitchen.

Addie's legs and feet seemed to weigh a ton as she attempted to follow him, every step harder to take than the last. Sweat beaded on her upper lip and trickled between her breasts, which seemed strange to her. She was so cold she shivered, but then why was she sweating?

The kitchen door came into view and her throat grew tight. The refrigerator, sink, and counter came next, and the pounding in her chest intensified. The walls seemed to close in and suddenly, she was pressed up against that counter again with JR's fetid breath in her face. He held her down with his greater size and weight, while his hands and mouth assaulted her body. Terror clamped down on her chest. She couldn't breathe, couldn't think! She could feel JR's hand tangled in her hair, pulling, tugging, forcing her to move with him.

Her vision blurred and she shook her head. "No…" she mumbled. "N-No…"

She didn't know who she was talking to, only that she had needed to get away from him, but he'd been too strong.

Her legs trembled so hard they threatened to collapse beneath her and everything inside her quivered with her need to escape. She inhaled and stepped backward, and then she screamed. Her shaky knees gave out and she tumbled to the floor as another scream ripped through her throat and then another. She began to crawl toward the closest exit, which happened to be the sliding glass door. If she could get to the backyard, she could run and get lost in the rolling hills of white. It didn't matter that the snow would inhibit her flight or that she'd freeze before she could reach her closest neighbor. All she could think about was getting away.

A hand touched her back and she screamed again. Spinning around with her fist raised, she swung at the man who tried to stop her. On his knees beside her, he reared back and she missed his chin by several inches, but the movement threw her off balance and she tumbled into his lap, sobbing.

"Addie? Please, sweetie, tell me what's wrong. What can I do?"

She looked up. *Cade?* It was Cade. He was here. He had risked his life to save her and had brought her home.

"I c-can't," she stuttered through her tears, scared and infuriated by her weakness. "I can't stay h-here. He…He would've—" She couldn't make herself say what JR would've done.

Understanding dawned on Cade's face and his shoulders slumped before he pulled her against his chest. "I know, sweetie," he murmured into her hair as he held her close and he rocked her gently. "He can't hurt you again. No one will ever hurt you again. I promise you that."

She nodded against his neck, squeezing him tighter, never wanting to let go. A moment later, he pushed her back, and with his hands on her shoulders, he held her steady.

"You do believe me, don't you?" he asked, his clear blue eyes filled with hope, trepidation, and…something warm and comforting. "Addie, please talk to me."

"I believe you," she whispered, the words barely getting through her achy throat. "But does that mean…?"

He cupped her face in his calloused hands. "Yes," he rasped and her heart fluttered. "Wherever you go, I'm going with you." The smile that lit his face warmed her as he brushed at the tears on her cheeks. "You're stuck with me now." His eyes turned serious. "Because I need you, Addie. I couldn't leave you if I wanted to."

She tried to swallow the lump in her throat. "But you…did."

He lowered his chin, a crestfallen expression on his face. Then he straightened and met her questioning gaze. "I never made it out of town. I couldn't leave you. I was coming back, but when I found you gone, I feared the worst. That I'd…"

A frown tugged at her brows as she tried to understand the panicked look in his eyes. "What? That you'd *what?*"

Lips parted, he inhaled and released a stuttering breath before his jaws clamped together again, and he swallowed. "I was afraid I'd never get to tell you that I…I love you, Addie. More than I've ever cared for anyone or anything in my life. I want to be with you. I want to love you, take care of you, and make a life with you."

Tears and terror forgotten, the fuzzy warmth of hope filled her chest, but she shook her head. "But…what about your home? What about Montana?"

He smiled. "I told you. *You* are my home, Addie. Whether here or in Montana or anywhere else, as long as I'm with you, I *am* home."

Everything seemed to stop. Addie couldn't believe her ears. He loved her! Falling forward, she wrapped her arms around his neck. "Then let's get out of here and find our home…together."

His body stilled and he pulled back. "But I thought you wanted to stay here?"

She shook her head and a tear slid down her cheek. "Not now. Not when I see *him* and everything he did around every corner. I can't sell, not yet, but I'll figure something out. I just can't stay in this house anymore."

Cade tucked a few strands of her long hair behind her ear and smiled. "*We'll* figure something out."

Addie returned his soft smile, feeling the warmth and security of his love wash over her, filling her with more happiness than she'd ever known. "Yes, *we* will."

CHAPTER 37

The clock on the dashboard read half past two in the afternoon as Addie gazed out at the snow-covered landscape that surrounded the gas station just off the highway. It was only a few days until Christmas, and they were starting a new life together in this winter wonderland of tall evergreens and taller mountains all covered in a thick blanket of fluffy white. It was gorgeous, but apprehension still made her muscles twitch.

This was a big change, and not only because it was a new state she had never been to before. They were moving into Cade's old home with his estranged brother, while living as a couple. Not that she was worried about Cord—they'd gotten on well when he came to visit. No, she worried about having to share a small space. No privacy, everyone in each other's way. She didn't want there to be any more family disputes, but she wasn't sure how to avoid them. She'd never had to deal with anyone but her boyfriend in a living situation before, and she wasn't sure what to expect.

Her knee bounced incessantly as thoughts tumbled through her mind while she waited for Cade to return from paying for the fuel and, no matter what she did or told herself, she couldn't make it cease.

They were only a few miles from the home Cade had left behind all those years ago, thinking never to return. Based on everything Cade had told her about the old place, Addie tried to imagine what it looked like. She envisioned a smallish two-story house with a barn and horse corral, the brothers working together, and Sunday dinners with the three of them and their friends. Was it too much to hope for more? For the children she'd always wanted but never dared to hope for? What if things didn't go well? What if Cade and Cord couldn't work together again, and worse, what if one or the other couldn't stand to live with her anymore? Her mouth went dry at that thought, but she pushed those dark possibilities aside. She was nervous about this, but she was also excited, and she could tell Cade was too as he jogged back to the truck and jumped in.

His infectious grin was a mile wide when he looked over at her, his eyes sparkling with excitement and happiness. "You ready?"

She nodded. "Yep, I can't wait to see it."

He glanced at her bouncing knee and reached over to place his hand on it, stilling its anxious motion. "You okay?" he asked, worry deepening the lines around his eyes as he studied her face.

"I'm fine," she said squeezing his hand. "Just nervous."

"Why?"

She could read what he was thinking all over his face. He'd pushed her into this, made her leave the home she'd wanted to keep, and she blamed him for it.

None of that was true, of course, but he worried about it and her anyway.

"It's just something new," she told him. "I'm looking forward to seeing your brother again and getting the tour of the house and property you promised me. I can't wait to see where you grew up."

"Are you sure you don't regret this?" His voice held a note of trepidation.

"Yes, I'm sure." She patted his hand and then, lifting it to her lips, she kissed his knuckles. "I'm exactly where I want to be."

He released a long sigh. "I'm glad to hear that."

"I'll say it as often as you need, but you should believe me by now."

He nodded and smiled again, but said no more as he pulled back his hand and started her truck. As the new snow tires churned through the snow and ice on the roadway, Addie thought back on the last week.

She had made her decision on the floor of her dining room the day they returned to her house. Afraid she'd made a rash decision, Cade had asked her to think about it a little more before they did something she might regret.

Though she didn't need to consider it any further, she'd followed his advice and thought about it during the first couple of days they'd spent staying with Helga and Dan. She'd also spent those nights alone because she still jumped at his touch or any little sound. She'd known Cade had wanted to stay with her, to hold her and nothing more, but he also hadn't wanted to rush into any physical intimacy she wasn't ready for, and she hadn't argued.

"You know where I am if you need me," he'd said the first night before he kissed her forehead and left the room for his own. Sleeping that night had been next to impossible, and she'd berated herself repeatedly for her weakness all the next day.

By midnight of the second night, she was tired of thinking about everything, tired of being afraid and alone, and just plain tired. She missed Cade's warmth and his solid strength beside her, and she'd made up her mind not to deny herself his company in her bed any longer.

Rolling out from beneath her blankets, she'd crept through Dan and Helga's darkened home, terrified of the darkness and angry with herself for the absurd emotion. The door to Cade's room had squeaked as she pushed it open and the sound swept an icicle of fear down her back.

You are fine, she had told herself. *Everyone's asleep and Cade is only a few feet away. No one else is around.*

Giving herself a little shake, she had stepped inside and closed the door behind her. Tiptoeing across the cold hardwood floor to the rug beside the bed, she'd held her breath, trying to figure out what to say when she woke him, but when she reached his side, she saw his white-toothed grin flash in the darkness.

"You couldn't resist me anymore, huh?" he'd teased and slowly reached for her hand.

She shrugged, but didn't pull away when his fingers entwined with hers.

"Would you like to stay?" His deep, sleepy voice had sounded far more serious with that question.

She tried to make out his expression, but it had been too dark to see much detail. "Would you like me to?" she'd asked, attempting to lighten the heaviness that had been pressing down on her for days.

"You know I would," he said softly, giving her hand a playful little tug, "but it's up to you. If you're ready, I'm waiting."

The air thickened and her breath stalled in her lungs.

He seemed to sense her fear because he spoke again. "I'll wait forever if you need me to, Addie, but I think we'd both be happier if we were together. You know I'd never hurt you, and that I'll always protect you. Right?"

Her chest had constricted at the uncertainty in his question. He loved her, he'd said it, and she'd refused to allow him into her bed. The sadness she remembered in his eyes the night before crushed her. She'd been cruel to deny him. He'd been hurt and afraid too, but he hadn't turned away from her. He'd opened his heart and given her everything.

"Addie...?" he had called when she didn't respond.

"Yes," she said in a breathless whisper, "I do know that, and I love you all the more for it."

He'd inhaled sharply at her words, but Addie had already moved to pull back the covers and slip in beside him. His arms instantly wrapped around her and she snuggled as close to his hard body as she could get.

"So," he'd murmured as he kissed the top of her head, "you love me, huh?"

She chuckled and hugged him a little harder. "Yes, I do." She looked up, a smile playing on her lips. "Don't let it go to your head."

Throwing back his head, he had laughed and the joyous sound had settled something inside her. She loved his laugh, loved him, and she was no longer worried that she would somehow lose Cade in some tragedy like she'd lost her last love. That terrified her more than anything. Seeing him hurt and hooked up to all those tubes had sent her back to that frightened young woman she'd been after Jared's death. But she had changed since then, and she'd found something stronger, better, something that had the power to last.

It was then that she knew her decision to move was the right one. It wasn't rash—she'd already considered leaving with Cade before this all happened—and she was ready to let everything else go. She'd made the right choice and did not regret a thing.

Unsurprisingly, she'd slept the whole night through and every night after with his arms around her. No manic thoughts or vivid nightmares troubled her, and she gave Cade all the credit.

The next day, Veta and Ivan had come to visit them at Dan and Helga's—to check on her, more like—and she'd discussed her thoughts with them. Ivan had made two very good suggestions that made the difference in her ability to move so quickly.

First, he'd suggested talking to Jorje about a lease to buy option for her property. "I think Jorje would jump at the opportunity."

"Yeah," Cade agreed, "he's talked about wanting his own place several times."

"But what about Pete?" she'd asked. "I promised him a percentage of the profits for the next few years. I can't just back out of that."

Ivan tilted his head and then brought up the second thing that had helped her move on with her life. "Why don't you talk to them both? I'm sure they'd be willing to work something out. I know Pete hates the senior home. He says he's bored and the home's too crowded and noisy. I think he misses the farm."

As it turned out, Ivan had been right. Pete missed the open land and Jorje was more than willing to work out something to get his own place at such a low price. To save Pete some money in exchange for a slightly lower return on the harvest profits, Jorje had offered Pete a place on the farm and even said his mother—who lived with him and needed something to keep her busy—could take over any of the care Pete might need. Pete showed no sign of the heart attack he'd suffered almost six months before, nor any other illness, and had been a little perturbed by the idea of being "looked after," but he couldn't hide his joy at the idea of returning home.

They'd checked with the bank the next day. Jorje was able to take over her loan and also agreed to pay her the amount she'd already invested in the property over the course of a few years. She wouldn't make much on her old dream, but she didn't care. She had a new dream that involved a tall, handsome, blue-eyed man who made her mouth water and her heart flutter and whose smile brightened her world.

Glancing at that man as he navigated the icy road, she grinned at the thrill that quivered inside her. Sometimes, like now, worries popped into her head about the future and where it would all end, but she shoved those thoughts aside and concentrated on the here and now.

"Are you excited," she asked and he glanced at her. The mile wide grin was back and his eyes glittered like aquamarine in the sun.

"Oh, yeah," he said and turned back to the road. Nervous energy seemed to zap around him, his body tense, his eyes taking in every detail before him. "Everything looks the same but different, if you know what I mean."

She nodded. "Well, you've been away a long time."

"Yeah…" He sounded sad.

"But you're back now," she said, not wanting to dampen his spirits.

The smile returned and he shot a quick look her way. "Yes, and I'm happier now, too."

The eagerness in his expression made her chuckle. "I'm glad."

"There it is," he said as they neared a wide turn surrounded by evergreens.

"Is that the driveway?"

"Yeah. It goes on for about half a mile. Then there's a small hill and when we get to the top, we'll be able to see the house." He was practically bouncing in his seat.

She giggled.

"What?" he asked, glancing her way.

She shook her head. "Nothing. You just look like a little kid on Christmas morning."

A chuckle rumbled up from his chest. "Well, it *is* the season."

She laughed at his animated expression as they turned onto the drive and bumped over the snow.

Someone had used a plow to clear the drive and left huge piles along either side, but she could just see some of the fence posts sticking out of the piles.

"Where are all the animals?" she asked.

"This time of year, they're probably in the barn or stabled closer to the house…" Cade replied, but his voice trailed off and he sounded uncertain.

She glanced at him and saw that his brows were drawn down. "What's wrong?"

"I'm not sure. It just looks different. See that?" He pointed toward his left at a good-sized barn. "That's new, at least, to me it's new." He shook his head, and when he spoke again, it seemed as if he was talking to himself. "Cord never said anything about making improvements… I didn't know he could afford it. I wonder what else he's changed."

The mood inside the truck shifted slightly and they remained quiet the rest of the way to the hill. Addie's stomach knotted with worry at Cade's silence, but she didn't know how to rekindle the joy that seemed to have faded.

When they finally reached the top of the hill, the valley opened up before them and Addie gasped in awe. It was beautiful. Like a Christmas card beautiful with everything covered in white. The main house was far larger than she'd imagined, like a giant cabin or mountain chateau, a rustic mansion. Another long, apartment-like structure built in the same style sat about two hundred yards beyond the house, with another smaller cabin set at a right angle to the main building several yards to the east. She saw a big red barn trimmed in white and three other large buildings Cade had never mentioned lined up beside it. There were trees and other landscaping near the house, but beyond it and the other buildings was a dark forest that encircled the open range.

"Oh, Cade," she whispered, "it's beautiful and so much more than I imagined."

"Yeah," he murmured, "me, too."

She slid over the seat to sit beside him and placed her hand on his leg. "You must be thrilled."

He took a breath as the tires continued to crunch over the brittle snow and let it out slowly. "I am, but…"

"But?"

"It's different," he said and Addie heard a touch of sadness in his tone.

"How so?"

"The house is a lot *bigger* for one, and all those other buildings in back weren't there before."

"But it's still home, right?"

He glanced at her and back at the house before he shrugged. "Yeah, I guess so."

As they approached, two people exited the main house and a third from the smaller cabin in the back. By the time they'd pulled up and parked beside Cord's truck, all three men had gathered on the deck. Addie recognized Cord and Zack, but the third man who'd come from the other cabin and looked several years older, she didn't.

"Do you know that other man?" she asked Cade as she handed him his hat and gloves from the seat beside her.

"Sure do," Cade replied. "That's Joe Baker. He used to work for my father. I guess he's still working with Cord. He's a very good rancher and a great guy." He turned to grin at her. "If you like those other two yahoos, you'll like him more."

Addie detected a note of respect in Cade's description. "Sounds like you were close…?"

"Yeah," he sighed and reached for the handle, "we were. He was kind of like a second father…or an uncle to us when Cord and I were kids. Even when we got older, too. Come on, I'll introduce you."

Cade hopped out of the cab and offered his hand to help her down.

Zack was the first to greet them as he skipped down the front steps. "Hey, you two. What took you so long? Did ya stop for a last private snuggle on the way?"

Cade shot him a dark look and, oddly, so did Cord, but Addie just laughed. She'd missed his open personality and rough humor. "If we did," she replied calmly as Cade slammed the truck door behind her, "I wouldn't tell you."

Zack laughed and rushed up to hug her. She immediately stiffened as his arms closed around her and he lifted her into the air. She forced her muscles to loosen. No one here would harm her and if they tried, Cade would stop them.

"It's really good to see you, pretty girl," Zack said as he set her back on her feet.

She grinned, once again thankful that her bruises had healed, but she could see Cade staring daggers at his friend. "Not cool, Zack."

"Hey, she *is* pretty."

"I know that, but—"

"It's all right, Cade," she said, touching his arm and felt him relax.

Zack slapped him on the shoulder. "See?"

Cade rolled his eyes, but a grin quirked his lips. Then pushed his friend back when Zack tried to give him a bear hug. Zack thought that was hilarious and stumbled back to the little group still chuckling.

"What happened to your truck?" Cord asked as he entered their little circle, shaking his head at Zack as he gave his brother a hug.

"I left it with a friend," Cade said as his brother released him, but Addie knew he'd left it with Jorje to use as a backup so she didn't have to drive.

"How are you doing, sis?" Cord asked as he leaned in to kiss her cheek. "I heard you had some trouble."

Heat swarmed up her neck and pulsed in her cheeks as Cord carefully examined her face, but a sense of belonging and acceptance replaced the embarrassment. Cade must have told him what had happened. "Yes, but it's all taken care of now."

"Good to hear," he said in a hard voice. "We don't take kindly to anyone messing with family."

She gave him a grateful smile, both for his support and cleverly stated protection, as well as for not saying any more about it. Not to mention claiming her as family. *Why did that feel so good?*

"You know these two idiots," Cade said, poking fun at his brother and best friend, "but you haven't met this guy." He waved a hand at the older man who'd entered their little gathering. "This is Joe."

Addie shook Joe's hand. It was warm and calloused, but gentle and friendly, as were his deep brown eyes. She liked him instantly.

"Hello, ma'am," he said in a low voice. "Good to meet you."

"It's very nice to meet you, Joe," she said and he grinned. The smile made him look younger. "And, please, call me Addie."

"Well, thank you, Addie. I'll do that."

Right then, a child's cry came from somewhere inside. Not a cry of surprise or delight. This was a baby's wail for mom...or dad in this case Addie didn't remember any of them saying anything about a baby. She looked up at Cade, who turned to his brother, who turned several shades of red.

"And *that* would be Bethany," Cord said by way of explanation as he rushed up the stairs and into the house.

"Who's Bethany?" Cade asked, his gaze bouncing between the two other men. "And who does she belong to?"

"Hey, don't look at me," Zack said, throwing his hands in the air and following Cord.

"Your brother will tell you when he's ready," Joe said as he started toward the stairs. "Come on inside. We'll get your stuff later."

Addie looked up at Cade's stunned face. Confusion wrinkled his brow and concern filled his eyes. "Cord. With a baby?" he murmured and then a smile broke across his face. He looked down at her and took her hand as he headed for the stairs. "Oh, baby, this I gotta see."

CHAPTER 38

Outside the sliding glass door, warm rays of June sunlight bathed the open meadow behind the Brody's remodeled home. The trees that surrounded the property were dark green against the achingly blue sky and birds tweeted happily as they darted from one location to another. Watching the pastoral scene, Addie brushed her hands over her ivory dress. Nervous flutters of excited anticipation danced in her stomach, but she couldn't stop smiling.

Her worries about moving in with Cord had been for naught. Always hoping to find Cade again, Cord had prepared for his brother's eventual return with new construction that would benefit everyone. The modifications he'd made to the house had enlarged the original building's main rooms and added two separate wings that allowed them each to have their own house-sized apartments. It gave her and Cade a private space to live and grow as a couple and Cord room to get to know his new baby daughter, as well as a common area where they could all meet as a family.

At the moment, Addie stood in the shared dining room waiting for Veta and her sister to return with information about the proceedings and how much longer she had to wait. Zack's mother, Janice, had volunteered to help with the planning for their big day and, in the process, had become like a second mother to Addie. When Helga and her husband arrived a week ago, she and Janice had joined forces and helped iron out the final details with far less stress than Addie had expected.

She was thankful for their help since she'd only had three months to bring this June wedding together, and when she'd called to tell them the good news, her friends had been ecstatic.

"They're getting married, aren't they?" Lana had asked in the background when Addie had called Veta last March.

"Yes," Veta replied with a cheerful note and Lana had squealed like a giddy schoolgirl.

"I knew it," she'd shouted. "I *knew* it!"

"Yes, yes. As you can hear, we are both very happy for you, Addie. You deserve it…" Veta was clearly shooing her sister out of the room before she whispered, "He does make you happy, right?"

A little pang struck her heart at the concern in her friend's tone. "Of course, he does. Cade's wonderful." She lowered her voice, mimicking her friend's. "I've never been this happy, Veta."

"Never?" Veta knew all about Addie's last major relationship and its tragic end.

Addie shook her head as she replied with heartfelt conviction, "Never."

Cade had proposed in early spring and they hadn't wanted to wait too long—after spending the months since Christmas making sure of their decision to be together, they hadn't wanted to waste one more day. But they'd also wanted a celebration, and Cade insisted she deserved the white dress, flowers, and a walk down the aisle.

Her smile widened as she remembered the day he'd finally popped the question. They had gone horseback riding, and Cade had picked out a gentle mare named Shiloh to be Addie's mount. They'd traveled far into the hills for a riverside picnic on a sunny spring day and she'd had no clue what he'd been planning.

Everywhere she'd looked that afternoon, the pale green of new growth caught her eyes and as they rode, her heart had soared like the eagles overhead. Once they stopped to lay out their meal, she'd enjoyed the loud gurgle of the river as they'd eaten and chatted before packing up. All through lunch, Addie had tried to remain cheerful, but Cade had seemed distant and preoccupied.

Did I do something wrong? she'd thought as she gathered her gear, suddenly nervous. It had been several months since she'd been attacked and in all that time, she hadn't felt comfortable enough to have sex again.

When it had come up a few months earlier on New Year's Day, Addie had felt ridiculous for being too apprehensive to be with the man she loved.

"I'm sorry," she'd cried on his shoulder after pulling away from Cade's ardent lips.

Cade had only smiled sweetly, love and understanding in his eyes. "It's okay, sweetheart. We'll get through this together," he'd said quietly.

"But I—"

"Shh." He'd pressed a finger to her lips. "I can wait until you're ready... I'll always wait for you, Addie. It doesn't matter how often or how long."

He'd held her that night instead, but her guilt for denying him had remained and it hadn't taken long for her to wonder if maybe her new aversion to intimacy bothered him more than he let on? She'd asked herself that question more than once in the months leading up to their picnic, but she'd been too afraid of his answer to ask.

As their picnic in the hills came to a close and his peculiar behavior had continued, Addie couldn't help but, once again, question his mood. *Why does he seem so...odd?*

"Is something wrong?" she'd finally mustered the courage to ask as he checked their saddles in preparation to ride back to the house.

He glanced over his shoulder. Surprise and then some other expression crossed his face. "Why do you ask?"

Her shoulders tightened when he didn't deny there was a problem. "You just seem..." She shrugged. "I don't know, like something's wrong."

He sighed and turned toward her. His beautiful blue eyes clouded with concern and it frightened her. He looked as if he was about to give her bad news or...or break up with her.

Her heart stuttered. *Oh, no...*

"Addie," he said as he took both of her hands in his and her throat closed up so much she could hardly breathe. "You've been through a lot and I know you've said you're okay, but I'm worried about you and..." His eyes dropped as he brushed his boot over the green grass. "There's something I want to say, I'm just not sure how to say it."

Dread curdled her stomach. She had wanted to tell him not to say it. That whatever it was, they could conquer it, but she couldn't speak.

When he lowered to one knee and gazed up at her with so much love glittering in his beautiful eyes, her heart had thudded into her breastbone and a joyful smile tugged at her lips.

"I love you, Addie," he'd said, his deep voice and normally steady hands both trembled as he pulled a small, red velvet box from his pocket. Addie inhaled sharply and pressed her hand to her open mouth, stunned, as he popped open the lid to reveal a delicately designed engagement ring. The diamonds had sparkled in the afternoon light as her eye's filled with tears. "I want you by my side," Cade continued. "I want to spend the rest of my life making you happy. Will you let me?" He shook his head. "That didn't come out right. I mean... Will you marry me, Addie?"

She'd been so overcome with emotion, her reply had been a garbled choke that had her coughing and crying at the same time.

"Please tell me those are happy tears," he'd said, only half joking.

She had dropped to her knees, her arms around his neck, kissing his face and crying like a sap. It had taken her a few seconds to clear the lump in her throat, but she wasted no time in accepting. "Yes, yes, yes!" A life with Cade was everything she had ever wanted. *He* was everything she wanted, and she'd told him so.

The memory of his proposal brought a smile to Addie's face as she adjusted the bell skirt of her strapless wedding dress, waiting for her cue to join her bridesmaids in walking down the aisle. The twinkle of her engagement ring—two thin bands, one set with tiny diamonds and the other, plain white gold, were woven together and swirled around a perfect-sized, princess cut diamond that Addie loved—glinted in the sun, drawing her eyes. Nervously, she ran her hands over the beads and crystals that adorned the bodice of her dress in a delicate swirling pattern, liking how the design complimented the elegant ring on her finger—as beautiful as the man who'd given it to her.

"You look like a princess," Cord said from the kitchen to her left.

She jumped and turned wide eyes toward him. Like Cade would be, Cord was dressed in a tux and black cowboy hat. He looked almost as handsome as she imagined Cade would be when she saw him.

She smiled and twirled around. "I feel like one."

He chuckled as he stepped up to her and kissed her cheek.

"But what are you doing in here?" she asked with a worried frown. "I thought all you boys were outside."

"I was," he said, patting his hip pocket, "but I forgot something small and round and sparkly upstairs."

Resting her hands on her hips, she gave him her best mock frown. "So you're the one who's holding up the show."

He grinned shyly. "I didn't want to ruin your day."

Dropping her arms back to her sides, she shook her head. "You could never do that, Cord."

"Yeah, well, my track record isn't all that great."

She tilted her head and lowered her brows. She didn't like the note of defeat she detected in his voice.

"Where's Bethany?"

"She's with Zack's mom. Aside from you and Cade, Mrs. MacEntier is about the only other person Bethany will tolerate."

"She loves her daddy," Addie said with a smile.

The grin that lit his face was like the sun brightening a dreary day. "That little girl's my whole world."

"I'm glad," Addie said and meant it. His first few months after the infant's mother had basically dropped the baby on his doorstep and took off had been rocky and, despite his misgivings about keeping Bethany with him, about being a single father, Cord had stuck it out with wonderful results.

"Enough about me," he said as his blue eyes brightened with his smile. "You look absolutely gorgeous."

She hugged him. "Thank you, Cord… Thanks for everything."

"You're family, Addie. You have been since you rescued my brother from his wandering. There's no need to thank me."

"You're so sweet." She patted his cheek affectionately. "But I know this has been a lot of work for everyone. I just want you to know how much I appreciate your help and support."

"That's what brothers are for," he said, pulling her in for another hug. When he stepped back, his eyes were suspiciously shiny. "I'm proud to call you my sister." He straightened his suit jacket as his eyes swept over her again. "My brother's a lucky man." He sounded so lonely and sad. "I wish you both the best. I always will."

"You'll find someone someday, too, Cord," she said as he tipped his black hat in farewell and stepped out the sliding glass door. As the best man, he was on his way to the flower-covered cedar arch in the massive backyard where the ceremony would take place.

"I hope so," he said, then smiled again, and was gone. She knew enough of Cord's story to know he'd had his heart broken, too. Because she loved him like the brother he'd become, Addie ached for him and the pain he carried, but she had no doubt the right woman would find him someday.

Straightening her back, she sighed. Today was not a day of sadness. *Today is a happy day,* she told herself, then wiggled her toes and giggled. Cord had called her a princess, but no one needed know that this princess wore cowboy boots beneath her bell skirt.

It seemed as if the six months she'd spent here with Cade had flown by—with the two of them growing closer every day. She'd also grown to love Montana and, though she missed her friends, she had gained so much more—a family to call her own, and soon, even more would be coming their way.

She wrapped her arms around her middle and sighed.

Working the ranch with the Brodys had given her the sense of peace and belonging she'd been looking for her whole life. The animals were a balm to her tattered spirit after she'd first arrived and had helped her overcome the trauma that she'd left behind. Learning to ride horseback and to care for the horses had soothed her, but Cade's ever-present love and affection had healed her heart.

Not that she'd forgotten what had happened, but she no longer jumped when someone spoke or touched her unexpectedly, nor did she have nightmares anymore. Cade's arms seemed to keep those at bay and his touch—she shivered in anticipation of their honeymoon, thankful that her aversion to sex had worn off the night Cade proposed. Ever since, she couldn't seem to get enough of him. It was as if she needed to make up for lost time.

She and Cade hadn't had much when they first came to the ranch, but Cord had done much better running it than he'd let on when he visited her place a little over seven months ago. With Cade working beside him now, the business was thriving like never before. She didn't know all the specifics, just that the brothers had come to an agreement about their past and the ranch that had left her and Cade in much better financial circumstances than when they'd arrived. They weren't billionaires or anything, but they were very well off. She just hoped Cade hadn't gone crazy with the honeymoon—not that she would complain. As long as he was with her, she didn't care where they went. But that didn't stop her from asking or joking with him about it as she had several times over the last two months. She'd been anxious to go somewhere far off and tropical, but at the same time, she'd also wanted to stay right where they were.

"You'll find out soon enough," Cade had teased when she brought it up again two nights ago. They'd just finished making love, a rousing round of kissing and connection that had left them both breathless and satiated.

"Not fair," she'd whined, playfully tugging on his chest hair.

"Ow!" He flattened her fingers against his chest with his hand and gave her a faux-stern stare. "Not nice."

"But it's my honeymoon, too," she'd pouted, continuing the play.

"And you'll love it." He squeezed her hand.

"Are you sure?"

He glanced down at her with a raised eyebrow. "You mean I'm not enough for you?"

She huffed out a breath and slapped his chest lightly. "Of course, you are, but you haven't told me *anything* about it. I'm...curious."

A slow grin spread across his face and he lightly bopped the end of her nose with his index finger. "You, my curious little cat, will have to wait."

"Are we going to Hawaii?"

He rolled his eyes.

"The Bahamas?"

Again with the eye roll.

"Europe?"

He gazed at her intently, something like worry wrinkling his brow. "Is that what you want? To jet around the world?"

Her chest tightened at his expression. "No, but someday I'd like to see the world."

His arms had tightened around her. "Me, too."

Addie sighed as she ran her hand over her fancy up-do, smoothing her hair and thinking back on that wonderful night, wishing now that time would speed up just a little bit. Enough to get things rolling so she could see Cade again.

I missed you last night, she thought suddenly, hugging herself. They'd both agreed to the one night apart, some old tradition that seemed right for them. But all she'd been able to think about was how he'd felt as she'd sprawled against his side the night before with one finger swirling through the light dusting of brown hair on his work-hardened chest. That memory—and the realization that in one day they'd never be apart again—had helped her find rest.

Now, as she waited for the word to exit the house and walk down the flower-lined aisle, she couldn't help but be thankful for Cade and his patience. She'd come so close to losing him and now she was looking at a lifetime of happiness with the man she loved.

Veta appeared at the glass door and hurried in with Lana and Helga right behind her. The sisters wore matching pale-blue dresses that shimmered in the light and reminded Addie of Cade's eyes.

"It's time," Veta said as she handed Addie her bouquet of mums, daisies, and white lilies.

Addie's heart stuttered as they stepped outside and went to where Ivan waited behind the landscaped brush that hid them from view until they were ready to walk down the aisle.

Zack's mother Janice stood beside Jorje and smiled, her dark eyes shining. "Addie, dear, you look beautiful."

Addie smiled at the compliment, but she was anxious to see Cade. Her heart longed for him, swelling with love and need at just the thought of seeing him again.

Damn, she scolded herself and her libido, *it's only been a few hours. Calm down.*

But her heart still beat too fast and her skin warmed, overly sensitive, and yearning for his touch. Her fingers practically itched to touch him, and her legs trembled with the desire to run to where she knew he'd be waiting with open arms.

When the Wedding March began to play a moment after they arrived, her heart gave a hard thump and butterflies took flight in her belly. "Soon," she muttered to herself. "Soon…"

"All right," Janice said as she quickly got everyone in line. "Time to get going. Lana," she pointed at the young woman who had her arm tucked into Jorje's crooked elbow—he'd arrived two days ago in Cade's old truck, and he and Lana had been inseparable ever since, "you two love birds are first. Okay, now, go!"

A blush had stained Jorje's cheeks at Janice's teasing, but Lana looked proud and in love. He smiled down at her as they took their first steps down the aisle.

They are so cute, but this is taking forever, Addie groaned inwardly, but she knew it was only a matter of minutes.

When Ivan finally led her to the aisle, Addie's heart leaped the moment her eyes met Cade's. The cloudless cerulean sky had nothing on the blue of his eyes and his smile put the bright summer sun to shame. He looked so handsome in his black tux and cowboy hat, and the love shining in his eyes—only for her—made her almost giddy.

Cade's grin never faltered as she made her way to his side and took his warm, calloused hand. He was all she saw. Not the gorgeous flowers in pretty bouquets decorating the aisle and every corner of the backyard. Not the white chairs lined up on the deep green lawn with the big white tulle bows tied around their backs. Not the flower-bedecked cedar arch framing Cade and the minister behind him, and not all their guests in their Sunday best, grinning and teary-eyed as she passed them. Only Cade, smiling at her with love pouring from his sparkling blue eyes as he took both of her hands. Her vision blurred and he gently wiped a tear from her cheek.

"Hey, sweetie," he murmured. "I hope those are happy tears."

"The happiest tears *ever*," she whispered back.

His smile was both tender and sweet. "Good," he said, then tucked her hand in his elbow and they turned to the preacher to take their vows.

EPILOGUE

Cade braced his booted feet against the floor of Cord's truck and ran frantic fingers through his already messy hair. *Damn this snow,* he thought as Cord carefully navigated the icy December roadway. If he had known Addie would go into labor *this* early, he'd never have agreed to help Zack with his troublesome heifer. The anxious, first-time momma had finally given birth, but it had been a long process. The call from Joe Baker with the news that an ambulance had just left their place with Addie inside had come right on the heels of the calf's birth.

Part of him was glad that Cord had driven them to Zack's, but another side wished he had his truck. "Can't you go any faster?"

Cord tossed a glare at him before concentrating on the road again. "Not if you want to get there in one piece. Addie would never forgive me, if I let that happen."

"I want to get there before it's all over."

"She's in good hands, Cade."

"Yes, I know that," Cade snapped, "but I'd still like to be there. She needs me."

"You need her, you mean."

Cade glanced at his brother, an angry retort on the tip of his tongue, but the teasing curl of Cord's lips stopped him, and his irritation drained out in a long sigh. "Yeah, that, too."

Cord chuckled. "She's strong, Cade, and the doctors know their stuff. We'll get there soon and you'll see, everything'll be fine."

"Yeah…" he growled, knowing his brother was right, but not liking the situation in the least. "I just… I want to be a good husband, a good father. I want to be there when my kid enters the world."

"You are all those things," Cord said, "and whether you see them all at the moment of birth or not, will not change any of that." He paused. "Addie seems to think you're the best husband in the world."

Cade's head snapped to the side. "She *told* you that?"

His brother shrugged. "Not in so many words, but after almost a year together, the way she still looks at you says it all."

The studded tires crunched over the ice-coated road as Cord maneuvered around a corner, only blocks from the hospital. The roads in town were far better than the outlying ones, but the going was still slower than Cade would've liked.

He'd been dreaming about this day since Addie had told him she was pregnant. The memory of that first night on their honeymoon filled his mind. He'd been so afraid that the plans he'd made would let her down, but the nice-sized cabin he'd had built for them in a secluded spot by the river and decorated himself had made her cry.

"Happy tears," she'd said when she turned to him. "They're happy tears, I promise. This is just so beautiful."

Her praise had filled him with pride. He'd installed comfortable furniture, a thick rug in front of the huge river-stone fireplace, and palm plants and flowers everywhere for a touch of the tropics she'd wanted. The edge of the roof, front windows, and deck had all been strung with Christmas lights that twinkled like stars and were almost as bright as Addie's eyes had been when they first pulled up.

"You did all this for me?" she'd asked, staring up into his eyes.

"For us," he'd replied, taking her hand in his. "It's our home away from home. Anytime we want to be alone…with no interruptions."

Grinning at his innuendo, she'd wrapped her arms around his waist and pressed her body against his. It had taken a while for her to trust im—and herself—again, but she'd finally broken the bonds of anxiety and fear that had kept them from deeper acts of intimacy. He would've waited forever, but he was thankful that he hadn't needed to. She was resilient, his beautiful little wife, and pride for her swelled his chest even as the softness of her breasts, her hardened nipples boring into him, and the promise in her eyes tightened his groin. It had only been one night that they'd spent apart, but it had felt like a year. Desire had flooded his veins like fire and he couldn't get her inside fast enough.

She had giggled when he swept her up in his arms to carry her over the threshold, and then kissed him soundly once they'd stepped inside. Their plans to unload their bags and get themselves set up for their weeklong stay had flown out the window the moment their lips met. Suddenly so hot for her, he couldn't wait another second. He carried her to the counter and lowered her beautiful backside onto the chilly granite surface.

"Burr," she said with a little shiver as she shifted her position and wrapped her legs around his waist. "I think you'd better keep kissing me. I'm getting cold."

He'd been so happy and more than willing to oblige. Without hesitation, her nimble hands tugged his dress shirt from the waistband of the black slacks he still wore and ducked inside. He inhaled sharply when her cool fingers splayed over his abdomen and slid up to his chest and then down again. She began plucking at the buttons of his shirt as he shoved the skirt of her knee-length ivory dress up to her hips and then reached around her to work the zipper seductively down her back. The sound of it opening and the soft, warm feel of her beneath made his skin tingle and heat, and sent a jolt of awareness to his already hardened shaft.

They'd both been so desperate to reconnect physically that it had taken less than a minute to push their clothes out of the way and for Cade to plunge deep inside her. She cried out, her hands clutching his shoulders and he slammed into her again. As his rhythm increased, her soft moans of pleasure were like music to his ears. They spurred him on, just as her legs and the heels of her feet against his backside encouraged him to move faster, drive deeper, until they were both crying out and clutching each other tight.

That had been a magical moment, but nothing compared to their evening after they'd unpacked and Cade had set up their meal in front of the large fireplace. He had planned everything to the last detail. The way he'd touch her as they ate. How he'd hold a plump strawberry up to her lips for dessert. How he'd relieve her of her clothes while he seduced her with his hands and mouth. He'd even planned out the orgasms he would give her in front of the flames. And he'd been very successful at all of it, but she'd been the one to give him the greatest gift.

It had been seven months since that night and he could still feel her body against him, her heart matching the thundering of his as she'd straddled his hips and joined their bodies once again. He couldn't take his eyes or hands off her.

Once they'd both cried out their release, Addie had collapsed onto his chest and his arms held her tight.

"I love you," she'd whispered, her warm breath cooling the sheen of perspiration on his skin.

"I love you, too, sweetheart."

She lifted her head to gaze into his eyes. "Will you love me when I'm fat and bloated, too?"

He laughed. "I'd love you no matter what."

She had frowned at his reply and he still felt like a fool for missing her hint.

"What?" he'd asked, unsure what he'd said wrong.

She'd rolled off him and rested her head on his shoulder. "I know you'd said you wanted a big family..." she started, but her voice trailed off.

With a finger under her chin, he lifted her gaze to his. His heart clenched at the doubt he read in her eyes. "Do you not want that now?"

They'd talked about it before and he'd thought they were on the same page, but it had been quite a while. Maybe she'd changed her mind after being attacked. *Why hadn't I thought to ask her about it again?*

Her eyes widened at his question and she shook her head. "Oh, no," she said quickly, "I still want that, it's just..." She dropped her gaze, but when she looked up again, she was smiling and a glimmer of mischief twinkled in her eyes. "When were you thinking of starting this big family?"

He had sighed in relief. "Well, maybe a year or two. Why?"

The smile on her face slipped just a bit. "How would you feel about his coming December?"

"I…well…I-I," he'd stammered, taken aback. December had only been seven months away at the time. He'd stared at her, confused, and then the truth hit him like a lightning bolt. "You… You're…?"

"Yes," she said with a huge grin. "Are you okay with that?"

"Okay? You're having my baby?"

"Yes."

"Oh, sweetheart," he'd said, turning on his side to pull her into his arms, "I'm fantastic! We're having a baby!"

The rest of their honeymoon had been filled with more lovemaking and talk about baby names. He'd repeatedly ran his hand over her soft belly, hardly able to believe that another of his dreams was growing inside her.

Addie had changed his life so drastically when she'd stopped to offer him a ride. She had healed his bitter heart, given him reason to dream and hope again, had even brought his brother and the life he'd missed back to him. Without even trying, she'd tilted his miserable life back onto its axis and made him happier than he'd ever thought he could be. He wanted to be there for her now.

"Cord," he said, the sense of urgency swelling inside him felt like a bomb about to explode, "please hurry."

Cord must have heard the note of fear in his voice, because he revved the engine a little more. "We're almost there."

They finally rolled down the street of the local hospital and turned into the parking lot. They found Joe Baker standing near the emergency entrance, shifting from foot to foot, waiting for them to arrive.

"You go in with Joe," Cord said as he pulled up to the entrance. "I'll park the truck and be right in."

Cade barely heard the last part of Cord's statement as he shoved open the truck's door and jumped outside. "Where is she?" he demanded.

"I'll show you," Joe said as he turned toward the sliding glass entryway.

Cade wanted to sprint down the hallway, but he didn't want them to throw him out either, so he measured his strides to Joe's rapid walk as he followed the older rancher down the white hall.

Cade's chest ached so much he could hardly breathe as they entered the maternity ward and stepped up to the front desk.

"This is the father," Joe said to the nurse behind the desk.

She glanced at Cade as she got to her feet. "Please leave your hat and coat with Mr. Baker and follow me."

Cade practically threw the clothing at Joe as he jogged to catch up with the nurse. "How is she? How's my wife?" he asked as they hurried down the hall.

"Her labor has been hard, but she hasn't given birth yet."

Cade sighed, but the knot in his chest tightened.

A scream echoed down the hall that made Cade's heart thump painfully against his breastbone. He recognized that voice. His feet moved faster and the nurse caught up to him before he could rush inside.

"You need to put on a gown and wash your hands before going in there."

"Why is she screaming like that?" His voice cracked with the panic that pulsed through him. "Is she hurt? In danger? What?"

"She's fine," the nurse said as she pulled him toward an alcove with a sink. "It's just a contraction." She pulled a gown off the shelf and held it open, gazing back at him with kind eyes. "Put this on and then wash your hands."

Cade shoved his arms into the sleeves then went to the sink while the nurse fastened the ties behind his back and pulled a cloth hat over his head. He scrubbed until she told him to rinse and dry his hands, his stomach twisting and tightening the whole time.

Addie's screams had died off once and started up again before he'd finished, but the nurse reassured him that was normal. "Her contractions are very close now, your wife must be almost there. You made it just in time." Her gentle smile didn't help him relax. He was too anxious to see Addie.

When they pushed into the room and he met Addie's tired eyes, something inside him untwisted a little. She was alive. Her face was flushed, sweat rolled down her cheeks, and her hair was a matted mess, but she was the most beautiful thing he'd ever seen.

"This is the father," the nurse said as Cade hastened to Addie's side.

He took her outstretched hand and she smiled. "You made it."

"Of course, I did. Did you really think I'd let you do this alone?"

"I knew you wou...ahh...!" Addie's happy smile turned into a grimace of pain as she squeezed his hand and screamed in what sounded like agony.

"Breathe, sweetie," he said, remembering his training from the Lamaze classes they'd attended. "Is she ready to push, doctor?"

"Almost," the doctor replied without looking up. "The next contraction should be it."

"You're doing so good," he told her as he used a piece of cloth to wipe the sweat from her face. "I'm so proud of you."

"I know," she murmured tiredly. "I'm glad you're here."

"Me, too."

Another contraction came. "Now," the doctor said. "Push!"

Several minutes passed while Addie struggled to bring their child into the world. Cade was worried about her, but anxious to meet their newborn.

"Push," the doctor shouted and Addie did as instructed. Cade was amazed by her strength and daunted by her pain. He had caused this. He'd been the one who wanted a big family. It killed him to know that his desires brought her this agony.

"Push, Addie," the doctor said again. "I can see the head, it's almost out. The next push should do it."

The next contraction hit and Addie pushed while Cade held and encouraged her. "I love you, sweetheart. I love you," he whispered in her ear.

A piercing cry suddenly filled the room and Cade's heart jumped into his throat. Addie's hand clung to his as they waited for the doctor. They hadn't wanted to know the sex of the baby, so it was time for the big reveal.

"It's a girl," the doctor said as he quickly handed the red, wailing, wiggling bundle to the nurse. Cade's eyes followed the tiny creature as the nurse cleaned her and wrapped her in a fluffy pink blanket. Tears burned his eyes as he stared at his daughter, unable to look away.

Then Addie screamed again and the doctor took a steadying breath "Okay, now for the other one."

Cade's mouth went dry. "The other one?"

"Surprise," Addie said between breaths.

"You knew?"

"I suspected," Addie breathed. "But the doctor confirmed it a few months ago. Remember that appointment you missed in October?"

He nodded dumbly as another contraction hit and she pushed.

"One more," the doctor said, "and you'll meet the twin."

"Twins?" Cade's brain seemed to be stuck in neutral. He'd known it was a possibility that he and Cord could produce twins, but it hadn't occurred to him to ask about it until now. He'd just assumed Addie would tell him if they were, and maybe she had tried.

"I tried to tell you," she said right before the next contraction, confirming his suspicion. He should've guessed, what with the amount of clothing she'd brought home alone, not to mention Addie "accidentally" purchasing two cribs.

"Good job, Addie," the doctor said a long moment later. "You now also have a son."

"A son?" Cade said stupidly, still trying to wrap his head around not only being a father, but to having a daughter *and* a son.

"Are you upset?" Addie asked quietly.

He looked down at her tired face and saw worry in her weary brown eyes. "No, sweetheart, I am not upset. You've done so much. Given me everything I ever wanted. You rest now, and when you're feeling better, we'll celebrate however you want."

"Hmm," she purred, closing her eyes. "I think I'd like to start with some kissing, and then I'd like to strip you naked and have my way with you."

When her lids lifted to meet his gaze with a meaningful glint in her eyes, he grinned. "You're insatiable."

"Only when you're involved."

"Would you like to hold your babies now?" the nurse asked, interrupting their flirting.

"Absolutely!" Addie's smile was wide and bright, though Cade could ell she was exhausted.

The nurse placed both children on her chest, their daughter still mewling a bit. Cade placed his hand on his daughter's back, feeling her warmth and the beat of her tiny heart. She settled instantly.

"Ah," Addie sighed. "She's going to be a Daddy's girl."

"I have no doubt." He nodded toward his son. "And he'll be as quiet and gentle as you." He kissed Addie's temple. "They're as beautiful as their mother," he rasped through his pinched and achy throat. "I can't wait to teach them how to ride and shoot and climb trees and—"

"Both of them, right?" Addie interrupted with a shrewd glance. "I won't have him learning something that she can't, and vice versa."

His head jerked back a little. "Of course, I'll teach them both. You think I wouldn't?"

"No, I don't think so, but I had to make sure." She looked down at the two small heads on her chest, both covered in wisps of dark hair. "It's important to me."

He lifted her face with a finger beneath her chin. "It's important to me, too, Addie. I'll teach them whatever they want to learn."

She smiled. "Good. I will, too."

"You should get some rest, Addie," the doctor said as he dried his recently washed hands on a paper towel.

Addie nodded. "Can my husband come with me? I'd sleep better with him beside me."

"You have a private room, so I don't see why not. As long as you *rest*." His tone and raised eyebrows indicated he'd heard their earlier flirting and was gently reminding them to wait a while for Addie to heal before working on creating their next child.

"She will, doctor," Cade promised. "After all this, I think we both could use a long nap."

* * *

Twenty minutes later, the babies were fed and fast asleep in the nursery. Cade had stopped by the waiting room to give Joe and his brother the news to find a frazzled-looking Cord pacing with worry. When Cade explained that Bethany had two cousins, Cord had grinned proudly and wrapped his brother in a bear hug.

"Congratulations!" Cord had shouted exuberantly and Cade laughed so filled with the love and joy of his family he couldn't contain it.

"How's Addie?" Joe had asked as he shook Cade's hand and Cord nodded, wanting to know that as well.

"She's good," Cade told them. "Tired, but good. I'm going to stay with her tonight, if you guys want to head home. You can come by in the morning to see the babies if you'd like."

"If we'd like?" Joe had chuckled, slapping Cade on the back. "We'll be here."

"Yeah," Cord said quietly. "I can't wait… I bet they're just beautiful. Have you named them yet?"

Cade shook his head. "Not just yet."

"Well, we'll have a whole mess of options in the morning," Cord said, giving Cade another hug—though a much tamer one this time. "I'm really happy for you, brother."

Then he turned and walked down the hall to join Joe at the elevator.

"You'll find a good woman, too, Cord," he murmured to himself, "and someday, I'll be congratulating you."

Not two minutes later, Cade climbed onto the wide hospital bed beside his wife and gently pulled her against his side. Addie snuggled in close and sighed as his arm wrapped around her.

"Did I worry you?" she asked softly.

"A little," he said, remembering their discussions about everything that could go wrong.

"I told you, I'd be fine. Even if you didn't make it here."

"I know," Cade said, brushing a stray hair from her damp forehead, "but I wanted to share this with you, be here for you."

She smiled. "I never doubted it."

He kissed the top of her head. "Good."

"So, shall we decide on the names?"

Cade smiled. "Caitlyn and Colton, Colt for short."

"Colt? Really? You're sticking with the cowboy name?" she teased.

"Of course," he said, "just like his pa and uncle. What do you expect?"

She giggled. "And you're okay with Caitlyn?"

"I'm sure your Irish grandma would've approved."

"I'm sure she would've," Addie said softly. "I guess it's settled then. Caitlyn and Colton the new terrors of the West."

Cade grinned at her joke and then they both lay silently, the soft sound of their breathing the only thing he could hear. Cade thought Addie had drifted off, but then she spoke again. "Did you think anything like this could happen when I stopped to give you a lift that day?" she asked, referring to how they'd met.

Cade chuckled. "No, I didn't think any of this would *ever* happen."

"Any of what, exactly?"

He hugged her close. "That I'd fall in love with the cute little blonde behind the wheel. That she'd give me a reason to love again. That because of her, I'd get my brother and my home back. That I'd actually have the family I always wanted."

"You thought I was cute?" she asked and he read trepidation in her wide-eyed gaze. "Even back then?"

Cade laughed again. She had a way of making him laugh, even at himself. "Hell yes, even back then. You were so gorgeous with your hair up in that messy bun and that tank top showing off your…curves."

"Really?" She tilted her head to pin him with a narrow-eyed look. "That's all you were interested in?"

He shrugged. "Hey, I'm a guy. Of course, I notice your natural beauty, but I quickly learned how smart and strong you are, too. I don't think I've ever told you that."

"No, I don't think you have."

"Well, it's true. I think I started falling in love with you when you slipped in all the oil on your garage floor and nearly smashed your head on the fender of your car."

"My hero," she said with a smile.

"Always," he whispered, and then leaned in to kiss her waiting mouth. She sighed when he pulled back. "Now, close your eyes. It's time to rest."

"Yes, sir," she teased as she tucked her head under his chin.

Several minutes later, her regular breathing told him she'd fallen asleep and he wasn't far behind. His body felt heavy as he relaxed, a happy warmth suffusing his chest, pulling him under. Happy, satisfied, content, he was all of those things and more.

Cade smiled as he drifted closer to sleep, pleased, knowing the love of his life lay in his arms and his new family slept down the hall. Soon, they'd all be back home to begin their new life together.

He chuckled a little as he realized that the blissful future he now faced had begun at the lowest point in his life when Addie's melodious voice had rung out from the cab of her truck to ask, "Need a ride, cowboy?" She'd awakened his heart on that dusty country road under the hot summer sun. Thanks to her, he'd regained everything he'd lost, and he would never hide behind walls of bitterness and heartache again. She filled him with happiness and love, and he intended to spend the rest of his days doing the same for her.

The End

If you enjoyed this book, turn the page for more books
by Jamie Schulz and the first chapter of the
Angel Eyes Series Prequel
Jake's Redemption.

THE ANGEL EYES SERIES
Award-winner in the Global Ebook Awards

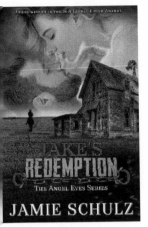

An imprisoned cowboy.
An empowered woman.
When true love is forbidden,
opening their hearts could destroy them
both...

Chained and enslaved, Jake Nichols is convinced he'll die alone. In this new order where men are stripped of all power, he endures brutal torture at the hands of his female captor. But when he's hired out to build a ranch home for an outspoken beauty, his dreams of escape transform into visions of passion.

Monica Avery struggles to fill her heart in a loveless society. With marriage outlawed and romantic partners reduced to pawns, she's given up hope of finding her soul mate. But watching the rugged rancher hard at work on her shelter awakens deeply buried desires.

As the project comes together, Monica discovers a kindred spirit in the tenderhearted Jake. But despite their growing attraction, he still belongs to a cruel woman who'd rather see him dead than free.

Can Monica save Jake, or will their love lead to a tragic tomorrow?

Jake's Redemption is a full-length book in the Angel Eyes cowboy dystopian romance series. If you like scorching-hot chemistry, clever post-apocalyptic worlds, and star-crossed love stories, then you'll adore Jamie Schulz's captivating tale.

Sound interesting?
Turn the page for a sneak peek of Jake's Redemption...

JAKE'S REDEMPTION

1

JAKE NICHOLS KNELT in defeat on the cold ground of the mountain meadow, directly beside his best friend, Bret Masters. Defenseless, with their fingers laced together behind their heads, their eyes scanned the surroundings for any escape from the Raiders who had attacked their camp in the early morning hours.

Both men scowled up at their captor, a woman Bret had foolishly—and against Jake's repeated warnings—loved to distraction. Jake risked a quick glance at his friend, knowing the pain Bret must be suffering in the wake of her betrayal. He felt the bite of it too, only for a different reason. Bret was family, and what hurt him, hurt Jake. His protective nature made him long to shield Bret from the misery this woman inflicted.

"I don't care for you," Amy had said only moments ago, indifferent to the devastation Jake saw in every line of Bret's granite-hard face. What made her confession even worse was the bit she added about only wanting to use his body.

"You do have such a pretty face, but no brains in your head," she went on, and then laughed at Bret's seething look. His expression made Jake ache for his friend, and he silently hoped she had nothing more to torment him with. But Amy wasn't done with Bret yet.

"How could you think any self-respecting woman would want you for anything more than your gorgeous face and hard body?" she asked, not waiting for a reply. "A decent woman would never accept you as an equal. Any woman who would is worse than the slave you will shortly become."

A deep growl rumbled up from Bret's chest, and to Jake's surprise Bret lunged to his feet and attacked her. Seeing an opportunity, Jake and all the other prisoners immediately joined him in a last, desperate attempt to gain their freedom. Their female adversaries, however, had a new genetic advantage. It may have taken a few seconds for the hysterical strength to kick in, but once it did, the fight, strength-wise, was no longer in the men's favor.

The skirmish didn't last long, but in a brief moment before it ended, Jake turned to see Amy about to drive a long-bladed knife into his best friend's back. Jake didn't think, he moved, tackling Amy as her weapon plunged downward from its high arch. Amy tried to wiggle away from him, but he held on, desperate to keep her from harming Bret.

"Run!" He heard Bret's frantic shout. "Run!" The sound of pounding feet and continued battle assaulted Jake's ears. He tried to roll away from Amy, but now she held on to him. On his hands and knees, he jerked his arm to shake her loose and follow his friend into the forest, but she wouldn't let go.

Pain bloomed sharp and bright in his ribs as a booted foot slammed into him—once, twice—and he fell. The boot kept coming. He curled up, protecting his vulnerable areas, but his assailant still landed several blows to his head and back.

"Enough!" Amy's voice rang out, and the assault ended. Jake spit blood from his mouth and struggled to catch his breath. The dizziness in his head and the stabbing ache in his side told him getting to his feet might be harder than it was a few minutes ago.

Definitely broke a rib or two, he thought, tonguing his split lip and rapidly cataloging the pain in the rest of his body.

"How many do we still have?" Amy shouted to someone nearby.

"Ten got away," a woman said. "With this one," Jake assumed she was pointing at him, "we still have twenty-seven men, along with some traitorous women and children too."

"Is there a tall man, black hair, green eyes, very good-looking, among those we recaptured?" Amy asked, describing Bret to a tee.

"No."

"That sappy, pretty-boy son of a bitch," Amy swore, undoubtedly meaning Bret. "I should've known he'd try something like that." She cursed again.

"You know their hiding places now," the other woman said. "We'll catch them and their friends too."

Jake and Bret had come across Amy by accident—or so they had thought at the time—almost seven months before as they traveled the mountains, hunting for food. She'd been hungry and in need of aid. Unsurprisingly, she took an immediate interest in Bret. Although he had a mistrusting nature, she spared little time wrapping his love-starved heart around her finger. Jake had never liked her and the two friends argued about her more than once, but despite his misgivings about Amy, Jake refused to alienate his boyhood friend. Yet as a result of her relationship with Bret, she now knew the location of most of their woodland hiding places.

"That's true," Amy replied to the other woman's comment. She tapped her chin with her index finger as if considering, and then she glanced down at Jake.

He had lain very still during their interaction, hoping against hope they might forget about him.

No such luck.

"And you," she said coming toward him. "You—"

He didn't give her a chance to finish; he had a fairly good idea of what came next. Instead, he ignored his dizziness and the pain in his chest as he surged to his feet, pushed her aside, and ran for the trees. He'd made it six feet when he heard a crack behind him. Then something hard and thin snapped around his neck and yanked him backward. He saw stars as his head and back slammed to the ground, sending a new wave of misery through his abused body. He groaned, trying to place what just happened, and then Amy was leaning over him.

She jammed her knee into his chest, and pain shot through hi damaged ribs. He lifted his arms to shove her away, but the leathery rop wrapped around his neck yanked at him again, choking off his air Desperate, needing to get her off him, needing to breathe, he tugged a the cord strangling him. His eyes widened as Amy grabbed him by th hair and tilted his head back to expose his throat. He reached for he again, but the minute the edge of her knife grazed his flesh, his arm collapsed to the ground and he froze.

The binding around his neck loosened and fell away as Amy glared into his face. Blessed air came freely, but the simple act of breathing caused his ribs to twinge more.

With the suffocating rope gone, his hands automatically lifted off the ground to defend himself. Amy's knife cut a tiny fraction deeper. Blood tickled his neck as the warm liquid trickled over his cool skin, and he froze once more, afraid to even breathe.

"Uh-uh," Amy warned as she increased the pressure slightly, widening the gash a bit more and digging the point of her blade into his Adam's apple.

His mouth went dry. *Is she going to slit my throat?*

"Looks like Bret didn't value your friendship as much as you thought, huh, Jake?" Amy said with a nasty smile, her dark brown eyes glittering down at him.

Jake cringed inwardly. He knew that wasn't the case. In the chaos, Bret probably hadn't even realized Jake had been captured, and wouldn't until he failed to show at their rendezvous point. But her implication twisted at his guts nonetheless.

A second woman stepped up behind Amy, coiling the long black length of a bullwhip in her hand.

So, that's what was strangling me...I should've known.

"You fucked up my plans, Jake, just as much as your damned friend," Amy hissed at him when he didn't respond to her earlier comment. "If it weren't for you, he'd be mine and you'd both make me rich. Now, I have to settle for you and those other losers we caught today."

"What're—you going—to do with me?" He stifled a groan for his alting speech and glared daggers at the woman hovering over him.

"Oh, I think you know what we do with captured men," Amy chuckled. She tilted her head, and a strand of her amber-blonde hair fell into her face as her eyes raked over him.

"You know, Jake," she said reflectively, "you're a good-looking guy. If Bret hadn't been around, you would've been my target. It's only next to a man like him that you'd seem second best. But then, you were always suspicious of me, weren't you? Maybe once you've been trained, I'll pay you another visit."

He clamped his jaws tight and didn't respond, but his mind was in overdrive. He wanted to fight, but moving meant death. He didn't want to know what it was like to bleed to death from a severed artery. Instead, he cowled all the more. If he wanted to live, it was all he could do.

The woman beside Amy crouched down, but he couldn't see what she was doing. The next thing he knew, he jumped as a needle jammed into his hip and something injected into his body.

Ah, shit… He knew what *that* was; he'd heard dozens of stories about it but luckily had never had to deal with the drug, until now.

It started working almost instantaneously, driving up his anxiety level, making him shake and cringe. A few seconds passed, while Amy's gaze bore into his, and the effect of the chemical doubled.

Oh, God, this is worse than I thought it would be. He had never felt so weak and vulnerable in his life.

"Now," Amy said as she removed the blade from his throat and stood. She tucked the knife in her boot and then plopped her rear down on his chest, knowing he would be too terrified, thanks to the drug, to do anything to save himself. "What shall I do with you?" She ran a finger down the side of his face.

He flinched away.

You could let me go, he thought and tried to force out the sarcastic remark, but the substance surging through him wouldn't allow it.

"I think you deserve a particularly horrible punishment for always interfering in my plans with Bret," she said, answering her own question while tapping his bearded chin with one finger. The slight contact amped up his anxiety, and he shivered. "He may have listened to you complain about me, but he *loved* me." Her derisive tone told him what she though about that. "He would've never turned me out the way you kept tellin him to do. And now, you've ruined my chance to have him how I alway wanted him: in chains. So, how shall I make you pay for all of it?"

Jake's body shook with fear, both real and chemically induced. Am was far more lethal than he had once thought.

"I know just the place you should go," she continued with a brigh smile, as if she'd come up with a brilliant idea. "I have an acquaintanc near here, a woman who's exceptionally adept at training men to b perfect little slaves. I'll bet she'd *jump* at the chance to make you a willin breeder. You'll make her a lot of money. Once she pays me a high pric for you that is."

"P-Please…" Jake pleaded involuntarily, the drug wreaking havoc with his willpower. No matter how much he wanted to resist begging, he couldn't stop now that he had started. "P-Please…" he muttered again, his voice shaking while fighting the drug—and losing. "Let me go…"

Amy laughed.

"Darla's going to tear you to pieces, Jake," she told him, her sinister smile sending waves of dread prickling up and down his spine. "A little bit at a time, she'll peel away your pride—"

A loud thud from down the hall jolted Jake's mind back to the present. Darkness surrounded his sweating, trembling body as terror from his nightmarish recollection lingered in his mind. As much as he hated the bleak confines of his concrete cell, he was thankful to be alone. No one expecting anything. No one demanding he perform acts that made him want to retch. No one hurting him. He waited for the sound in the hallway to repeat, but when it didn't, he exhaled in a grateful rush and ran an unsteady hand over his face.

Why can't I stop obsessing about what happened that day?

He slumped against the cold stone walls of his tiny prison cell, staring into the midnight-black nothingness. Scurrying sounds of small creatures sounded nearby, and in the distance he heard the soft sobs of another slave. A burning wetness welled in Jake's eyes, and a thick ache formed in the back of his throat for the other man's suffering. Or maybe it was for is own. He shook his head, wiped at his face again, and tried to block out the other man's weeping.

The concrete chamber in which he sat was smaller than the walk-in closet in the tiny two-bedroom apartment he'd rented years ago. That room had seemed huge back then; this one felt claustrophobic. He had enough room to lie down and turn over, but that was about it.

His first frantic attempt to find a way out yielded nothing. Several times since, his hands had methodically slid over the wet, rough stones of his cell. His fingers dug into the concrete joints, every nook and cranny, until they hurt; still, he found no way out. Even if he had, he couldn't have gone anywhere. The chains connected to the heavy shackles around his neck, wrists, and ankles anchored him to the wall, but he kept trying. So many times, sweat had trickled down his face and chest as he gritted his teeth, his fingers gripping the chains with a desperate strength. He strained every muscle in his body, but after hours of repeated yanking, he released them with a despondent cry and sprawled on the damp floor in exhausted defeat.

The lump in his throat returned. Would he ever see the sun again? Ever see his friends? But then, only one of those remained. Bret Masters.

He sighed and rubbed his forehead, attempting to ease the ache caused by thinking about Bret. He dropped his hand and sighed again. The long story of their friendship had led Jake to this fate. A part of him blamed Bret for everything that had happened to him in this place, which was unfair, but rationalizing didn't stop him from being angry.

His fingers unconsciously moved to his chest. They kneaded rhythmically, trying to release the knot of despair tangled around his heart. In constant battle, resentment warred with the brotherly regard he still harbored for Bret, and the victor was, as yet, undecided.

Jake rubbed at his temples and shivered. *This damn room is freezing.*

Even in the spring, the room was damp and cool. Of course, being naked all the time didn't help, but his Mistress, Darla Cain, couldn't be bothered with clothing her slaves. Only when required to work in the cold and wet or the sweltering heat were they given the minimal basics to cover their nudity. The rest of the time, they were all bare and vulnerable to whatever their Mistress wanted from them. Or what she wanted to do to them. After witnessing much of her cruelty personally, Jake suspected she hated men—she took too much enjoyment from their agony not to Adept at causing pain, she tormented her captives, changed them, ruling them utterly. When she tired of them, they were tossed aside and left to molder as Jake was doing now.

Jake had to admit, Amy's choice of punishment had been well made. The things his Mistress did to him were terrible—demoralizing and humiliating—and he didn't want to remember, but he had nothing else to do here in the lonely, oppressive darkness.

As the memories came, his mind flinched from the incident that had landed him in this cell.

Piercing agony burned across his back, and he screamed. Over and over he screamed, but he refused to give them what they demanded, would not provide them their sick pleasure.

A moan escaped him. He shivered at the memory of his short-lived rebellion, hating himself more for his eventual submittal, for being weak, and for the loss that eventually came of it.

The act that followed his failing though—when his Mistress tried to force him into another vile game for her entertainment—that one he relished.

"You sick bitch!" he had roared at his Mistress as he surged against the three guards who blocked his way. Fear trembled in the back of his mind, but reckless rage kept it there. "I'm going to fucking kill you!"

When alarm crossed his Mistress' face, his lips twitched upward as satisfaction flooded his system. *Good, she's scared,* he thought bitterly. *She should be!* Then his muscles tightened and he redoubled his efforts.

He lunged with all his strength, his gaze locked on his target, determined to reach the red-headed bitch and end her for good. His bigger, heavier body drove the guards back several steps before more joined in. He swung at them, but the chains on his wrists hindered his movement. Again, he gathered his diminishing strength and strove to reach the cause of all his pain and fury. He surged against the human barrier, but too many bodies now stood between them. He hadn't moved fast enough. Hysterical-strength kicked in, and the women guarding his Mistress grew stronger.

A sharp yank on the chain attached to the collar around his neck wrenched him off his feet. He landed on his back, knocking the breath from his lungs and cracking his head on the hard floor. Dazed, he blinked, and then saw the next blow coming. The end of his own lead chain slammed across his heaving chest with a loud thud. Ribs vibrating with pain, he grunted and rolled into a ball as the next strike fell, knowing he had lost the fight. Knowing his Mistress' treatment of him would now grow much, much worse.

And it did.

Instead of preventing his Mistress from ever forcing something so terrible on him or anyone else again, the guards had stopped him, beat him severely, and dragged him down here. For hours, he'd lain almost lifeless where they dropped him, licking his wounds and berating himself. He didn't know how long ago that was now. Days, weeks, months—they all blended into one. Regret for his inability to end his Mistress' reign of terror left him feeling hollow and weighted down by the enormity of his failure. Though, if he'd succeeded, they would've killed him, disappointment still pierced his heart like a flaming arrow.

But that first act, the unthinkable thing his Mistress forced him to do—the one that led to his futile assault and lonely imprisonment—that event *haunted* him.

"Leave it alone," he growled into the abyss of his cell, his heart heavy in his chest. "You can't change anything now."

But he couldn't leave the memory alone.

Her soft brown eyes filled with terror and tears.

Her trembling body, cringing against him.

Quiet whimpers wrenching at his heart.

Her misplaced trust in *him*.

Jake's hands curled into fists and he shook his head, the recollection tearing at his insides, killing him slowly.

I was supposed to protect her.

A sob bubbled into his throat, but he swallowed it down and rushed to his feet as self-loathing roared in his ears. His chains rattled along the rock as he paced, five steps one way, five steps back. *A path should've worn through the stone by now from all my pacing*, he thought.

He stopped at the door imprisoning him. His hands clenched tightly at his sides, and in his helpless anguish, he hammered on the steel with his fists.

"Let me out!" he bellowed in a cracked voice, welcoming the pain in his knuckles, his hands, his wrists. "God damn you. Let me out!"

His cries and the dull pounding of his fists ricocheted through the long corridor outside, the echoes mocking him with their freedom. The cries of the other slave stilled as inarticulate roars of fury ripped through Jake's aching throat, every muscle in his body quivering as he released the rage inside him.

You're being stupid! a voice in his head shouted. *Stop it!*

His throbbing fists ceased pummeling the immovable metal, and his hands splayed out over its cold surface.

His forehead fell against steel with a muffled thud.

Waves of shudders crashed through him.

Despair, like a living thing, coiled tightly around his heart, and a sob finally escaped him.

Squeezing his eyes closed, he concentrated on breathing.

I will not give them any more.

No more blood. No more sweat. No more tears.

Pushing away from the cell door, he wiped his hand over his face, brushed at his damp lashes, and sat back down.

Maybe Bret had it right all these years, he thought. *No more trust either.*

He shook in the aftermath of emotion. Or perhaps he should blame the drug. He was more than a day overdue for his booster of the nasty stuff, so the fear and submission it caused were minimal now. In nearly two years, he'd never gone so long without an injection. He wondered if they figured his obedience didn't matter because he was chained, locked up, and half-starved.

His fingers rubbed at his chest again. Still sore from the beating they had given him after his ill-fated, rage-induced attack, he felt weak and tired, and he didn't care anymore.

Again, resentment burned in his chest.

"Run!" Bret had screamed that day, and—after all they'd been through together and all Jake had done for him over the years—Bret had left him behind to be captured and enslaved.

You know that's not fair, a part of Jake murmured, the familiar war waging inside him. Despite their agreement not to attempt to rescue each other, the fact that Bret didn't even try made Jake unreasonably angry.

"He couldn't have saved you from this," Jake mumbled into the gloom, "and you would hate yourself worse if he had gotten captured or killed by trying. Let it go."

"Jake?"

The sound of the soft voice filtering through the steel door made him jump. Only a few minutes had passed since he howled his rage at the world. She must've heard him screaming because she sounded uneasy. Not nervous or afraid, just uncertain of what she would find when she opened the door.

The voice belonged to one of the handful of halfway-decent guards working for his Mistress. The guard's name was Hailey Tate, and there weren't enough like her. She talked about leaving this place one day to move into her own home with her own slaves. Though he didn't know her well, he would miss the kindness she had shown him and the other slaves. When she eventually did leave, there would be one fewer of the kindly guards working here, just one more face forgotten.

He didn't answer her call. They would come in whether he wanted them to or not, and though she had been kind to him in the past, he would no longer cooperate. They could fill him up with the fear drug, beat him unconscious, but he wouldn't do one more thing for them. Or so he kept telling himself. Trying to stay alive for the hope of escape was like slow, agonizing torture, and he would not do that to himself, not anymore—unless they dosed him with the drug again. Then its effects would leave him no choice but to submit.

A key fit into the lock. The mechanism clicked, and the heavy door slowly swung open on squeaky hinges.

"Jake?" Hailey called again, but he refused to respond.

He closed his eyes and turned away from the intolerable brightness coming from the lantern she carried. After sitting in the dark for so long, even the dim illumination burned.

"Jake? Are you all right?"

He chuckled, an unpleasant sound bouncing off the walls of his small stone prison. "Well," he croaked, "if you count being beaten, starved, and chained to a wall as *all right*, then I'm just dandy."

"I know it's been a while. I tried to get some food to you yesterday," she said as she crouched down beside him, "but there was a problem."

He glared at her but didn't speak. Even through his hurt and anger, he appreciated her aid, especially since she didn't have to offer it.

"Someone's here to see you," she said, changing the subject.

"There's no one out there I want to see."

"It's one of the council members."

Jake laughed, still bitter. He looked down at his filthy, naked body and reached up to scratch his bearded cheek. "I'm not in any condition to perform sexual favors. Send her away."

Hailey frowned and glanced over her shoulder at the open doorway.

"Keep your voice down, Jake," she hissed, leaning closer to him, her tone hardening as she spoke. "And mind what you say. I might not agree with all the rules here, but I will enforce them if I must."

He cringed inwardly as his last comment replayed in his head. He didn't intend for it to, but it did come out like a command. A shiver of dread slid up his spine. Hailey might not punish him for that, but he didn't know about his visitor if she had overheard. Quickly, he changed the focus of their murmured discussion.

"I'm going to die down here, Hailey." He couldn't help the forlorn note in his voice.

"Don't use my name, Jake."

"Sorry. Ms. Tate. My Mistress doesn't care if I live or die, and I will die down here, just like all the others."

"I don't think so," she corrected, and he aimed another sharp glance in her direction.

"No?"

"No. That's what your visitor's here about."

His brows twitched together in confusion. "What?"

"She has an offer for you," Hailey told him. "If you give me your word you won't try to harm her, I won't restrain you as *she* ordered me to do."

Ordered. He knew who ordered that: his Mistress. A slave attacking a

ellow council member in Darla's house would make her look bad, but
even if he failed, the effort might also set him free from his unbearable
existence. *Is it worth it?*

Jake sighed. "She won't take it well if she finds out you disregarded her
orders."

"Do you plan to try to harm your visitor?"

He stared at Hailey and then shook his head. "I don't want to hurt
anyone, even though you all will hurt me."

That sounded sufficiently noble, he mocked himself. *What happened to not
giving them any more?*

"Just do it," he said when she didn't move or respond, not caring how
his words could be construed.

It didn't matter anyway.

She didn't argue, and soon his wrists were locked together above his
head, connected to a steel ring embedded in the wall. She glanced down at
him, still seated on the cold stones.

"Take the offer, Jake," she whispered as she bent over him, and his
eyes snapped up to hers in surprise. He opened his mouth, but she
straightened and stepped out of the room before he could speak.

An older woman entered. She was impressive; her gray-streaked black
hair, pulled into a bun at the nape of her neck, exposed a pretty face, now
lined with wisdom. She wore jeans and a lightweight white work shirt. She
appeared stern, but a kindness resided in her amber eyes that calmed his
initial fear. When she smiled, her whole face changed, and he relaxed even
more, before reminding himself to stay on guard.

"Good afternoon, Mr. Nichols," she said in a clear voice.

Jake only nodded and stared at the floor.

It's what they expected of slaves.

Whatever she wants, I will not give it.

"My name is Jewel Stewart. I'm a member of the section's governing
council, and I have a few questions for you."

He flicked a withering glare at her and looked away again, but still
refused to answer.

She paused, and he could feel her eyes assessing him like ants crawling
over his skin. He wanted to squirm under her perusal, but he forced

himself to remain still.

At length, she spoke again. "Do you like living here?"

Astonished by the idiotic question, he met her gaze and barked out rude answer before he could stop himself. "That's a stupid question."

"Does that mean yes or no?"

Is she dense?

"No."

"I didn't think so," she said and smiled again as she joined him on the floor, sitting directly across from him. Her actions, disarming as they were clearly meant to be, shocked him too. The floor was filthy, and the room stank from his unwashed body and his waste—which hadn't been emptied from the overflowing bucket in the corner since before they last fed him three days ago.

What's she up to?

"Tell me about yourself, Mr. Nichols."

"What do you want to know?" Curious now, he told himself that talking required nothing from him. Besides, he had been alone too long. Seeing and speaking with another human being was...nice.

"How did you come to be here?"

He scowled at her. "The same way every other man came to be enslaved."

"A raiding party took you?"

"We fought a war and lost."

"I meant something a little more recently."

Jake hesitated. This was his most civil conversation with a woman since before the war, which sent people running for their lives while its destruction leveled cities and towns across the globe. Again, a pang of regret twisted inside him. So many had died in the war that destroyed their world and altered its social conventions completely. Women, no longer considered the weaker sex, controlled everything now. Men were their slaves, thanks to losing a second civil war they foolishly started themselves.

Raiding parties, like the one that had captured Jake, traveled into the mountains searching for runaways, uncaptured men, and the women who helped them, to sell at auction. In Jake's case, the Raiders had help in cquiring him.

Another reason for his resentment of Bret Masters.

"A woman fooled my friend and betrayed us," he finally responded to her question. "The Raiders showed up, I was taken, and sold at the Auction Hall to Dar...uh...Miss Cain. When she got tired of abusing me, he locked me up down here and left me to rot." He sounded angry and bitter, but he didn't care.

"Tell me what you did before the wars. What kind of work did you do?"

He glared at her, wondering again what her game was, but he saw no reason not to tell her. Giving her the answers was far preferable to another beating.

"I worked in construction for a number of years," he said, "and did some ranching for several more after that."

"So, you're trained in building houses and caring for livestock?"

"Yeah..." he said warily.

Jewel asked for more details about the work he did and he told her, but his suspicions amped up his anxiety level once more. He sat taller, his whole body and consciousness on alert. *What the hell does my work history have to do with anything?* No one had asked him any of this before. No one cared.

"That's quite a resume," she said, smiling again.

Jake grunted in reply and averted his gaze.

"Would you like a chance to leave here for a few months?"

His eyes snapped up to her face. He frowned as his heart rate sped up and he waited for the punchline. Was she screwing with his head like Darla? Dangling a carrot in front of him, getting his hopes up, only to snatch it away again?

"It's not a trick," she told him, apparently reading his thoughts. "There's a job in need of your particular skills if you're interested."

"What kind of job?" he asked, still cautious. This seemed too good to be true. "And where?"

"A friend of one of the other council members is building a new home," Jewel told him. "Her ranch foreman, who also happened to be responsible for the construction, had an accident and died. She has a number of decent workers, but no one with enough experience to oversee the work now. She asked the council if we knew of anyone who could fill in, and your name came up."

He croaked out a rusty laugh. No way did his Mistress tell anyone about him. She wanted him to suffer. Jewel smiled when he said as much.

"I didn't say it was Darla."

He scowled at her again. *Is this for real?*

"The job would last about six months or so," she said as if he'd asked "Do you want it?"

He stared mutely at the floor. Could he trust her or believe her story? *What if this was just another one of Darla's mind games?*

He was silent so long she must've assumed he wasn't interested, because she stood up and dusted herself off. "I'm sorry we couldn't come to an agreement," she murmured and stepped toward the door.

"Wait!" The chains connected to his wrist shackles rattled against the wall as he abruptly sat forward.

She turned back to him and looked down into his upturned face, her expression impatient now. "You have something to say?"

He took a deep breath, wavered, and then dived in. "What's the woman like? The one who needs the house built?"

Jewel smiled again, the annoyance melting away.

"She's nothing like Darla if that's what you're worried about. She won't beat you or starve you. You'll be working in the sun, have three meals a day, and a bed to sleep in at night."

He dropped his eyes to the floor. His mind blazed through the assorted possibilities, while his chest tightened with uncertainty.

Sobs from the slave down the hall had started up again. The other man's torment spurred Jake's decision.

Jewel shifted her feet, and Jake tilted his head to meet her amber gaze. "Are you interested, Mr. Nichols?"

He hesitated. Wary prickles crept over his skin and his heart stuttered, but there really wasn't any other choice.

"Yes," he said, and a shudder of hope passed through him. The reemergence of the once-lost emotion sent another wave of terrified tingles racing up and down his spine.

"Very good," she replied with a smile. "Let's get you out of here. Your temporary Mistress is anxious for you to start right away." She turned to the guard outside. "Hailey, would you unchain him, please?"

As Hailey released his shackles from the wall and helped him to his feet, Jake's stomach fluttered with the shock of escaping this hellhole, where he had expected to die. Heart racing, he reeled and stumbled into the wall, but Hailey steadied him. His head spun and his stomach churned from lack of food, but he fought down the nausea and clenched his jaw, determined to keep going. He would not stay in this place one second longer than it took to get on a horse, or in a cart, or whatever transportation waited to take him away from here.

One foot in front of the other, he thought, his whole body feeling somehow lighter with every step. *Just keep going.*

"Lead the way, ma'am," he told Jewel when he stood beside her in the hallway, swaying slightly, but resolutely staying on his feet.

She smiled and started down the hall.

Jake Nichols, with a rapidly lightening heart, followed in her wake.

* * *

If you've enjoyed the story so far and would like to find out what happens next, go to Amazon and buy your copy of Jake's Redemption today. If you're a Kindle Unlimited reader, you can read the rest for free.

Turn the page for more on this gripping series.

* * *

ALSO BY JAMIE SCHULZ

THE ANGEL EYES SERIES BOOK 1

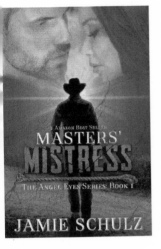

A man bound by chains.
A woman burdened by regret.
Will love set this tortured pair free?

In this nightmarish future where women own men, Bret Masters refuses to serve anyone. But after spending years evading slavers in the mountains of the Pacific Northwest, he's furious when he's finally caught and sold. So, although his mistress has a pretty face and deliciously tempting curves, he vows to escape.

Angel Aldridge hides her pain behind fences as sturdy and vast as her ranch. And even though her newly acquired slave is a ruggedly handsome cowboy, she's not about to let her fantasies endanger the people she swore to protect. But between her always-watching enemies and her wounded heart, she's reluctant to admit she may need him in more ways than one...

As the two toil side by side, Bret is surprised to discover Angel's vulnerability and her compassionate nature. And the more time they spend together, the harder she finds it to resist her feelings and to soothe her lonely soul. But when they're stranded alone together, the barriers between mistress and slave may not be strong enough to withstand their red-hot attraction.

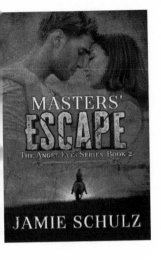

He refuses to be tamed.
She can't let him go.
Will they break down their walls
and allow love to grow?

Bret Masters thought he'd finally found a glimmer of hope in his nightmarish existence. But after a night of sweet passion, the woman he trusted throws him out of her bedroom and returns him solely to worker status. His ego crushed, a rash escape attempt only results in him being dragged back in chains.

Angel Aldridge hates herself for yielding to her foreman's cowboy charm. Furious when he runs away, she resolves to keep him on a tight leash as her personal servant. And with a rival due for her annual visit, the frustrated cattle rancher can afford no signs of weakness.

Nursing his injured pride and estranged from his fellow slaves, Bret struggles to balance shame and desire as he endures his punishment. And with trouble brewing with her enemy, Angel must deny her feelings for her handsome ranch-hand if she's to protect those under her care.

* * *

Masters' Promise book 3 in the Angel Eyes series
is schedule for release in late 2021...

ACKNOWLEDGMENTS

'd like to say a special "Thank You" to my editor Silvia Curry. I'd also like to thank all my beta readers and proofreaders especially Angela Cross, Kate Amberg, Lady Elizabeth, Rosemary Kenny, Sandy at the Reading Café, Diane Wilson, Sherri Daschner, Lesley Walsh, Linda Tenda, Dasha Fehrenbacher, Staci, Becky, KRosa, Stacie Davis, my BookBub and Goodreads followers, and all the others I may have missed.

'd also like to send a heartfelt thank you to my family and friends. Without all of you, none of this would have happened. Thanks, once again, to Sam and TJ, the Facebook groups, Miss N. for everything, Bryan Cohen, all my newsletter swap author friends, and everyone else!

About the Author

Jamie was born and raised in the wonderful Pacific Northwest and she has always wanted to be a storyteller. As a child and young adult, she spent countless hours dreaming up stories to entertain herself and her friends. She kept long-running, developing stories in her head for years, knowing someday she would write them all down.

She still has many stories still floating around the back of her cluttered mind (and haunting her hard drive as well). She hopes they will all make their way out into the world for your enjoyment someday (soon)!

She still lives in Pacific Northwest with her family and her fur-babies.

You can learn more about Jamie and her books on her website: www.thejamieschulz.com

And you can follow her on her social media pages:
Facebook (@TheJamieSchulz)
Twitter (@TheJamieSchulz)
Instagram (thejamieschulz)
Jamie's Amazon Page
Goodreads
BookBub

Made in the USA
Middletown, DE
07 September 2023

38116761R00208